SECRETS OF OUR HEARTS

Sheelagh Kelly was born in York. She left school at fifteen and went to work as a book-keeper. She has written for pleasure since she was a small child, but not until 1980 were the seeds sown for her first novel, *A Long Way from Heaven*, when she developed an interest in genealogy and local history and decided to trace her ancestors' story. She has since completed many bestselling sagas, most of which are set in or around the city of York.

Visit www.AuthorTracker.co.uk for exclusive information on Sheelagh Kelly.

SHEELAGH KELLY

Secrets of our Hearts

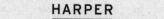

Harper
An imprint of HarperCollins*Publishers*
77–85 Fulham Palace Road,
Hammersmith, London W6 8JB

www.harpercollins.co.uk

This paperback edition (2007)
2

First published in Great Britain by
HarperCollins*Publishers* 2007

Copyright © Sheelagh Kelly 2007

Sheelagh Kelly asserts the moral right to
be identified as the author of this work

A catalogue record for this book
is available from the British Library

ISBN-13: 978 0 00 721157 9
ISBN-10: 0 00 721157 0

Typeset in Sabon by Palimpsest Book Production Limited,
Grangemouth, Stirlingshire

Printed and bound in Great Britain by
Clays Ltd, St Ives plc

In loving memory of my parents.

1

He had been dying to tell them all day. But, also dying for his tea, he had saved his announcement for later, as one might reserve the best bit on one's plate until last. Now replete, Niall Doran gave a little groan of satisfaction, a leisurely stretch, and prepared to regale his family. Then he remembered what day it was.

Perhaps this was not the time for frivolity. His thoughtful blue eyes moved to the fireplace, half expecting still to see the old Yorkshire range, but that had been ripped out weeks ago and replaced by a modern one with shiny beige tiles. Upon its mantelpiece, twixt two posies of flowers, stood a soldier's photograph. Today marked the eighteenth anniversary of Brendan's death; killed one week after his birthday on the Somme in 1916, forever twenty-five. Twenty-five, thought Niall with a mental shake of head – why, even the blasted sideboard had been allowed to survive more years than that! Without turning his head, he felt its dark presence. It seemed to glare at him, as if knowing he had always hated it – this heavily carved Jacobean-style monstrosity that took up an entire wall, its funereal bulk alleviated only by scraps of white lacework and the photographs of his children at their confirmation. Having his mother-in-law living here was oppressive enough, without putting up all her old-fashioned stuff too. It felt like a blasted funeral parlour . . .

Still, he noted, the occupants of the household didn't appear overly sombre. From the front room came the sound of female muttering: his wife, Ellen, her younger sisters, Harriet and Dolly, and their sixty-five-year-old mother having converged there a few moments ago, probably to spy on some neighbour, as women were prone to do. But Niall would soon have them pricking up their ears.

'You'll never guess what I saw today,' his deep Yorkshire voice called teasingly, 'not even in a million years.'

Seated at the table alongside him in the living room of their small terraced house, five brown-haired, blue-eyed children waited expectantly.

'A wolf!' came their father's grandiose announcement.

Whilst his offspring gasped in awe, only a half-amused reply came from the other room. 'I thought they were extinct in this country?' Ellen remarked.

'Obviously not, for I saw one today with me own eyes!' Niall sounded pleased with himself.

'You know what happened to the boy who cried

wolf,' jeered Nora Beasty, his mother-in-law, her concentration still fixed on the street beyond the window.

'I'm not having you on!' objected Niall, with a laugh. 'I swear I saw it.' And he began to recount today's adventure on the country line, all five children leaning on the table, their pixie-like faces holding him with rapt attention – the girls, Honora and Judith, with their delicate bone structure, the youngest, Brian, too, whilst the remaining pair of boys were more robust – all paying respectful heed. 'I'd just chased an old moorjock off the line—'

'What's a moorjock, Dad?' interrupted Bartholomew, a rascally-looking five-year-old.

'It's a sheep, Batty – and I were bending down with me spanner to tighten a crossover rod, and I looked up and there was Mr Wolf, jogging across the line as bold as brass!' His thrill conveyed to the children, Niall delighted in watching them hang on his every word. There came a display of excitement from the women too, but not because of anything Niall had said.

'See! I told you – he's off to meet a woman!' declared Nora, her flint-like eyes piercing the lace curtain and following the suspect's passage up the terrace.

The three younger females, who craned their necks beside their mother, gave angry murmurs of agreement. Then one of the disembodied voices manifested itself: Dolly thrusting her toothy,

3

unattractive face round the brown varnished jamb to summon her brother-in-law. 'Go after him, Nye, and see where he's off.'

'Who, in God's name?' He showed slight exasperation, which was mirrored by his informant.

'Your Sean!'

'Spy on my own brother? That's a bit devious.' But Niall had turned grim, annoyed as much that his own bit of glory had been spoiled as over his brother's purported wrongdoing, though he spared a warm and grateful smile for his eldest, who removed his empty plate and brought him the evening newspaper.

'There's your press, Dad.'

'By, you're a good lass – thanks, Honor.' He touched her affectionately. Quiet and conscientious like her father, the eleven-year-old merely smiled back, as Niall raised his voice again for the benefit of those in the parlour. 'Anyhow, he said he's off to play billiards with a chap from work!'

This drew sounds of faint contempt from the other room, his mother-in-law's answer relaying a sneer. 'I heard what he said, but you don't get dressed up like he is to knock a few balls about – and he couldn't look us in the eye when he said it. It's a woman, I'm telling you.'

'It'd bloody well better not be or I'll flatten him.' Despite the Irish name and facial characteristics, the Celtic knick-knacks and shamrock-laden, proverb-bearing plaques that dotted his house,

Niall was Yorkshire personified in his tight-buttoned, blunt-speaking manner. Irritated, he snatched a mouthful of dark brew from his glass and unfolded his newspaper. It had been a long hot day, he had laboured hard on the railway and, with his tale about the wolf overshadowed, all he desired was to be left in peace to finish his Guinness and read the press. Trained to accept this, his boys scrambled off their chairs and went to play outside. But, as ever, the women wouldn't let him rest.

Ellen broke off spying to bustle in and urge her husband persuasively, 'Go on, darlin', before he gets too far ahead. He's the one who's devious – he knows he's in the wrong otherwise why would he lie?'

'We don't know he is lying.' But at the back of his mind Niall knew they were right: his brother *had* looked shifty when questioned as to his intended whereabouts. Sean had rarely ventured out since his wife had died three months ago; then, last evening when he had come over for tea – which Nora had kindly taken to cooking for him since his bereavement – he had made an announcement that he wouldn't be over the next night, would just grab a quick bite at home as he was going to meet a friend from work. Niall recalled how he had offered to accompany his brother, for he felt like a night out himself, but had been met by a hasty refusal, Sean explaining that his workmate was not the sort to welcome such an intrusion. Niall had put little significance on this at the time, for past experience had shown that Sean's choice of friends was not his. But now, with his glass of Guinness only half drained, he abandoned it, wiping the froth from his long upper lip and casting aside the newspaper as he went to join the suspicious tribe by the window.

The front room was strong with cocoa, emanating from Harriet and Dolly, whose clothes and hair – even their skin – seemed impregnated by the factory in which both worked. The grey head with its severe parting, and hair tied in a bun, moved aside so that Niall could take her place.

'Now will you go after him?' bawled an impatient Nora, once he had seen for himself.

Far from being cowed, he responded with sour amazement. 'Don't me legs carry me enough miles a day?' But even as he said it he knew he would cave in for the sake of a quiet life, as he always did against this unforgiving wall of women.

Still, he vacillated, unwilling to do their underhand bidding, yet inquisitive to know himself. 'Well, I might just go . . .'

'Can I go with you, Daddy?' Unnoticed, six-year-old Judith had followed him in here and, fond of such cloak-and-dagger shenanigans, dragged at his legs and tilted her face at him pleadingly. 'Aw, can I?'

'Eh, Juggy Doran, what are you doing creeping up behind me? You're as bad as this lot!' Much as he joked, he did not care for the example being set for her. 'You should be out playing on a lovely night like this.'

'Go on!' nagged Ellen with a helpful push. 'You'll lose him.'

Niall was still looking down with fondness at Juggy, whose warm little body was clinging to his thigh. This morning she had sported a neat bow in her long, dark brown hair, but the latter was now tousled from play, and the ribbon dangled loosely about her face as she tried to seduce him with those shining blue eyes. '*Please!* I want to hear about your wolf.'

'I should be glad somebody does!' growled her father. Judged on this unsmiling appearance Niall could have been a wolf himself – sharp of feature, keen and intelligent of eye, his dark, wiry hair grizzled around the temples, at thirty-three in his prime, lean and raw-boned and rather menacing. In nature he was quite the reverse. Not exactly a sheep in wolf's clothing, and as far from being meek and mild as one could be, he was nevertheless as moral a fellow as ever stood, anything untoward or underhand offending him deeply, and he was not averse to using his fists in defence of those values. However, this side of his character was never visited upon his womenfolk, whose every whim he chose to grant in order to enjoy the quiet life he yearned. All in all a soft-hearted soul, especially at the hands of his children, Niall would take much goading before his teeth were bared. Yet here now before him was the one thing guaranteed to raise his hackles, and it was his brother who provided it.

'For heaven's sake, will you stop faffing and get after him – please!' This addendum was swiftly issued, for Nora knew him well enough to know that he did not respond to bullying. But she could not hide her exasperation and, unlike her son-in-law's, Nora Beasty's appearance was not so deceptive. With those cold grey eyes, she looked as if she'd enjoy torturing people and, by God, Niall knew if he didn't do as she wanted now she'd make his life a misery for weeks in all manner of small ways.

But it was from a sense of curiosity rather than obeying Nora that he finally agreed to act, and, with a gasp of aggravation, also to take Juggy with him. 'Flamin' 'eck, if it means I'll get some blasted peace, all right I'll go!' Juggy laughed in triumph. 'But keep your gob shut,' he warned her. 'We don't want Uncle Sean thinking we're after him.' Even if we are, he fumed to himself. Still in his grubby shirtsleeves, he hauled his grinning little daughter by the hand and left.

Outside, he paused only to sling Juggy onto his shoulders, then set off after his brother. She was a delicate, gangly creature, and no more than a featherweight to bear. On consideration he was glad to have her with him for it might look less suspicious. If Sean should turn and confront his pursuer the latter could always say he was only taking his child somewhere – though why he should lie when Sean was obviously the one at fault . . . However, he had not been found guilty yet and must be granted the benefit of the doubt.

Employing the bat his father had painstakingly carved for him, Dominic was now involved in a game of cricket with a dozen other raggle-taggle young residents of this slightly impoverished but happy area, his smaller brothers hovering in the avid hope they might be allowed to run after the ball. So concentrated, none of them noticed as their father went by with their sister on his shoulders.

'Ooh, just the very fellow!' old Mrs Powers accosted him as he was passing her open doorway. Mr Doran was a man who kept himself to himself, but knowing him to be charitable too, she entreated him, 'Could you just give us a hand to get a lid off, if you're not in too much of a rush?'

Unable to ignore the elderly widow's smiling plea, the chivalrous Niall turned to follow her lame figure indoors, only remembering he had Juggy on his shoulders when she yelled in alarm, and ducking swiftly to avoid injuring her.

With the lid removed, and the old lady's thanks ringing in his ears, Niall did not tarry but called over his shoulder, 'You're all right, love!' Then he hurried to regain surveillance of his brother, who had now turned a corner, the bony little buttocks grinding his shoulders as he jogged.

Thenceforth, he loped along Walmgate in the manner of the wolf that he had seen crossing the railway line that morning, occasionally responding to his daughter's questions about his encounter with it, though his mind was on other things now.

Well, Sean wasn't going to play billiards, that was for sure. He was travelling in the wrong direction. Still, Niall conceded that the local billiard hall was not the only one in York, and to be fair to his brother he tried his best to keep an open mind as, with the ancient limestone bar to his rear, he shadowed him towards town.

A tram came gliding past, the odd motor car, and argumentative voices from the Chinese laundry, but apart from these intrusions the way was quiet. If not for the task in hand it would have been a very pleasant walk. This evening, with its occupants basking peacefully in the sunshine – gentle old Irish grandmothers in black dresses, shawls and bonnets, seated upon chairs on the pavement and puffing on their clay pipes – it might be hard for a stranger to imagine that he was in one of the roughest quarters of York. Contained on two sides, the east and the south, by a medieval limestone wall, the rest of the area was enclosed by the River Foss, as it snaked its way to meet the Ouse at Castle Mills; the road that Niall trod was its main artery, a network of veins to either side.

Notwithstanding the garish posters daubed on every space, the odd smashed windowpane and derelict property, Walmgate itself did not look particularly rough. In fact many of its structures were immensely graceful, and it boasted a fine array of shops. Even the dosshouse looked genteel nowadays, the dirty crumbling stucco Niall remembered from his youth having been removed to expose fifteen-century timbers, and the gaps between them whitewashed. But Niall kenned that, with a few drinks down them, those same old grandmothers who waved to him so benignly might be tearing out each other's hair, and their sons trading blows. Likewise, behind those Victorian establishments with their sedate awnings to ward off the sun, and the symmetrical Georgian façades, at the other end of those narrow, urine-reeking alleys that ran between them were the most appalling courtyard slums.

However, of late there had been a definite change in the air. Along his way, Niall was pleased to note that a few of the worst offenders had gone, others in the process of being razed too, though the awful smell of their midden privies lingered on, overpowering the more pleasing aroma of fish and chips. Such dwellings had been there since he was a boy – his father and mother had said the same – and he would be glad when all were finally eradicated. How sad that it had taken a world war to instigate progress. Holding his breath and warning Juggy to do the same as they passed one such demolition site, he hurried on up Walmgate.

Linked to Fossgate by a small stone bridge that lay some way ahead of him, this was one of the longest thoroughfares in the city, its thriving commercial premises interspersed by ironworks, forges, breweries and tanneries, all of which emitted a sooty effluvia that was indiscriminate in its resting place, coating elegant Regency pediment and sagging medieval beam alike. Amidst these grimy edifices were butchers' shops with attached slaughterhouses. A few ancient churches were outnumbered by public houses: the King William, the Spread Eagle, The Clock, and eleven others. The combined smell of beer fumes and unsanitary middens billowed out from every entry on this warm summer evening – too warm to be dressed up like a dog's dinner, came Niall's inner pronouncement, as he noted the carefree manner in which his brother walked. The bouncing, cock-sure gait of his grey-flannelled legs, the swagger of his shoulders under the best jacket, the cap at a jaunty angle, the rhythmic clitter-clatter of his steel-tipped soles as he danced off the pavement and onto the cobbles in order to get round the small crowd that had gathered to hear the tingalary man – hardly the demeanour of a fellow recently bereaved.

Involuntarily, Niall's mind was cast back to poor Evelyn's death, for which he held himself partly responsible. It was from one of his children, the nephews and nieces on whom she doted, that Sean's wife had caught chickenpox. Whilst the youngsters had been barely incommoded, other than by an irritating rash, Evelyn had become critically affected. Her death had come as a complete and terrible shock. Niall remembered how devastated Sean had been and unable, as some might, to take solace in his offspring, for, despite being with Evelyn several years, their marriage had been unfruitful. There was no sign of that devastation now, thought Niall with disgust, as the gay tune from the tingalary affected his brother's gait.

He shouldn't have been surprised. Sean had always seemed to get over things quicker than he himself did – he could still weep over the death of their mother if he thought about it too deeply, though she had been dead more than thirteen years. But then he'd always enjoyed a closer relationship with her. His father had died when he was twelve and Niall had become the man of the family, insisting that he leave school and get a job to support his mother and younger brother – younger by only three years but it made all the difference between their levels of maturity. Even in adulthood Sean had continued to be the less responsible of the two. It annoyed Niall slightly that their mother allowed the younger brother to get away with it, whilst demanding a more grown-up attitude from himself and going mad at him if not receiving it. Still, he had adored her and had been heartbroken by her death on his twentieth birthday.

Then, soon afterwards had come Ellen to stem his grief. Susceptible to her comforting arms, deeply grateful for someone to organise his domestic affairs – for there was no way this clumsy labourer could do justice to the house he had inherited – he had married her within weeks of their getting together, their first child conceived on honeymoon. Yet, maintaining filial responsibility, he had not abandoned Sean, nor even tried to buy him out, but had welcomed him into the fold of newly wedded bliss, until, a few years later, Sean married one of Ellen's sisters. But even then, Niall's supportive role was not over, for, with great financial hardship to himself, he had taken out a mortgage in order to release Sean's half of the inheritance so that his younger brother could buy a house of his own. And, when Ellen's father had died, who was it took care of his widow and two unmarried daughters, and invited them to come and live under his roof, even though it was overcrowded already? Certainly not Sean.

With a snort of annoyance, Niall became aware that his little rider had slipped on his shoulders, and with one deft movement jerked her back into position. 'Sit straight, darlin'.'

'Sorry, Dad.' Juggy sat bolt upright, her hot little hands pressed to his skull.

The glazed brick frontage of the Lord Nelson signified that Walmgate was almost at an end. Thereafter came only a few shops, and two more public houses. Then, beyond the jagged, moss-coated roofs of derelict warehouse and broken Dutch gable that nibbled the skyline like rotten teeth, the Minster rose into view, its gargoyles and pinnacles defaced by the same centuries-old grime,

14

yet still towering spectacularly over all. Niall, barely aware of this colossus or any other antiquity, was deep in thought about his relationship with his brother, when a sudden cry made him jump in alarm that he had been found out.

But Sean was only calling to a woman on the other side of the street: 'Charlie's dead!'

Immediately interpreting the phrase to mean that her petticoat could be seen, the recipient of Sean's impudence automatically glanced down at her calf-length skirt, and made deft adjustment of its waistband, and the show of underwear was gone. Then, with an embarrassed laugh for her grinning informant, she minced off with a click of high heels. Niall scowled. What sort of respect was that to show a dead wife? Similar in looks, maybe, but the antithesis of his elder brother, Sean had always been a flirt; even when he had been married it had not stopped him. No, it hasn't taken you long to get over her, has it? Niall noted grimly.

Had this been Sean's only transgression that evening, it would have been bad enough, but he had just walked straight past another billiard saloon. As the tramlines and their overhead wires veered left, Niall carried straight on, his face even grimmer as he hurried across the road to avoid being run over by a car, his little passenger clasping tightly to his head. The street became narrower now, flanked by bulbous stone balusters, between which flashed glimpses of an oily river. The muscles in Niall's thighs tensed effortlessly as they met the incline of Foss Bridge, and thereby began another series of pubs. 'King's Arms Hotel, Parties Catered For', shouted the huge advertisement painted on an end gable; whilst some fifty paces ahead, Sean was passing beneath a sign for Magnet Ales. And in between were narrow jetty-fronted shops and grand emporia, an exotic-looking picture house, a barber and a confectioner, fresh fish and iron-monger, wagon repair, garage and cycle dealer . . .

Finally reaching the Army and Navy Stores, which marked the end of the thoroughfare, his quarry rounded a corner. Niall rushed to catch up, and his mood darkened into fury. Nora had been right. Waiting beneath the gold-painted carving of a ram, which dangled from a bracket and was an emblem of the Golden Fleece public house, stood a pretty young woman, obviously well acquainted with Sean. At his arrival her face lit up, and she touched his arm with such famil-iarity that there could be no mistake.

'Sorry I'm late,' Niall heard his brother say as he himself made a swift diversion to avoid catching up with them, almost dislodging Juggy in the process, and pretended to be looking in a shop window.

'You're not, I'm early,' the woman replied. Then, to Niall's horror, she added curiously, 'Is that little girl waving at you?'

As Sean wheeled to face him with a guilty look on his face, a childish voice hissed, 'They've seen us, Dad! But don't worry, I'll fix it.' And she called cheerfully from her father's shoulders, 'It's all right, Uncle Sean, we're not following you! Me dad's just come to buy summat from this shop!'

'Since when has he worn women's corsets?' muttered Sean, glaring knowingly at Niall.

For a few angry seconds the brothers faced each other, sharing the same defiant pose. Then, as ever, it was Sean who turned away first, steering his bemused lady friend from the scene and leaving an equally disgruntled Niall to return home.

'And where did they go?' demanded his outraged wife and in-laws, when he had reported all this to them several minutes later.

'How do I know?' Divested of Juggy, who had gone to get ready for bed, even though it was still light, Niall flexed his cramped shoulder muscles. 'I stopped following them.'

'Clot!' accused the cold-eyed Nora, to supportive murmurs from her daughters, who were gathered round him.

Already simmering, Niall fixed her with a warning glare. 'I wasn't going to have an embarrassing confrontation in the street!'

Ellen recognised that her mother had tested his good nature too far, and said hurriedly as he carved a passage through the women, 'Well, it's sufficient to know that Sean was with that woman, Mam. It doesn't really matter where they went, does it?'

'No, indeed, the snake-eyed traitor!' Nora

backed off from Niall, though it did not stop her venting her disgust on his brother.

Harriet too spoke her piece, obviously expecting Niall to listen. With strained patience he beheld her objectionable face, which was shaped like a cardboard shoe box, its expression and features similarly hard. 'So what are you going to do about it?' she demanded.

'Don't fret! The minute he gets home I'll be waiting for him. I'm not having this family brought into disrepute.' With a look of grim determination, Niall finally got to rest his aching body in an armchair, the brown artificial leather creaking as he slumped upon it. Purchased in a moment of rebellion against having his home cluttered with Nora's belongings, aside from the fireplace it was one of the few tokens of modernity about the house. Faced with that looming monstrous presence that was the sideboard, Niall bent to remove his boots, then thought better of it. Nora would no doubt start wittering at him, and besides, he'd only have to put them on again when he went to confront Sean. Contenting himself with loosening their laces, he threw an abstracted smile of gratitude at Ellen, who had replenished his glass with Guinness, and whilst she herself supervised the children's bedtime prayers, he opened the evening newspaper.

But, as before, he found himself reading the same line several times due to the angry commentary of his mother-in-law as she waited by the front window for the perpetrator's return. Normally he could ignore her, but tonight his own annoyance with Sean made this impossible, and eventually he left the room to seek refuge in the outside lavatory. How could someone of five foot two make her presence so felt? For if there was one anomaly about Nora Beasty it was that she looked much larger in photographs than in real life. Niall recalled his first sighting of her, when his relationship with Ellen had grown serious and she had produced a family snapshot as a preview to what Niall could expect upon making their acquaintance. If he had felt intimidated then by those steel-grey eyes, the iron jaw and hawkish nose, he had felt even more so at meeting Nora in the flesh, for her personality filled the room – much like her sideboard. Yet he had been astounded at how short she was. Short and stout and determined. Wide those hips might be, yet there was barely a hint of femininity about Nora, rather an armour-platedness; and despite the scallops of lace at collar and cuffs, the delicate chain of the locket she wore, and the slender gold band of her wristwatch, there was a mannish strength to her arm. Niall had been quite alarmed, for was it not said that a woman grew into her mother?

Thankfully, Ellen's jaw was not so square, her face softened by a fringe of brown curls; she had a maternal tenderness in her clear blue eyes that Nora could never have possessed, even in girl-hood. For although Nora had been very good to him in many respects, there lurked behind that initial smile of welcome the hint of a nastier side, which he had quickly discovered could be evoked at the drop of some harmless comment, and woe betide anyone who crossed her. A much younger man then, he had avoided doing or saying anything that might upset his mother-in-law – not that Niall was the type to go around upsetting folk just for the sake of it, nor was he someone who shrank from a fight, it was simply that he couldn't see the point in disrupting an otherwise ordered life by indulging in petty squabbles with the matriarch, even if she did regularly test his patience. But short of hitting her, he could not alter her wilful character – and one could not hit a woman. So for the sake of keeping everyone happy, if things got too much he would simply leave the room, and for the next thirteen years this was the way he had orchestrated his marriage. He could not say that he himself was ecstatically happy – what labouring man could boast contentment with his lot? – but so long as he had a steady job, a roof over his head, and his children were healthy and well fed, he would never complain. It could have been far worse. The rest of the daughters – not just the younger pair, Dolly and Harriet, but also the other two who had flown the nest – all were quite plain, their eyes slightly protuberant and grey like their mother's, their hair nondescript and their figures unappealing, and he counted himself lucky to have landed the only one amongst them who was reasonable-looking. Whilst no raving beauty, Ellen had the ability to look clean and trim, even when she was up to her eyes in housework, always having a tasty meal ready for him, and she was a wonderful mother to his children. The only characteristic she shared with her sisters was those thin lips, which showed a proclivity for intolerance and spite. Niall had come to know that this was not mere fancy, the amount of times they had ganged up on folk over the years. For a second he rather pitied his brother, who looked set to experience the full strength of their wrath; but for only a second. Never by any stretch of the imagination would he himself behave in such an overhasty manner should anything befall Ellen.

Which was why, the instant his lookout gave warning that Sean had arrived home, Niall was out of the door and over the road in the time it took to tie his bootlaces.

'Don't try creeping in!'

About to cross the threshold, Sean jumped and spun round, then retorted in anger, 'Why should I creep into me own house?'

'You know bloody well why!' accused Niall.

Sean scoffed in disgust. 'If you think I'm going to explain myself to you – you're t'one who should be explaining, spying on me like that!'

'I wouldn't have to spy if you had any sense of right and wrong!' Niall's dark, shaggy eyebrows were arched in disbelief. 'For God's sake, your wife's hardly cold!'

'Three months is a long time when you're on your own!' There was a hint of supplication in the face that was very like that of its accuser, with dark hair and vivid blue eyes, if slightly younger and not so healthy, for Sean worked in a factory. 'You don't know what it's like coming in to an empty house . . .'

But Niall was not to be won over. 'If that's your only excuse then get a lodger.'

All vestige of peace-making drained from the younger brother's face, usurped by contempt. 'You clever sod! You know what your trouble is? You're just jealous because you resent me having a bit of happiness when you're so bloody miserable.'

A second of stunned silence – then, 'Don't talk bull!'

'It's bloody right! You'd love to escape from Ellen and her lot, given the chance.'

'*Right?*' sputtered Niall, angered by the insult and coming dangerously close to his opponent's face. 'What would you know about right?'

'I know what's right for me,' parried Sean, 'and I intend to get on with it, so you can go back and tell that to the ones who are pulling your strings!'

Now totally incensed at being portrayed as only here to do the women's bidding, Niall returned fire, dappling his brother's face with saliva. 'It's not just them as thinks you're a traitor! For Christ's sake, can't you even do the decent thing and wait a year at least?'

'A year – who's to say what's a reasonable time?'

This penchant for sticking to the rules had always annoyed Sean. 'Why do you *always* have to do things by the letter? Why can't you take into account that some people aren't as regimented as yourself and might just happen to fall in love?'

'*Love* – you? Pff!' Niall laughed, but his eyes bulged with danger. 'We both know what you're after!'

'I don't give a damn what you think of me, but don't you dare insult my friends with your mucky insinuations!' Restricted by his collar and tie, Sean's brow had broken out in a sweat, his face cherry red, his eyes brimming with fury. 'Emma's a good, decent woman and that was the first time we've walked out together.'

'Well . . . I meant no slur on her.' Blood still pounding through the veins in his temples, Niall's reply was tempered by remorse, though only for the woman who might be innocent. 'Maybe she's unaware of your position; maybe you misled her like you've misled us.'

'She knows all there is to know about me,' retorted Sean to this double-edged apology, he too becoming less vociferous now, if no less firm. 'And I didn't lie to you. I said I was going out with somebody from work. You just assumed it was a bloke.'

'It was natural to assume it when you said you were off to play billiards!' countered Niall.

'Women can play billiards too, you know! As a matter of fact she's a very good player, and we did go for a game.' Normally a much less volatile character, Sean managed to bring his annoyance under control and tried reason instead. 'Look, I don't want to fall out with you, Nye. Can't you just be happy that I've found someone again? She's really lovely. I know you'll like her when you meet her.'

'I don't want to bloody meet her!' Niall exploded again and, one foot on the doorstep, he dealt his brother's chest an angry shove. 'If she knows everything about you she must think it's all right to go out with a man so recently widowed, and that doesn't constitute decency in my book.'

'Then bugger you and bugger your book!' Equally angered, Sean pushed his assaulter back into the street. 'I'm seeing her whether you approve or not. You might be an angel, but I'm just a normal bloke. The trouble with you is you can't put yourself in anybody else's shoes, you've got no bloody imagination!' And thus saying, he slammed the door in his detractor's face.

Absolutely fuming, Niall dealt the barrier a vicious thump, then wheeled away. No imagination indeed – how little his brother knew him. Oh, he had imagination in bucketsful! But it was not the sort that could be disclosed. What kind of man had daydreams of his wife being killed in an accident and tried to imagine how he'd feel at the news?

He felt this way now as he strode back to his own house and saw those tight-lipped expressions at the window, knew that the moment he was through the door Ellen, her mother and sisters would be pestering to hear what Sean had had to say, and demanding that he do something about it. For, since marrying into a family that came to lose all its men, Niall had been bestowed with the mantle of leader; in name at least. There was a time when he had been flattered to act as surrogate for Nora's dead son, Brendan, to be treated like a king in never having to lift a finger, his every requirement brought to hand. But callow vanity had soon been ousted by a truer sense of place. Now he was mature enough to see that Nora and her daughters regarded him as just another child to be manipulated, that he held no real importance for them other than to be the provider; for if ever he was to offer an opinion on anything they would regard it with amusement or, even worse, might scoff. Only in time of crisis, when there was some onerous duty that they could not perform themselves, did they deign to treat him like a man – yet even then instructing him how to do it.

So, yes, perhaps Sean knew him better than he cared to admit. At times like this, when all he wanted was to sink into bed after a hard day's labour, he did regret marrying Ellen – yearned to be free of those carping bloody women. But he'd never do it, for it wouldn't be right to walk out on his kids. And so he dreamed instead that one day she would just be taken from him, and tried

25

to imagine how he'd feel upon hearing the news, and how long it would be before he could get shot of her mother from his house. And then, of course, being the moral soul he was, Niall felt guilty and sad because there was no valid reason for wanting to be rid of Ellen, apart from her clan. There was a certain affection between them, they shared five children to whom she was a good mother, and she was a good housekeeper. He was sure he and his wife would have been fine if not for others' influence. But he could not fight all of them. And so he was left to his imagination . . .

But imagining something wasn't the same as reality, Niall told himself angrily upon reaching his door, nor was it a crime. Had he been in his brother's shoes he knew he would never choose to act like Sean. He would do the right thing. He cared what people thought of him, cared about his good name. And by association with his brother, that name had been plunged in the mire.

2

Steeped in such troubles, Niall had almost forgotten about the wolf when he saw it again the next day, bounding across the stretch of track he and the gang had just laid, not ten feet ahead, and making him cry out in alarm so that his companions dived onto the embankment thinking he was alerting them to danger. As before, it caused quite a stir amongst the labourers, many of whom dropped what they were doing to scramble up the grassy embankment. One of picked up a stone and hurled it with such accuracy that it drew forth a yelp. Objecting to this, Niall preferred to stand and watch the wolf escape across a pasture, scattering cattle as it ran, and leaving tufts of moulting hair in its wake from a coat that seemed almost red in the sunlight. One would have expected the noise to deter a wild animal, he thought, all that steam and clanking from the locomotives and the cranes, the grinding and hammering – not to mention the human activity. One would have assumed the wolf would take a wide berth, but no, there he was, giving his observers a devil-may-care backwards glance over his shoulder as he finally vanished into the trees.

Their excitement dying down, the labourers were ordered back to work by their foreman, and soon all were busy again renewing the track. Around fifty in all, some worked with picks, some in a wagon casting down shale with their spades, others shovelling earth into corves, yet more manoeuvring the girders and tracks that were suspended from the crane, guiding them into position, whilst a host of others worked with spanners and hammers to secure it, the whole site a cacophony.

His boots crunching the ballast, his ears ringing with the sound of steel upon steel, Niall narrowed his eyes against the smoke from the cigarette that now dangled from the corner of his long Irish lips, as he squatted to wrestle with metal and timber, and his thoughts turned once again to his errant brother.

A fair man, after a night's sleep he had pondered Sean's dilemma more objectively, yet for all he tried to put himself in the other's shoes he could not condone such behaviour. Sean might like to think that the matter was ended, but he had another think coming. From now on Niall would be alert to his every move.

Thus, that evening, tipped off by a watcher that Sean was heading out again, he pre-empted Nora's instruction to follow him by dashing straight out for confrontation.

'You'd better not be going to see *her* again!'

Clean-shaven, his hair slicked with brilliantine and smartly dressed in tweed jacket, white open-necked shirt and grey flannels, Sean merely eyed the challenging stance with disdain before continuing on his way up the sunny terraced street.

'Hark on!' Niall barked after him. 'If you do this you won't be regarded as part of this family any more! This is the last time I'll be talking to you.'

Once there was a time when Sean had worshipped his big brother, but with Niall become so judgmental and strait-laced, all respect vanished in a trice. Still walking, he flung a nonchalant reply over his shoulder. 'I'll consider meself told then.'

His threat so blithely unheeded, Niall strangled his intended retort, wasted no time standing there fulminating, but returned to his womenfolk, immediately to form a pact of war.

Henceforth, the women took it in turns to stand by the parlour window, noting what time Sean left and what time he returned, no matter how late. Even whilst detesting such methods, Niall was to play his part too, refusing to speak to his brother and darting him arrows of contempt whenever they came face to face.

It was a measure of their combined depth of loathing, their desire to arrest Sean's wicked descent, that these tactics were to be maintained for eight tense weeks. Until, one Friday evening in late August, when a day of high wind had already whipped up tempers, the lid of restraint was about to be blown clean off: Sean arrived home with his scarlet woman in tow.

Following the collective gasp of outrage, Nora blurted, 'He can't do that – that's our Evelyn's house!'

But Sean could and did proceed to escort the woman right to his threshold, both of them laughing as the wind swept her hair from back to front so that it totally obscured her face, then whipped Sean's cap into the street, causing him to make an acrobatic leap for it, before they finally managed to slam the door.

His mother-in-law was almost apoplectic over this presumption. 'Well, I'm not having it!' Heaving her solid carcass forth, surprising nimble of foot, she rushed outside to stand on the pavement and glare, closely followed by her daughters, all bracing themselves against the gale, whilst their hair was whipped and their pinafores billowed and ruffled, and paper flew all about the street.

Unable to see how this would help matters, Niall chose to remain indoors, as disgusted as the rest, though not so vocal. But no matter that Sean and his lady friend had gone inside, Nora and her deputies were to brave the elements for extra moments, standing firm and Medusa-like in the gale, so as those looking out could be under no illusion.

'They'll have to come out sometime,' declared Ellen, eyes narrowed and watering, arms folded under her indignant bosom, whilst her clothes flapped about her.

'What if they don't?' enquired Dolly, the least forceful of them, trying to keep a wisp of hair from her mouth. 'What'll we do then?'

'They'll have to!' From inside, Niall heard his wife reiterate.

'Not if she stays the night.' When they all turned to frown at her, Dolly explained quickly, 'Well, if she's the type of brazen article who takes up with a man whose wife's barely cold, she'll hardly have qualms about anything else.'

'Just let her try it!' Nora propelled this verbal gauntlet at the wall of the house opposite, before leading the return indoors to maintain her surveillance in comfort. 'I'll be over there and drag her out by her frizzy hair.'

Inwardly balking at such a bad example for a grandmother to set the children, Niall sought to distract them, especially the older ones, who were exchanging knowledgeable looks of concern.

'Is that your homework you're trying to do on the edge of that newspaper?' Recently turned twelve, Honor was seated at the table chewing the end of a pencil, as if more concentrated on the row from outside.

She broke away from her trance and went back to studying the pencilled words that were crammed into the white border around the newsprint. 'No, I'm just making a list of my sins for confession.'

Her father smiled. 'I thought school had run out of money for books. Sins, eh? You'd better get a bigger piece of paper then, all the things you've been up to.'

Her serene posture was cracked by a laugh of quiet outrage. 'Dad, stop it, you're putting me off!' Then her face became serous again as she tried to recall every offence committed during the week, for an imperfect confession meant damnation.

'Sorry.' Her father smiled and stopped teasing her, knowing how seriously she viewed the act of confession. Then he turned his attention to three-year-old Brian, who was pressed to one of his knees, unnerved by the howling of the wind through the gaps in the windows, and he pulled the child onto his lap. 'Don't worry, Bri, it's just the silly old wind making that noise – you know like your dad makes when he's eaten pea soup.'

There was collective laughter from his children.

'That doesn't hurt you, does it?' reasoned Niall.

'I don't know about that, Dad,' laughed Dominic, holding his nose.

'Oy, mister!' His father levelled a threatening finger, but his eyes were full of fun. 'You want to watch it or I'll be confiscating all of that five bob you've lined up for yourself tomorrow, instead of letting you keep some of it.'

Dominic adopted a non-comprehending frown. 'Don't you mean half a crown?' He would be performing his duties as altar boy at a wedding ceremony.

'I mean five bob!' Niall was stern but amused. 'I happen to know there are two weddings tomorrow – thought you'd pulled the wool over me eyes, didn't you? Well, think again! You'll have to get up early to hoodwink your dad.' He projected a grin of rebuke at his son who, in feature, took after Ellen's side of the family, and could be sly, but was redeemed by possession of a charming smile, which bounced back at Niall now.

'I only just found out myself there was another wedding!' protested Dom with a laugh.

Momentarily reassured by the smiling banter, Brian rested his head on his father's chest, though his ears still adhered to the external noises – as did Juggy's.

'Has Uncle Sean been naughty?' she finally dared to ask.

'That's none of your business,' retorted a stern father, but Niall felt the sharp eyes of his eldest son on him, and, annoyed at Sean for putting him in this position, sought to let Dominic know, without giving too much away, that this was no way for a man to behave. 'Suffice to say that a man's good name is everything,' he declared to all.

'I think Doran's a good name,' mused Juggy, kneeling by the fire and cradling her doll. 'Though I'd quite like to be called Pretty – that's what they call the girl who sits next to me in class.'

Niall responded with a chuckle and a compliment.

'You don't need to be called Pretty when you're already pretty.'

'Father didn't mean it *sounded* good,' Honor broke off her list of sins to explain quietly to her little sister. 'He meant that when people hear your name they think of you with respect, for the way you behave, and that you've got nothing to be ashamed off.' She looked to Niall for confirmation, and when he gave a pleased nod, she added, 'And Father's got a very good name.'

'So, is it the lady what's got the bad name?' persisted Juggy, having received more than an inkling from the angry voices that competed with the gale outside.

Her father decided enough was enough. 'None of that need concern you,' he said firmly, and designing to take his children's minds off this, and also the eerie whistling of the wind, he instructed Batty, 'Chuck us that book, little un – we'll have a story before bed!' Opening the tome, he set upon imbuing them with one of its moral tales in an effort to drown out their grandmother's voice.

'I will! If they're not out in five minutes I'll go in and drag them out!'

However, the threat was not to be carried out.

A couple of hours later, around nine, when the youngsters were safely upstairs, Sean and his partner in crime finally emerged. Immediately the Beasty women rushed out to hurl insults.

'Well, I'm glad she has the grace to blush – Ah say, you do right blush!' scathed Nora from across the street, amid a mass drawing-in of chins and glaring and huffing from her equally irate daughters.

Struggling to pull his door shut against the wind, Sean did not even look at them as he took a protective hold of his companion's arm.

'That's right, take her home – take her back to her sty, and good riddance!' This from Harriet.

'I like your hair, love!' Dolly mocked loudly, then declared to her abettors, 'Nobody has hair *that* colour – she must dye it!'

'With a bucket of rusty water by the look of it!' brayed Harriet. Even as she spoke the words were ripped from her mouth and dispersed on the gale along with a noisy collection of debris, yet a few of them hit their target.

'The cheek of them!' an indignant Emma told her companion, all windswept and troubled as they made their departure. 'It's my own natural chestnut.'

'I know that. They're just jealous, ignore them – and don't take any notice of their threats neither; they're all mouth,' advised Sean. He put a firm arm around her and quickly steered her away from further insult. 'They can just get used to it.'

Alas, far from growing used to it, tireless in their determination, one or another of the Beasty women was there to mutter and to scowl on each future occasion that Sean's lover came to visit. Even more humiliatingly, the neighbours had become aware of the rift. At his current arrival, there was a small audience to witness the antics of his reception committee. Worst of all, though, for an uncle who loved them, Niall's children were being indoctrinated by this bitterness.

'Don't do that!' Ellen slapped a hand that had come up to wave as she and her mother took their turn at observation, crammed into their doorway in an effort to shield themselves from providing entertainment for the neighbours, whilst at the same time maintaining their vigilance towards Sean and his fancy piece.

'I wasn't waving at the lady,' protested a forlorn Juggy, rubbing her hand, her skinny body squeezed between mother and grandmother's hips. 'Only at Uncle Sean.'

'You don't wave to either of them!' her mother bent to warn her in a manner and tone that could not be misinterpreted. 'And she's certainly no lady!'

Though Sean translated the comment only too well as he closed the door upon it, his little niece asked innocently: 'What do you mean?'

'Never mind!' Ellen shoved her daughter back inside, she and her mother following. 'You do as you're told and don't say a word nor make a gesture to either of them. He's not your uncle any more.'

The child's father was to endorse this, both in word and deed. In a change of tactic, from then on whenever encountering his brother, Niall would simply walk past as if the other were invisible. Hence, his children were to act by example.

It was all very sad for one who had doted upon them.

Yet however some might like to pretend that Sean did not exist, others continued to watch and to criticise his every move. Which was how they were to discover that the hussy had finally stayed the night.

This was the ultimate outrage. At the sight of Sean and Emma emerging together at eleven thirty that Sunday morning, Nora abandoned her sentry duty and charged like a rhinoceros from the house, running directly across the street and arriving at such a velocity that she almost bowled her son-in-law over in her attempt to slap his face. She would have struck Emma too had Sean not quickly recovered from his shock to grab her arm.

'You're disgusting, the pair of you!' Nora was snarling at them by the time Niall rushed over to referee, and to try to hold her back as she strained to be at those who had demeaned her kin. Ellen, Dolly and Harriet had rushed to join in the hounding, forming a barrier around Sean and the woman so that they could not escape. 'Besmirching my daughter's memory with that guttersnipe – where did she sleep, that's what I want to know!'

Though deeply embarrassed by the attention this was drawing – everyone dressed for the performance in Sunday clothes – Niall wanted to know too.

The mark of retribution glowing on his cheek, an angry Sean tried to disentangle himself, whilst at the same time trying to protect Emma from Harriet, the most dominant of his sisters-in-law, who kept aiming vicious prods. 'We don't have to put up with this!'

But Niall caught his arm, 'Yes you do! You owe Nora an explanation as to how you've got the gall to have another woman in your wife's bed!'

Cornered, Sean managed to wrench his arm free, then drew a frightened Emma closer to him, barking at his accusers, 'If you'd have been talking to me you might have found out before this – might have been invited to our wedding!'

Totally shocked, they stopped to gawp at him, lending him the chance to carve an exit from their oppressive circle, though once free he did not run but stood his ground and faced them.

Nora was first to recover, her accusation shrill with disbelief. 'You can't be married. We'd have heard from Father Finnegan!'

Ruffled of temper and clothing, Sean was still putting them to order as he explained, 'We got married at Emma's church.'

'Where's that then?' grilled Niall.

'St Oswald's.'

There was a consensus of derision over the Protestant venue. 'Well, you're not really married then!' countered Nora.

Sean remained firm. 'The certificate says we are.'

'If you think I'm letting you bring your floozie to live in my daughter's house—'

'*Nora!*' A lock of black hair tumbling over his

brow, Sean leaned towards her with an expression of determination. 'I'm very sorry but Evelyn's dead. She isn't coming back. I loved her but I can't keep the house as a shrine. I've got to get on with my life. So it isn't Evelyn's house any more, it's Emma's.' Taking advantage of their stunned faces, he dashed his hair back into place, straightened his spine, then said, with more equanimity than he felt, 'If you'd like me to introduce you . . . ?'

'No, we bloody wouldn't!' yelled Harriet who, at twenty-five, might be the youngest, but had inherited the lion's share of her mother's obnoxious character. Whilst there might be name-calling from Ellen and Dolly there was the definite threat of violence here, and Sean had no wish to hang around and sample it.

In an act of finality, he turned his back on them all, muttering, 'I knew it'd be a waste of time,' as he and his wife escaped up the street, shoulders braced against a tirade of insults.

'You needn't think you're getting away with this!'

'I don't see as there's much you can do about it,' sighed Niall to his mother-in-law, who was to repeat this threat as he shepherded her and everyone else indoors. 'I'm as angry as the next person. I think he's despicable, but—'

'There's one thing I *can* do about it right now!' declared Nora, in warlike form, gathering her daughters. 'Come on – you an' all!' And her hand made a graphic summons at Niall as she led the procession back to Sean's house.

No one locked their doors around here for there was nothing to steal; Nora found something though, as she barged straight in and made for a cottage piano. 'We'll have this, for a start! Ellen, grab that end.' She herself took hold of the piano and started to heave it, groaning and squeaking, across the brown lino, her daughter shoving from the other end. 'Dolly, grab them Staffordshire dogs! Hat, you do the kitchen!'

'You're taking all his stuff?' questioned a slightly amazed Niall, for the moment hanging back.

'It's not his property, it's ours!' Nora grunted and grimaced over the shifting of the piano, banging her shins as she fought to manoeuvre it over the bunched-up carpet that acted as a wedge against its wheel, her anger anaesthetising the pain. 'I gave our Eve most of the things in this house when she got married, and I'm damned if that little bitch is having the benefit – now are you going to help us or just stand there gawping?'

It took Niall only a few seconds to realise that what Nora said was quite true: she had donated most of the furniture here and many of the utensils, for she had done the same for all her daughters. With only the briefest qualm that Sean would come home and have no chair to sit on – but had he not brought it on himself? – he began to assist with the removal. Nudging Nora aside and telling his wife to leave this to him, he freed the piano from the bunched-up carpet, then hauled it along the passage, its castors emitting an ear-splitting squeal of protest before he hefted it over the doorstep, bumped it onto the pavement, down the kerb and across the street, eventually to install it in his own front parlour alongside Nora's bed – for this was where she slept.

'I'd rather have to climb over the blasted thing to get to me bed than let him keep it!' rasped his mother-in-law.

Then, under the curious eyes of the neighbours and anxious children, he and his angry female bandits proceeded to travel back and forth, transporting piece after piece of furniture, box after box of utensils and pictures, until there was no further room to cram in anything more. All that remained in Sean's living room was a table, an old sofa, and the echo of contemptuous voices.

For once, having washed their hands of the affair, Niall and his womenfolk were not outside to meet Sean's return. Had they been so, they might have glimpsed through that window, denuded of its lace curtains, the heartbreaking scene of a man come home to such wanton pillage that he broke down in tears.

'What have we done to them that's so bad, Em?' he sobbed quietly to the wife who tried to comfort him. 'My own brother treating me like this – I know he was in on it – leaving you with not even a kettle.'

Emma crooned and patted him tenderly, donating her handkerchief. 'Don't worry about me, dear. Look!' Temporarily she rushed away, trying to sound cheerful and to salvage a ray of hope. 'There's a little pan here we can use to boil some water, then we'll have a cup of tea and make a list of the things we need to buy.'

'It's hard to believe, isn't it?' Sean's tone was desolate as he looked about him at the plundered room. 'Yesterday was the happiest time of my life . . .'

'Aw, mine too!' Teary-eyed, she hurried back, linked his arm and squeezed her support, trying to bolster him. 'It still can be if we refuse to let this get us down. I'm sorry about all your things, but we can get some second-ha—'

'It's not pots and pans I'm bothered about!' He dashed away his angry tears. 'What gets me is the spite that's behind it – that they left you with nothing to manage your house with!'

'I think that's the whole point,' Emma told him quietly with a sad little smile, knowing he was not cross with her but with them. 'They don't see it as my house . . . and neither do I, truth be known.'

He dealt a rapid nod of understanding. 'Well, we can soon remedy that! After we've had our cup of tea, I'm off back out to put it up for sale – in fact I don't think I can even bear to spend another night near that wicked lot.'

'You might not have to,' came the sardonic reply

from Emma, and she made for the stairs to check whether Nora had taken their bed too.

But no, it was still there, scorned and all alone in the bedroom.

'Well, she wouldn't take that, would she?' scathed Sean, wandering up to join her, his face bleak.

'No, but she's pinched all the spare linen.' Having opened a cupboard, Emma quickly closed the door on empty shelves, again trying to make light of the incident. 'There's one good thing: we won't have much to shift, will we?'

Sean tried his best to raise a chuckle, saying as he embraced her tightly, 'As long as I've got you I'm not bothered about owt else.' But it was only half true, for he just could not get over the fact that such a deed had been perpetrated by his own flesh and blood. He doubted he could ever forgive that.

And upon leaving to throw themselves on the charity of Emma's parents, for however long it might take to sell his house, he threw one final look of disgust at Niall's abode.

'Well, that's me and him finished. As far as I'm concerned he's dead. I wouldn't even go to his bloody funeral.'

'Don't say that. It's not Christian,' his wife scolded softly.

'Neither is reducing your own brother to a pauper,' muttered Sean. 'From now on, he's no kin of mine.'

3

Whilst continuing to be the subject of gossip for many a day amongst the neighbours, Sean was rarely mentioned in his brother's household again, except for when Father Finnegan or one of the nuns dropped in on their parishioners, whereupon the sinner was roundly castigated in his absence, for marrying out of the Church. Other than this, the mere whisper of his name became taboo.

And yet, Niall observed, when any residue of anger was allowed a voice, it was not over Sean's disloyalty, but more his financial gain.

'Is there no justice?' spat Ellen, on learning from their next-door neighbour, on this autumn Saturday afternoon, how much her brother-in-law had netted from the sale of his house. 'The jammy bloody devil, why should he and that tart be rewarded when it's our lass who put all the hard work into it?'

Though similarly angry, after a brief outpouring, her mother gave stoical reply. 'Well, we did what we could to rescue Eve's things. Short of taking t'house down brick by brick there's nowt much else we could have done. Thanks for letting us know, though, Mrs Lavelle. Will you stay and have a cup of tea?'

Clad in black, with an air that nothing good would ever happen to her again, the neighbour gave one of her typically heavy widow's sighs. 'Aye, I might as well; I've nowt else to see to.' And she flopped her rear onto an Edwardian armchair, signalling for her daughter, Gloria, who accompanied her, to do the same.

Nora hefted the teapot at the prettier, but slightly vacant-looking woman with the limpid blue eyes. 'Will you have one, Gloria?'

'Aye, she will.'

Her mother answering for her, having rarely been allowed to make a decision in all her thirty-nine years, the downtrodden Gloria took a seat. Though she needed no encouragement to take an interest in her neighbours – at least in one of them – and whilst her mother did all the talking for her, Gloria herself proceeded to cast a series of adoring smiles at Niall. Sadly, none of these was noticed, for Niall was involved with making shuttlecocks for the children with the bunch of feathers he had collected on his travels along the railway line, trying to concentrate on this whilst the women speculated over the people who had moved into his brother's old house.

'We've been wondering what he does for a living,' said Harriet. 'Do you know, Mrs Lavelle?'

'We think he's a gunslinger, from the way he walks,' cackled Dolly, holding her arms away from her sides to demonstrate.

'That's from hefting stretchers for ten years.' Mrs Lavelle knew everything. 'He's an ambulance man.'

Nora had been studying Gloria. 'Where's them nice new teeth you bought, Glo?'

'They hurt her, so she only wears 'em on Sundays,' provided Mrs Lavelle.

Juggy's head popped around the jamb then. 'It's spitting. Can I go play in Kathleen's passage?'

'Yes,' said her mother, 'so long as you take Brian.'

'I will!' called Juggy on her way back out. 'He's gonna be the patient.'

'Well, don't be doing any operations on him!' shouted Ellen, then murmuring to the women, 'We don't want any bits missing when he comes home.'

Dolly's laugh was like the high-pitched bleating of a goat. A length of twine nipped between his teeth, Niall's face tensed in irritation, whilst his wife briefly left the gathering to look from the window and check on the whereabouts of their other offspring.

After exhausting all the latest scandals, Mrs Lavelle said, 'Well, we'll have to be going soon. Oh, I nearly forgot!' She grabbed the paper carrier that her daughter had been patiently nursing, and proceeded to display a tablecloth. 'We really came in to show you what we found for our Gloria in Rhodes Brown's sale.'

Harriet, before even remarking on any attribute of the cloth itself, asked immediately, 'How much was it?'

Niall glanced at Ellen and shook his head – Harriet always demanded to know the price of everything – then he returned his attention to the shuttlecock and tried to ignore the female babble.

'Two bob!' came the boastful reply.

There were murmurs of admiration over the bargain. Where Gloria was toothless, Dolly had an overabundance, and these were bared like a row of tombstones as she inspected the purchase with exaggerated interest. 'And is this for your bottom drawer, Gloria?' From the way she addressed the woman, who was twelve years her senior, one would think Gloria was a little child. 'Eh, you must have loads of stuff by now, you are a lucky lass . . .'

But after the visitors had gone this sentiment underwent an addition, a gleam of malicious laughter in Dolly's eye. 'She'll be lucky if she ever gets to use them, an' all. Bottom drawer'll collapse under the weight of all that stuff before she finds anyone who'll have her.'

'Ooh, you mean cat,' scolded Ellen. Niall also cast a disapproving look for this two-faced conduct, which was another thing that irritated him besides Dolly's bleating laugh, the latter grating his ears yet again.

'Well, she doesn't do herself any favours, does she?' pointed out Dolly, her face creased in mirth.

'You'd think by the time she reached that age her mother would have bought her a brassiere. She looks like a sackful of piglets off to the butcher's.'

'Well, at least she's got some piglets.' Harriet spoke bluntly, as she rose to take away the cups, her eyes upon the other's flat chest. 'You want to watch it, you might have to eat your words – you being the last one of us left on the shelf.'

Niall shared a wince with Ellen, but at least with Harriet one knew where one stood; she always said things to your face. Satisfied with the positioning of the feathers around the cork, he secured the twine.

Dolly bridled, though waited until her more forceful sister was out of the room to mutter, 'Smug devil. Just because she's cornered herself a man doesn't mean he'll be daft enough to wed her. You'd think she was going out with the Prince of Wales. It's not as if he's anything to write home about – even our Nye's better-looking than him.'

Whilst Ellen and Nora chuckled, Niall gasped offence. 'What do you mean, "even"?' Using his palm to bat the shuttlecock onto the table, he leaned back and picked up a newspaper.

'Well, at any rate, Gloria seems to think you're the bee's knees,' Nora told him, with a sly look at her daughters.

'Yes, I shall have to watch her,' teased Ellen.

Niall blustered with embarrassment and rustled the pages of his newspaper. 'What're you on about, you daft beggars?'

48

'Oh, we've seen her making sheep's eyes at you! Why do you think she's always popping in here?'

'She'll have to ask her mam's permission first,' bleated Dolly.

'You're all bloody daft,' muttered Niall grumpily. Then, as three drenched children swept in to ask if he would partake in a game of cards, he threw aside the newspaper with a cry of surrender. 'I can see I'm not going to be allowed to read!'

'Eh, don't go tearing it,' warned Ellen with a wink at her mother. 'You might miss seeing a report about your wolf.'

Whilst this was a jest, the children took it seriously, each of them jumping in with their own query, ten-year-old Dominic being first. 'Have you seen it kill owt, Dad?'

'Not yet.' Niall lit a cigarette, its smoke overpowering the reek of wet hair and clothing.

'John Mahoney's dog killed Reg Wilson's rabbit this morning, and there was all this blood, and purple guts hanging ou—'

'Yes, thank you!' Niall called a halt to spare the younger ones' sensitivities, then addressed the boy's mother. 'You'll have to stop feeding him meat. He's getting to be a right bloodthirsty devil.'

Dom's smile burst forth.

'Are you scared of it, Dad?' tendered five-year-old Batty, his cheeks pink with cold.

'Father's not scared of anything, are you?' Honor informed her brother in a quietly disapproving voice that said, how could he even ask.

Yes, thought Niall, sometimes I am scared, scared that this is all there is to life, to undergo the same routine day after day, being tormented by female drivel year after year until I die; to be nothing more than the wage earner. But to his offspring he said, 'Me, scared? Nah? If he shows them big teeth at me I'll flatten him with me shovel and bring him home to make a fur coat for your mam.'

Re-entering to the children's giggles, Harriet pricked up her ears. 'Our Nell's getting a fur coat?'

Ellen hooted. 'On the pittance he earns? That'll be the day.'

'Shame, I could have borrowed it when I go to meet Pete's family.' Harriet's young man was a comparatively recent acquisition, but already both were smitten.

'I doubt it would impress them,' smirked Ellen. 'It's that so-called wolf he's supposed to have seen again. I reckon he needs specs.'

'I've told you, it's not just me!' objected Niall, a smile on his face yet slightly annoyed that his wife should denigrate him thus, and in front of his children too. Even if it was intended as a jest it was no way for a woman to address the bread-winner. 'All the other lads have seen it.'

'They're having you on!' Ellen was relentless in her teasing. 'I bet one of them's got hold of a big dog and touched it up with a tin of paint.'

'Don't believe me then!' Cigarette in mouth, Niall

dismissed the laughing doubters, but remained adamant as he dealt out cards to his children for a game of Happy Families. 'Dick Kelly says he's going to set a trap for it. You'll be laughing on the other side of your faces when he does.'

'Well, don't be fetching the stinky old thing home here,' warned his wife. 'If I'm ever lucky enough to get a fur coat I'd like it to be genuine.'

However, by the time autumn was in full flush, what Ellen had assumed to be a figment of her husband's imagination turned out to be quite real. Niall and his workmates had seen it a few times now; but more pertinently it had earned a wider notoriety for killing and partly devouring sheep, its gruesome attacks being reported in the newspapers. It was definitely not a dog, said the experts. And there was Niall's name in print, being one of those witnesses interviewed. So they had to believe him now, didn't they?

On the contrary, they teased and tormented him even more, Nora and her daughters, that the following Sunday during dinner, Harriet decreeing mockingly, 'Eh, he'll do anything to make himself look important!'

Smarting beneath his fixed grin, feeling his children's eyes on him as they watched for a reaction, Niall continued in his stoic silent manner to eat his dinner, and awaited his wife's contribution. But for a change Ellen stuck up for her husband, laying down her knife to lean over and pat him, saying with genuine affection, 'Aw, he's important to us, aren't you, dear?'

Niall returned her smile, half-expecting some clever comment from one of the others.

So it was no surprise when Dolly added, 'Aye, if we didn't have him who else could we poke fun at?'

'I'm sure you'd find somebody, Dol,' muttered Niall, which everyone took as a joke.

Then the clink of cutlery displaced chatter as all became intent on the delicious roast.

After dinner, with Nora and Dolly in the scullery washing the pots, Harriet ironing work overalls, and Ellen escorting her children to Sunday school, Niall relaxed in his brown leatherette armchair and took up the newspaper, which had so far remained unread due to morning Mass. This was his favourite time of day.

He must have been napping though, for when the children came home he was jolted awake to find the paper in a crumpled heap on his lap. Refreshed, he laughed at himself and greeted them.

'Look what I've got, Dad!' From under his jacket Batty presented a small toy car.

'Why, you little demon!' scolded his mother, then quickly explained to her husband, 'The fly beggar must have picked it up whilst I wasn't looking.'

Niall was at once stern. 'Eh, now then, Bartholomew Doran, what have I told you? You can't have things unless you've got the money to pay for them.'

'It doesn't belong to anybody,' protested the innocent. 'It were just there on the road.'

'Is this the sort of thing you've learned at Sunday school?' demanded his father. 'No! Now, take it back. There'll be a little boy looking for that.'

'But he wouldn't have lost it if he'd looked after it,' reasoned Batty. 'You told me people don't deserve to have things if they don't look after them.'

'Never mind what I said!' retorted Niall firmly, his voice rising. 'And you can stop trying to wheedle your way round me. It's not yours, now take it back to where you found it.' He shook his head in disbelief at Ellen. 'How did we raise such a freebooter?'

Covering a smile, his wife led the little boy away to replace the stolen item. Niall spent a few moments chatting to his other offspring before they were made to attend certain duties, at which point he rustled his newspaper to order and resumed reading.

The rest of the afternoon was comparatively peaceful, everyone sitting reading or sewing or other suitably quiet pursuits. Towards five o'clock Nora went to put the kettle on and, discovering there was no tin of peaches in the pantry for tea, returned to appoint an errand boy. Despite this being the Sabbath one could always buy what one needed around here from those who were not observers.

'Dom, nip out and get me some.' His grandmother delved in her purse.

Engrossed in an adventure story, Dominic seemed reluctant to tear his eyes from it, and was tardy in moving to obey. 'To Mrs Madden's?'

'No, she's too pious to open on Sunday. You'll have to go to that one by Navigation Road.' Nora handed her eldest grandson a coin.

'I'll go, Mam.' Ellen jumped up to intercept it. 'I need something meself.'

'He's nearly eleven,' scolded Nora, 'I think he can find his way.'

'I know that!' Her daughter gave a light reply and performed a quick tug of her silky blue jumper over trim hips. 'But I said, I need something myself.'

They all knew it for a lie. Ellen was much too protective of her children, never allowing them to cross the road on their own, standing at the school gates to wait until they had gone in safely, waiting for them again at home time, even though the school was close by, ever fearful that something would befall them, unable to relax unless they were safely under her care.

'What is it then?' challenged her mother.

'Just something!' Ellen gasped. 'Bloomin' heck, do we have to have an inquest?'

Niall hardly lifted his eyes from the newspaper. The children were his wife's concern and he rarely interfered.

But Nora shook her head in exasperation. 'You'll still be holding his hand when he walks up the aisle, you will! Stop mollycoddling the lad.'

Dom looked most insulted, flopping back in his chair and huffing as he reached for his book. 'There's no need for me to go if me mam's off then.'

'You'll go if you're told to go,' cautioned his father from behind the *News of the World*.

'It's all right, he doesn't have to,' negated Ellen.

Dom might have been excused but his five-year-old brother leaped up to accompany her.

'There'll be no sweets,' warned his mother, in strict manner, 'especially for those who take things that belong to other little boys. Don't think there will.' But from the indulgent twinkle in her eye Batty knew she could easily be persuaded.

Aware that this brother was in possession of such a knack, Honora's head shot up from her exercise book. 'I'm coming if he's off!'

'No, Honor! You've got that school work to finish . . .'

'Oh, but—'

'For heaven's sake!' Unable to read his newspaper with all the argument that was going on, Niall slapped it onto his knee with a heavy sigh. 'Look, why don't I save everyone the bother and go meself? I might as well go for a walk, I'll get no peace here.' He began to rise.

Ellen pushed him back in his chair, saying sternly, '*I'm* going!'

'Good, bugger off then,' grumbled Niall, only half joking as his wife made for the door, the five-year-old tagging on to her skirt.

* * *

With Batty hopping alongside her – protesting when she dragged him past the sweet shop on the corner – Ellen journeyed along a warren of short streets, going out of her way to call in on a friend and to spend some ten minutes chatting whilst her bored infant was made to sit and wait. Finally, she resumed her errand, a relieved little boy almost dragging her along the street as they made for the main thoroughfare, where he knew there to be other sweet shops.

They had reached the corner, and were about to turn into Walmgate, when suddenly two bicycles appeared on the pavement as if from nowhere, racing at full speed side by side. Two shocked faces loomed large, the young riders displaying panic as all parties realised there was about to be a collision. Her instinct to protect her child, a horrified Ellen yanked on the little arm, lifting Batty off his feet and out of the path of danger, crying out as she herself was hit by one of the speeding bikes, and falling into the path of the other, its rider flying through the air and landing on his head in the road.

'I wonder who she's met this time,' sighed Nora when her daughter had not returned after half an hour, and the table had been laid with bread and butter for tea. Ellen was an incorrigible gossip, who had been known to spend two hours over a short trip to the corner shop. 'Go and see what's keeping her, Dom. Tell her we'd like those peaches for tonight's tea, not Christmas.'

From his chair, Niall threw her a wry smile and went back to reading the newspaper.

But his eldest son had not reached the door before there came a series of knocks on it, a rapid, urgent summons.

Niall lowered his *News of the World* and exchanged puzzled looks with the others, whilst his son revealed the caller.

'Oh, Mrs Beasty!' Gloria's limpid blue eyes brimmed with tears as she addressed Nora first, then directed her look of compassion at Niall, clutching a handful of blouse as she spoke. 'It's your Ellen . . . you'd better come . . .'

They all rose as one then and converged anxiously on Gloria, demanding to know what was amiss.

'Knocked over . . . ambulance . . .' Words tumbled disjointedly between the unaccustomed dentures, invoking panic in the listeners.

And then they were all running in the direction of her pointed finger, Niall, Harriet, Dolly and Nora – and the children.

'*Stay!*' their father turned back to command them harshly, then ran on, not knowing what he was running to, his heart almost pounding out of his chest as he headed for Walmgate, the terrified mother and sisters in his wake.

Immediately they saw the ambulance. But even as Niall ran towards it, the vehicle was pulling away from the crowd of onlookers. He and the women called after it, frantically waving, yelling and shrieking for it to stop.

'Here's the husband!' People were pointing and gesturing, amongst them Father Finnegan, who also tried to arrest the vehicle, dashing into the road and waving both arms, but its driver paid no heed as it departed, bell ringing.

His senses ripped apart, Niall thudded to a halt as he reached the scene to be met by the priest, but his frantic blue eyes were to travel beyond Father Finnegan's entreating features, taking in fresh horror. There were smears of blood on the road and on the pavement. Then he saw Batty in the arms of a nun, not a scratch on him, and his whole being was swamped by relief. Ignoring Father Finnegan's attempt at ministration – 'I'm sure she'll be all right, Nye!' – he shoved his way through the curious onlookers and took charge of his little boy, kissing and hugging him, but the child did not say a word, his eyes round with shock. Nora, Harriet and Dolly came screaming after him, frightening the child further with their reaction, whilst the priest and the nun tried ineffectively to calm them.

They were all taken in charge then by a policeman who, quickly ascertaining that these were relatives of one of the victims, gave brief explanation as he hurried them to a car, which took them to the hospital; where, after a long wait, they were met by an apology and the abrupt announcement that Ellen had died.

Mingled with the cries of grief was incomprehension. How could she be dead? The sun was shining! This same thought served all. But for Niall the shock was manifold, his mind harbouring a deeper, darker impact of guilt. He had wondered, imagined time and again, what he would feel if his wife were to meet with a fatal accident, and here it was, happened.

It was all right for them. They were women, they could wail and weep and sob and beat their breasts. Men couldn't do that – well, his brother might have done when Evelyn died, but Sean was weak, and everyone knew just how genuine that display had been when he'd married someone else five minutes later. No, Niall could not do that. Consumed by guilt that he had wished it on her – caring Ellen, so loving of her children, so missed by them – he could only stare and hang his head. In previous imaginings he had rehearsed his own role as one of affected grief. But it wasn't pretend. He truly did throb with sorrow. How could he not?

Prior to an investigation, there had been anguished debate amongst family and friends – how could one be killed by so innocuous a vehicle as a bicycle? Then the inquest had revealed that Ellen had died due to a fractured skull, received not directly from a bike but from the kerb upon which she had fallen. Whilst the youth who had landed on his head had suffered only a gash, Ellen's skull had been as fragile as an eggshell.

Pending any more serious charge, the youths

had been summoned for riding their bicycles on the pavement, their fate yet to be decided – not that it could ever be as bad as Ellen's, condemned those who had loved her. At the Requiem Mass Father Finnegan had asked the mourners to pray for those wretched sinners. Stupefied as he was by this trauma, Niall had felt the palpable wave of anger that emanated from Ellen's womenfolk, rippling like magma along the pew, but they had voiced no comment until now, when, in the privacy of their home, they gave vent to their revulsion, protesting vociferously about the priest's request.

'I don't care if they are repentant!' raged Harriet to the throng of grief-stricken relatives, friends and neighbours crammed alongside that monstrous sideboard on borrowed chairs, who sipped respectfully from their glasses of sherry, the plates of ham sandwiches and fruit cake barely touched. 'I'd kill them myself if I had them here before me!' Agitated fingers picked at a black-edged handkerchief, seeking a patch that was not sodden. In the puffy face, her eyes were as dull and empty as stones, but her angular jaw oozed resentment. 'I mean, one of them landed on his bloody head, for Christ's sake! How come he walks away scot-free, and poor Nell . . . ?' Faced with her sister's bereaved children seated all forlorn in black, her nasal anguish was to terminate in a fresh bout of sobbing.

'Murderers,' denounced a red-eyed Nora, her own voice leaden and morose. 'That's what they are. God might forgive them, I never will.' There was a combined rumble of agreement from the gathering.

Two more of Ellen's sisters, Mary and Kate, continued to sob quietly, their husbands offering awkward condolence, their movements stiff and unaccustomed to these black suits and starched collars. Distant relations of Niall were here too, and his friend Reilly, whom he hardly ever saw, had hurried to his side with characteristic loyalty, but these were outnumbered by the Beasty followers.

One of the neighbours, Mrs Dunphy, sighed pityingly and shook her head. 'Eh, two in one year, Nora.'

'At least there was nobody at fault in poor Eve's case,' sniffled Dolly, blowing her nose for the umpteenth time, her eyes similarly lifeless. 'I mean, it was terrible to lose her but there's not much you can do against a disease, is there? But there's plenty can be done about those buggers – I'm sorry to swear but that's what they are! And how Father Finnegan can even ask us to forgive them – they deserve hanging!' There were more murmurs of agreement and more tears.

Then she and everyone else looked to Niall for similar declaration. Soused in guilt as he was for the many times he had imagined his wife dead, the best he could deliver was a shuddering sigh and a shake of head.

Taking this to indicate that the widower was

too choked by grief for words, the tearful women rallied to him, reached out supportive hands, assuring him they would be here to assist in his hour of need and ever after.

'Don't you worry, lad,' murmured Nora in stalwart tone. 'We'll always be here.'

You would think that something like that would turn one's routine on its head, thought Niall, but no. Weeks after the mourners had taken home their chairs, here he was doing exactly the same things at the same hour, amongst the same people, albeit one less of them. And the strange thing about it was, he still expected her to be here when he came home on an evening.

The routine might be the same but life was not – how could it be, burdened as he was by such tremendous remorse? Never in his selfish imaginings had he stopped to think what Ellen's death would do to her offspring. But he did now. If he had been left prostrate at the age of twenty by the loss of his mother, what agony must such little children feel? Even though they had gone back to school the day after the funeral, and were once again to be seen playing their childish games in the street, the devastation they had suffered could so easily be resurrected, tears never far from the surface. One might have expected little Batty to be worst hit, he being witness to his mother's death; and perhaps this was true, for no one could see into another's head. Yet the five-year-old seemed to have suffered few ill effects. No, it was Brian and Juggy who were most clingy, the latter seemingly terrified to let Niall out of her sight, lest her one remaining parent not return.

For the third time that week he heard footsteps behind him and looked over his shoulder to find himself shadowed. With a doomed sigh, he stalled and waited for his younger daughter to catch up. Scolding her gently, he told her to go home and get ready for class, and remained there for a moment to make sure she obeyed, casting a stern expression in response to the beseeching one that she threw over her shoulder.

Whilst he stood watching, another figure came out with a bag in her hand, crouched towards the child and spoke gently for a mere second, before running up the street to accost the father. Having been about to turn away, Niall gave another inward sigh and waited for Gloria, trying to avoid looking at those breasts that appeared to have no synchronisation as they bounced this way and that beneath the floral pinafore.

'Me mam says I have to bring you these to have with your break, Niall!' Earnest of face, failing to hide her admiration of him, Gloria pressed the paper bag in his hand; it contained two buns. 'I made them meself,' she lisped through toothless gums.

With his smiling nod of gratitude, she hovered for a second, then, with a last adoring look, turned and ran back down the street. Upon reaching her doorstep she turned to fling a last gaze at him, but by this time another neighbour had accosted Niall to donate yet another gift, and, robbed of his smile, Gloria turned sadly indoors.

'Here, take these with you, love,' whispered old Mrs Powers, the skin of her hand paper thin and displaying a network of veins as she donated a small package. 'Two rashers of bacon – you've got a stove in your hut, haven't you?'

Niall replaced the cap he had just tipped. 'Aye, I'm grateful of it an' all, what with these nippy mornings.' Gracing her with a polite smile, he took off his haversack and inserted the package, and even though his needs had been well provided by Nora, he told the donor, 'I'll have them for me dinner. Thank you very much, it's very kind of you.'

'It's no more than you've been towards me, dear.' With a beneficent nod, old Mrs Powers backed indoors – only to be replaced by her neighbour, Mrs Whelan, who had come out to collect her milk from the step.

This time, though, there was only verbal contribution. 'Eh, how's them poor little mites of yours, Mr Doran?' No one looked their best in a morning, but Mrs Whelan's appearance would not improve during the day, the worry of her husband's constant unemployment adding years to her scraggy features. 'I wish there was some way I could help . . .'

'There's nowt much anybody can do, love – but

thanks.' Niall gave a tight smile, his eyes straying to check on Juggy, as he itched to be off.

'I know,' sighed Mrs Whelan, 'but I just wish I could make it right for you. You've done so much for us over this past year. I'd never make ends meet without all them rabbits and coal you've given us—'

'Ooh, keep it under your hat, love!' he said hastily, 'or I'll be losing my job.' By rights everything on the line, whether it be a few lumps of coal or a rabbit caught in a snare, belonged to the LNER. A soul of great integrity, Niall would steal from none, but in this case he had no regret: what loss was a few bits of coal to a huge railway company? And what was moral about a soldier who had fought for his country being subjected to the means test?

Tipping his hat to Mrs Whelan, and checking that Juggy had finally gone indoors, he resumed his eager stride. However inhospitable the conditions, he had become glad of his work, for it took him away from that pain-filled mien and that of her siblings; for the daytime at least.

But it would always be waiting for him when he got home.

'I don't know how I'd cope without you, Nora,' he informed his mother-in-law, having arrived home after dark on that same day, to an ordered house, a nourishing meal on the table, and his offspring washed and ready for bed, he himself now sated. 'I'm really grateful for you looking after them so well.'

Her hawkish face calm, yet still etched with the pain of losing too many children, Nora waved aside her role as she supervised the reluctant exodus to bed, then removed Niall's empty plate. 'It keeps me busy. Anyhow, I've got Hat and Dolly to help.'

Niall acknowledged this too as he accepted a cup of tea from the latter. 'I know how hard it must have been for you all.' Any denigrating opinion he might have of them was swept aside; no one could have been kinder to him.

'It's the least we can do for our Ellen's husband,' replied Harriet, touching his shoulder.

Niall felt himself blushing and thanked God they could not peer into his soul. But he simply nodded and to cover his awkwardness said, 'Mrs Powers gave me some bacon as I was on me way to work this morning, and Gloria ran after me with a couple of buns.'

Dolly smirked. 'You'll be needing a new set of teeth then.'

'She's only trying to help,' said her mother, more generously. 'I've been glad of her and Mrs Lavelle meself, I can tell you.'

Niall agreed that everyone had been so good, many of the neighbours continuing to play their part in helping the bereaved husband, running after him in the street to offer some little bit of comfort. 'But I wish they'd just leave off a bit now—' He broke off abruptly as there came a tap, and the face of yet another neighbour appeared round the door.

'I've not come to bother you, Mrs Beasty.' In respectful manner, the monkey-like Mrs Hutchinson set a tin of peaches on the table. 'I've just brought you these from town. It's nice to have a little treat through the week, isn't it?'

Niall saw his mother-in-law's jaw twitch in anger. And though she managed to contain it under a veil of politeness, as she thanked the woman for her thoughtfulness, Mrs Hutchinson was sufficiently intimidated by that steely-eyed face to remove herself from it within seconds. 'Well, let me know if you need anything else, dear!'

Immediately the door closed, Nora said of the peach tin – the kind that Ellen had gone to purchase on the day of her death – 'Stick 'em in the cupboard, Dolly! I couldn't stomach the blasted things if I was starving.' Her tone was one of deep loathing. 'You can't say anything when they're only showing concern but, by God, I don't know how I stopped meself from crowning her with it.'

Niall's eyes followed Dolly as she relegated the peaches to the back of a cupboard, his voice hollow. 'Aye, I were just about to say, when she came in, I wish they'd just leave me to get on with it now. Every time I open the front door I can feel their eyes on me, brimming with pity.'

The women agreed that it was the same for them, Dolly voicing what all had experienced.

'Whenever you see any of them gathered together they clam up – you can tell they've been talking about Nell.'

'People love a tragedy,' pronounced Nora, her eye and tone become bitter.

'They make me sick,' seethed Harriet, revisited by her own grief. 'Acting all teary and concerned – it's not their tragedy it's ours.'

Niall chewed his lip, noting how quickly they turned, how they hated to be on the receiving end of the gossip. So did he.

'And the worst thing is,' declared Nora mournfully, 'they'll have got over it in a few weeks. We never will.'

Dreading Christmas, Niall found it even worse when it finally arrived not crisp and white but wet and miserable. Telling himself it was for the children's sake, he tried to make the best of an overcast celebration, scrimped on his own pleasures to take them all to a pantomime, and to buy each the type of present they would normally not receive. Yet, at the end of a very testing day, there remained an empty bed and a sobering indictment: no gift he had bestowed could replace their mother.

The winter months of 1935 were tough. Battling his way up the line through flurries of January snow, he had never felt so desolate. The wolf was obviously finding it arduous too in these foot-high drifts, for the vulpine spoor that defaced the pristine blanket led investigators not to a savaged sheep but to the remains of tinier mammals. Despite these giveaway tracks, the predator continued to remain at large. Wishing he too was a lesser beast, so as not to think and to feel emotion, Niall tried to inject himself with hope; told himself that spring was just around the corner.

But even after the upland streams and tributaries had thawed and their icy contents came tumbling down from the hills to swell the Ouse and Foss and threaten the city, before mercifully receding, Niall was to remain swamped in desolation.

Is this it? he was often to ask during the months after Ellen's funeral. Was this what he had wished upon himself? Why, he was even worse off than before. At least he had had a wife to cuddle up to on a night. However much she might nag him over his shortcomings, Ellen had been good at heart, knitting him jumpers and socks, making sure he was warm and well fed before setting off to work on winter mornings, treating him to his favourite sweets whenever she went into town. How could he have been so lacking in imagination, so perverse as to think he would not miss her as much as anyone else in this house? Steeped in melancholia, for months he had crucified himself over his last words to her. He had told her to bugger off, and she had. For good. And all over a tin of bloody peaches! Grief superseded by anger, he raged at the stupidity of it all. I *told* her I'd go for them! Why does she never listen? And then the anger had reverted to misery, for that was another thing: the habit of referring to her in the present tense; expecting her still to be there when he got home on a night, waiting to take his coat and to rub his cold hands with her warm ones, to steer him towards the fire . . .

But he had imagined her dead and now he had got his just deserts. Life held no further pleasure than to see his children become adults, and marry, and hopefully make better decisions than he himself had done. And isn't that sufficiently worthwhile, a sudden, inner voice demanded at his lowest ebb. At least you can help to guide them, make up for your failure as a husband. And there would be grandchildren. Yes, yes, of course there were things that were still meaningful. And thereupon the tide of self-pity began to recede. Never even to contemplate re-marriage, Niall decided then that, with his mother-in-law willing to cook and to wash and to lay out his clean underwear for him, his children would be enough; *must* be enough. Accordingly, from that point of catharsis, it was to Nora he handed his wage packet, and she who took over from Ellen in the running of his life.

4

Despite the apparent return to normality, both for Niall and those who lived alongside him, there remained an air of emptiness in the house, and the women could not help but feel how unsatisfactory this was for a man.

'He's lonely, is the lad,' Niall overheard his mother-in-law murmuring to her daughters one night in early March, with greater understanding than he gave her credit for. 'God knows, I miss Nell, but her husband must miss her twice as much.'

Drying his hands in the scullery, he cringed and gripped the rough towel, listening to the three talking about him for a while, and taking a few moments to compose himself before hanging the towel on its hook and wandering in to join them.

The only one still draped in black, Nora glanced up sympathetically from her knitting as he entered. 'All right, love?'

He nodded, his face pensive and his voice loaded with regret. 'I shouldn't have let her go on her

71

own. If the bike had hit me it wouldn't have done any damage . . .'

Stricken by a bolt of agony, she rebuked him, 'Eh, now don't start that!'

'How can you be to blame?' demanded Harriet and Dolly, both misty-eyed.

'Here!' Resting her knitting on her lap, full of bluster to mask her grief, Nora made a grab for her purse and dug out some coppers. 'We were just saying you need summat to take your mind off things. Get yourself out for a little bevy.'

Having enjoyed this pursuit only a handful of times during his entire marriage, Niall was taken aback, and did not seem particularly keen to go, for instead of taking the money from her he stared at the manly wrist in its delicate little gold watch-band and shook his head.

But his mother-in-law's hand remained extended, gesturing deliberately as she urged in a kind but forceful manner, 'Go on! It doesn't do you any good to be sitting with us women night after night. Go and find some male company. Anyway, you earned it.'

As of course he had. And so, in reluctant fashion he took the money, donned his cap and his army surplus greatcoat, and picked up the evening paper, saying, 'I'll take the press with me in case there's nobody to talk to.'

The night was dark and cold; the kind of damp, depressing cold that permeates one's bones and dilutes the marrow. Set between two rivers, which ever-threatened to break their banks, in its scooped-out saucer of land this city was not a good place to be in winter; like an overfilled cup in a puddle of tea, its lower reaches constantly a-drip. Niall was glad of his greatcoat, tugging its collar around his neck, chin and ears against the drizzle, as he made his way towards Walmgate, welcoming each intermittent splash of lamplight, before being plunged into gloom once more.

From behind a closed door came the sound of a man and women arguing violently, and pots being thrown; from another, a child's pathetic wail. Niall jumped and stopped dead as a dog came barking at him out of an alley, and he kept a wary eye on it as he walked on. Seeking a drinking partner, he went straightaway to the abode of his friend Reilly, a short distance away on the other side of Walmgate. Pals since their schooldays, the two had gone their separate ways upon leaving there – Niall to the railway, and Reilly to Terry's factory – and had met only a couple of times a year since then. They had last reunited at Ellen's funeral. It might seem odd to some that such close friends did not get together more regularly – especially at such time of strife – but Reilly had said genuinely then, if Niall ever needed him he knew where to come, and that provided solace enough. It would be nice to meet again in happier circumstances and Niall found himself looking forward to it, as, just before the Bar, he turned off this main artery that was Walmgate, and entered a primary vein. Travelling beyond its many capillaries – the overcrowded alleyways and courts – he went down to its far end where, by a cut of the River Foss, was to be found his friend's dwelling, a similar two-up, two-down to his own.

Reilly's wife, Eileen, answered the door, warily at first, until she discerned his identity through the darkness – then she was immediately pleased to see him. An attractive little woman, dark of hair and eye, her face cracked into a munificent smile and she threw open the door.

'Eh, look who it is after all this time – what's your name again?' And she gave a bubbling laugh. But in the next breath she was to issue disappointment. 'Oh, you do right come when he's working nights! He'll be that mad at having missed you, Nye. Anyway, come in and have a cup of tea with me and get the neighbours talking. Eh, how lovely to see you!' With an encouraging sweep of her hand she prepared to welcome him in.

Reminded of how this might appear to others, Niall went only as far as the doormat, though he retained his friendly smile as he took off his cap. 'Er, no, I won't stop, Eileen, thanks all the same. Me mother-in-law's given me the money for a pint. I daren't waste it; she might not grant me the opportunity again!' Nevertheless, he did not leave immediately, taking a few moments to enquire after Eileen's wellbeing – for he liked this small, but generously proportioned woman very much – and to share with her news of his children, about whom she was always quick to ask. If ever a woman was made for motherhood, this was she, with her soft ample bosom upon which a small head could rest, and her kind eyes and patient nature. It was a great shame the Reillys were childless.

'Eh dear,' she sighed, when he had finished bringing her up to date on his sons and daughters' emotional welfare – particularly Juggy, 'you never can tell what's running through a bairn's mind, can you?'

Niall gave a sombre shake of his head. 'I try to buck them up as best I can, but—'

'Oh, I'm sure you do, love!' Eileen pressed his arm.

'—it's not the same as their mam, is it?' he finished.

'I'll tell you, lad,' bolstered Eileen, 'you do a lot better than most.' Acquainted with Niall for many years, she had never met a man so mindful of his children's happiness. That alone would have earned her admiration, but he had also proved a loyal friend to her and Reilly too, at short notice – even in the middle of the night – coming to their aid when the flood waters threatened their furniture, and helping to shift it to higher ground. 'They're lucky to have you as a father – and you're lucky to have them.'

'Well, I don't know about the first bit,' came his self-effacing reply. 'But you're right about the second.' Absent-mindedly, he wrung his cap.

Eileen studied his abstracted pose. 'And how are you managing without her?'

'So, so . . .'

She served a thoughtful nod, knowing that Ellen had been the only buffer between Niall and his awful in-laws. Personally, she had never been enamoured of Ellen either, thinking the pair badly suited, but one could not say this to a bereaved husband.

'Anyway!' Niall broke away from the spell that thoughts of Ellen had created. 'I won't keep you standing here being nithered to death.' He gave a smile and a shiver, before backing away and replacing his cap. 'Tell me laddo I'll catch up with him another time.'

'I will, love!' With a brisk, smiling gesture, Eileen waved him off. 'He'll be that jealous I've seen you and he hasn't!' And with a last warm farewell, she closed the door.

Niall felt at a loss now as he made his way back towards Walmgate. There were a dozen public houses in this vicinity and he had no idea of where to dispose of his coppers. Eschewing the most notorious hostelries, which were a regular feature in the local press, he re-examined the one on the corner of the road from which he had just emerged. This might sport the usual advertising posters on its side wall, its brickwork chipped and scruffy, but it did not emit rowdy voices. He paused for a while, trying to see through the window but its glass was frosted and etched with fancy scrolls that advertised the commodities within: Wines, Spirits and Beer. The light from a gas jet illuminated a sign overhead: 'The Angel'. He couldn't get into much trouble in there, could he?

His self-conscious entry was quickly allayed by the bright warm atmosphere: a fire burning merrily in the hearth, gleaming brass, polished tables, sparkling mirrors, and pictures on the walls depicting scenes of fox-hunting and horse-racing. The bar shimmered with rows of spotless glasses. On its top shelf, above a row of optics, was an assortment of brightly coloured ceramic barrels, and other such decorative items relating to the trade. Removing his cap and flicking it to remove the droplets of rain, Niall folded it inside out, put it into his pocket and strolled across the tiled floor towards the counter of polished mahogany. The woman behind it smiled at him in a friendly but polite fashion – amply proportioned, but not one of your blowsy types, he decided with relief, more of a country lass, fair-skinned, fresh-complexioned, blue-eyed, and competent-looking – and there was a Celtic lilt to her tongue. Asking for a pint of bitter, he noted her strong-looking fingers on the pump. Strong, but not those of a peasant, for the nails were trimmed short and clean, and the skin was smooth with no blemish, as was that of her face. She was wearing lipstick, he suspected, though it was not heavily applied. Having lived here all his life, he knew most of the folk round this area, if not by name then by sight, but he had never laid eyes on this one before.

He would have remembered that smile, that shape . . .

His inspection was knocked aside by guilt. It was not yet five months since his wife had died, scarcely time for her blood to be washed from the pavement, and here he was looking at another. He was as bad as Sean. Handing over his coppers, he gave peremptory thanks, then glanced around for a nook in which to sit and read his paper. First, though, he blew his nose, which had developed a dewdrop, courtesy of the roaring fire. Much too warm now to sit in his overcoat, he hung it on a stand before settling down to read.

But for some reason he could not concentrate on the pages and found his gaze being dragged back to the barmaid. He liked the honest way she had looked him straight in the eye when serving him, her face a sweet, open book. There was someone who would never belittle a man, thought Niall, someone who'd never cheat or lie or steal. Part of this assumption was to be proved correct a few moments later when she called out to a chap who had forgotten his change. She could just have kept quiet and pocketed it, but she hadn't. Niall liked that. Affecting to read his paper, casting surreptitious glances from the print, he continued to observe as she chatted and laughed with other customers, his interest in part for the nice manner she had about her, but mainly for the attractive swellings under her jumper. Embarrassed to find himself reacting to them in base fashion, he tore his eyes away. What was the point in tormenting oneself over something one could not have? With no hope of concentrating on the press, after downing his pint, he went home.

Nora was there alone, waiting up for him. Harriet and Dolly had gone up to bed, the only trace of them being the scent of cocoa that wafted from their coats as he brushed against them in the passage. The elderly widow was partially ready for bed too, for her grey hair was dangling in a long plait over one shoulder. But for now, she sat by the firelight, employing its weak glow and that from the one remaining lamp as she squinted over her mending. Her iron jaw relaxed into a smile, as he hung his coat on a hook and came to join her by the fire. 'You weren't long. Didn't you enjoy it?'

His nose beginning to run again from the sudden change in temperature, Niall pulled out a frayed handkerchief and trumpeted into it before answering, 'Aye, it was a nice break, but I were hoping to have Reilly as company and he was working.' His tone was dull and he made absent-minded dabs at his nose. 'No point being sat on me own. I might as well be in bed.'

Nora put aside her mending, lifted heavily corseted hips from her chair and went to fetch him some cocoa. 'Never mind, he might be available next time.'

Her son-in-law nodded, shoved his handkerchief away, then sat rubbing his hands and staring into the glowing embers, conjuring pictures from them. Yet even then he could not concentrate, for he found his absent thoughts depicting not Reilly, but the smiling girl behind the bar.

Is this some fluke, asked a wary Niall, when his moment of wakening failed to produce that sensation of dread, or is it some miracle? Seemingly overnight, the weather had taken a turn for the better too. The sun shone, the air was crisp instead of damp, and the sky was clear and blue. The odd daffodil began to flutter along the grassy ramparts of the city walls. Where yesterday had been a brown and barren tangle of dormant briar along the railway embankment, there were primroses, and bees that zigzagged between them. At the shrieking whistle and clattering wheels of a train, startled lambs bucked and skittered, kicking their heels in the air. A stoat came out of hiding to enjoy the sun, his beady little eye ever alert for the delighted man who watched him as he darted like quicksilver among the rocks at the side of the track, his lissom body dipping and gyrating into nook and cranny, the sunlight gleaming on his russet coat, his entire being conveying the sense of rejuvenation that Niall himself felt.

With the following days proving that this was no aberration, at the end of the week when his mother-in-law doled out pocket money from the wage packet he had just handed her, Niall clinked it thoughtfully, before saying, 'You know, I reckon you were right about that little trip to the pub doing me good . . .'

'It must have done.' She cast a shrewd eye at him. 'If it's made you visit the barber at last.'

Niall rubbed his shorn neck defensively, and sat at the table with his children. 'Aye, well, I thought I'd better smarten meself up. I got a few disapproving looks from the landlady the last time I was in. I thought I might just trot along for another pint later on – don't worry!' He saw Juggy's face turn anxious. 'I'll only be half an hour – that's if Gran doesn't mind?'

Pleased to be able to ease the widower's unhappiness, Nora said generously as she served his meal first, 'Why would I mind?'

'Well, it is Lent . . .' A time of self-denial.

'Ah, yes,' replied Nora and, to his consternation, she said nothing more on the subject as Harriet and Dolly finished bringing the rest of the plates. Whereupon, she sat down to murmur grace.

Niggled by disappointment, Niall hardly tasted the fish upon his fork, as he inserted it time after time into his mouth, all the while machinating how to get around this problem. But it turned out he did not have to, for later, after the children had gone to bed, Nora spoke again on the subject. 'I've been thinking, you've been through enough deprivation lately – and it's not as if you'll be overindulging.'

Startled, Niall looked to Harriet and Dolly for agreement. 'I don't want to go upsetting anybody . . .'

'You won't upset me.' Hardly seeming to care, Harriet flicked over the pages of her magazine, Dolly too murmuring permission as she mended the hem of her overall.

'Oh, thanks!' He projected a somewhat relieved gratitude at all of them.

'I almost wish I could join you myself.' Neither she nor her daughters would ever frequent such a venue, but, added Nora, 'It'd be good to have a change of scenery sometimes.'

Niall was keen to oblige with the next best thing. 'Well, if you can't go there it'll have to come to you. I'll bring a couple of bottles home for you and the lasses – maybe some chips an' all if you're good,' he added with a wry smile, as he went to towards the scullery, intending to tidy himself up.

'Aren't you forgetting something?'

He swirled round at Harriet's sardonic query.

'Lent?' she reminded him with a smirk. 'Some of us are good little Catholics.'

Dolly emitted her goatish bleat of a laugh. 'Don't believe her, Nye! She reckons to have given up sweets, but she's got a bag of mint humbugs tucked down the side of her chair. Don't think I haven't seen you cramming them in when you think nobody's looking!' She gave another mocking laugh at her sister's outrage.

'Mints don't count as proper sweets,' retorted Harriet, under her mother's disapproving eye.

Niall feigned to wince, and said to Nora, 'So, no beer and chips then – I'd better get out while the going's good.' And he shut the scullery door on them.

But Nora's disapproval had only been pretence, and in his absence she exchanged warmer words with Harriet and Dolly. 'He seems a lot chirpier does the lad, doesn't he? Aye . . . I'm glad there's something made him feel better, poor soul.' Then she gave a heavy sigh and reverted to her faraway state of bereavement, her face haggard, and uttering wistfully, 'I wish a glass of beer'd have the same magic properties for me.'

After a quick wash and shave, and a change of attire, Niall went upstairs and popped his head into the children's bedrooms to bid them good night and also deliver a word of warning for them not to read too long in bed.

'Dad, will you tell her to stop kicking me?' begged Honor, from her cramped corner of the room that had been divided into two in order to separate boys from girls. 'I keep reading the same sentence over and over.' Lifting herself from the pillow, she tugged one of her plaits from beneath her head, with exasperation.

'I'm not doing it on purpose!' The small face protruding from the other end of the bed burst into angry tears. 'There's a lump under me bum.'

Niall laughed softly as he came to perch on their bed and to mop the tears. 'I don't think I want to know what it is.'

'I mean the bed!' Juggy sat up and gave a furious thump at the mattress.

'You're doing it again!' Honor laid down her book in despair, and whilst her father tried to settle the younger child, she indicated the empty bed that was only eighteen inches away. 'Couldn't I just lie on that while I finish me chapter? I promise I'll pull the covers straight and be off it before Aunty Doll and Aunty Harriet come up.' Her aunts would be cross if they found their bed rumpled.

Since their mother had died, Niall had found it hard to deny them anything. 'Go on then, but don't fall asleep on it – and don't let on it were me who gave you permission!' Giving each girl a fond peck, he made for the other side of the partitioned room.

'Right, untie your brother and get into bed now!' His expression turned stern as he waited for Batty and Brian to remove the gag from Dominic's mouth.

'It's all right, Dad,' reassured his eldest boy with a grin, 'I'm just letting them practise.'

'For what – getting themselves a prison sentence?' Impatient to be off, Niall seized Brian, who was seated astride Dominic's torso, and put him in his rightful place in the bed, then helped free Dominic's wrists from the bonds that Batty had tied. 'That's my belt! Now lie down, the lot of you, or I'll be taking it to your backsides!' But the boys saw him laugh to himself as he left.

''Night, Dad!'

'Good night, sleep tight, mind the bugs don't bite!' called Niall cheerfully.

Downstairs, set to depart, he experienced a thrill of anticipation.

'I hope your friend's in this time,' Nora called after him as he left.

'Who?' Niall stopped by the door, and wheeled quickly to frown.

'Reilly, you clot!'

'Oh!' He had not even considered visiting his friend, but laughed swiftly now to cover his guilt, 'Aye, well, if he is he is, and if he isn't he isn't. See you later.'

The night was still as dark and still as cold, yet not half so damp as it had been earlier in the week, and any chill he felt at being without his greatcoat was soon overcome by an eagerness of step. Neglecting Reilly, Niall went without delay to the public house he had visited last time, wondering whether *she* would be there to serve him.

She was. The saloon being almost devoid of other patrons, apart from one grizzled old toothless codger puffing on his pipe by the fire and a couple more playing darts, the golden-haired young woman approached him immediately with a smile of enquiry. Niall asked for a pint, then fell silent to await it being poured, snatching a glance at her whilst she concentrated on her task. Taking in as much about her as was possible without staring, he saw that her hair was shortish, though not, he noted with gladness, that severe kind of shingle that some women had adopted since the war, that looked as if it had been hacked at by garden shears;

there was still enough of it to afford her femininity, and it certainly did the job for him, rippling in soft waves about her neck. In fact, despite the pink lipstick she didn't seem one of those modern types at all, her face being in a way rather old-fashioned, which could have belonged to any period in history. No film-star glamour, just an overall impression of a really nice girl – well, he called her a girl but it was just a manner of speech; she was probably thirty or even more. But although he liked the look of her, and despite being the only customer at the bar, he made no attempt to engage her in conversation, for being a shy sort, Niall was hopeless at small talk. Segregated from females by his Catholic upbringing for the entirety of his schooldays, he had never really been able to relate to them since.

Wondering what she saw when she looked at him, he sought a glimpse of his own reflection, and was immediately dismayed at the wolfish face that stared back. There was a jaw that held too many teeth, and in consequence a few of them crossed over others – only slightly, but enough to annoy him. He had hoped to conceal them behind a close-lipped smile, yet this only made his mouth look bigger, for his lips were long and curled up at the outer edges, this prominent feature emphasised by the deep lines that ran from either side of his mouth to his sharp nose. His cheeks were tattooed with high colour by the elements. It was, in general, the raw-boned countenance of one who laboured hard to make an honest living, yet not, he decided, one to inspire female trust. The women in his street had known him since childhood, but strangers were another matter. And so, for fear of humiliation, Niall held his tongue.

Yet he was to experience a wave of pleasure when she herself instigated a dialogue, if only about the weather, saying in her soft Irish lilt, 'How lovely it is to see the sun again, don't ye think?' She had been eating a cachou. Her breath smelled of violets, wafting all the way over the counter at him, raising foreign but deeply pleasurable emotions. 'I could hardly believe it, winter just behind us and the yard like a sun trap – oh, it must have been seventy degrees! Sure, I only sat out for half an hour to take my break and came in like a tomato – well, half a tomato.' She laughed and cocked her head, presenting one pink cheek for him to view.

Possessed of the kind of smile that came from nowhere, a chink of blue sky amongst grey cloud, Niall forgot any attempt at hiding his teeth and used them to full effect now. His eyes came bright with amusement, the skin around them crinkling, as he noted how very fair her skin was, and how easily it would burn. 'Ooh dear, I bet you suffer in a real heat wave.' It might not be eloquent, but Niall was rather pleased with himself for managing to uphold the discourse.

'Aw, I certainly do! If I stay out too long I peel in strips – I look like the hanging gardens of Babylon.'

He laughed. 'Wouldn't suit you to work outside every day like I do, then.'

A fair, swan's-wing eyebrow was arched, showing interest. 'Oh, and what line of employment would you be in?'

'I'm a platelayer on the railway.' Niall leaned on the bar, thought better of it and stood erect again.

'And what does that involve?' she asked, her hand still on the pump and a careful eye on the beer that had almost reached the top of the glass.

'Well, besides initially laying the track, I maintain it every day, walking along making sure it's in good repair and that . . .' It didn't sound much of a job; he wished he had given a better explanation. 'To make sure it's safe.'

'A very important position then.' Handing over the beer, she took his money.

He gave a self-effacing shrug. 'That's not for me to say.'

'Ah well, you look very fit on it. 'Tis a lovely complexion ye have.'

It was not in the least artful, but Niall felt a blush spread over his cheeks, and he took a quick sip of beer. Despite having managed to shake off the acute shyness of his youth, outside the family home he remained self-consciousness and he did not appreciate being stared at so directly. When confronted thus, in the manner of a dog his eyes would flick away as if to divert the watcher's gaze. This time, however, it failed to have the required effect, and he was compelled to blurt: 'I thought it'd be busier than this, being payday!'

Seeing not the miserable countenance that Niall conjured of himself, but the face that his friends and neighbour saw, one that was quiet and strong and approachable, she removed her eyes from it to steal a quick glance at the mahogany clock on the wall. 'Oh, don't worry, they're just biding their time for a good night. We'll be rushed off our feet in half an hour.' She took his money to the till, saying on her way, 'I haven't seen you in here before. Just passing through, are ye?'

Disappointed, though unsurprised, that his previous visit had made no impact on her, Niall chuckled softly. 'No, I've lived round here all me life.'

'A bit longer than me then. This is only my fourth week of working here.' She beamed as she gave him his change.

This would be the time for him to move away from the bar and find a table. He could have taken his pick tonight, but chose to remain where he was for the moment, wanting to continue the dialogue but not sure how. He took another sip of beer, hoping she would help him. Instead she began to potter about the bar, refilling shelves with bottles. It was perforce left to him.

He licked the foam from his long upper lip and cleared his throat nervously as she came past, and said, 'You're from Ireland then?'

'How very perspicacious of you.' A smile removed the barb from what might be misinterpreted as snide.

However, this comment instantly demoted her in Niall's estimation – he had enough of such sarcasm at home, people thinking they were being clever or witty – and the fact that she did not appear to intuit his annoyance served to deplete her standing even further. Instantly he revised his former opinion of her as a kind, old-fashioned type. Nevertheless, he was forced to stay put for she was still speaking and it would have been rude to turn his back.

'I know what you're thinking – how the divil did I get away with a heathen name like this in Ireland!'

Eyes fixed on his glass, he shook his head, still annoyed about her previous sarcasm. 'I wasn't even aware of your name.'

'There's me told then.' She grinned, but was obviously stricken with embarrassment from the way she seized a cloth and began to polish a non-existent smear on the mahogany counter.

'Sorry . . . I just haven't heard anyone mention it.' Despite himself, he wanted to make her feel better, and asked, 'What is it then?'

This appeared to restore her friendliness. 'Aw, me and my big mouth – I could've got away with it. I'm not sure I want to tell you now.' She tilted her head as if paying the matter great considera-tion, but this was merely play-acting. 'Ah, go on then. It's Boadicea Merrifield.'

Niall couldn't help but be impressed. 'That is a rum'n!'

She laughed gaily at his expression. 'Don't I know it – and all my father's fault.' Still only the two of them at the bar, she leaned both forearms on it and, without the slightest prompting, launched into the story of her life whilst Niall sipped his drink and listened.

Her father, a sergeant in the army and resolutely English, had fallen in love with a colleen whilst on duty in Ireland, and against natural disdain of its inhabitants had sought permission to marry her. This had been refused at first by her family, until he had become a convert. With Boadicea's father often away for years at a time on foreign service, and her mother declining to go with him, she had been born and brought up amongst her mother's kin. Hence the Irish accent. Up against them and the Church, her father had been forced to baptise his child Mary, but in his presence she continued to be Boadicea, and the brother who followed her, Arthur. Her name had caused all sorts of friction, and even without the nuns' insistence on it she would have called herself plain Mary at school so as not to draw attention to herself. 'Even when I came over here I got an awful lot of leg-pulling – 'tis a wonder I'm not walking round with one leg longer than the other, the amount I got. Not that I care. 'Twas the name my father chose for me and I'm sticking to it.' Her smile showed that she was immensely fond of her father. 'I rather like having a name that no one else has – well, not many, anyhow.'

'So how come you are over here, then?' asked Niall, having warmed to her again.

Her face clouded slightly and she tapped her short fingernails on the bar. 'Oh, things . . .'

'Are your parents still there?'

'No, my mother died—'

'Oh, sorry, I didn't mean to upset you.' His softly uttered sentiment was genuine; he knew what that felt like.

'Thanks,' she was equally sincere in her response, 'but it's been a good few years now. Anyway, with her gone, there was no reason for Dad to be in Ireland, what with all the back-biting he suffered. So he came back here with Arthur. He'd left the army by then, o' course, though they did call him up to train the recruits during the war – I suppose you'd have been too young to see any fighting?'

Niall nodded quickly. Like many of his age, it was rather a sore point that he had not contributed.

She mimicked his nod. 'Anyway, as I say, he and Arthur came back to live here. I stayed on for a while with Mammy's folks, but I couldn't get work, so that's why I came over, and also to be nearer to Dad and me brother – although I'm not so near as I was, me being in York now and they in Manchester. I only get to visit them a couple of times a year.' Seeming to think she had spoken long on herself, she smiled and asked 'Have you any brothers or sisters?'

Immediately Niall shook his head, then looked awkward. 'Well, I did have a brother, but we don't see each other.' Before she could ask why, he posed a query of his own. 'Don't you miss Ireland?'

'Oh, sure.' Her eye was momentarily wistful. 'It'll always be home.'

'Whereabouts are you from?'

The wistfulness turned to impudence. 'Would you be any wiser if I told ye?'

Niall felt his jaw twitch in irritation; she was doing it again. 'I just meant what county.'

'Mayo,' she eventually revealed.

'That's where we're from!' exclaimed Niall.

Boadicea seemed to find this hilarious. 'Sure, ye don't sound like it!'

That really annoyed him, for he was immensely proud of his Irish heritage. But he kept his tone equable. 'Aye, well, maybe that's because we've been here sixty years.'

'Nor do you look that old,' came her teasing addition.

'I *meant* my great-grandparents.' He decided to end this humiliation there and then by tipping back his head, draining his glass and bidding the barmaid a curt farewell, leaving her smile fading to bewilderment.

'Have you been upsetting my customers again, Miss Merrifield?' quipped the landlady, a no-nonsense type of Yorkshire woman, having witnessed the terse departure, moving to stand beside her.

'Heaven knows.' Totally mystified, Boadicea shook her head. 'And here's me thinking I was giving him compliments. Sorry for losing you business, Mrs Langan.'

'Nay,' the woman's tone was dismissive, 'he's only a one-pint Willie. It'll hardly break the bank.'

Boadicea laughed at the terminology, and prepared to welcome the group of more amiable-looking customers who had just barged into the saloon, and from that instant was run off her feet for the rest of the night. Nevertheless, she was to remain disappointed over her miscommunication with the shy and handsome man with the serious face and the smile that came from nowhere. When he came in again she would have to apologise.

However, she was not to get the chance, for Niall had decided to abandon his foolish notion. Having emptied his conscience at confession on Saturday and been absolved for his lustful thoughts, he had assumed that to be the end of the matter. Had he not bumped into her in the street during the following week he doubted he would have seen the rude biddy ever again.

It was a somewhat embarrassing encounter. There had been a cattle market and, that Monday evening, the main route to his house was splattered with dung, the air rich with its scent. He had successfully evaded it so far, then had rounded the corner and encountered a great quantity on the pavement.

Too late to dodge this one, he was standing under a streetlamp and using the kerb to scrape it from his boot and so avoid taking it home, when someone said in a familiar Irish lilt: 'Blasted nuisance, is it not?'

And he spun round to see Boadicea emerge into the pool of lamplight. The weather having turned cool again, she wore a long fitted coat with a golden fur collar that was almost the same shade as her hair. As wide as a shawl, it enveloped her shoulders, making her seem smaller, more vulnerable than the person who had issued such impudent banter last week.

'Oh . . . hello,' Niall muttered lamely, then went back to cleaning his boot.

Ignoring the hint, she explained her presence: 'I just thought I'd nip to evening Mass before going to work.'

'Right.' Niall moved his head in acknowledgement.

Her smile was tentative, her voice soft and her breath visible on the cold evening air. 'Ye haven't been in to see us for a while . . .'

'No.' Niall felt ill at ease, wishing she would not watch as he dragged his boot along the kerb this way and that.

'I've been hoping ye would, Mr . . . ?' Blue eyes fixed upon his face, she waited for his name.

Eventually he said it, obviously reluctant and not a little morose. 'Doran.'

'Mr Doran, I think I might owe you an apology. Maybe you thought I was being rude to ye last time ye came in.'

Still occupied in ridding his footwear of cow dung, Niall frowned, pretending not to know what she was talking about.

'You might've thought I was mocking your Yorkshire accent – I wasn't, I think it's lovely.'

How could one remain hard-hearted to such charm? He donned a self-effacing attitude and stopped cleaning his boot, attending more politely as she went on, 'Sure, I ought to know better, folk taking a rise out of me with their top o' the mornings and begorrahs and all manner of rubbish. Anyhow,' she inclined her head graciously, 'I apologise. I meant no harm.'

'None done. I can't even remember it,' lied Niall, but hoped his attitude projected how happy he was to see her again.

'Well . . . that's all I wanted to say, really.' Obviously relieved, she flashed him a smile, then turned and began to melt into the darkness, but paused in anticipation when it looked as if Niall was eager to speak.

But he simply blurted, 'Er, thank you anyway – even if there was no need!'

Her lips retained their smile, though Niall thought he saw a hint of disappointment in her blue eyes as she gave a little nod, then went on her way and he on his. And, as he went, he thought about what she had said about going to evening Mass, and made a note to himself to look out for her at church on Sunday, for he had not noticed her there before, being too involved in his devotions. He hoped, though, that he would see her again much sooner than that.

For the first time in days he felt his spirits elevate, thoroughly restored from the gloom that had descended since his altercation with her. Hence, upon nearing home and seeing his boys playing football under a streetlamp, he cantered up to join in a lively kickabout until, remembering that he was supposed to be grieving for Ellen, he swiftly composed himself, gave his boots a last rake on the iron scraper set into the wall, then went indoors, though his mood was to remain light-hearted.

That night he started visiting The Angel again.

Gradually becoming inebriated by the woman who served it, rather than the alcohol itself, Niall increased his excursions to five nights of the week from then on. Whilst this was all very well on a Monday, or even a Wednesday, when, the bar being relatively quiet, he could sit and watch her to his heart's content – perhaps even be lucky enough to share a word or two with her when he acquired the pint he had rationed himself – Friday turned out to be a different matter. Having arrived somewhat later than on previous visits, he encountered a wall of people the moment he came through the door. The place was so packed, he had to navigate his way through a labyrinth of elbows to acquire his drink. At last, there she was. Forced to raise his voice above the hubbub, he returned Boadicea's smile of welcome and asked for the usual. He noted briefly that there was something different about her tonight, but didn't know what it was until a few moments later he heard one of the female customers call to her from the passage, 'I love your new dress, dear!' And the recipient of this praise joked, 'I'm glad somebody noticed.'

Ah, that was what it was. Niall hardly ever paid attention to such detail, but studied her garment more closely now. It was blue with flowers on it, and made of silky stuff that emphasised every curve – which was probably why he had noticed neither the pattern nor colour before. With all the tables occupied and his usual nook taken, he remained at the bar to watch and to yearn. But sadly there was to be no chat with her tonight, for after serving him she was instantly off to serve another, maintaining this hectic pace all the while he was there.

Crammed in from all sides, alert to straying elbows that might jolt and spill his pint, he made tentative sips of it, whilst his eyes followed Boadicea to and fro behind the bar. His ears too strained to attend her, to decipher her Irish lilt from the blunt Yorkshire vowels that obscured it, to detect every word from her smiling lips – and were just becoming attuned when a roar went up. Niall turned his head in vexation to see what had ruined his evening. Unable to discern the origin, he was soon to be made aware, as a piano was set upon with gusto, the whole pub erupting into lively accompaniment.

His faint disgust must have been apparent, for

when his eyes returned to Boadicea, he received a signalled command from her to cheer up and join in with the singing, her mouth pretending to mimic his in an exaggerated sulk, and though he didn't sing he was forced to smile back. She responded with a grin of commendation, every feature of her face participating in that smile and her warm eyes focused completely on him, which made him feel on top of the world. It was not to last for long, her services required elsewhere, but Niall was to treasure this little piece of attention as if she had pinned a medal to his chest.

With a practice born of necessity, the level of his glass was reduced sip by sip over the next hour. Whilst around him others grew merrier and more boisterous, singing at the top of their voices, he remained sober, all the better for watching the object of his desire, making out, when she caught him studying her, that he was enjoying the singsong with the rest. Seeing others treat her to a drink, he wished he could buy her one too. Maybe next week, he could wangle extra allowance from Nora. But if he were to stand Boadicea a drink, he would make sure it bought him her full attention.

'Are you ready for another, sir?'

Realising the question was directed at him, Niall tore his eyes from Boadicea and glanced at the landlord who asked it, before checking his almost empty glass. 'Er, no, thanks, I'm all right.'

'I just thought as you'd been stood there for a while,' persevered Mr Langan, a respectful yet commanding figure in his black suit, his brawny hands pressed to the counter, 'you might be waiting to get served.'

'No, no.' Niall's reply was casual. 'I'm just here 'cause I can't get a seat.'

The firmly patient tone became strained and the large face was thrust deliberately closer. 'Only you're keeping other customers from the bar!'

Not until then did Niall realise he was being castigated. 'Oh – right, sorry!' He could have retained his place by buying another half – might have done had it been Boadicea who hovered to serve him. Alas, she was away at the far end of the bar, so he picked up his glass and began to squeeze himself away through the throng, seeking another space from which to watch her. But there was none. Nor was there a way back: immediately he had moved, another rushed to fill his slot and that was the last chance Niall had of speaking to her for the remainder of his time there.

Still, by drawing himself up to full height, he could glimpse her golden head bobbing its way back and forth along the row of drunken patrons, whilst he sipped his drink and the crowd bawled in unison, 'Oh, Danny Boy, the pipes, the pipes are ca-a-lling!'

The songs, the sentiments bequeathed by their grandfathers, were Irish, though the voices were not, the lyrics delivered mainly in loud Yorkshire tones as the participants sang of the old country that their ancestors had departed long ago. And in this alone, despite his Yorkshire name and his Yorkshire accent, Niall felt his Irish heart at one with them.

Inevitably, after stretching it out for so long, he was finally unable to drain another drop from the glass. Even so, he continued to stand there. Thwarted at having to share her with so many others, he was loath to depart – though not from this mob, who had grown increasingly drunk. How irritating it was to be amongst such a crush when oneself was sober. Look at them – how foolish they appeared as the maudlin tune gave way to a gayer refrain and set them jigging. No matter that it was crowded, one of their number was performing a strenuous dance, arms akimbo, lifting his knees in the air. The big Irish drover was well known in the area, usually good-natured, but boisterous in his cups. Niall could see what was about to happen – tried to warn the drunken buffoon that there was someone about to pass behind him with a tray of drinks – but his voice was lost amid the deafening entertainment. The drover hopped backwards, bashed into the man with the tray and there came the sound of shattering glass. A few heads turned, there were groans from behind the bar, but these were lost amid a cacophony of ivory keys and discordant voices. Nothing could still the dancers, who proceeded to crunch across the carpet of shards, singing to their hearts' content whilst the poor fellow who had just paid for the drinks was left to stare in dismay at his empty tray.

''Scuse me!'

Niall looked on sympathetically as the victim tried to catch the attention of the big Irish fool who continued to dance about like a lunatic, eventually managing to tug at his sleeve.

'You might offer to pay for them!'

But the author of the disaster stopped only briefly to weigh up the little fellow, and to demand with a contemptuous sneer and a thick Irish brogue, 'What're ye going to do about it if I don't, Johnny-boy?' Then he cackled out loud and went back to his dancing, flailing his arms and legs about like a maniac.

He was not to do so for long. His victim might be a foot shorter but he had a weapon in his hand. Lifting the tray, he dealt the Irishman an almighty blow to the back of his head, so hard that the tray instantly buckled and so did the man's legs – but only for an instant, for he wheeled round in anger and was about to take a swing at the one who had assaulted him, when another grasped his arm.

'I think you ought to pay for his drinks,' demanded Niall.

Restricted by the iron grip, the drover turned his hostility on the one who held him and, wrenching himself free, threw a punch at Niall, which was easily parried. With this insufficient to halt the attack there was only one way to terminate it: Niall dealt a blow that knocked him to the ground.

The crowd, which had drawn aside like two

separate curtains at the first sign of trouble, now swept back together, laughing and singing along with the piano player, who had not even missed a beat, whilst the avenging angel Niall rubbed his knuckles and looked down at the bully, who lay out cold on the glass-sprinkled tiles.

'Sure, I wouldn't want to be upsetting you!' laughed an Irish voice close to his ear, a kinder female one this time.

It was Boadicea, come to try to sweep up the mess, though she was not allowed to do so until the obstacle had been removed by his friends. The piano player changed to a gentler tempo and the crowd took an interval from their dancing.

'Sorry, I just can't stand people like him!' Niall increased his pitch against the raucous strains of 'I'll Take You Home Again, Kathleen'.

She wrinkled her nose and bent to her task. 'Aw, he's all right really. 'Twas just the drink talking.'

Realising this did not present him in a good light, Niall felt he should justify his action. 'I'm not usually so quick to hit somebody! He gave me no option; it was him or me.'

'Sure, I know that!' She did not sound at all recriminatory. 'He was asking for a few tours of the parade ground, as my old dad would say, and you were only looking out for the little fella. Your man'll be regretting it tomorrow, so he will. Likely be offering to buy you a drink!'

'That's probably true,' agreed Niall, still rubbing his scuffed knuckles, his attention more on

Boadicea now, for it was suddenly and delightfully brought home to him that he usually only ever saw her from the waist up. Taking advantage of this new perspective – the young woman crouching unawares – he examined first the wide hips, then followed the line of a rather shapely calf in a tan silk stocking, to the finely boned ankle that protruded from the high-heeled court shoe. 'They're a strange lot, the Irish,' he concluded.

'Ye cheeky article!'

He was forced to tear his eyes from her leg as she came upright with a look of faked offence, and dealt him a dig with her arm.

'I hope you're including yourself in that remark?'

So, she had remembered what he had told her then, about being of Irish stock. This and the little nudge of familiarity pleased him no end, and he grinned at her. 'Aye, well, there's some'd say I'm nobbut strange meself.'

Boadicea grinned back, her eyes sparkling, but already her attention was being stolen by another who was thrusting a coin in her hand to pay for the spilled drinks, and soon she was set to return to the bar, her shovel piled with glass. Still, she included Niall in an afterthought as she left him. 'Would you be after a refill an' all?'

'No, thanks, I've had my quota for the night.'

'See you again then!' called Boadicea, before being swallowed up by the revellers.

Aye, you'll see me again, thought Niall warmly, her final smiling comment topping off the evening nicely for him, as he took one last covetous look, then went out into the night.

Friday's episode being too boisterous for one of such a quiet disposition, he decided it was point-less to call in at the pub over the rest of the weekend, for he would see very little of Boadicea. But oh, the aching emptiness this involved... Being without her for two nights was as hard a separation as he had ever experienced, tearing at his gut in a way that was almost physical in its intensity. It was a crime in itself to attend confes-sion and be forgiven for his sinful thoughts, when he had every intention of repeating that sin, but Niall went along anyway, if simply for the fact that his parish priest was one of the few to whom he could unload such a burden – though he did not name names, of course, but restricted the infor-mation to a generalised confession of impure thoughts. So long as those thoughts were not put to deed he could rely on Father Finnegan's under-standing; he was a man himself, after all.

Already conscious of the worried looks that were exchanged between Nora and her daughters, as he had gone off to the pub night after night, he dared not extend his itinerary to the Sabbath, though he would dearly have loved to, for come Sunday he was as thoroughly depressed and agitated over his withdrawal from Boadicea as an alcoholic might be from his whisky. Hence, by Thursday of the following week, his good intentions of limiting his visits looked set to collapse, for he had been to The Angel four times in as many days, and in all probability would be there on a fifth.

It did not matter that often he had not even the chance to converse with her other than to obtain his drink of choice; he was content be in her presence, to watch and to listen and to admire. Barely able to afford even the one pint per visit, he had foregone other things, walked miles to work where once he might have caught the bus, in order just to sit nursing the glass that permitted him to be near her; a nearness that became almost unbearable as he witnessed others do what he himself would love to be doing. He was deeply jealous of the ease with which they chatted to her, though he told himself he had no right to be. It was not as if she belonged to him.

Which in turn made him ask, did he want her to? Sitting there on his own, night after night, levered away from the bar by those more extrovert, and by his own lack of confidence, in his unobtrusive corner he had been privy to all manner of discussion about the fair Irish barmaid, and would have known if there had been a rival. He had even heard one fool comment that she was a bonny enough lass but there must be 'summat up with her' to remain a spinster at her age. Well, here was one who would have her.

Acutely conscious where this would lead, and how it would hurt Ellen's family and possibly his children, and that he was a hypocrite for the way he had condemned his brother yet was following the same route himself, Niall tried hard to overcome his feelings . . . but maybe not hard enough . . . or maybe it was just that he did not really want to. He could not remember experiencing such a reaction over anyone, not even Ellen in the first flush of courtship. He had not even known it was possible to feel a passion that took over one's entire life. Which was why, finally abandoning all self-delusion, all pretence of noble resistance, and surrendering to a baser, masculine selfishness, he decided he must pluck up the courage and ask her to go out with him.

Yet, whilst his happiness flourished over this decision, so too did his guilt, for, acting totally against character, he had lied to those at home about the recent change in his social habits, had made out that he had joined the Railway Institute where there were all kind of activities to take one's mind off one's sorrows – feeling guiltier still at using a dead wife as his excuse. But nothing could have deterred him now from seeing that lovely Celtic lass.

Obsessed as he had become in his mission, hoping like some callow schoolboy to disguise his tracks by way of sucking peppermints, Niall did not realise for a while that such uncharacteristic behaviour had spurred others into action. Not until that Friday evening did he see disaster loom. He had opened the door of the pub, about to enter, when, alerted by a police whistle, he turned swiftly to see two officers bearing down on a youth who ran for his life, their truncheons at the ready. But it was something even more unnerving that caught his eye. Looking as startled as he himself felt, Harriet stopped dead in her tracks, making it obvious she had been following him.

Instantly defensive, Niall took a step backwards into the street, allowing the door to swing shut as he turned to confront her, his stance indignant. 'What do you think you're playing at?'

His sister-in-law's expression of guilt was quickly replaced with one of determination, as she bustled up and thrust her face at him. 'And what are *you* playing at? Cracking on you were going to the Institute—'

'Can't a bloke change his mind? I decided I couldn't be bothered to trail all that way – me legs do get enough punishment at work, you know!'

She tapped his chest knowingly. 'You can't pull the wool over my eyes! What's going on, Nye?'

'Nothing!' But Niall felt the heat of embarrassment as it rose up his neck, turning his face red. 'I don't know what you're on about.'

Confronted by his anger, Harriet failed to interpret the underlying guilt, but instead took it as indication that her mother had been correct, he *was* trying to conceal something. 'I'll bet you've been nowhere near the Institute. You've been coming here all the time, haven't you?'

'I haven't!'

'I don't believe you!' came the blunt accusation.

'And what if I have?' he demanded testily. 'What has it got to do with anybody else? You've no right to be following me!'

Harriet grasped his upper arm in an act of concern. 'Look, Nye, it's only for your own good. We can see how you miss Ellen. I still can't believe she's gone so it must be ten times worse for you, losing your wife . . .'

At the sound of her name his belly flipped again. How could he have let himself be caught out in such shameful fashion? Now he guessed how his brother must have felt.

'But you can't drown your sorrows, you know,' said Harriet. 'You'll just pickle your liver, and then where will your children be?'

When her victim continued to frown at her blankly, obviously unwilling to admit his problem, she added a lively incitement. 'If you think you've been covering it up with peppermints you're wrong!'

In the wonderful realisation that he was not being accused of anything worse, Niall felt his chest flood with relief, eventually demanding with a forced, dry bark, 'You think I'm turning into an alcoholic?'

'You might not accept it, but this is how it starts,' reasoned Harriet.

But this evinced only humour, Niall shaking his head and his face creased with laughter, such was his relief. 'You daft bugger! How could I afford it with your mam doling out my spending money?'

At this, Harriet let go of his arm and paused to consider the matter, her face undergoing a gradual dawning.

'In fact,' Niall went on strenuously, 'I've been told off by t'landlord for making my pint last an hour and a half. Come and ask him if you don't believe me.' It was a safe enough invitation; she would never be seen in a bar.

'No, no!' His sister-in-law was looking somewhat relieved herself now. 'I'll take your word for it . . . of course it makes sense . . . sorry, it's just that we've all been so worried for you, Nye.' She inclined her square jaw in an attitude of repentance, her glassy grey orbs searching his.

'Thanks,' he said with gratitude, though suddenly awash with renewed penitence at so deceiving her. 'But don't be. I just need to get out of the house for a while. These dark evenings are getting me down . . .'

'Well, I hope you're not staring into your glass, moping.' She wagged a finger at him, though satisfied enough with his explanation.

'No, there's usually a game of darts or dominoes to occupy me.' That was true; at least there would have been had he wanted to disrupt his happier pursuit for a more trivial one.

Accepting this at last, Harriet apologised again. 'Well, I'm sorry we thought the worst of you. Carry on and enjoy yourself.' And with that she backed away into the darkness, saying she would go home now and vindicate him with her mother and sister.

Glad of her departure, Niall considered himself lucky, told himself he should be more careful and should not pursue this doomed liaison. And at that moment he seriously considered it. But, pushing open the door to the saloon, his eyes lit up as they settled upon Boadicea, and just as quickly, his former resolution was quashed.

Tonight would mark a turning point, he decided, as she greeted his arrival at the bar more warmly, more personally than usual. There was a definite connection between them – he was sure of it from her eyes. The exchange with Harriet had fired him up. Upon asking for his pint in the normal fashion, he found the nerve to blurt an additional request. 'Could you get tomorrow night off and come out with me?'

There was fleeting disconcertment. Then Boadicea raised her fair eyebrows and, with a rather mocking chuckle, said, 'It's good to tell you're not accustomed to pubs.'

Taken aback by this unexpected response, he looked blank.

'Saturday's our busiest night!' she declared.

His embarrassed laughter joined hers. 'Oh aye, sorry, I was forgetting what day it is!' She had done that to him – made it so he could think of nothing else. Sometimes he was unsure what planet he was on, never mind what day of the week it was. Undeterred, he blurted quickly, 'Sunday then?'

'I'm afraid I'll be working that too. Sorry.' Wearing an apologetic smile, she finished pulling his pint and handed it over.

Not wanting to sound desperate in asking which night she was free, he nodded quickly, handed over payment and murmured, 'Maybe another time then,' and he hid his discomfiture in his glass.

Boadicea dealt him another brief smile, though not another word, before moving on to serve someone else. Receiving no encouragement, Niall retired to his usual corner to nurse his wounded pride.

Deeply disappointed and utterly confused by her attitude – one minute seeming to welcome his attentions, the next giving him the brush-off – he chose not to go to the pub on Saturday, almost managing to remove his mind from her by helping his children prepare for their coming roles in the St Patrick's Day procession.

At least, though, he did manage to grab sight of her on Sunday, if only at Mass. She looked so lovely, so angelic with her rosy cheeks, and her golden hair curling from under a new green hat, he couldn't understand why no other man seemed as interested as he. But to feast his eyes on her would give him away, though the glimpse he allowed himself was totally insufficient, and the thought of another evening without her unbearable.

His eye on the clock for opening time, directly after tea he decided to risk his mother-in-law's wrath and visit Boadicea at her place of work.

There were more stunned faces, naturally, over this detour from the normal Sabbath routine.

'Not going to Benediction? But you always love to go!'

It was indeed Niall's favourite service, but, 'Not tonight. I don't feel like it.' However, it was obvious he was intent on some venture for he had risen.

'Where you off then, Dad?' asked Juggy.

'Mm?' Niall examined himself in the mirror. Seeing that the sprig of shamrock in his lapel was rather wilted, he went to the scullery and delved into the bucket for a fresh one and was pinning it on as his daughter asked again: 'Where you off?'

He looked down at her now. 'Oh . . . nowhere.'

'The same place he goes the rest of the week,' muttered Nora, casting a tight-lipped expression at Harriet and Dolly, who looked similarly disapproving.

Niall ignored this, but catching the six-year-old's fearful expression, he addressed her more gently. 'Don't worry, Jug, I'll be here when you get home from Mass.'

Hardly noting that his daughter was not fully reassured, he turned to Nora. 'Would you mind taking the kids?'

'I suppose I'll have to,' retorted his mother-in-law somewhat sniffily at being taken for granted.

'Thanks.' Warning his children to be good, Niall

went directly along the passage to the front door, as he did so overhearing a stern addendum from Nora.

'A good job there are more dutiful souls around to maintain the children's religion whilst others fall prey to the evils of drink!'

But he chose not to heed the disparaging comment, and soon his entire thoughts were once again fixed on Boadicea, determined that she would be swayed.

Needing no other alibi than it was Sunday, his weekday casual garb was displaced by a navy-blue double-breasted suit and tie, a silver watch chain gleamed upon his waistcoat, his shoes were buffed to a high gloss, and his dark hair also groomed. How could she turn him down? There was a fresh confidence to his step, a sparkle to his eye, as he swung open the door of the saloon, marred only by the fact that she was not behind the bar when he arrived, and so did not immediately witness this new Mr Doran. For the moment that did not concern him, for she might be serving in the snug. It was busier tonight, being St Patrick's Day, the bar all decorated in green.

Provided with his glass of Guinness by the landlord, Niall remained at the counter in the expectation of chatting to Boadicea when she did finally come around this side, occasionally running a finger around the inside of his starched collar, and admiring his reflection in the mirrored glass behind the bar, what little there was of it between the bottles of liquor and the row of green pennants. The pint had been three-quarters consumed by the time he accepted that she was not coming.

Forcing himself to sound casual, swilling the dregs of his pint round his glass as a prelude to buying another, he remarked, 'Barmaid's late tonight.'

'She doesn't work on a Sunday,' Mr Langan informed him.

Niall's heart dropped. And then he immediately stiffened, the surge of disappointment being quickly overwhelmed by anger that she had lied to him – lied simply to get rid of his unwanted advances. Tossing the last of his drink down his throat, he wished the man a curt good night and left.

5

'Not going out?' enquired Nora on Monday evening, when her son-in-law remained in his work clothes for longer than was usual – long after the children were in bed – and sat in preoccupied fashion staring into the fire.

Still deep in thought and brooding over being made a fool of, Niall took a moment to glance up at her and the other women who closely examined him, then shook the frown from his brow. 'No, I think I'll have an early night . . .'

Harriet and Dolly exchanged looks of relief that he was not resorting to alcohol again; though both were to feel concerned that his recent good mood should have relapsed so quickly, as he added in lacklustre voice, 'I just can't bring meself to go to bed.'

Nora empathised with his reluctance. 'Too much room in it, I know. 'Sfunny, when my Dom was alive I was forever bashing and prodding him, trying to grab meself more space, but afterwards . . .' Her voice trailed off in a wistful sigh.

His mind somewhere else, Niall picked at the hard skin on his workman's fingers. 'Seems a bit daft, me having that double bed all to meself, and the rest of you squashed in together. Why don't we have a shuffle round, and I share with the boys?' His suggestion came out of the blue.

Though it choked Nora to say it, she broached a possibility; for if one brother could do it, then so could the other. 'Well, I didn't like to suggest it meself. I thought maybe you might decide you want to get married again some day.'

He looked shocked that she might have guessed what had been behind his nocturnal jaunts, and tried to read what was in her eyes whilst delivering adamant rebuttal. 'No, no, there'll never be anyone else for me.' After his humiliation by Boadicea, he had finally decided to be content with his lot. 'Unless of course I lose my chief cook and bottle-washer,' came the half-jocular addendum.

His mother-in-law looked gladdened by this show of allegiance, her masculine face and steely grey eyes projecting warmth, as much as they were able. 'No, I'll always be here to see you're fed and watered. I just thought I'd make sure. Wouldn't want to hold you back . . . I should have known you better,' she concluded fondly. Harriet and Dolly too looked pleased about his loyal decision.

'Well then,' Nora rubbed her hands thoughtfully, as if intending business, 'if you're quite sure, Nye, we will have that shift about tomorrow.'

His soulless nod conveyed certainty. 'If you wait till I get home I'll give you a ha—'

'Nay, just you leave it to us!' Nora's tone impressed upon him that she would not dream of this. 'You work hard enough as it is, me and the lasses'll organise everything, won't we?'

'Well, if you don't mind—' began Niall.

'Mind?' cried Harriet, springing up to make cups of cocoa and tweaking his cheek playfully in passing. 'I thought you'd never ask! After twelve years of having our Dolly's toes stuck in me face, I'll be up at the crack of dawn to turf you out of bed.'

There was soft laughter then, and discussion over who would sleep where.

Hence, for Niall, it was his last night alone. From then onwards, he would sleep alongside his boys.

For a whole week he managed to stay away from the pub. Yet try as he might, he could not forget Boadicea, nor her lie that had so hurt and insulted him. It niggled at him day after day, demanding an explanation. If nothing else, he would have that.

Staving off any qualm from Nora and her daughters, he convinced them that tonight's venture was not a regression to his previous drinking habits. 'But I reckon I should force meself to go out once a week, if only for the sake of sanity – mindst, I could have changed me mind by the time I come in!' That was certainly true, the outcome dependant on Boadicea's apology.

It might have been an idea, thought Niall after a catastrophic evening, to grant her the chance to offer one first, before steaming in with a smart comment. The look on her face as he said it . . .

'You must have long arms, being able to pull pints when you're somewhere else.'

It was obvious she had translated the remark, for she had the grace to blush. 'Oh, yes, Mr Langan said you'd been in . . .' Slightly flustered, she picked up a glass and prepared to fulfil his requirement.

'Get a better offer, did you?' He did not meet her eye, hoping it was obvious that underneath his stiff exterior he was furious with her.

'No,' she said firmly, grasping the ivory handle of the pump. 'I was at home. I had things to do.'

'If you didn't want to go out with me why didn't you just say?'

'It's not that . . .' She fought for an explanation. 'I was just thunderstruck that you'd even ask. I wasn't expecting it from a married man. I didn't know what to say.'

Niall's blue eyes brimmed with indignation. 'You think I'd ask you out if I was married?'

Her own eyes were cynical. 'A bachelor has no reason to visit a pub in order to get his newspaper read. Sure, I know a married man looking for a bolthole when I see one.'

'Oh, so now I'm a liar as well!' He was grossly insulted.

'If I'm wrong then I beg your pardon, but either way it proves we don't really know each other, doesn't it?' Ill at ease, she worked the pump, filling the selected glass to a creamy head. 'I think it's best if we just keep our conversation for the pub.'

'Suits me! On second thoughts, don't bother with that!' And thus saying he turned his back on the glass she had presented, went directly from the bar, and was to prowl in the darkness for half an hour in the hope of composing himself by the time he got home.

He might have succeeded in pulling the wool over Nora's eyes. He might even have convinced himself that all was well, as he went on to perform his usual tasks during the ten days that followed. But all was not well, for despite every effort he failed to overcome his obsession with Boadicea. His face might often bear a smile but his heart was a vacuum. And eventually, that inconsolable longing was to drive him back.

That others might suffer because of this deci-sion he was hardly to notice. Coming home that evening, his sole intention to fill his belly before going straight out again to The Angel, he found that the rain that drenched his clothing had also driven his children indoors. Juggy and her friend had set up a 'house' in the passage, laying out blankets and pillows for their dolls, talking to them as if they were naughty children. On seeing her adored father, the little girl beamed, and looked set to jump up.

'Do you want me to come in now, Dad?' she asked him.

But, intent on one pursuit, Niall was to stride over the obstruction she had created. 'No, you're all right to play for a while, love,' he told her, briefly ruffling her hair before moving straight to the living room, and leaving a crestfallen face in his wake.

Her siblings were to fare no better, their pleasure at seeing him rewarded with a smile of lesser value, the younger ones' request for a bedtime story receiving short shrift.

'Oh, I'm a bit tired tonight, lads,' was all their father murmured abstractedly, as he gulped down his tea. 'Maybe somebody else'll oblige.'

'I'll read you one,' a kind-hearted Dominic told his little brothers. But it did not escape his notice that Father seemed not too tired to go out again.

The moment Niall walked into that pub his spirits miraculously soared. However, they were soon to plummet, for the object of his dreams appeared not to have missed him at all. She was chatting to some other man when he went up to the counter, and seemed reluctant to tear herself away, until the landlord prompted from the other end of the bar, 'Eh, missus, are you going to serve Rockefeller?'

Smirking at Mr Langan's pun, Boadicea came up to enquire of Niall, 'The usual, is it?'

No apology, no *how are you*, even. Cut to the quick by her indifference, he nodded and placed the correct money on the bar. She served him as politely as she would anyone else, then wandered back to her previous conversation partner. Niall carried his pint to a table, pulled out a stool and sat with his back to her, inwardly sobbing with anger and frustration. Before he knew it his glass was empty. Against habit, he took it back to the bar for a refill.

It was the landlord who served him this time, affecting great astonishment. '*Another*? 'Struth! Don't tell the taxman I've doubled me profits.'

Niall gave a sour smile, but accepted the teasing in good part, and, instead of returning to his table he remained at the bar to share a few desultory words with Mr Langan, cheered up slightly by the latter's humorous ancedotes. Soon, though, the landlord was called away, and with no one to entertain him, Niall took a self-conscious sip of his beer, put down the glass and stared into its depths, his heart aching.

'I feel a bit responsible.'

He knew it was her but did not glance up. 'For what?' he asked dully.

'Driving you to drink.'

He could have said *don't flatter yourself*, in fact

he did consider it, but he was not so openly rude, and he liked her too much. Oh God, how he liked her, and how it hurt that she didn't care for him. And so he said nothing.

'Do you always sulk when women turn you down?'

He did present his face then.

Taken aback by the intense sadness upon it, she flinched and appeared repentant. Still he did not reply. This was not a man for games. A glint of compassion in her eyes, Boadicea weighed her words carefully. 'It isn't that I don't want to go out with you personally, just that I've made it a rule never to go out with customers. If I do it for one I'd have to do it for another.'

Niall continued to stare at her unhappily, feeling no better at learning that she regarded him as just another customer. 'So why didn't you just tell me that there and then? I'd rather be told the truth than all that palaver . . .'

This stung her to irony. 'Like the palaver you fed me?'

Niall forced himself to remain calm. 'If you're on about me being married—'

'Don't kid me you're not.' She showed disbelief.

'I used to be, but my wife died.'

'Aw, God, I'm so sorry!' Boadicea's face was momentarily distorted, and she covered her mouth, imagining how difficult it must have been for him. 'And me accusing you of such indecency! She must have been young . . . how long is it since ye lost her?'

He was ashamed to say six months, didn't want to see those sympathetic eyes turn hard and to hear her say *you don't waste your time, do you?* Hence his reply was ambiguous and his gaze downcast. 'Oh . . . a fair while now.'

'Still, it's awful! I hope you'll accept my apology.' She formed a quick, sad smile. 'Sure, I always seem to be apologising, don't I?'

'Ah well, no harm done,' murmured Niall, lifting his eyes to her again.

'You're very gracious.' Even now she remained annoyed with herself. 'After I treated you like that, not even granting you the chance to say otherwise . . .' She shook her head in self-punishment.

Forgiving her everything, Niall took advantage, smiling warmly as he said, 'Does that mean you'll reconsider my invitation?'

She looked at first amazed. 'You still want me to go out with you after that?' Then, at his keen nod, she became flustered. 'Well . . . I would, but you see . . .'

'You don't go out with customers,' he provided.

'No, yes, no, what I mean is—'

'Some might say I deserve to be exempt from that rule, having putting up with such injury.' How daring that was for him to say!

Her attempts to explain were stilted. ''Tis awkward . . . you don't really know me . . .'

But this only gave Niall further encouragement,

for it was plain from her expression and the lack of an outright no that she very much wanted to say yes. Now it was he who was the better orator, his tone calm and reasonable and kind. 'I thought that's why people went out together, so they can get to know each other.'

'Sometimes you never really get to know a person.' In the course of those few moments, despite her apparent attraction towards him, Boadicea seemed to have become inexplicably edgy. 'Anyhow, what I really meant was, you've no idea what you'd be getting yourself into.'

'I won't know unless I'm granted the chance.' From the way she had uttered her latest remark, and her determination to hold him at arm's length, Niall got the strong impression that she had been hurt by someone; could see a struggle taking place behind that fair visage. He was about to reassure her, but just at that moment a customer slammed his glass on the other end of the counter and bawled for a refill. Apparently relieved at being rescued, Boadicea swiftly excused herself and hurried away.

Niall continued to watch her closely, denouncing his former lack of confidence as he did so, for he saw now that although she did use that smile of hers to great effect on others, her eyes did not behold them in the way they did him. And so, for once undeterred, he was content to bide his time while she rushed about and pretended to be busy. If he had to stand there all night he would have a positive answer.

This he told her after she had been compelled to return to the vicinity, unable to ignore his signal for a top-up. 'If I have to drink meself to death in order to get your attention then so be it.' Encouraged that she did not immediately dismiss him, he leaned nearer to her, conscious that he might be overheard, issuing his plea in a low earnest murmur. 'Just give us a chance. Then if you decide you don't want to go out with me again I'll gladly stand aside – well, not gladly, but you know what I mean.' He wondered if she did know what he meant; if his roundabout bumbling fashion had been sufficient to let her know how he truly felt about her.

Somehow, it must have struck a chord, for she too leaned forward to whisper, 'Look, Mr Doran, I like you—'

His face and spirits brightened considerably, though his voice was gruff. 'I like you, an' all. And me name's Niall.'

But she sought to temper any excitement her remark may have caused. '– so I'm going to tell you something and I'm not sure you'll feel the same afterwards.' She waited a second, checked that no one else could hear, then whispered, 'I'm married.'

Immediately she saw his shocked eyes go to her ring finger. With the thumb and forefinger of her right hand, she rubbed self-consciously at the denuded digit. 'I took it off when he left me. I don't know where he is and I don't care.'

'I *knew* you'd been hurt!' Niall exclaimed.

'Ssh! Nobody else knows, not even the people I board with.'

'Why? It's none of your fault. I'd say he's the one to blame for running out on you.' Niall found himself full of hatred for the one who had got there first.

'I just don't like people knowing my private affairs,' whispered Boadicea firmly.

'Neither do I.' Still shaken, but pleased to find something that they shared, he confirmed, 'They won't hear it from me.'

She smiled and tilted her head in appreciation. 'But now you can see why I'm not really free to walk out with you or anybody. Much as I'd like to,' came her sincere addition, her eyes endorsing this as they held his face.

Searching them, he pondered her answer for a while. In fact he was not to say anything else on the matter, for Boadicea was taken from him again. When she returned he had almost finished his pint. Deep in thought, mainly ones of jealousy, he emerged to ask, 'What will you do if you never see him again?'

She shrugged, took up a cloth and wiped spills from the counter. 'It's no loss.'

Niall shook his head. 'No, I meant it's not much of a life being on your own.'

Instead of identifying with this statement she exclaimed with a smile, 'Oh, I wouldn't say that. Sure, I'm happy enough with the folk in my boarding house.'

He kept his voice low, their conversation interspersed by the sporadic thud of darts into a board and occasional applause. 'So you'd never contemplate marrying anyone else? I'm not hinting or anything!' he hastened to add with a laugh. 'I'm just interested to know, being in a similar position. Even if you were free—'

'Never,' she said adamantly. 'Once bitten and all that.'

Stricken by bitter disappointment, Niall wondered if this showed. 'Still, it can't feel good knowing you're tied to somebody, yet not married in the real sense.'

'Marriage isn't for me,' she said with certainty.

It hadn't been for him a couple of weeks ago. How swiftly could one's life change. Desperate, utterly consumed by his need to possess her one way or another, he exclaimed, 'Tell you what! How about coming out with me just as a friend then? We both know where we stand. I can't see it'd do any harm and we like each other's company – least I think we do,' he ended with an embarrassed laugh.

She hesitated, probing his eyes warily, before replying, 'I suppose so . . .'

'Next week?' Having rationed himself to one night out per week, it might look suspicious to Nora if he were to start making regular outings again. 'What day?' He half expected another excuse.

But no. 'I've got next Monday evening off,' she

told him. 'In fact every Monday evening from now on 'cause they're changed my hours.'

Niall's heart soared in triumph, and though he tried his best to disguise this for fear of scaring her away, his face appeared brighter than she had seen it for weeks. 'Do you like the pictures?' At her enthusiastic nod, he began to list the options. 'There's Boris Karloff and Bela Lugosi at the Rialto – or maybe you prefer Greta Garbo?'

'No, give me a good fright any day.' She cocked her head knowingly. 'I see you've already checked to see what's on. I admire your confidence.'

'I wasn't confident at all, just hopeful.'

Her eyes were warm but stern. 'Remember we're just friends.'

'Just friends.' But his gut was taut with excitement.

'The Rialto it is then.'

He grinned his delight at the venue so easily being agreed. Then, with a care as to who might see them, he added, 'Shall I meet you outside? It'll have to be second house 'cause I'm working away and I sometimes don't get home while seven.'

'That'll be grand,' smiled Boadicea.

And the deal was struck.

Niall could hardly believe this was happening – would refuse to believe it until she was standing there outside the cinema – and he bade himself not to become overexhilarated. Even so, there were plans to construct. For a start he would need more than his usual pocket money from Nora. Without wanting to explain what the extra amount was for, he took it from his wage packet on Friday before handing it over. The slightest hesitation as she opened it showed that she had noticed the packet had been tampered with, though to his relief she did not remark on it.

Then there was the question of his whereabouts. Having allotted Monday as his night out there would be no trouble getting away, but with two films and a newsreel to watch, he would be out much longer than usual. Whilst he laboured on the railway line, he was to mull over a list of excuses. But why not be truthful? At least half truthful? It wasn't illegal for a man to go to the pictures on his own and that was what he would let them assume.

Having made that decision, his next concern was what to wear. It bothered him that he could not dress in suit and tie, and he fretted over this as he donned these for Mass on Sunday. But there was much more to bother him that morning, for this was no ordinary Sabbath. Only the most thick-skinned of men would have enquired what ailed the children, who sat all misty-eyed and forlorn in preparation of their trip to church. Where others would offer flowers and prayers of gladness on this, Mothering Sunday, Honor, Dom, Juggy, Batty and Brian would only be reminded of their still raw loss, and Niall's heart went out to them, knowing how empty was this festival for those without a mother. His eyes pricked with tears when Juggy was the one to articulate her own despair and that of her siblings. 'I wanted to make one for you, Gran,' she murmured sadly, as she examined the cards on the sideboard that had been sent by Nora's daughters, 'but, 'teacher wouldn't let me. She said we could only make one for our mothers . . .'

Everyone looked round as Honor rushed outside. Not knowing what to do, a concerned Niall glanced at Nora, but she shook her head as if to say leave the child be.

Whilst the boys hung their heads, Juggy turned her attention back to the cards. 'I told her I didn't have a mam any more – Mary Kelly put her hand up, an' all – but 'teacher said it wasn't called Grannying Sunday and those of us who didn't have a mam could do jobs instead, so I had to bash the chalk out of the blackboard duster.'

'Stupid bloody woman,' muttered a tearful Harriet to her mother, as she turned away to put on her hat.

Niall was angry too, but his voice was soft as he bent over to address his little daughter. 'If you want to make your mam a card,' he said firmly, 'then you can. And this afternoon we'll go on Low Moor and pick her some flowers and lay them where your mam's put to rest.'

'Will we see her when she's had her rest?' came the hopeful query from Brian.

131

'No, son, you won't.' Niall shook his head and, straightening, he chucked his youngest with sad affection before turning away.

'Away now,' said Nora in a gruff voice that betrayed deep emotion. 'Let's get to Mass.'

Whilst the women put last-minute touches to the youngsters' appearance, Niall wandered outside to where Honor lingered miserably by the front window. A dejected figure in her grammar school uniform and beret, she remained with eyes downcast, so as not to see her friends with their bunches of flowers.

'It'll get better,' he murmured, trying to convey in his manly way that he understood how it felt to lose one's mother. 'I know you won't think so at the moment, but it will. And when it does, you'll feel guilty for laughing or whatever . . .' The face beneath the school beret looked up at him then, giving away a hint that Honor had already experienced this sensation. 'But you shouldn't,' he added quickly, 'because your mam wants you to be happy. Still . . . it's only fitting that you'll feel sad today.' He placed a helpful hand to steer her. 'Come on, you and me'll set off and let t'others follow.'

As they walked, Honor was quiet for a while, before blurting, 'I feel guilty about something else, Dad.'

Niall looked down at her, his face kind and quizzical.

'I can't tell you what it is. It's too awful.' She

was obviously racked with conscience. 'I can't even tell Father Finnegan at confession, but if I don't . . .' Her face told what would befall her.

Niall was becoming worried, but had to coax this out of her with a gentle squeeze of her shoulder. 'I can't think you've done anything so bad—'

'I wished it were Gran who died instead of Mother!' She hardly dared look at him.

But her father seemed relieved it was not worse. 'Don't think too badly of yourself, Honey. Your gran's old; she'd probably wish exactly the same thing.'

Taught by nuns, Honor remained anxious. 'But God knows all the secrets of our hearts . . .' She saw the look of shock that pulled her father up in his tracks.

Niall recovered his step quickly, but felt totally wretched, for if Honor only knew, his own secret was so much worse. It was one he had to live with, but his child did not. 'Yes, He can see into your heart and He can tell it's a good and pure one, and that you didn't mean it,' came his words of comfort, he desperately trying to draw comfort from them himself as he assuaged his daughter's worry. 'He wouldn't punish you for wanting to keep your mam alive. I'm sure of it.' Whether or not God would punish him for imagining Ellen dead, was another matter. Try as he might to allay his child's fears, to convince her of a merciful Creator, the doctrine that had been impressed upon him both mentally and physically from childhood caused him to fear for his own soul.

However, it seemed to help Honor. Appreciating the firm pressure of his hand on her shoulder in its navy blazer, she did not look up but took reassurance in the love of her one remaining parent, and, leaning into Niall's steadfast presence, she accompanied him to church.

Despite his having reassured her, all in all, it was a melancholy day for Niall, the trip to the cemetery where his children laid flowers on their mother's grave overshadowing all thoughts of Boadicea.

Not until he removed his clothes for bed did he allow her to steal into his mind again. Placing the suit on a hanger, and giving it a gentle brush before putting it away and climbing into bed gingerly so as not to wake Brian, he was reminded of his thoughts upon donning it that morning, and before he fell asleep he wondered again if there was any way he could wear it for his date tomorrow night.

Awakening to that same image on Monday morning, he was forced to relinquish it, for there was no way round this. He was desperate to look his best for Boadicea, but that would immediately give the game away. Best clothes on a weekday? Must be going to see a woman! It was with some irony that he recalled a similar phrase directed at his brother. And now he was taking the same furtive path as Sean – not that they were cast from the same mould; no, he wouldn't have that. Sean's only reason for deceiving his mother-in-law had been to save his own skin, whereas Niall's action was to prevent her being hurt. For as much as he had condemned Nora in the past for her tyrannical nagging, she had been so good since Ellen's death, so compassionate in her handling of him, he could not have expected better treatment from his own mother. How could he hurt her by announcing that he had met someone else? The time would come when he would have to tell her. But not yet, not until there was really something to tell.

Yet despite this professed noble reason, his choice of venue was not without guile. The dark interior of the picture house would help to shroud him, and make it less likely that he be spotted. Imagining himself there beside Boadicea, perhaps with his arm around her to quell her squeals of fright at the horror film, the feelings of anticipation and sexual excitement grew, so that by Monday tea-time he could barely sit still for five minutes – not that he had the luxury for there was less than half an hour before the rendezvous, leaving him little time for ablutions.

To this purpose, unaware that he was being watched, he wolfed down his tea.

'You'll give yourself bellyache,' observed Harriet, turning a page of the evening newspaper. 'What's the rush?'

'I'm off to the flicks.' He had been dreading this moment of explanation. But apart from the murmur of slight surprise, Nora and her girls seemed pleased about his change of pastime.

'Well, I hope you weren't thinking of going to the Rye,' Harriet chuckled, without looking up from the paper.

Pricked by guilt, Niall hoped she would not comment on his blush. 'Why's that?' he asked, head lowered, still eating.

'It's burned down.'

'What?' His eyes shot up. 'When?'

'Saturday. It's in here.' She held up the print for him to see. 'I was just saying to Mam, that explains all the fire engine racket we heard.'

His fork still poised midway between plate and mouth, his plans so unexpectedly demolished, Niall groaned.

Misreading his dismay, Nora asked, 'Was it something you really wanted to see?'

'What?' He turned vague eyes on his mother-in-law who, with his children lined up before her, was performing her weekly search for nits, roughly positioning each head over a white cloth on her lap before running her comb through it. Breaking away from his thoughts about Boadicea, he set upon his meal again, saying hastily, 'Oh no . . . no, it doesn't matter. I'll go somewhere else.'

'There's a good one on at the Picture House!' Dolly jumped in eagerly. 'I wouldn't mind coming with you.'

Luckily, Niall had researched the programme. 'That's one o' them soppy ones, isn't it? I don't really fancy that. I might try George's instead.'

'Oh, if it's that historical thing about the Duke of Wellington you can stick it,' sniffed Dolly, as he had known she would, and she went back to plaiting Juggy's hair ready for bed.

'It won't go, Dad!' On his hands and knees, little Brian had been attempting to shove a home-made toy lorry across the square of carpet at the centre of the room, but now hurled it away in frustration.

'Eh! We'll have less of that,' warned Niall. Then, at a show of repentance, 'It'll wheel better on lino, son.' And he indicated the brown linoleum around the edge of the room, to where Brian quickly shuffled.

'Well, I'd best get ready then.' Still chewing, Niall clattered his knife and fork onto the empty plate and carried it briskly towards the scullery. 'Can I just have a wash before you do the pots?' Nora granting his wish, he climbed over Brian, and pulled the door shut after him.

Ensconced in the tiny scullery, he underwent a quick wipe with a flannel, generally smartening himself up, exchanging his working trousers for less ragged ones, his dusty boots for shoes. But that was the easy part. What the hell would he do about Boadicea now? What if she had heard of the Rialto fire and was in this same dilemma? He had no idea how to let her know, nor where she lived. The only thing for it was to head for the original venue and hope that she had reached the same conclusion.

His mind on this, he emerged from the scullery, again having to avoid Brian.

Hair in neat plaits, and in her nightgown, Juggy came straight to him. 'Can I have a story, Dad?'

His thoughts interrupted, anxious to be off, Niall glanced down at the elfin face, still forlorn from yesterday, and immediately his glazed expression melted. Grabbing a book from a shelf, he led her to his chair. 'Away then, sparrowshanks!' He pulled her onto his lap, where she snuggled in, her head against his chest. 'But don't get too comfy, 'cause it's just a quick'n!' But this was issued with a hug. Batty came running too, in his striped pyjamas and with happy round cheeks, reminding his father of a character from a comic. 'Away then, Tiger Tim!' Niall hauled him onto the other knee, then shouted to the youngest – 'Put that lorry down, Bri!' – finally to read them four pages from *All the Mowgli Stories*, before thoughts of Boadicea were to overrule his good intentions.

After a swift good night kiss to his little ones – for there was now less than ten minutes to get there – he was on his way.

Sunny by day, it might have been, but it was still only April and the nights retained their wintry chill. Without his greatcoat and feeling the nip, Niall huddled into his jacket, his excitement tempered by concern as he travelled briskly through the dark, passing from the labyrinth of terraced streets and alleys, under the thick stone archway of Fishergate Bar and its crenellated battlements that were scarred both by time and civil rebellion, past the row of stinking cattle pens that ran directly parallel to these same medieval walls, along Fawcett Street, with its public houses crammed full of drovers from today's fat-stock market, and on towards Fishergate.

An ominous smell of carbon hung in the air. Approaching the charred hulk of the cinema, he saw that he was not to be alone. A small number of other cinemagoers, unacquainted with the disaster, had turned up to see the film and were standing there in bemusement. To his great relief Boadicea was amongst them.

She did not see him for the moment, her profile slightly hidden behind her fur collar, which she had tugged around her neck and cheeks, but he knew it was her. Relaxing, he eased his pace and made a quick check of his attire before continuing, his lips twitching in fun as he moved up silently behind her.

'If you didn't want to go out with me you only had to say, you know. You didn't have to burn the place down.'

She spun round at his comment, looking as relieved as he was, then giggling heartily at the joke. Then she covered her mouth in guilt. 'Oh God, you're terrible! It's people's livelihoods – we really shouldn't be laughing!' But all the same she expressed further mirth at the ironic concurrence and so did Niall.

'I wasn't sure you'd be here.' He continued to appraise her lovingly, his smiling eyes fixed to hers, which were shining and alert, her cheeks and nose reddened by the keen air. 'I didn't find out meself till I got home, and then I realised I'd no idea where you live so I couldn't let you know.' Not expecting her to be so forthcoming, he was delighted when she did not hide her address.

'You know where Dorothy Wilson's Hospital is on Foss Bridge? Well, between there and the old Malt Shovel in Walmgate you might've seen an archway, go down there and you'll find a Georgian mansion – sounds grand, doesn't it? Oh, I'm terribly grand!' She stuck her nose in the air, flicked it haughtily, then laughed at her own quip. 'No, it's just a boarding house, dropping to bits really, and we're right next to a tripe dresser – stinks to high heaven – but the people are awfully nice. What about you? Do you live on Walmgate itself?'

Unlike her, he was imprecise, though not through any reason of concealment. 'No, I live down one of the streets, down t'other end, near the Bar.' He hovered self-consciously over what to do next, rubbing his large hands and looking around as if in search of a venue. 'Well, we can't hang about here in the cold . . . where would you like to go now?'

She followed his gaze to the Edinburgh Arms, and gave a cryptic smile. 'Not in there, for sure.'

'Aye, it'd be a bit of a busman's holiday for you, wouldn't it?' laughed Niall. 'Come on then, it'll only take us ten minutes into town. We can make our minds up when we get there.'

They embarked on a long stretch of pavement that sloped in gentle descent through the darkness towards the floodlit Minster and bar walls, walking independently of each other yet with an air of closeness between them. To their left, merging with the night sky, loomed the tall, smoking chimney of the glassworks, and along the way lurked other sinister intrusions; yet, totally in thrall to his companion, Niall saw none of them, his eyes remaining steadfastly on the lighted path ahead.

As usual it was Boadicea who initiated the conversation, enquiring cheerfully, 'Well then, Mr Niall Doran, and what have you done today at work?'

Having been struggling to think of a topic, he perked up instantly to tell her. 'Have you read about the wolf that's going round eating sheep?'

'Oh, yes!'

'Well, I saw him again today.'

Boadicea showed deep interest, sucking in her breath. 'You've seen him before then?'

'Aye! I was the first to report him – well, me and the rest of the gang!' Niall hurried to correct the impression that he was bragging. 'We've seen it plenty of times.'

'Come on then, tell me all about it!' she urged.

And so he did, this providing enough conversation to take them right the way into town.

Uninformed as to York's picture theatres, and asked which one she would care to visit, Boadicea plumped for the Electric, simply because it was near to where she lived and, in passing, she had liked the look of it. This caused Niall a moment's awkwardness. It might look like an ancient Greek palace, with its tall pillars, its huge archway graced with plaster garlands and swags and a theatrical mask, and be guarded by a grandly uniformed commissionaire, but beyond that entrance was a fleapit. However, there was another source to his discomfort as the usherette's torch showed them to their seats, namely the main film on show, ironically titled *The Man With Two Faces*. What would Nora think if she could see him? As if this were not enough, he was to suffer more self-torment at finding himself surrounded by courting couples, each squashed as closely together as decency would allow, whilst he sat there rigid and uncertain in his seat beside his companion in the dark. Still, Boadicea seemed to enjoy the show, despite the frequent scratching at her legs, and a good laugh was to be had not only from the accompanying comedy film, but from the newsreel showing German troops marching in goosestep.

'What kind of an army marches in that silly fashion?' Boadicea made fun of them as, after the closing National Anthem, she and Niall emerged from the cinema. 'They look as though they're auditioning as dance girls, kicking their legs in the air.'

He echoed her amusement, whilst stepping around her in chivalrous fashion onto the outside edge of the pavement. 'Aye, not much of a threat, are they?'

'You didn't enjoy the main picture very much, did ye?' she asked as they strolled side by side in the lamplight.

Niall glanced at her quickly. 'What makes you think that?'

''Twas just that ye looked a bit glum.'

'Oh, no, that was just my normal face!' he joked. 'I thought you'd know that by now.'

'Thank God,' she laughed in relief. 'I was afraid my choice might not have been to your taste.'

'No! I like anything with Edward G. Robinson in it.' How could he tell her that it had been the title that had caused his unrest, that had made him ashamed to be with her?

'Good, because I enjoyed it.' She smiled up at him. 'And the company. Thank you, Niall.'

'My pleasure.' Any residue of guilt was instantly quashed by that smile, and by the sound of his name on her lips. He would have liked to remain in her company for much longer, but she lived only a few hundred yards from the cinema and here they were on Foss Bridge already.

Not wanting the journey to end, he paused and leaned over the dirty stonework of the parapet, affecting to see something in the water.

'Must've been mistaken,' he smiled at her as they set into motion again, using this excuse to slacken his pace even further. Then both fell quiet for a moment, the only sound that of their shoes clip-clopping alongside each other on the pavement.

The bridge was all too short; they were almost to her lodgings. The smell from the fried fish shop growing ever stronger, and making him salivate, Niall wished he could afford to offer her some. He did have enough left in his pocket for two bags of chips, but it would be a total embarrassment if she asked for fish as well.

He struggled to think of something else with which to detain her. 'It's the King's birthday this year, isn't it?'

'Doesn't he have one every year like the rest of us then?'

Niall stopped in his tracks, unable to prevent a frustrated gasp.

His companion stopped too. 'What's wrong?'

'I thought I'd heard the last of them!' His reply was quietly forceful.

'Last of what?' Boadicea's face was clothed in amazement.

'Them bloody smart remarks!'

She issued a laugh of astonishment. 'Sure, I was only cracking a joke – least I thought it was!'

'Well, it sounded as if the joke was at my expense and I get enough of that at home. All I meant was, it'll be his blasted thingertikite – his jubilee! Anyhow, it's not important,' he finished rather huffily and moved off again. 'I was only going to ask if you're off to a party.'

'Mrs Langan will organise something at the pub, I'm sure.' Boadicea glanced at him curiously as they walked. 'God, you're a touchy little soul, aren't ye? I'll hardly dare say another word.'

After a moment's defiance, he hung his head. 'Well, maybe it's me, having to put up with too many catty remarks from my in-laws.'

She stopped again, her tone reassuring but slightly reproving too. 'Niall, there's a great difference between catty and witty. I'd never try and make fun of ye – in fact I'm really quite offended that ye'd think I would.'

'Sorry, it's me being daft,' he offered quietly.

As they walked on, Boadicea tried to offer encouragement, leaning into him for a moment with a smile that cajoled. 'Sure, there's nothing to stop you giving as good as ye get, ye know. I rather like the odd verbal joust.'

Niall's gaze was focused on his shoes. 'Nay, it'd take me a week to think up summat clever.'

She laughed, but her face showed sympathy. 'God love ye, I didn't mean ye have to be a genius, just offer a bit o' backchat, ye know.'

He continued to look at his feet. 'I can't see why you have to make snide remarks to people if you like them.'

'Oh, don't be such a stuffed shirt!' she took a risk in teasing him.

'I'm not, honestly!' he protested, lifting his eyes from the pavement to look at her. 'It's only that I prefer to call a spade a spade, so's everyone knows where they stand. I like a laugh as much as the next bloke.'

'Is that so?' She indicated a building. 'Well, at that house there lives the meanest, grumpiest old divil you're ever likely to meet. I dare ye to knock on his door and run away.'

'That's just childish,' he accused, but she had made him smile.

'I'll bet ye never even did it when you were a child,' challenged Boadicea.

'Yes, I did!'

'When?'

He had to cast his mind a long way back. 'Probably when I was about ten.'

'Time ye did it again then.' She stood there defiantly, obviously waiting for him to take up the challenge, but he refused with a laugh. 'Spoilsport!' She pretended to sulk. 'In that case I'll bid you good night, Mr Doran.'

For a second, Niall's face was clouded by dismay until he realised that all she meant was that they had reached the archway that led to her home. Then he smiled, though this was tinged with disappointment as he escorted her down the unlit alleyway to the crumbling mansion in which she lodged.

Here, uncertain how to leave her, he asked with some trepidation, 'Would you come with me again next week?'

'If you've a mind for the baiting.'

'I'm sure I'll get used to it.' He bared his teeth, covering them with a self-conscious hand, though his voice remained uncertain.

'Then I will,' she told him. 'Thank you.'

Relieved that his good behaviour had been rewarded, thinking that he had never felt so happy, Niall cocked his smiling face. 'I think Gary Cooper's coming to t'Picture House. They're showing Our Gang an' all – I like them.'

'Ah, already prepared again, I see!' Even now she could not resist teasing him. Staving off his protestations with soft calming laughter, and agreeing to the time and place, she concluded with an impish expression, 'Let's hope that place doesn't burn down too.'

Niall chuckled. He wanted very much to kiss her, but, having not so much as held her hand, dared do nothing now that might jeopardise this fragile friendship. 'Well, good night then. See you next Monday . . .' Still smiling, he backed away, not wanting to tear his eyes from her, until she turned and entered the lodging house, then he too went home with a bounce to his step.

6

Could anything ever come of this? Niall did not know. But for now he was glowingly content to sit beside her in the darkness of the Picture House, praying that his good behaviour would eventually lead to more. Braced with an excuse for those at home, he had been amazed at how easily they had accepted this second outing, had expected them to tease him over coming here alone, or at least to question; but they hadn't. If anything, they seemed pleased at his abrupt abandonment of the public house. That was all well and good, but, having allotted himself this one night out per week, Niall could not now turn round and say he was off for a drink, which meant that from now on he would only see Boadicea once every seven days, which in turn meant he had to make the most of her company whilst he had it.

And make the most of it he had, on the way to the cinema asking her questions about herself, never too intrusive or personal, merely enquiring about her likes and dislikes so that he might better please her if she consented to come out with him again.

He might not dare to ask personal questions, but Boadicea supplied the answers all the same, telling him much more about the place she had lived before coming to York, the various jobs she had had since arriving in England and the towns she had inhabited, rattling out so much information in that talkative manner of hers that he could never hope to remember it all. It had been almost a disappointment to reach the cinema; he would much rather have watched and listened to her than the film.

Still, it was wonderful to be seated here so tantalisingly close to her, the episode marred only by an awful grating noise from the woman nearby, who seemed determined to suck every last dreg of melted ice cream from its cardboard container, this causing much amusement to Boadicea.

Later, as they drifted through the foyer along with the other filmgoers, Niall noticed that some of them were now heading for the café above the Picture House. Not wanting the night to end, he asked impulsively, 'Do you fancy some supper?'

'Not one for self-denial, are ye, Niall?' But her eyes were bright. 'Neither am I – and sure, isn't Lent almost over?'

And with her smiling nod of approval, he escorted her up the staircase, adding, 'Let's hope that woman with the ice cream doesn't follow us in. She might start licking the plates.'

Boadicea chuckled. 'Yes, that's the only disadvantage of coming to a cinema: you have to put up with all that slurping and crunching. Not to mention some of the mucky pups ye get sitting next to ye. I've often gone home with more than I bargained for.' She pretended to scratch at vermin.

Having been shown to a table, and both having chosen from the menu, Niall mused with a thought as to their previous discussion. 'What we need is that television thing they've been on about in the papers. Wouldn't it be grand to have your own personal screen in your living room?'

'Aye, but then ye'd never have to leave the house except to work,' pointed out his companion. 'A bit boring, don't ye think? Besides, I doubt the likes of me will be able to afford it.'

'Me neither,' Niall smiled at her fondly. 'Not with five kids.'

This served to elevate Boadicea's eyebrows, not for the amount of children, which was a normal enough number for any Irish family, but the fact of the widower having to cope alone. She sought to reassure him. 'Well, don't worry, I'll be paying for the meal.'

'Nay, you won't!' He looked mildly offended, not least because the waitress had just come back to supply the glasses of water he had requested. 'I wasn't hinting, for heaven's sake.'

Boadicea said hurriedly for the benefit of the waitress, 'Oh, I know you weren't, but—'

'I wouldn't dream of asking a woman for money,' Niall cut her off. 'I was the one who invited you out.'

'Yes, but it isn't that sort of outing,' she reminded him as the waitress left. 'When I come out with friends I usually expect to pay my own way. You paid for the pictures, I'll pay for the meal.'

'I'd rather you didn't.'

Examining his face, she saw that he might feel insulted if she took out her purse in front of others, and so told him, 'Well, we'll settle up later.'

'No, we won't.' Niall remained firm.

'You're making it very difficult for me to come out with you again if you insist on paying every time,' she objected.

'It's hardly worth arguing over coppers, is it?' he pointed out with an air of finality.

'I should think it is when you've five children depending on ye.' Nevertheless, Boadicea used this subject to deflect further argument. Like Niall she had thus far refrained from being invasive, not even asking how many children he had, though now that he had made reference to his family, she did initiate gentle query. 'And who's looking after them, might I ask, whilst you're out enjoying your-self?'

'My mother-in-law. She looks after all of us.'

'Would I know her?'

Niall provided Nora's name.

His companion blurted laughter. 'No, I think I

would've remembered if I'd met someone called Mrs Beasty! Ah, look, I'm not one to be poking fun at someone's name – I'm sure she's very nice.'

'Well, I don't know about that,' grimaced Niall, imagining what Nora would say if she knew of his female companion. 'She can be a beasty by nature too, sometimes. But she's grand with the kids.'

'And what're they called? How old are they?'

He tweaked absent-mindedly at the tablecloth as he listed them. 'Dominic's eleven, he's named after Nora's husband—'

'Not after your father then?' she chipped in. 'I'd have taken you to be the traditional kind.'

'Aye, well, maybe I would if I'd had any say.' Niall looked rueful before going on, 'Honora's thirteen this summer, she's named after her granny, of course,' another regretful smile, 'Judith – Juggy – after me mam, she's six, nearly seven; then there's Bartholomew, after my father, he's nearly six, and Brian's the babby, he's three.'

Boadicea nodded, then was silent for a time. He wondered what she might be thinking. But she didn't enlighten him. In fact it was left to Niall to proceed with the dialogue, turning his attention to the cruet as he did so, correcting the position of the salt and pepper pots that were out of line. 'Two of Nora's daughters live with us as well.' He grinned. 'Sounds as if I have a right big house, what with nine people living in it, but it's just a two up, two down.'

'And here's me thinking I'd latched on to a millionaire,' said Boadicea drily. 'In God's name, where do you manage to stow them all?'

'Nora sleeps downstairs, and I built a partition wall in the back bedroom.'

She watched his workmanlike fingers tinkering with the condiments. 'That's a very handy man you are, Mr Doran. Just as well. Why, there're more people in your house than in Mrs Precious's.'

'Is that your landlady?' asked Niall.

She nodded, then glanced around to gauge when they might expect their meal. 'And she'll be locking me out, if I'm not careful.'

'Strict is she?'

'Strict? As a sergeant major! If I break the curfew it'll be six circuits of the parade ground for me, and peeling spuds for a week.' She emitted a gay laugh. 'Ah, not really – but she worries if we're out too late. Oh drat, is that rain on the window? I knew I should've brought my brolly. My hair detests this weather. It'll be all frizzy by the time I get home.'

'Will you have to put them curler things in it?'

Her blue eyes gleamed with amusement. 'God, no! 'Tis bad enough as it is. I'd be like Harpo Marx if I used those. No, I shall just have to get Mrs Precious to run it under the iron for me.'

Niall almost choked on his glass of water. 'D'you mean a proper iron – what you use on shirts?' At her smiling nod he laughed more heartily.

She chuckled affectionately with him. 'It's the only thing that keeps it under control.'

'Well, make sure you don't flatten all them lovely waves,' he warned.

'You like them, do you? All completely natural.' She affected to preen them with her fingers, then wrinkled her nose to show she was joking. 'Well, actually I do have to enhance them a little by the time I've finished smoothing the rest of it out.'

'Oh, don't tell me!' Niall exclaimed with an amused groan. 'You use them big metal things with the crocodile jaws!'

She gave a surprised exclamation. 'How did you know?'

''Cause I once got attacked with one of 'em, that's how – nearly took me blasted nose off.' He rushed to explain this bizarre situation. 'Ellen thought it were funny to stick it on whilst I was napping, good grief did it hurt!' He shook his head at the memory, becoming suddenly reflective. 'Row upon row of them she used to put in – so did her sisters. Bloomin' heck, when they'd all washed their hair it was like an armoured division in our house.'

'Was Ellen your wife?' Boadicea's voice was softer now.

He nodded, wondering what had made him refer to her by name. Suddenly guilty at being here, he glanced around for people who might know him. When a thoughtful Boadicea opened her mouth to pose another question, he feared it would be, *do you miss her?* But instead she asked, 'Was she born here like yourself?'

'Aye, but her lot came over much later than mine. She still has family over there – her dad's side. They're farmers.'

'And what about yourself?'

'No, any relatives I might have had are long gone. They all came over here.'

She nodded thoughtfully, then laughed. "Sfunny, isn't it? Here's me with my oh-so-English name and an Irish accent, and you with not a drop of English blood and looking every scrap the Irishman, sounding as local as a Yorkshire pudding – no offence!'

For once he took no insult, agreeing that life was odd.

'I don't suppose you've any reason to go back then?' she hazarded.

'Not to where my lot come from, but we've been to stay with Ellen's mob once or twice.' In the past, the family had been lucky enough to spend the occasional summer on the relatives' farm in Mayo. He went there now in his head.

'And where is this farm?' Boadicea enquired casually.

Niall gave a lopsided grin. 'Well, they call it a farm; it's actually a cottage and two fields. It's near Ballyhaunis.' He asked if she knew the town.

Her expression turned vague, and she appeared less relaxed, for she began to fidget. 'I went there once, but our place was miles away, almost into

Sligo. Is it just my imagination or have we been sitting here half an hour?' She snatched a look at her wristwatch.

Niall looked initially stunned at how quickly the time had gone, then annoyed that they seemed to have been forgotten. Glancing around at others who were being served, he murmured to Boadicea, 'Didn't those people come in after us?'

She gave an anxious nod. 'If it doesn't come in a minute I'm afraid I'll have to go – sorry.'

He showed dismay at the prospect of his wonderful evening being cut short due to this lack of service. 'I'll go and – oh, hang on, this must be ours she's bringing now.' The waitress was heading towards them, two plates in hand. 'About time.' But as Niall expectantly fingered his cutlery, the girl sailed past.

'Excuse me, miss!' He tried to attract her attention, but his voice was too soft, and he was forced to turn to Boadicea with a foolish smile that covered deeper annoyance. 'I'll try again when she comes back.' However, his manufactured patience was to fade, for on her way back the waitress looked set to ignore him again. 'Excuse me! Can you tell me when we'll get attended to?'

She turned with a harassed expression. 'We're very busy—'

'I can see that.' Niall did not care for the way she was regarding him as a nuisance, and held her responsible for robbing him of Boadicea's company. 'But we've been here half an hour, and you've just served some people who came in after us.'

The waitress frowned. 'Oh, have I . . . ?'

'Yes, you have!' he said stiffly. 'So, I'd be obliged if you'd fetch what we ordered.'

Looking fraught, she riffled the pages of her notepad. 'What did you order?'

'Fish, chips and peas!'

'Ah, that's what I just gave them. Hang on, I'll go and check.' And before he could say anything she rushed away to the kitchen.

'Not to worry,' Boadicea tried to laugh away the situation. 'I'm sure it won't be long.'

'Better not be,' said Niall ominously, drumming his fingers on the table. Then, lest she get the idea that he was holding her to blame for having to leave, he added genuinely, 'I'm really sorry about this . . .'

There followed more waiting, during which Boadicea tried to uphold a leisurely conversation in order to keep the situation calm, for it had become obvious that Niall was simmering with annoyance.

Eventually the waitress returned. 'There's been some mix-up with the orders. Would you like to give me it again?'

Niall slammed his palms on the table. 'Right, that's it!'

'Let's just leave . . .' Boadicea began to rise, for other diners were now craning their necks to see what the fuss was about.

'No!' He motioned for her to sit down. 'Why should we, when we were here first? Fetch the manager!'

The waitress scurried away, leaving Niall to fume and Boadicea to grow increasingly uncomfortable. 'Really, Niall, I'd rather—'

'Look, he's here now!' Desperate to impede her premature departure, Niall sprang to his feet as the manager appeared.

'May I be of assistance, sir?'

'Well, it's a bit late for that! You should have been here half an hour ago, making sure your staff were doing their job instead of ignoring us as if we don't exist!'

'Sir, I appreciate your annoyance, and I apologise sincerely if you feel that our service was less than perfect—'

'Perfect? It's non-existent!'

'Then I apologise again,' continued the manager in a deferential tone. 'And may I invite you to select anything from our menu in recompense, free and gratis?'

Niall shot a beseeching glance at Boadicea, who told him reluctantly, 'I'm sorry, Niall, I can't wait. I'll really have to go—'

'So, my guest has to go home hungry because of you!' Niall vented his frustration on the manager.

'Maybe sir would care to take up our offer on another night?'

'You think I'd come back here? No, you can shove it where the sun doesn't shine!'

'As sir pleases.'

Fully wound up and further incensed at the calm demeanour, Niall leaned his face towards that of the manager. 'You couldn't care less that you've ruined our evening, could you? You jumped-up—'

'Sir, I have tried to make amends!' The man backed away. 'But if you continue to be abusive I shall have no recourse but to send for the police.'

At this, a look of shock flashed across Boadicea's face. She was out of her chair and down the stairs before her partner had the chance to utter another insult.

Equally jolted, not by the manager's threat but by Boadicea's action, Niall rushed after her. She was out in the street by the time he was able to catch up and hurry through the darkness alongside her, both of them dodging people along the way, but before he could offer regret, she cast harsh aspersion.

'Do you always make such a damned fuss when you can't get your own way?'

Despite it being evident from her crimson face that he had caused her deep humiliation, Niall was still wound up, and transferred his annoyance to her, upset that she didn't see the matter the way he did. 'So you'd just have sat there and let them ignore us, would you? If there's one thing I hate it's bad service and rudeness—'

'Maybe!' snapped Boadicea from the side of

her mouth. 'But she was run off her feet. I know what that's like!'

'If she'd apologised straightaway I might have forgiven it,' retorted Niall, striding along to keep pace with her, 'but I wasn't about to let her get away with treating me like that, and certainly not my guest!'

'It still hardly warranted almost getting yourself arrested. For God's sake, I thought I'd come out to enjoy myself!' Boadicea was as angry as he now. 'If that's the way it's going to be I don't think I'll bother in future!'

Her legs moving like pistons along the dark and greasy cobblestones, weaving their way around happier couples who sauntered too leisurely for Boadicea's liking, she attempted to put a space between herself and Niall, prancing towards home, determination on her face.

His anger transformed to horror that he was going to lose her, Niall lengthened his gait to keep abreast. 'Wait, Bo, wait, I'm sorry! I didn't mean to embarrass you. I only wanted it to be special, and when it wasn't I was just that mad!'

'That's your problem, Niall!' Boadicea's heels clickety-clicked across Parliament Street, one of the few wide expanses in York, moving her way between the ranks of empty market stalls that ran the length of it. 'You fly off the handle far too easily!'

'Only when it's important!' Niall slithered on a wet cabbage leaf, wanted to swear but quickly righted himself. 'I'm sorry! I promise I'll tone it down for next time.'

She gave a bitter laugh. 'You think I want there to be a next time?'

'Oh, don't say that!' He grabbed her arm.

'Let go, damn ye!' She stopped dead and tried to shake him off, her teeth bared at this hindrance, her eyes impaling Niall with so fierce a look of determination that he immediately released her.

But he injected his words with such conviction that she would surely have to listen, 'I'm sorry, Bo, I'm that stupid, it's just that I really like you – I mean *really*.'

'*Look!*' Her eyes were wide and glistening with exasperation. 'I made it plain that I was just going out with you as a friend – well, my friends don't embarrass me like that, Niall. It's very clear to me that you're taking this far too seriously, that you're intent on making more of this than I'm willing to give. So let's just call it a day.'

Devastated, he gasped – then tried to grab her again. 'You don't mean that!' he pleaded. 'I can tell you feel the same from the way you look at me—'

'I *mean* it!' Her glare staved him off. 'It's finished. Now, I'd be obliged if you'd let me go home – *alone*!'

So saying, she tottered briskly away.

Assailed by misery, still shocked at how quickly this had occurred, Niall stared at her retreating form, the shoulders stiff with anger. Then, after a few melancholy moments, he began to drag his feet in her wake, trailing her from a distance, but only to ensure she encountered no peril along the way. When her prancing silhouette finally disappeared under the archway, he felt as if his world had come to an end.

He should have given up, had he listened to his conscience and not his heart, for to pursue a married woman was morally repugnant. He *would* have given up, had not a tiny spur of hope managed to pierce that crust of desolation: how could it be wrong when his every waking moment was consumed by such deep longing for her, when he had seen that affection returned in those gentian-blue eyes? She felt the same compelling need as he did, Niall was certain of it, if only she would forget about past failures and allow herself to be happy.

Fighting his urge to run and confront her with this, he let a few days pass before visiting The Angel, hoping by then she would have calmed down. She accused him of having a quick temper, which was totally inaccurate, for only under the greatest provocation did he lose it – and even if he did have a temper, then by God, her own could equal his. However, it would not do to argue this point, for the look on her face when he did finally enter told him that she had not yet relented, and any optimism he might have cultured on the way here was brought to an abrupt halt.

Wearing a cautious smile, he approached the bar.

'What can I get ye?' Her voice was unusually cool, her eyes emotionless and refusing to connect with his.

'I just came to apologise . . .' began Niall softly.

'Right – a pint is it?' Still terse, Boadicea grabbed the pump.

'I know I can be hot-tempered,' he confessed, 'but it's only when I get upset about something that really matters to me. Please don't let it spoil things.'

'There's nothing to spoil.' She was growing agitated. 'Now would you be wanting this or not? 'Cause I've others to serve.'

Niall did not even bother to point out that the taproom held few customers. 'Why won't you talk to me about it?'

Her voice rose an octave. 'There's nothing to talk about!'

'If I thought you hated me I'd never come here again, but I know you feel the same way as I do, and I'm not giving up.' Seeing that she was about to fend him off again, he made a swift gesture of acceptance with his hands. 'All right! You're still mad with me, I can see that. You don't want to talk to me tonight, so I'll just have to keep coming back till you will.'

But this only procured an outraged roar, and there was a hint of anguished desperation to her eye as she stormed off into the kitchen.

The landlady emerged from a different direction. Finding one of her customers unattended, she tilted her chin at Niall and enquired what she could get for him.

'Nothing, thanks. I've changed my mind,' he told Mrs Langan quietly, before he turned and left.

But, undaunted by the frosty reception, he was to return the following evening. This time, Boadicea would not even serve him, conveniently vanishing for the duration of his visit. Hence he was forced to leave without so much as a word passing between them.

Good Friday was similarly barren. With no work to go to, the shops all closed and the streets deserted, not even a newspaper to take his mind off his dilemma, there was good reason for Niall's sombre outlook, and therefore no suspicions were raised at home. The entire day composed of matters religious, like a dutiful Catholic he attended morning and evening Mass with his family, and, prohibited from the pub, went early to bed alongside his boys. But all this did not stop him plotting his next visit to The Angel. And on Saturday evening there he was again, as dogged as he had promised.

Making his way through the drinkers, returning convivial nods along his way, Niall arrived at the bar. His money at the ready, he glanced around in search of Boadicea. She was not immediately evident. The landlord, his wife and barman were working their way through the noisy queue of customers. Niall waited his turn, idly clicking his pennies together whilst maintaining his surveillance, trying to pick her out amid the sea of heads, and eventually was served.

Mr Langan appeared vexed as he pulled the glass of stout, for once not displaying his usual bonhomie and not open to trivial conversation, but Niall asked him anyway.

'Is Boadicea about?'

The landlord paused to glare. 'Hang on, I'll just go and find her for you – does it bloody look like it when we're rushing about like blue-arsed flies?' His contemptuous reply was pursued by a rebuke. 'And I reckon you're the one responsible for her leaving us in the lurch!'

Niall's lips parted in surprise as the scolding continued.

'Coming in pestering her,' mumbled Langan, who had resumed filling the glass. 'By rights I shouldn't even be serving thee! Losing us our best barmaid . . .'

'You mean, she's left for good?' Niall looked stunned.

'Give the man a coconut!' The landlord firmly placed a glass of Guinness before him and held out a hand.

Dazed and upset by this unexpected outcome of his adoring attentions, Niall placed the coppers on the man's upheld palm; then he turned away from the bar and sought out a place in which to consume it. But a pub on a Saturday was no place for quiet contemplation, and he sat there for only a few moments before rising again to leave. What was the point in staying when the woman he loved no longer worked here? Such a drastic reaction said one thing: she really did have no wish to see him again. Utterly crushed, he went home.

There was plenty of time for contemplation afterwards, though it was a deeply miserable state to be in. Maintaining a vigil with the faithful, in a church pitch-black as death, Niall waited piously for midnight, confident of Christ's return. But even in the midst of such devotion, he fought to keep his mind from straying to Boadicea, and his heart was much less confident about her.

Even with the joy of the Resurrection, his brain remained quite numb, making it hard for him to summon much enthusiasm on Easter Sunday, as he gathered with a crowd of friends and neighbours along the roadside in Walmgate. Whilst Grandma, Aunts Dolly and Harriet keenly awaited his children in the religious procession that would bring the ornaments back to church, his eyes were seeking another. Of course, had he wanted merely to see Boadicea, he could have positioned himself outside her boarding house. He had indeed considered the possibility many times since last night, but one recurring thought prevented it: if she had given up her job in desperation to avoid him, then she could equally have given up her lodgings and left the area altogether. Unable to bear the thought of having driven her away, he chose to remain in ignorance, desperate to see her even in passing, holding tightly to this last tendril of hope as his eyes flitted back and forth over the crowd of bystanders.

'They're here!'

His thoughts momentarily jerked away from Boadicea by an excited voice in the crowd, Niall glanced to his right and leaned forward, craning his neck to see beyond the jutting row of heads, which extended all the way to Walmgate Bar and beyond, into Lawrence Street, right up to the Poor Clares' convent from where the procession had set out, and was now entering the dim tunnel of the barbican into Walmgate. First to emerge were Father Finnegan and his two fellow priests, and their acolytes strewing flowers upon the road, Father Finnegan in his biretta and Easter robes, swinging his incense burner to right and left, the smaller altar boys with clasped hands and earnest intent.

'Eh, look at our Dom!' Niall's womenfolk smiled and nudged each other at the sight of his son's angelic appearance in his crisp white surplice over red soutane, pacing dutifully beside the priest, ahead of the platforms bedecked with flowers that carried the holy statues, followed by hundreds of little boys and girls all veiled in white.

Women's eyes brimmed with tears at the vision

– men's eyes too – all watching proud and loving as, upon the air drifted the sound of childish singing, the scent of crushed flora, their offspring making an unhurried way towards them along the road, their pace faltering as they came under the parental gaze, all eager for a smile of approval, and then onwards, finally to turn off the main thoroughfare. At which point the watchers fell in behind the procession as it wound its way along a side street to St George's church.

Proud and emotional though he was over his children, once they had gone ahead, Niall's thoughts were soon returned to Boadicea. Head downcast and crammed with pictures of her, he joined the multitude, and began to amble towards the double bell-cote that protruded above the roofs of houses at the far end of the street.

Meanwhile, from another direction could be heard the loud approach of a military band, competing with the joyous ringing of bells, as those Catholic soldiers from the barracks made their way to worship too. Through sheer volume of numbers, it took a little longer than the usual two minutes for Niall and his in-laws to reach their destination, the separate parties finally converging at the junction of two streets – whereupon sat an uninspiring church, unadorned, save for a cross upon each of its stone gables, yet its open door revealing a friendly and inviting interior. By the time he arrived, the music had stopped and the players were storing their brass instruments behind the low outer wall for safekeeping. This, and the accommodation of many bodies taking a further period, Niall's shuffling approach to the entrance was slow, so his fantasies had ample time to take a grip, and as he squashed through the gateway with others, his mind was miles away. On the verge of entering church, he stood back to allow his womenfolk to go before him, when he lifted his eyes, and came face to face with the adored one.

His gut lurched and he could not prevent a smile of delight as he fixed his gaze to that dear face. Neither could Boadicea – though hers was obviously performed on impulse, for just as quickly she appeared angry at herself over this display of weakness and, turning her face away, she squeezed through a gap in the crowd and into the flower-bedecked and candlelit church.

It had all occurred in seconds. The smile had not yet had time to fade from Niall's lips as his mother-in-law inched her way past him. Experiencing a slight note of panic alongside his heartache, he pretended the smile was for her, before composing his face into a more suitably religious mien. Then, nursing mixed emotions, he too wandered into the church, surrendering to the embrace of incense, freesia, lavender polish and candle wax.

Slightly ahead, Nora crossed herself with holy water, genuflected before the stone altar, then moved into a pew and knelt. A set of rosary beads dangling from her mitts, she clasped them, and bowed her head in meditation, such a demeanour betraying no hint of mistrust. But she had noticed the way her widowed son-in-law had feasted his eyes on that buxom woman, and, mingled with her prayer was a note of resolve that something must be done about this.

Assuming that his shared illicit smile had gone unnoticed, for Nora would surely have commented otherwise, Niall remained untroubled by any fear of being found out, burdened by a greater dilemma: should he corner Boadicea at home, demand that she listen whilst he poured out his heart, and perhaps run the risk that this would drive her away altogether, or should he do as she purportedly desired and leave her be, and perhaps run the risk that she might depart from his life anyway, without ever knowing how deeply he cared?

With a bank holiday lending much time to stew over this horrible quandary, Niall remained in bed for longer than was usual that Monday, trying to lose himself in sleep, whilst downstairs the children consumed the chocolate eggs that their aunts had brought home from the factory. Though when he finally decided to shift his unkempt carcass for a late breakfast, it looked as if it might be not such a slothful day as he had anticipated, for Nora proposed they take the children to the Museum Gardens.

'In fact, it's such a lovely day,' she announced, 'I reckon we'll have a picnic lunch – that's when your father decides to get his whiskers off.'

The children were exuberant, Juggy most of all, as she leaped up to balance on tiptoe beside her father's dining chair, running a chocolate-scented hand over his stubbled jaw, only to receive a tired grumble. 'Oy, don't go clarting me up with Easter egg, missus.'

Whilst the youngsters might jump for joy, there was insurrection from Harriet. 'I had planned to go and see Pete . . .'

'You can see your fancy man later,' retorted her mother. 'Easter's a time for families.' Her face remained stern as she muttered to Dolly, who had also preferred a lie-in to Mass, 'Don't think you're jibbing out neither, sat there with your hair like a haystack – you can get yourself smartened up.'

Her face creased from oversleep, Dolly bleated, 'I was going to!'

'I can't manage these children on my own and they haven't been out in ages,' Nora continued to rally. 'It'll do you all good.'

Feeling that her comment was directed mainly at him, even whilst resenting her interference, Niall accepted that in the midst of his own troubles he had been somewhat remiss towards his offspring. Which was why, without objection, he went to wash and shave, and to dress in his best suit, and, when everyone was ready, accompanied the family to the other side of town.

En route, they were to pause at the end of the street to chat with some neighbours. After fifteen years of marriage, the middle-aged couple were parading their firstborn, eager and proud to display him to anyone they might meet. Whilst Niall stood back, the women crowded round to bestow congratulations, the smaller children craning on tiptoe to see into the pram.

'Ooh, isn't he gorgeous?' Harriet shoved her face towards the pram and extended a forefinger, which the baby immediately grasped. Not so overtly maternal, Nora nevertheless managed to offer a compliment, though not to her own child.

'Don't bend so close to the poor bairn,' she warned Dolly, who was baring her overabundant teeth to the little occupant. 'You'll frighten the life out of him.'

'Can I push him, Mrs Fry?' Approaching womanhood, Honor had developed a keenness for such pastimes.

'Maybe later,' said the new mother, unconvincingly.

Smarting from her mother's insult, Dolly lifted her head away from the pram, and for something to say, was overly gushing to the parents. 'After all this time, a little miracle!'

'Delivered by the angels,' declared the doting father.

'Delivered by the angels,' muttered Dolly from the side of her mouth, as the two groups moved off in opposite directions. 'Delivered by Pickford's more like – did you see the size of it? What a brute!' she tittered. 'And there's our Honor asking to push him. She'd need a crane just to get him into the pram.'

Niall chose not to join in the cruel humour, but walked on ahead. Juggy ran to catch him up, slipping her hand into his, though he seemed hardly aware of it. All the way to town, his mind was to remain preoccupied.

Whilst there had been a stream of bank holiday traffic carrying locals to the coast since early morning, there had been influx too from other parts of England, with tourists eager to view York's antiquities. By midday hundreds were scattered along the banks of the Ouse, and upon the grassy ramparts of the city walls where daffodils fluttered in profusion, and across the lawns of the Museum Gardens. Struggling to find a patch of daisy-laden turf that was large enough to take her extended clan, Nora finally spotted a vacant lot and charged ahead to stake her claim, her sturdy ankles in their thick lisle stockings striding over outstretched limbs, not caring if she trod on one or two of them in her rush. Dolly and Harriet followed with the baskets, whilst Niall took up the rear, the rest of his tribe scampering in between.

Though the sun shone brilliantly today, the grass was still damp from recent snowfalls. Wise to this, the women had brought their mackintoshes and these were spread to form a groundsheet upon which everyone contorted themselves into position, then sat like basking seals, closing their eyes against the sun's glare and tilting their smiling faces to its warmth, pending lunch. And it was not long before this juncture was reached, a brown paper parcel of sandwiches hauled from Nora's bag, and divided.

Half-heartedly devouring one potted meat sandwich after another, Niall wondered what Boadicea might be doing, his fantasies transporting him into a trancelike state, until a Thermos flask was rudely thrust under his nose.

'Get the top off this blasted thing for me, will you?' demanded Nora.

The spell broken, he removed the stopper easily and handed the flask back to his mother-in-law.

'Eh, I don't know what we'd do without you!' praised Nora, and handed him the first serving of tea in reward.

Responding with a thoughtful half-smile, Niall took a sip from the Bakelite beaker, attempting to tear his mind from Boadicea, instead to concentrate on the sights and sounds and scents around him: the chirruping of sparrows that bobbed amongst the picnickers, appealing for crumbs; the excited laughter of his three-year-old son in white knitted jersey and shorts, as big sister Honor helped him do tipple-tails on the sloping lawn; the pungent scent of blossom; the cries of wonder from his children at the sudden glorious spectacle of colour, as one of the resident peacocks displayed his tail feathers. For a time these were sufficient to distract him. But then his attention was ensnared by those who promenaded along the sloping rockery pathways that led in different directions around the gardens: happy couples arm in arm, some of whom made detours into a shady arbour, obviously to share a secret kiss; and his mind returned to his own loved one.

A sudden yell jolted him from his stupor. A squirrel, which Juggy had been trying to befriend, had run up her leg and bitten her.

By the time Niall jumped forth to receive his crying child the furry bandit was halfway up a tree.

'You ought to have been watching her!' Nora scolded him. 'I was busy seeing to Brian. I haven't got eyes in the back of me head.'

Fighting his annoyance, Niall comforted the snuffling child. 'Come on, let's go buy you an ice cream.'

'Can I have one, Dad?' yelled Batty from afar, now coming running.

'I'm sure he's got ears in his bum,' muttered Niall to his wounded daughter, making her laugh as he had intended to do. Then he summoned the lad, and the rest of his brood. 'Aye, come on then, Tiger Tim! We'll all have one.' And they tore across the lawns to join the queue by an ice-cream vendor's van under the magnificent spread of a horse chestnut tree.

In Niall's absence, Nora rebuked her daughters. 'You're supposed to be helping me cheer him up!'

'We can't make him talk if he doesn't want to,' objected Harriet. Then as an afterthought she jumped up and brushed herself off, adding, 'And I'm not even bothering to waste my time. I've better things to do!' And with this she was hurrying away towards the wrought-iron exit.

'Eh, I'll swing for her when she gets in!' spat Nora, then informed Dolly, 'And you might as well not be here for the contribution you've made. Buck your ideas up.'

'What do I say?' wailed her daughter.

'Just chuck him some of your usual scintillating conversation!' chafed Nora, with a despairing shake of head. 'At least let him know you're alive.'

Thinking to lend his mother-in-law some respite, once his children had been served their ice creams, Niall ushered them to the nearby bank of the river, from where they sat and licked their cornets, and watched as teams of rowers sculled by. Even after the treat was consumed, a majestic flotilla of swans was to hold their attention for a further ten minutes. Finally, though, he was compelled to return to where the women were seated.

'Aunty Harriet's gone,' noticed Honor as they came across the lawn.

'Mm,' replied Niall, with scant interest. Though he began to study Nora and Dolly a little more closely now. By their attitude and by the way they clammed up and smiled at his arrival with the children, he guessed they had been discussing him and, from the opening remark, he was to deduce it had not been complimentary

'Eh, look at this one, he's clarted up to beggary!' Immediately out came his mother-in-law's handkerchief, which was given a lick and, using a fistful of his white jersey, she hauled little Brian to her and proceeded to wipe the daubs of dried ice cream from his cheeks and nostrils, giving Dolly a prompting glare as she did so.

'And look at all them grass stains.' Taking the hint, Dolly remarked on the little boy's soiled knitted garments, and those of the other children. 'Good job they've got their aunty to scrub for them.'

In the act of sitting down, Niall looked at her sharply. He said nothing, but it was obvious that he had taken umbrage.

'Still, they are here to enjoy themselves,' added Dolly with a hurried grin.

There was a long silence. Niall thought he saw a nudge pass between the women. They were up to something, he was sure of it now. Irritated by the soggy remnants of sandwich lodged between those tombstone teeth, he looked away.

Dolly spoke again. 'Mam and me were just discussing the Jubilee. Only another week and we're into May.' Easter had fallen late this year. 'There's heaps to be done if we're to have a decent street party. For a start we'll need to know what everyone wants to dress up as, so we can start making the costumes. What do you want to come as, Nye?'

'The Invisible Man,' he told her.

Dolly turned crimson. 'Well, there's no need to be like that!'

'Like what?' he demanded testily.

'If it were a woman who'd said it I'd call her catty!' she told him.

'And you'd know all about catty, wouldn't you?' muttered Niall under his breath as he turned away in annoyance.

Dolly leaned forward with a hurt frown. 'What?'

'Nothing.' He refused to look at her but stared into the distance.

'She was only trying to cheer you up, miseryguts,' Nora objected.

Niall gave a cynical laugh. 'Has it occurred to you that some of us have nowt to celebrate?'

'And has it occurred to you that *some* of us are putting a brave face on for the sake of others?' retorted Nora, making a poorly veiled gesture at the children, who were looking decidedly uncomfortable at the exchange.

Chastened over his selfish behaviour, Niall was grudgingly repentant. 'Aye, well . . . I'm sorry. I weren't thinking . . .'

'The trouble with you is you think too much,' corrected Nora. 'Just snap yourself out of it, for heaven's sake, and concentrate on your family. Things'll come better if you do. You might even get a nice surprise.'

Curious over the smug expression that accompanied this last part of her remark, Niall remained pensive for a second, then he reached out to the nearest child, rubbing Honora's bony shoulders through the gymslip, and saying as cheerfully as he could muster, 'All right, you've roped me into this blessed party!' And for a few merciful moments he was to forget about Boadicea as, grabbing Dom, he set to wrestling with him on the grass. Whereupon, all the other children piled in to tickle Father, the afternoon rounded off nicely by his announcement that they would visit the Easter funfair on their way home.

7

But contrary to the promise of that afternoon, despite all the cheerful shop window displays that were to appear in the month of May, the red, white and blue bunting, and the special costumes made by Nora and her girls for the children to wear at the party, it looked like the intended celebrations were to be halted by a severe and unexpected snowstorm. So that instead of helping to set up the trestles in preparation of the weekend party, Niall found himself, with others from his gang, called upon to fight his way through the early morning blizzard to ensure the railway lines were cleared. And in the deathly hush of that white world, as his boots trudged their way through the frigid mantle that served to suffocate all vestige of spring, he found himself in despair again.

Still unsure what to do about Boadicea he had tried his best to immerse himself in family life, yet still lived for Sundays, when he strove for a glimpse of her in church, overjoyed that she was still around, but having to exist on this morsel for an entire week.

The wolf was in no such straits – his menu so plenteous with the glut of spring lambs that he chose not to eat them at one sitting, but seemingly killed them just for fun, or perhaps to devour later, secreting them under bushes, often close to the railway line. It was as if he enjoyed the danger, thought Niall, stumbling across one such carcass now. Narrowing his eyes against the icy flakes that settled upon his lashes, in the act of bending to pick up a rabbit that had been caught a glancing blow by train, he spotted a grey fleece protruding from the snow, and dashed away the layer to reveal a larger mammal. He peered down at it for a moment, feeling as stiff and lifeless as the sheep, wondering if it had been poisoned. Tired of waiting with their guns, sometimes throughout the night, the farmers had adopted dirtier methods. But so far to his knowledge their only bag had been birds of prey and some crows.

A horn sounded, the lookout alerting the gang to an oncoming train, and Niall moved swiftly to safe ground, waiting until the locomotive steamed past before returning to examine the rabbit. Finding it recently killed, he shoved it in his haversack, having no qualm that what he did was illegal. In his view, wildlife was no one person's property. It was part of nature, provided by God, and every man had a right to feed his family. Rejoining the gang, and proceeding to battle his way along the track with his lamp, he wondered if the wolf had a family, a mate. Or did it feel as cold and isolated as he?

However, the fates that had ostensibly conspired to rob his children of their party were once again smiling by Saturday. The sun had burst forth and, under its brilliance, the layer of snow had begun rapidly to melt, so that by the time Niall got home that midday all trace of it had gone from the street. And, under that glow, with that drip, drip, drip of melting ice, it was as if his own problem had begun to melt too. For he had reached a brave decision: he would visit her at home on Monday.

It had to be a week day. Loath to incur any scrap of suspicion from Nora, he would call on his way home from work. Then, if he was lucky enough to spend an hour or two with Boadicea, he could pretend he had been doing overtime, though in fact he would seek permission to knock off earlier than usual under pretence of having toothache. It was not quite the lie it seemed, for every cell of his body did ache, in anticipation of seeing her again.

But for today he was determined to have fun with his children, and to have a pictorial record of this fine occasion – wielding his box camera as if to compete with the Monarch himself – for, as Niall rightly announced to those gathered, most of them here would never witness another Jubilee. He was even persuaded to join in the games, and to dance, once with Dolly, and again with Gloria from next door, which seemed to please them both more than it did Niall, though he managed to conjure a grin of enjoyment. But no amount of Jubilee celebration could completely erase Boadicea from his mind. Even in the midst of all this toasting – 'To the King, God bless him!' – he longed for Monday, when he would carry out his plan.

The clock above a shop told him it was half-past four as he turned into Fossgate. Even having cleaned himself up as best he could in a public convenience, the fact remained that he was in his working clothes. Under this combination of sweat, ragged collar and cuffs, a greasy cap and muddy boots, he guessed that he must appear like something from the bottom of a dustbin. But all this was of little consequence. For his gay mood of Saturday had been somewhat dashed in church the day after, when he had managed to catch her eye, only to have her look straight through him. So, she would probably reject him anyway. She might not even be there.

Even so, he refused to give up without one last try and, along the way, he inserted a penny into a chewing-gum machine with a view to freshening his breath. On the bridge now, his nerves almost got the better of him. Had he not wanted her so very badly, he might have gone straight past the archway and continued home. But giving his face a last wipe with a handkerchief, he went through the short alleyway and into the yard. Here he was to pause nervously before the Georgian mansion, with its scaling brown paint, its once graceful fanlight now rotten, and its windows bereft of putty, and he lifted his eyes to the upper windows, wondering which room was Boadicea's. She had been right about her neighbours. In addition to the tripe being prepared in the building next door came an even more atrocious stench of intestines being washed and boiled to make chitterlings. Almost balking with disgust, Niall averted his senses and braced himself for the task ahead, took the two steps that led up to the large door, lifted its tarnished brass knocker and rapped out a summons. Too late to run away now. Cap in hand, he stood back to wait, his stomach bubbling.

His knock was answered by Mrs Precious, the landlady. At least he assumed it was she, for the elderly woman whose figure filled the doorway had the build and attitude of a warrant officer, and, upon receiving his request to speak to Miss Merrifield she boomed a series of orders at him: 'Come in! Wipe your feet! Wait here!' Then she left him standing in the hall whilst she herself performed three manly strides to an elegant but badly neglected staircase, the ancient wallpaper hanging off it in fronds, and bawled up it.

'Miss Merrifield – visitor!'

Receiving a faint response, she wheeled to address Niall again, hands on hips, her voice demanding, 'Friend or foe?'

'Er, friend, I hope . . .' Facing this rather intim-idating woman, whose gun-metal hair was divided into plaits that were wound into buns and fixed on each side of her head in the manner of earphones, Niall struggled to explain his reason for being here. 'Sorry for troubling you. I tried to have a word with her at the pub, but Mr Langan said she'd given in her notice.'

Mrs Precious narrowed her sharp brown eyes, then exclaimed in a loud and knowing voice, 'Oh, you're *that* one, are you?' And she looked him up and down as if he were the Prince of Darkness.

Her victim was still stumbling over an answer when Boadicea appeared at the top of the stairs. He had forgotten how lovely she was. His belly turned a somersault as she leaned over the balustrade to see who it was, and afforded him a generous glimpse up her silken flowered skirt, almost to her thigh. Upon seeing him she faltered and looked as if she had been rammed from different directions by panic and gladness at the same time, and at one stage he feared she was about to rush back into her room, but she chose not to.

Following Niall's gaze, Mrs Precious saw the look of startlement that was still in evidence upon the young woman's face, and barked, 'Shall I get rid?'

The yoke of Boadicea's turquoise blouse was emphasised with a frill; he watched her toy with this for a number of seconds before she came to a decision. 'No, no, that's all right, Ma, I'll see him.' And her peep-toed shoes made their descent, her eyes fixed upon them as they trod the stairs, and not once looking at the man who had come to visit her. But when Niall lifted his own inspection above those slender legs in the tan stockings, and breasts that trembled 'neath the turquoise silk, he saw that her face remained worried, as if she were still in a quandary over what to do about him.

Her landlady snorted, and dealt him a less than affectionate whack on the arm. 'Think yourself lucky I don't chuck you out on your ear. You've caused this lass nowt but grief these last few weeks! Having to leave her job because of you—'

'Ma, it wasn't that bad.' Now arrived, Boadicea hurried to reassure her, and extended this reassurance to Niall, who was looking flushed with remorse. ''Twas less than a week's pay I lost. I'll be able to settle up with ye this week.'

'I'm not bothered about cash! I'm bothered about what this one's put you through!' The woman in the incongruous floral pinafore continued verbally to assault Niall, who was beginning to wonder what on earth had been said about him.

'No, no!' pleaded a slightly impatient Boadicea. 'Look, 'twas all just a bit of a misunderstanding. Mr Doran wasn't responsible for me leaving and I'm back there now so—'

'You're back at The Angel?' Niall had come alert.

She nodded. 'I realised what a big mistake I'd made.'

He searched her eyes, wondering if her comment held a double meaning.

'So no harm done,' finished Boadicea, looking

away and giving absolutely no hint as to her feelings for him.

'We-ell, if you say so, dear.' But the landlady remained suspicious as she announced loudly to Niall, 'Are you stopping for your tea then?'

Not daring to express how ecstatic he was to hear that she was back at the pub, he looked awkwardly at Boadicea, who dealt her landlady a brief nod to indicate consent.

'Don't talk much, do you?' accused Mrs Precious. 'We'd better fetch you a cup of tea right away, so's to wet your whistle.'

'Don't put yourself to any trouble,' said Niall hurriedly.

The sergeant major in the floral pinafore beheld him as an idiot. 'Would I offer if it were any trouble? Do you want one or not?'

'Well, only if you're having one,' he replied, trying not to make any more fuss than necessary, but only succeeding in drawing more pithy comment from Mrs Precious.

'God help us! No, I'm not having one! But I'll make one for you if ever I can get a straight answer!'

Only using it as an excuse to get rid of the woman so that he could speak to Boadicea in private did Niall respond, 'All right, thank you, I will have one.'

Mrs Precious threw another order at him. 'Right, now that's established, you can get your backside in here and give account of yourself!'

Passing an uncomfortable grimace at Boadicea,

and slightly encouraged by her smile, meekly he followed the landlady.

'Visitor, Georgie, get the kettle on!' Mrs Precious bawled ahead of her. Then, seeing the room was vacant, she demanded, '*Now* where's he gone?' And she glared around the room as if hoping to find her husband in some corner.

Niall too looked around, astonished by what he saw. Stepping into the Preciouses' living room was like being plunged back into the Victorian era. It was all aspidistras, Landseer prints and stuffed animals under glass domes. One display of flowers and foliage, birds, field mice and squirrels was so gigantic it took up an entire corner. The furniture was battered and second-hand, but had obviously been acquired from a much wealthier household, there being much mahogany, marquetry and inlay. He was still awaiting an invitation to take a seat when a cat strolled in, stalked up to him and rubbed its scent against his legs, before moving on to piss against several chairs, strutting around as if it owned the place, before having an altercation with its reflection in a broken mirror that was leaning to no particular purpose against a wall, finally to walk out in a huff.

'Sit down!' said Mrs Precious, with what she saw as a friendly inflection, though it emerged as more of an order than an invitation, her deep voice ricocheting off the walls.

'If you can find a place,' murmured Boadicea, only half joking, for every surface was cluttered.

She cleared herself a spot, in the process having gently to disturb another cat, a female, which Niall had not previously noticed, it being fast asleep and blending with the silvery colour of the brocade. This one too left the room.

Fazed by the jumble of his surroundings, Niall selected a chair that had not received the attentions of the tomcat, at least not today, though judging by the smell it had been visited many times before – and he had been bothered about coming here in his work clothes! Discommoded that Mrs Precious was still there, he remained silent and, trying to think of what to say when she did finally grant him and Boadicea some privacy, he perched stiffly against a background of dark, elaborate wallpaper with crimson roses and acanthus leaves, and brown varnish on the woodwork, such as favoured by Nora, and a velvet sofa the pile of which was so worn that it was all but bald. In fact velvet, tassels and other ostensibly plush furnishings abounded, not to mention more fantastic ones.

Following his intrigued gaze to a black and tan rug complete with head, Mrs Precious beamed, 'Like it, do you? That was Rex, one of our favourite dogs.' Then she disappeared into the scullery to make a pot of tea.

Laughter on his face, Niall tore his eyes from the lifeless glassy ones of the rug to engage Boadicea with an amazed whisper. 'If that was her favourite I'd hate to see what she doled out to one she didn't like! My God, she's as tough as my mother-in-law.'

Though there was no outright merriment, she did seem to share his amusement, and there was a gleam in Boadicea's eye as she whispered back, 'Will we pit them against each other and lay bets on who wins?'

He surveyed her lovely face, so overwhelmingly pleased that they were speaking again, and grasping the moment told her, 'I'm really sorry about your job . . .'

'Ah, not to worry.' Her reply was calm, almost carefree. 'I've got it back now.' And after a second, she added, 'I was surprised not to see you in the pub.'

This was going better than he could ever have anticipated. Yet his happiness was tinged with frustration. 'What point was there in going?' he bewailed of her. 'I only went there because of you, and once you'd gone . . . I can't tell you how—' He was about to say how much he had missed her, but to his dismay someone else wandered in then through another entrance.

'Ah, hello, Pop!' Boadicea smiled at the intruder, who was accompanied by a ginger Pomeranian dog, which immediately trotted up to sniff at the visitor. 'This is my friend, Mr Niall Doran.'

Glad at being referred to as her friend, Niall put aside any exasperation over the man's intrusion, plus his repugnance of the stinking little dog, which had jumped onto his lap. He rose to greet its owner, so ridding himself of the animal without appearing a heartless brute, as he bade Mr Precious a polite, 'How do?'

'Champion, thanks!' The speaker appeared a kindly old man, slightly built with thinning silver hair but still obviously both mentally and physically alert, for at Boadicea's introduction he had leaped forth like a stripling. It was clear he was still fit enough to work, for his clothes were those of a labourer, and the hand he extended was obviously a tool of his trade; its fingernails were gnarled and split and stained with varnish. Niall marvelled at the strength of the handshake, which was issued with more beaming enthusiasm than he had received from the man's spouse.

Mrs Precious returned then, to exclaim loudly with not a little indignation, 'There you are, Georgie! Where've you been? I've had to make this tea myself.'

'Sorry, dearie!' The old man released Niall's hand, and rushed forth to divest her of the tray, thenceforth to sit alongside her on the sofa and lay his head on her shoulder. 'Just wanted to get my equipment in good order so I can devote my entire attention to you tonight.'

Miraculously appeased by the little man's petting, Mrs Precious explained to a bemused Niall, 'Pop's a wizard on the squeeze-box – in fact with all musical instruments. Make 'em, mend 'em, play 'em – why he can turn his hand to anything!'

Her husband beamed modestly at Niall. 'But without my dear wife I'd be nothing at all. I'm the luckiest man alive.'

At this, Niall enjoyed an inward laugh. However,

now that Mrs Precious had decided he was not such a threat as she had feared, she too began to view him more kindly. It was also evident from the way they both addressed Boadicea that they looked upon her as much more than a paying guest and that she returned this affection in equal amounts, calling them Ma and Pop as if they were family. It was clear too they each doted on the other. Watching them snuggle together on the sofa like a pair of old slippers, Niall wondered whether he and Boadicea would ever achieve such status – not unless he were soon granted some privacy, they wouldn't. Beginning to feel irritated by the couple's presence, however cosy, he tried to convey that he wished to speak to Boadicea alone.

'Well, that was very nice,' he announced, having drunk barely half a cup of tea before handing it back towards his hosts. 'But I'll have to go in a minute.'

'I thought you were stopping for your tea?' Mrs Precious accused with a frown.

Niall looked momentarily confused, then exclaimed. 'Oh, sorry! When you said tea I thought you just meant a *cup* of tea.'

'Nay, that was just to keep you going!' scoffed his hostess.

He looked thoughtfully at Boadicea. There would be a meal for him at home, but he would much rather extend his stay here if it meant he would eventually get to speak to her.

Mrs Precious misread his hesitation. 'You needn't

think you'll be getting Sunday's leftovers. We're having cutlets!'

He tried to negate any insult, 'Oh, I wasn't—'

'This isn't your run-of-the-mill lodgings where guests are fleeced all ends up, and have to look after themselves! Everybody's welcome at my table. We're like one big family, aren't we, Bo? You never go hungry here, do you?'

'I do not,' confirmed Boadicea with a smile.

'I'm not a vain woman,' continued Mrs Precious, 'but if there's one thing I do pride myself on, it's cooking them a nice wholesome meal every single night.' She noticed the grandfather clock. 'By the by, isn't it time you were getting those spuds peeled, Georgie?'

'I shall do it right away, deary.' And off went the meek and gentle old man to do her bidding, a beatific smile on his face.

If Niall had been hoping the landlady would also soon depart, he was wrong, for as much as she boasted of her hospitality, it turned out that Georgie Precious was the one who performed all the chores around here, and his wife merely gave the orders. But she could obviously do no wrong by him, for as he scuttled in and out to receive instruction, his face wore a contented beam, and he patted her affectionately at every opportunity. Meanwhile, Niall had given up any hope of baring his soul to Boadicea, and had forced himself to be content with breathing the same foisty air.

With her other half so employed, Mrs Precious

sat forward, legs apart to display long bloomers, a hand on each sturdy knee and announced forthrightly to Niall, 'Let's be having it then! What're your intentions towards our lass?'

He looked shocked.

'That's quite enough, Ma!' scolded Boadicea.

'Is it?' Mrs Precious was immediately put in her place, her expression on the verge of mildness. 'Right, I know when to shut up.' But she could not help herself from adding forcefully to Niall, 'Just think on how you treat her in future!'

'Ma!' Boadicea dealt stern warning.

'All right, all right, I'll not say another word.' Chastened, Mrs Precious sat back for a while, though Niall was to receive further keen inspection, her eyes trying to penetrate him, whilst he sat there feeling most uncomfortable. 'Well, he's not such a slimy cad as I was expecting, I must say.'

Niall could not help an inquisitive gasp at Boadicea.

'Sure, you'll have him think I've been running him down! I didn't say a word about ye,' she told Niall quickly, 'Well, other than a few choice ones, when the only way I could get ye to leave me alone was to give up my job.'

'I can't imagine why you'd want him to leave you alone,' opined Mrs Precious, eyeing Niall up and down. 'He's not a bad-looking chap at all.'

Boadicea blushed and shook her head in smiling exasperation. 'No, he's just got a foul temper on him.'

Niall was embarrassed, and somewhat annoyed at having to discuss this before an audience. 'Only 'cause we'd had our night spoiled! I did try to apologise but you wouldn't let me.'

'Let bygones be bygones,' intervened Mrs Precious.

'I have,' replied Boadicea evenly. 'Why do think he's still here?'

Looking into her face, Niall's feelings of upset began to subside. He warned himself that, however frustrating it was not to have her to himself, he must not show any sign of temper. That he managed this during the hours that followed was an indication of how desperately he wanted her, for as the other boarders began to trickle in he found them even more testing than their landlady.

Mr Yarker was the first of these to arrive. Niall looked up expectantly at the tall and slender, sour-faced individual in the gabardine mackintosh, and decided immediately that he did not like him. The countenance might be faded by middle age, but Mr Yarker's tongue had an energetic edge, as it delivered not so much as a word of acknowledgement for those gathered, but launched into a tirade about the vermin menace in town.

'Blasted pigeons again – look!' He stood arms apart, to display the stain down the front of his fawn mackintosh; his accent was cultured but its tone was not. 'Every bloody day alike, pigeons overhead, pigeons to the right, pigeons to the left – talk about the Valley of Death – I shouldn't be surprised if there's one in my bloody room when I go up! I almost broke my neck tripping over one of the wretched things just now.' His diatribe ended on a note of glee. 'Managed to land it a decent whack with my brolly though.'

'Oh, Mr Yarker, how cruel,' objected Boadicea.

'Don't fret, my dear young woman!' Yarker held up his palm. 'Its name was obviously Lazarus. Filthy blighter dropped another bomb as it flew off.' And he flourished his tarnished trilby with a look of contempt. 'Flying rats, that's what they are, the bastards – please excuse my French,' he added as swift afterthought to the women.

Catching Niall's disapproving frown, Bo quickly explained that this was a regular gripe of Mr Yarker, and in the same breath introduced the two men.

Having removed the mackintosh to expose a crumpled business suit, Yarker exuded, 'Delighted to meet you, dear boy!' And the two shook hands, though Niall detected this was out of politeness rather than sincerity. He himself hated anyone superficial, and merely nodded. Moreover he was growing exasperated at these constant obstacles to his love life.

Alas there was to be no hope of having Boadicea to himself, for by the time Mr Precious announced that tea was ready there were three more boarders to be served: Mr Allardyce, a clerk, whose greeting was quiet and polite, before he merged unobtrusively into the background; and two young cattle-drovers who were brothers, Johnny and Eamonn

Mulloy. These two were much worse an intrusion, for their roughspun clothes had a combined smell of dung and alcohol, and judging by the happy demeanours above their neckerchiefs they had had one too many a tot after a day at the cattle market. However, Niall chose not to object to their overly boisterous handshakes, for they were much more genuinely affable than Mr Yarker, and being Irish had more in common with him than the very British middle-aged one, who now sat opposite with an air of open disdain for his table companions.

'Serve the visitor first, Georgie!' commanded Mrs Precious as her husband was about to place a meal before her.

'As you wish, dearie!' Beaming and dancing his way round the table, Mr Precious diverted his attention to Niall, donating three cutlets alongside two huge mounds of mashed potato and cabbage, so much of it, that it almost spilled over the rim of the plate.

'That's a very generous helping.' Niall stared in awe.

'Oh, he always likes to provide a bigun, don't you, Georgie?' boomed Mrs Precious.

Unsure whether this was an intentional double entendre, Niall gave her a swift glance; her face remained straight, but her eyelid fluttered in a barely perceptible wink. Somewhat shocked, he found himself blushing and quickly bent his head, though he sensed that Boadicea was amused, seated as she was so closely next to him.

'One tries, dearie!' Mr Precious sang to his wife, then continued to rush around the table, laying down plates.

Eventually, all were served. Unsure whether grace would be observed, Niall held back until his hostess tucked straight in, then he too picked up his knife and fork, surprised to experience the weight of solid silver, before putting them to work. He could feel the Pomeranian sniffing round his ankles under the table, and wished he dared kick it away with his boot, but seated next to Boadicea he would not risk injuring her instead. Casting surreptitious glances from the corner of his eye whilst he ate, he watched her separate the meat from the bone and carve it into dainty portions.

'You haven't got much gravy,' Mrs Precious observed loudly. 'Can I get you some more?'

Niall swallowed before answering. 'No, I'm fine thanks.'

'Georgie, you've skimped on the gravy. Fetch this lad some more!'

Mr Precious, who had just sat down, now leaped up and scuttled back to the kitchen, returning with a saucepan of gravy, which he tipped at Niall's meal. 'Anyone else?'

'No, sit down now, dear,' his wife instructed. Whereupon he left the pan of gravy balanced inelegantly on a sideboard and returned to his place at the head of the table.

Resuming his own meal, Niall shot another side-ways glance at Boadicea, watching her hands wield the cutlery, studying the fine bones in her wrists. He was not allowed this pleasure for long, for Mrs Precious seemed bent on chattering to him.

'Do you sing, Mr Doran? We like a bit of entertainment after tea, don't we, Pop?'

Niall parted his lips to speak, but was to suffer a rude interruption.

'You fucking little bastard!' Eamonn, the young cow-walloper seated to his left, had snatched one of his brother's cutlets and gnawed a huge bite out of it before the other could stop him. But as the laughing perpetrator threw the cutlet back on its rightful owner's plate, the victim plunged his fork into his brother's hand.

His guffaws abruptly terminated in a yell, which also set the dog yapping, Eamonn observed his bleeding mitt for a split second, then used his own cutlery to similar effect, jabbing the tines into Johnny's forearm. Whereupon, the prank escalated into a violent struggle, each seizing a knife and trying to impale the other – luckily only the table knives, and blunt ones at that, but still able to inflict damage as they were aimed in vicious stabbing motions again and again until, in their berserk efforts to avoid them, the brothers knocked each other from their chairs. Still they proceeded to tussle violently on the ground, the dog yapping and dancing frantically around them, whilst they tried to outdo its noise, snarling and calling each other all the names under the sun. It was no great mercy that, spilling from Irish tongues, and coming as fast and numerous as machine-gun bullets, the expletives were barely discernible; it was enough that they merged into one huge assault on the senses.

Niall was horrified. He tried to shield Boadicea, knowing how much she detested displays of temper, whilst at the same time attempting to separate the fighters. But, in danger of being bitten by the dog, or injured by flailing limbs, he was eventually forced to look to the other males for support. To his astonishment, Mr Yarker continued to wade through his meal, his only contribution a look of deep disgust.

'Right, that's enough, boys!' boomed Mrs Precious cheerfully. 'Visitor present!'

But the dog's shrill yapping and the brothers' violence continued unabated. In fact the situation grew even worse as one of the knives found its target, and blood began to fly.

Still, trying to protect Boadicea, Niall was poised to make a grab, when Mr Allardyce suddenly rose like a jack-in-the-box. Presuming the man's mission was to assist him, he was instead to witness a display of near hysteria. 'Stop it! For Christ's sake, *stop*!' screamed Allardyce.

Just as mayhem looked set to reign, Mrs Precious boomed one decisive word. 'Georgie!'

And, seeming to know her every wish, a determined smile upon his face, old Georgie grabbed the pan of gravy from the sideboard, tipped the residue on his plate, and, with remarkably calm and accurate aim, dealt first Johnny, then Eamonn, a resounding blow to the head. Niall felt Boadicea wince as the sound of metal against bone reverberated the brothers' teeth. Though it did not knock the fighters out cold, it certainly stunned them to order, and, fearing similar treatment, the dog backed off too. There followed a pained hiatus, as the young drovers, still sprawled upon the carpet, observed their assailant, each rubbing his gravy-speckled head whilst the dog ventured back to laugh at them, wagging its tail and sneezing with excitement. Then, like castigated schoolboys, and regarding each other sullenly, Eamonn and Johnny dragged themselves back to their places, as did everyone else.

'As I was saying,' continued Mrs Precious to Niall, 'we like a bit of entertainment, though we usually wait till after tea.'

Apart from a lot of bone-sucking, the meal was to proceed without further racket. In fact, by the time it was over, so too was any animosity between the brothers, leaving their visitor amazed at how genial they had once again become, even to each other. That was the way families should behave, thought Niall, not bearing grudges like he had towards his own brother. And in that second, he wished he could make it up with Sean, but having no idea of his whereabouts, this was impossible.

Afterwards, everyone was to repair to Mrs Precious's sitting room. First, though, Boadicea helped Mr Precious stack the plates.

'Do you want a hand?' Niall thought to ask.

'No need!' sang Mr Precious gaily, as he rattled his way to the scullery.

'There's a girl comes in to wash up,' explained Boadicea. 'Go sit down. I'll be with you anon.'

Niall moved on his way, but once there he remained standing to await her. Languid of expression and movement, Mr Yarker moved past him, sank into a brocade armchair, and crossed one leg over the other, displaying a length of tartan sock.

'Sit down!' invited Mrs Precious noisily, flopping onto the sofa and lifting the ginger dog onto her lap.

But Niall ignored this cheerful command, letting the others seat themselves first, not due to politeness, simply hanging fire until Boadicea re-entered to select her chair, then taking the seat beside her.

She had brought some mending with her. He watched as if it were the most fascinating thing in the world whilst she snipped off a length of black thread and proceeded to secure the press stud that had come loose on a skirt.

Mr Allardyce had merged into the background, so quiet that Niall forgot he was even there. Somewhat noisier, their stomachs replete and the whisky fumes from their belches filling the room, the inebriated Eamonn and Johnny were already nodding off.

Mr Yarker appeared irked by the sound of their heavy breathing, for the foot at the end of his tartan sock began to twitch. He leaned over to prod the nearest offender, but finding he could not reach, sat back with a look of resignation. After studying his fingernails for a second, he made a gesture towards the visitor. 'Pass me that, will you?'

Despite the lack of a please, Niall picked up the newspaper that lay on a cluttered occasional table beside his chair. 'This?'

'No, that!' Yarker's finger jabbed more forcefully. 'Thing!'

'This?' Niall reached for a pen.

'*No!*' The voice became more and more impatient, the hand gesture more agitated. '*That* wretched thing there, the blasted what-the-hell-do-you-call-it!' Whilst an obviously offended Niall sought to interpret the command, moving his hand over a dozen objects that might be the relevant item, Yarker uttered further gasps of frustration, which instantly turned to gratitude as Niall finally hit on the correct object: a nail file. 'That's it! Thank you so much, dear boy.' And magically calm again, he leaned over and thrust the file into Eamonn's arm to rouse him. This having the desired effect – at least it lessened the volume of breathing – he sat back and proceeded to give himself a manicure.

Seeking to ease the annoyed furrows from Niall's brow, Boadicea leaned over the arm of her chair with an explanatory whisper. 'He just gets frustrated with himself when he can't remember the words for things.'

Niall himself was becoming increasingly frustrated with these oddities who were Boadicea's living companions, though he managed to cling on to his temper, not daring to do anything to upset his restored friendship with her. Still frowning over Yarker's apparent lack of respect, he caught her eye and found himself instantly melted by the smile she bestowed. He had been here over three hours. Would he ever be allowed to speak to her alone? As she finished repairing her skirt, and sat back to rub her neck muscles and smile at him, he decided to make a move.

'Are you working tonight? I could walk with you . . .'

She shook her head, still smiling. 'Night off. It's Monday, remember.'

Niall groaned inwardly. Had he questioned her earlier, they might have gone somewhere together. Still, there was nothing to stop him asking her now. 'Would you like to go to the pictures, then?'

'You don't want to be wasting your money on that rubbish!' hollered Mrs Precious. 'Pop, run and get your squeeze-box!'

Mr Precious's buttocks had barely touched the sofa, but at his wife's behest he now leaped up willingly, the dog jumping off its mistress's lap to follow him. Boadicea gave an apologetic shrug at her would-be suitor as off went Georgie again to do his wife's bidding.

To Niall's disconcertment, it appeared there was to be a concert. It was something of a relief to find that Mrs Precious did not expect him to join in, her attention being solely for the one who serenaded her with romantic lyrics on his concertina.

"'I'll be your sweetheart, if you will be mine!
All my life, I'll be your Valentine.'"

Turning to Boadicea in surprise, Niall was soon giving Mr Precious his rapt concentration, for even though the fingernails upon the buttons were gnarled and worn and stained brown from varnish, his voice had the sweetness and clarity of youth, and it was obvious his spouse was the love of his life, for he gazed adoringly into her eyes, as he continued to play and croon as if there were no one else in the room:

'Roses are shining in Picardy,
In the hush of the sil-ver dew,
Roses are flowering in Picardy,
But there's never a rose like you!
And the roses will die with the summertime,
And our paths may be fa-ar apart.
But there's one rose that died not in Picardy!
'Tis the rose that I keep in my heart!'

At the old man's tender conclusion, someone trumpeted into a handkerchief. Not looking round to see who it was, averse to anyone spotting his tears, Niall dashed them away with the back of his hand, then gave an embarrassed sideways smile as he saw that Boadicea had caught him. It didn't matter, for her eyes too glittered with moisture. Sharing a wet chuckle, they looked away from each other, as Mr Precious continued his sentimental repertoire.

Three more songs were performed. Even in this

smelly old armchair, seated beside the woman he loved, Niall felt so relaxed and happy by now that he was almost falling asleep, when Mrs Precious announced loudly, 'Right, time you were going!'

Startled, he sat upright and looked around. An ebony timepiece told him it was eight o'clock.

'You can come again,' bawled Mrs Precious, as if to a well-behaved child. And with this he was unceremoniously ejected.

Thankfully, only Boadicea accompanying him to the exit, donning a cardigan as she went.

'So, what do you think to the house of curiosities?' she enquired as they stood, at last alone, in the yard.

'Where do I start?' Niall puffed out his cheeks with a laugh, then threw his eyes skywards. It was barely dark, the moon a pale sliver in a greyish-blue sky, though a gaslamp cast its yellow glow upon his face. 'God's truth, I feel as if I've been involved in a Three Stooges picture – and I can't believe that's the woman you entrust to iron your hair! It's a wonder you've any left.'

'Ma's a bit rough and ready but she's a good heart,' replied Boadicea quietly, her smile fond as she hugged herself against the cool night. 'Ye saw the way she treated us all as if we're family – well, I suppose we are; her and Pop have none of their own. I've only been here a few months, yet you'd think they'd known me ages the way they treat me. Mr Yarker and Mr Allardyce have been with them fifteen years, so she can't be so bad. And Pop's just marvellous, isn't he? What a voice!'

'Aye, he's a grand old chap. I liked him,' agreed Niall. Then added less cordially, 'Wish I could say the same about t'other fella.'

She guessed who he meant. 'Mr Yarker?'

'Aye. Arrogant devil, looking down his nose at folk . . .'

'Appearances can be deceptive,' murmured Boadicea. 'You'd never know he was a war hero, would ye?'

There was a sceptical edge to Niall's response. 'He told you that, did he?'

'No, he did not.' She looked at him intently, her tone level. 'Nor will you ever hear it from his lips. He'd prefer you to think he's unfeeling – didn't you hear him blowing his nose furiously during Pop's serenade? Mr Allardyce told me all about it – he was a corporal in the same company. Mr Yarker – or Captain Yarker, as he was then – saved the lives of three of his men who'd been badly wounded, by carrying them back one after the other to the lines under heavy fire, Mr Allardyce being one of them. He still has funny turns over it – Mr Allardyce, I mean. In fact he often goes quite doolally, the poor soul. Ye saw how upset he was by the boys scrapping over tea. It was in having to explain his odd behaviour that he told me all about their terrible exploits in the war. So, ye shouldn't always judge by appearances, should ye?'

Niall gave a thoughtful shake of head. 'He's not an easy bloke to like, though.'

'Nor would you be,' she told him, 'if ye got back from the war with your medals, to find your wife's run off with somebody else.'

Niall performed a wince of sympathy. Then, after a pensive moment, he referred to the Irish drovers. 'And what about Larry and Moe, what's their story?'

'Oh, they're just mad buggers,' quipped Boadicea lightly. Then she gave a hearty laugh.

So did Niall, though his face betrayed some anxiety.

'Ah, they're not dangerous, save to each other,' she assured him softly.

'I'm relieved to hear it,' breathed Niall. 'By, they don't half swear in your house.'

'Aye, 'tis no place for shrinking violets,' agreed Boadicea. 'I've a foul mouth meself after living with them. Sure, I've never heard folk swear so much as they do in York.'

Niall felt something brush his calf, but a quick glance downwards told him it was only one of the cats, and he was soon once again devoting his attention to Boadicea. His eyes loath to tear themselves from her smiling face, he reverted to the previous subject. 'It's a good job I didn't take Mr Yarker to task then. I would've done, only I thought you might throw me out if I lost my rag. Although . . .' Still holding her gaze, he underwent some thought on this, 'I'm a bit confused as to why you don't seem half as frightened by the bad bahaviour of that lot in there as you did by mine in the café—'

'I wasn't frightened, I was bloody angry!' she interjected.

'—not to mention that you've got a bit of a temper yourself,' he finished with a crooked grin.

'That's different!' she shot back.

'Aye, it always is for women.' He gave her a mild scolding, his expression wry, being accustomed enough to living amongst females, and intimate enough with their behaviour to have noticed that they reacted with undue aggression at particular times of the month.

Boadicea conceded this with a smiling shrug.

Suddenly wondering if her errant spouse might have offered physical abuse, he added quickly, 'If you're worried I'd hit you, then don't. I've never hit a woman in me life.'

'I'd never even think that of you, Niall,' she was swift to allay his fears. 'I can tell what a lovely man you are just by looking at ye.'

Whilst bucked that she held him to be a lovely man, he was momentarily disconcerted. 'What, even with this "foul temper"? How can you tell?'

Boadicea hesitated, then pronounced, 'You've got eyes.'

He laughed. 'Well, I'd be a bit stuck if I hadn't!'

'Ah, but there's eyes, and *eyes*,' she relayed with a sage expression. 'You've got *eyes*.'

Under this warmly issued compliment, his frown

dissolved, though not his concern. 'You're very good at changing the subject, but did I strike a nerve? Did *he* used to hit you? You seemed almost terrified that night.'

'No, no, you're exaggerating!' she said lightly. 'I was angry, certainly . . .'

'But did your husband—'

'Ssh!' She grabbed his arm to silence him. 'Have ye forgotten? Nobody knows about him but you.'

'As if I'd forget,' replied Niall, rather flattered that she had shared her secret with him alone. 'And I know you don't like to talk about him, but all I'd like to know is, was he violent?'

Boadicea released his arm. 'No, no he wasn't.' Such was the firmness of her reply that he was convinced as to the truth of it. He waited for her to go on. Eventually, she spoke again, paying great effort into forming her explanation. 'It wasn't so much your temper that did it, Niall. You're right, I have been known to throw the odd tantrum meself. It was just . . . well, I hate having that sort of attention drawn to me, everyone looking, I was so embarrassed . . .'

He appeared dubious. 'I would've thought you'd be used to unwanted attention with a name like yours.'

'Now who's being insulting!' she gasped.

'Sorry,' he said quickly, 'but you did say yourself—'

'I *said* I've no care if people take the mickey out of my name,' she retorted hotly. 'It's a different

210

thing entirely to be threatened with the police when ye thought you were just off for a pleasant night out!'

Niall cringed at his own behaviour. 'Aye, I suppose I did go overboard. I'm ever so sorry.' He touched her arm, and felt the warmth of her through the soft cardigan. 'So are we friends again?'

She beheld him with slight exasperation, but it was an exasperation born of being hopelessly attracted to him, in the knowledge that they had no future. But, unwilling to give him up, she finally nodded acceptance. 'Ah well, it was hardly the crime of the century, was it?' Having heard him explain that his exhibition had been due only to the frustration and disappointment of wanting to please her, and having someone else ruin this for him, she could empathise with that. So much so that she even chuckled. 'I suppose I should be flattered ye still want to know me, after meeting that lot in there.'

Vastly relieved, Niall studied her smiling, upturned face. There was something different in her attitude tonight, the way she stood so close to him, her eyes twinkling through the darkness, as if that defensive shield had been lowered. He knew he shouldn't do it. He knew he was taking a huge risk, but he just could not resist. Intoxicated by her laughter, the intimacy of her conversation, her sentimental tears over those love songs, he swooped his lips towards her own.

But before they could make contact she turned

her head away, begging him to be content with friendship. 'Niall, have ye forgotten already?'

Not to be thwarted, he moved to close the gap she had created, gripping her arms and appealing into her face, 'I *know* what we said, but I can't help how I feel and there's no point lying!'

Undergoing struggle, both without and within, she tried to avert her cheek from his warm breath. 'I really like you too. It's been awful not seeing you—'

'I *knew* you felt the same!' His voice was half jubilant, half distressed as he clutched her arms. 'Then why keep me dangling like this?'

'Is that what you think?' she cried hotly. 'That I'm some sort o' flirt?'

'No – for pity's sake!' He could have shaken her. 'I just don't understand why you're putting us both through all this, when you feel the same as I do!'

'Because I don't see how anything can come of it – I'm not free!'

'I don't care – well, that's just it, I *do* care!' Niall spoke passionately, tightening his hold on her, looking earnestly into her face. 'I detest the thought of you belonging to somebody else. I know I'm going to hurt Nora and Ellen's family, when they've been so good to me, but I can't give you up! I want you, Bo.'

She made a weak attempt to release herself, but his grip remained strong, much stronger than Boadicea's resolve to remain platonic, for, somehow, despite all the inner anguish, she was suddenly kissing him more passionately, more ravenously than either of them could have anticipated.

Overwhelmed, yet still with an eye to public decency, Niall sought to manoeuvre her into the shadows, maintaining the kiss for as long as they were able to breathe, then both breaking apart with a gasp, his of triumphant joy, hers of apprehension over what she might have started.

'Well, you've really gone and done it now, haven't ye?' she breathed, laying her head upon his chest that smelled of honest labour, feeling his heart thudding in time with hers.

'Sorry, I just couldn't help it.' He wasn't sorry at all as he hugged and stroked her, kissing the top of her head, imbibing the scent of her.

'I warned ye what ye'd be getting into,' pleaded Boadicea, her emotions torn. 'I don't know where he is . . .'

'Then we'll find him and set you free and then I'm going to marry you.'

'The Church might have something to say about that!'

This concerned Niall too. Since discovering Bo was married he had not been to confession. 'I didn't say it was going to be easy.' He studied her. 'Forgive me if I've got you all wrong, but you don't strike me as particularly devout.' He had never seen her go up for Holy Communion, nor in the queue for confession, come to that.

Bo agreed that whilst she believed totally in God, her Roman Catholic conviction was not all it should be. Even though she had been raised mainly by her mother's kin, and the nuns who taught her had held great influence, her father's had been greater. As one with no particular loyalty to any denomination, only a true Christian with a spirit of compassion, his humour had helped dispel much of the destructive elements of Catholic dogma.

'Then it wouldn't bother you too much that we couldn't get married in church?' ventured Niall.

She lifted her tormented face, which was creased in weary protest. 'Niall, we've only been out a couple of times, you hardly know—'

Her objection was smothered under his deeply persuasive kiss, Boadicea responding again with pleasure. Still, he was unsure what would be her verbal response to his next question. 'Don't you want to be with me?' He sounded plaintive.

Lifting her eyes to examine his, she eventually nodded, yet it was a sad little effort. 'God help me, you know well enough I do. You're the loveliest man I ever met. For all sorts of reasons I just can't promise marriage. So please, Niall, let's just see how it goes . . .'

Boosted by her compliment, Niall could see no obstacle. 'If we want it badly enough we'll find a way,' he told her, kissing her again – could have kissed her all night.

Only at a startled utterance did he finally let her go, reacting with embarrassment to the comment of the man who accidentally stumbled upon their embrace. 'Disgraceful!'

Eyes gleaming through the darkness, Boadicea covered her lips to hide an impish smile as, after quick arrangements to meet again, she rushed indoors. But Niall took the remark to heart, as he went home nursing it in his chest where it jostled with his happiness. Had Nora been the witness, he would have heard much worse – *would* hear much worse. How on earth was he going to tell her?

8

Upon great consideration, there seemed no point in telling Nora anything for the time being. For, despite their increasing intimacy over the next couple of months, Boadicea steadfastly refused to countenance marriage. And after all, as she herself said, they had only been together a short time; it just felt like years. The more he got to know her, the more she was a total mystery to him. Sometimes he felt he knew everything about her, other times not at all. But throughout these fluctuations, there was one constant: he loved her. He could not say why, for at times she deeply hurt him with her thoughtless quips and actions – but that very ability to hurt showed that he *did* love her, was crazy about her, otherwise he would not hang around eager for more. But, for the moment, Niall must be content with these weekly liaisons to watch a film and perhaps to receive a kiss at the end of it, all talk of marriage forbidden.

It came as a shock, therefore, when Nora herself was the one to broach the subject.

The children were in bed that Friday night, though with the onset of summer and longer daylight hours, it had been harder to get them there, and they could be heard still talking and giggling at nine o'clock. Harriet had gone to meet her own amour, leaving only Niall, his mother-in-law and Dolly sitting in the living room, reading their various books and periodicals.

Nora suddenly lifted her head, and asked her daughter, 'Didn't you mention you were having an early night?'

Without so much as an argument at not receiving any supper – almost as if it had been prearranged, thought a suspicious Niall – Dolly closed her novel and rose. 'Yes, I think I'll finish this in bed. 'Night, all.'

With the door closed, Nora eased her impregnable torso from the chair and began to dabble around the stove. 'Right, you and me'll have a cup of tea, Nye.' Rinsing the teapot with hot water, she waited for the kettle to return to the boil, meanwhile delving into the caddy with a spoon. 'Eh dear, how time flies when you're getting old . . . I was just remarking to the girls, it's been fifteen months since our Evelyn died, and nearly ten since our Ellen . . .' There was a casual air to her introduction, but Niall had heard that tone before, and knew that it prefaced some deeper intent. He tensed in readiness. Had she found out he had been seeing Boadicea?

'I can't believe it, can you?' She turned sad eyes on him.

Still wary, he lowered his dark head and shook it respectfully.

'It still seems like yesterday I lost my Dom, so I know how lonely you feel.' Padding the hot handle with a knitted square, Nora tipped the kettle towards the pot. 'It's harder for a man, I think. I know you said you'd never marry again, but if you were just saying it for my sake . . . then I want you to reconsider.'

Shocked, but inwardly delighted at being granted this opening to confess about Boadicea, Niall instinctively shook his head, 'Oh, well, I don't—'

Nora stopped him with one of the authoritative stares at which she was so good. 'I'm not saying you have to rush into it. But just sit and listen to my proposition.' She stirred the teapot, and tapped the spoon on its edge. 'Before you say anything, I know she hasn't got the looks, but she's good with children and a decent housekeeper . . .'

Niall was thoroughly perplexed. 'Sorry, Nora,' he hunched forward and frowned at her, 'who's this we're on about?'

Setting out the cups, the elderly woman laughed at herself. 'Oh, I thought I'd said – our Dolly!'

Deeply shocked and perturbed, Niall struggled to reply, coming up with the first objection he could think of: 'Is it legal to marry your sister-in-law?'

Nora was not to be fooled. Seeing the look of undisguised horror on his face, she gave a perceptive nod, as she waited for the tea to brew. 'Aye, I thought you might not be keen.'

'It's not that I don't admire her!' That was only part of it. My God, Dolly of all people! It took him all his time to deliver a peck on the cheek at Christmas, let alone kiss that mouth with its tomb-stone teeth that collected half a loaf between them whenever she ate a sandwich. Why, the goat-like bleat of her laugh was enough to drive him into the next room.

Nora dismissed his interjection. 'I can't say I blame you, after being married to our Ellen. As I say, Dolly's not exactly your Botticelli Venus. I just thought this might be a good opportunity to find her a husband. Nobody else seems to want the poor lass – not that I'm trying to palm her off on you.' She lifted the teapot, staring wistfully into the distance. 'It would have been nice to keep things in the family . . . but anyway, don't worry, I warned her you might not take to the idea.'

Eavesdropping on the other side of the door, Dolly had already pulled away with a silent gasp of indignation at being so discussed. Now, at Niall's tacit rebuttal, she dashed up the stairs to pour humil-iated tears into her pillow.

Meanwhile, Niall's gush of relief at not being obliged to marry her was stanched at first flow as his mother-in-law handed him a cup of tea, along with a confidence. 'So, I've been putting out feelers to Gloria next door. I know you always treated it as a joke, but she really does think you're the bee's knees! Mrs Lavelle says she's always twittering away about you. Anyway,' Nora's tone was conspiratorial, 'I thought I'd invite her for tea on Sunday, let you get to know each other better. She's a bonny enough lass when she has her teeth in. I know she's not the sharpest knife in the box, but she's got a good heart.'

She was also very malleable. Hiding his dismay in his cup, Niall knew that Gloria would easily succumb to Nora's bullying, whether she wanted the match or not. Unable to bring himself to hurt his mother-in-law's feelings by giving outright refusal of both candidates, he formed his words carefully. 'It's a very brave decision on your part, Nora, thinking to do this for me . . .'

She sat down, nursing her own cup of tea on her lap. 'Not really.' Not at all, in fact. Having guessed it was inevitable that her son-in-law would eventually seek another wife, and wanting to maintain control of her grandchildren, Nora had deemed it shrewder to line up her own contender. 'I won't always be here to look after you, and I'd like to see you settled.' She took a sip from her cup.

'Well, as a matter of fact—' About to take advantage of her generosity, and reveal that he had found a prospective bride of his own, Niall broke off as Harriet burst through the door, shrieking.

'You'll never guess what!'

'Christ!' exclaimed Nora, clutching her cup and saucer with one large mitt, and her chest with the other. 'You stupid cat, I almost scalded me lap!'

'I'm engaged!' Harriet's usually hard face was radiant as she thrust out a hand adorned with a tiny diamond, and wiggled her fingers. 'Look what Pete's bought me! He got down on one knee and everything!'

Still recovering from her fright, Nora examined the ring with a critical eye. 'Couldn't he have found one smaller?'

'*Mam!*' Harriet scowled, then studied her diamond protectively. 'It's not small, it's subtle. I think it's lovely.'

'Congratulations.' Niall manufactured a beam, despite harbouring feelings of anticlimax.

'Mine too,' said Nora, her voice more genuine now. 'Well, at least we'll have one wedding this year,' she declared in pleased fashion.

'Oh, didn't it work?' Harriet's eyes went straight to Niall, proving that the discussion of his remarriage had not been spontaneous, but had been previously concocted between them. 'Don't suppose our Dolly'll be very interested in my ring then. Didn't you fancy Gloria either, Nye?'

He could not withhold a surge of resentment, directed mainly at Nora. 'How come you didn't offer Harriet all this assistance you've shown me? Do you think I can't be trusted to find a spouse – assuming I should want one?'

Nora sighed. 'Of course you can't be trusted – you're a man, aren't you? No idea what's good for you.' She pre-empted his reply. 'And if you think you were the one to choose Ellen, then think again!

She had her sights set on you before you knew she existed!' She gave a sad laugh at the thought of her once lively girl, then gave Niall a fond pat. 'Aye, she knew how to pick a good un . . .'

This took him by surprise, for such praise was rare. And again there was conflict in his breast, his anger at her interference dissolving into guilt as she bestowed this compliment.

'And Harriet's the same,' explained Nora. 'She's her mother's daughter; her choice doesn't need vetting.'

'Aye, we know how to keep them in line, Mam, don't we?'

That's what you think, simmered Niall. Wouldn't they get a shock when he told them? But not wanting an argument at this time of night, he chose not to proceed with this topic for now. And from this point, with all talk of marriage deflected onto his sister-in-law, Niall did as he usually did when they annoyed him. He left them to it, and went to bed.

Talk at breakfast the next morning was still about marriage, Harriet nattering on to the children about what bridesmaid dresses they would be wearing.

'And I hope you won't be charging me half a crown for your services, Dom!' she quipped to her altar boy nephew. 'I'll expect them for nowt.'

He sucked in his breath and looked dubious. ''Tisn't me what sets the rates, Aunt. You'll have to speak to Father Finnegan.'

'You can wangle me a rebate if you have the mind,' Harriet teased the grinning boy.

Throughout this banter, her sister remained sullenly intent on her cornflakes, Niall getting no word in at all either. It was hopeless now to mention Boadicea; the opportunity had passed. He wondered whether to apologise to Dolly, who had obviously been informed that he had turned her down, for if she looked at him at all it was only to glare. What with this, and Harriet making her even more peeved by flashing her diamond all over the place, he decided it was better to remain quiet.

If only Harriet had felt the same.

'We shall have to get our thinking caps on again,' she told everyone cheerfully. 'There must be somebody suitable among all our relations for Niall.'

Niall dealt her a glaring rebuke for speaking thus in front of his children. But if the subject showed offence, it was mild compared to another's. Dolly dropped her spoon into her half-finished cereal, dealt Harriet the most splenetic glare and retorted, 'You just can't help rubbing my nose in it, can you?'

'Oh, stop being so jealous,' said Harriet airily.

With the children gaping from one argumentative face to the other, their grandmother intervened, saying calmly to Dolly, 'We can't force him to marry you, dear.'

'I *knew* you'd be on her side!' Dolly's eyes brimmed with angry tears. 'I heard the things you said about me last night!'

'Well, you've got to admit,' replied her mother,

'you'll never win any beauty prizes. Just simmer down. I'm sure we'll find *somebody* who wants to wed you.'

'See, that's what I mean!' Dolly bared her large teeth in anguish. 'You make it sound – oh, don't bother yourself!' And she fled to the stairs, pounding up them for all she was worth, then, in no time at all, thundering down again with a small suitcase in her hand. 'I'm off to stay with Aunty Peggy. She's always appreciated me!'

''Course she has,' laughed her mother uncaringly, watching as her daughter grabbed a work overall that had been drying near the fire, and shoved it into her case. 'She wants an unpaid skivvy.'

'Well, at least I won't get insulted like I do here!' Dolly snapped her case shut, and, hurling a last defiant look at Niall and a hasty farewell to all the children, she rushed out, slamming the door behind her.

'She'll be back,' Nora gave a confident prediction to the gathering. And breakfast continued.

It turned out that Nora was wrong in her forecast: Dolly was not to live there again. Though she did briefly return to make things up with her mother and sister during an evening of the following week, this truce was not to extend to Niall.

'I'm sorry, Mam, you were right about Aunty Peggy, but I just can't live here any more.' From the scullery, he heard her anguished confidence. 'I couldn't bear the humiliation of seeing him marry somebody else.'

Then he felt enormously sorry and, after a further uncomfortable half-hour in her presence, sought to rectify the situation as she was leaving. 'It was nothing I had against you, Dol,' he rose to explain, hoping that he sounded sincere. 'Just that, well, it wouldn't have felt right, you being Ellen's sister . . .'

But it didn't work, the tone of Dolly's reply making it very clear as to the depth of the hurt he had inflicted. 'Ellen would have preferred me as a mother to her children, rather than some stranger you've chosen!'

'I've no intention of choosing anybody!' Niall could have kicked himself. Why did he protest such innocence? It felt like a betrayal of Boadicea. But there was no way he could mention her at the moment, not with feelings running so high.

Dolly bestowed one last scornful glance, before taking leave of the others. 'Anyway, I'm off.'

'So, I'll have to make do without your wages then,' came her mother's sigh of resignation.

Dolly shrugged an apology. 'I'll let you have summat when I can.'

'You're still going to be my maid of honour, aren't you?' demanded Harriet insensitively, as her sister reached the door.

Without enthusiasm, Dolly delivered a nod, before finally making her exit.

'I feel terrible about all this . . .' began Niall to his in-laws, after Dolly had gone.

'Don't you worry about her, son.' Nora offered a crumb of comfort. 'She's a Beasty, she'll survive.

She might even meet a fellow next week who wants to marry her.'

Out of politeness, Niall voiced the hope that this was true. But, aside from the guilt over hurting Dolly, he was in fact singularly unworried by her departure. For with her out of the way, there would be one less Beasty to fight against, when the war over his true marriage partner erupted.

With Harriet's wedding planned for the last week in August, which was almost upon them, and a smart new house beckoning on the council estate at Tang Hall, there would soon be another one less to fight against too. Much encouraged by this, by the following week Niall had forgotten all about the upset with Dolly, as he set off with a spring in his step to meet Boadicea – perhaps there would be a wedding for him too this year. At least there had been a slight improvement in their partnership, in that he was able to escort her to and from her home instead of meeting outside the cinema like strangers. Indeed, he had become a regular visitor to the Precious household, and seemed to have been accepted by her surrogate family. By now, he had come to enjoy his visits to the boarding house. Despite all the chaotic clutter, its atmosphere was not in the least oppressive; in fact, there was a lightness, a homeliness that emanated from the people who ran it. Contrary to her military manner, Ma Precious was a very friendly soul, and if she did approach everyone with the same bossy attitude as

Niall's mother-in-law, one was left with the impression that she had one's best interests at heart. There was no malice at all, and he felt totally welcome. Alas, it would be a while before he could reciprocate. Ever conscious that Harriet might interpret his buoyant mood, and take to following him again, he had continued to conduct his liaison on an evening, as if on a trip to the pub. Thankfully, tonight she and Nora were safe at home stitching bridesmaids' gowns, too busy to follow him.

On his way along Walmgate, he paused to fish a cigarette from his pocket. Striking a match, he happened to glance into the empty window of a bakery where, with the dying of the sun, two black-clock beetles had deemed it safe to emerge, and now scuttled furtively from crumb to crumb, trying to avoid being seen. And in that moment of clarity, Niall looked upon himself: a dirty, devious beetle scuttling in the night, trying to hide his sins from the world. How could he say he wanted to marry Boadicea when he continued to regard her as some sordid secret? Accosted by this truth, he asked himself what on earth he was doing. Remembering the viciousness that had been meted out to his errant brother, he did not relish the same happening to him, but he knew in that moment that he must treat Boadicea with the respect she deserved. The next time they met, Niall decided, it would be in daylight.

If Boadicea had been surprised by his announcement that night, she made no adverse comment, but had agreed to meet him on Saturday afternoon, when they would go to the art gallery – the latter being one of the places in York she had yet to see. Though it might be a rushed visit, for, as she reminded him, 'I've to be back for opening time.'

On his way home, and indeed all that week, Niall had had much more to concern him than getting her to work on time. It had been a gallant decision, but one that would restrict his own movements, if it meant that the only time he could take her out was on a weekend. And if this was to become a habit, it would also require ever more ingenious excuses for those at home. He could not pretend to be going to any sporting event, for the boys would expect to come too. No, it would have to be suitably mundane. But that was to present other difficulties

'Painting?' Nora looked up from the bridesmaid's dress she and Harriet were working on, both of them eyeing him up and down, as he prepared to depart that Saturday afternoon, having told them he was off to help a workmate decorate his front room. 'In your decent trousers?'

'No!' Niall sounded slightly exasperated, as he picked up the bundle he had made of his work clothes. 'I'm taking these to change into. If John's missus asks me to stay for my tea, in return for helping him, I don't want to be sitting on her sofa in me muck, do I?'

But he was to deposit the bundle of clothes at Boadicea's lodgings until his return.

The choice of indoor venue was to be fortuitous. As he and Boadicea set off the sky was leaden, and besides wearing her trenchcoat she brought along an umbrella just in case. In the event, they were to reach the art gallery just as the heavens opened, and hurried laughingly to join the crowd of people inside. Browsing the collection, shifting slowly between massive works of genius, and miniature ones, little was said between them other than the odd murmur of respect over a particular painting. This was something of a respite to Niall, for whom the art of intimate conversation was a skill not yet conquered. For him, it was sufficient just to be in her company. Yet he knew how Boadicea enjoyed a chinwag, and was so open in her revelations that he feared she might find him boring if he did not make some kind of effort. Thus, all the way round the gallery he worried about how to entertain her when their tour came to an end.

He need not have done, for as usual Boadicea was the one to set the ball rolling as they came out to find that the downpour had eased, though there remained a steady drizzle.

'Oh, wouldn't ye know it!' She swiftly erected her umbrella, inviting in her lovely Irish lilt, 'Come on, squeeze yourself next to me. We can both fit under.'

Crouched beneath its inadequate canopy, they jostled against each other as they splashed their way across Exhibition Square towards another limestone bar in the city walls. Whilst it was lovely being in such proximity to her, and stimulating to feel the warmth and scent reflected from her face, Niall quickly found it impossible to travel in this fashion.

'Nay, you're holding it too low for me. You keep knocking me cap askew!' So saying, he emerged to brave the drizzle with a typically wry grin, setting his cap straight, and dipping around her to walk on the outside edge of the pavement, as they came under Bootham Bar. 'You have it all. A bit of rain won't bother me.'

'You're lucky!' She sounded most emphatic, railing against the moisture. 'My hair detests this weather – I'll look such a state for work.'

'You never look a state,' complimented Niall.

'Sure, you haven't seen me first thing in the morning,' replied Boadicea, then she blushed, for his eyes told her he would like to.

It was much too glib for Niall to say he hoped she would grant him the chance once day. Besides, there were too many others using the narrow pavement who might overhear. However, her comment had raised the spectre of one who *had* seen her in the mornings, and he underwent a moment's thought, waiting for the couple behind to overtake, before addressing the subject again.

'I know I'm slow, but it's only just struck me . . . your surname, Merrifield . . . your husband must have been English, was he?'

But the mention of her errant spouse was not welcomed. 'No,' she said crisply, 'I preferred to go back to my maiden name after he left me.' Sensing an inquisitive gaze, she snapped an addition. 'It's not illegal, you know.'

'No, no, I'm not saying it is!' Niall wanted to ask what her married name had been, but it was obvious she did not like being reminded of it. She had fallen quiet, and seemed unconcerned now with the state of her hair, for her umbrella had been allowed to slip to one side. Hoping to divert her from this trance, Niall took hold of a spoke and set the umbrella straight, then grinned as she suddenly appeared to remember where she was and emerged from her pensive mood to smile back at him.

'Sorry,' she issued softly.

'Nay, it's just me being nosy,' soothed Niall. 'I don't know why I even mentioned it. I don't want to know about him, I just want to know about you.'

She cocked her head as they passed the Minster. 'Don't ye know everything already?'

It was true she had been very forthcoming. But, 'Tell me anything,' said Niall. 'About when you were a bairn in Ireland.'

And quite happily she did as, dwarfed by the cathedral and under constant surveillance from its ancient gargoyles, along the narrow streets they pattered, barely mindful of the rain, intent only on each other. So obsessed was Niall that he wanted to know every trivial detail about her. 'And did you have dolls?'

'Of course I did,' Boadicea laughed from beneath her umbrella. 'I'm a girl, aren't I?'

'You certainly are.' Walking in the gutter now, in order to be on a level with her face, his eyes were warmly admiring. 'And did you play houses like my lasses do in our passageway? Sometimes I can hardly get into me own place, what with all the prams and blankets and clothes horses they've set up. Leastwise, Juggy does. Her sister, Honor's, a bit old for it at thirteen, though she sometimes has a game if she's nowt better to do – or so she cracks on.' His laughing expression faded. 'It's a bit sad really, seeing them grow up so fast.'

Boadicea responded kindly to his wistfulness. 'Still, you've a good few years before a man comes along to take the younger one off your hands. Is she six, did ye say?'

He brightened again. 'Seven now, she's had a birthday.'

'Ah!' Boadicea made a thoughtful sound. 'And when is her daddy's birthday, by the way?'

'Oh, I don't bother with 'em meself,' mumbled Niall dismissively.

'You've gone all gritty Yorkshireman on me again,' she teased him.

He laughed and tugged self-consciously at the peak of his rain-dappled cap, though it had no need of adjustment. 'What I really mean is, other folk don't bother with my birthdays.'

''Tis a crime!' she announced in determined

fashion. 'I shall send you a card – tell me, when is it?'

But he still refused to tell her, maintaining his smile as he replied, 'Honestly, I'd rather not bother.' At her doubtful scrutiny, he admitted with a sigh, 'It just reminds me of when me mam died.'

She stopped, causing the person walking behind almost to bump into them before having to go around with a click of impatience. 'Your mother died on your birthday? Niall, how awful. I knew she and your father were dead, but ye never told me that!'

'I didn't want to bore you,' he smiled, leading her on again.

'Nothing you have to say could bore me,' she told him warmly, trying to get nearer to him, whilst taking care to avoid his eyes with the umbrella spokes. 'Least of all that – you poor soul. How long ago was it?'

'Oh, a long time – fourteen years.'

'But it still hurts, doesn't it?' she recognised sadly. 'And how long is it, did ye say, since your wife died?'

Niall felt a jolt. His face must have altered at this unwanted reminder of Ellen, for before he could respond, Boadicea spoke again, and there was a perceptive quality to her remark. 'Seems there's things we both don't want to talk about.'

He nodded and, acting automatically as they came to a busy open square, began to check the identity of each face in the crowd, alert for any spy who might go running to Nora. But in seconds he was focused on Boadicea again. 'It's not so much talking about it that bothers me . . . it's that you'll think less of me if I tell you.' He sighed. 'But I should do anyway. Ellen only died last October.'

After a quick calculation, she understood his reluctance. 'So, she'd only been gone five or six months that first time you asked me out?'

He moved his head in affirmation. 'I knew you'd be shocked. That's why I didn't want to tell you, not before you'd had a chance to really get to know me. And now that you have, you must realise I'd only act like that when it was something I felt so strongly about. I'd never have done it on a whim. I was crackers about you, still am.' There was a self-conscious pause. 'But you've been straight with me about being married, so you had a right to know.' Looking chastened, Niall lowered his gaze from her face to the ground. The bottom of his grey flannels were sodden and covered in dirty splashes that his shoes had flicked up from the pavement. 'I'll understand if you give me the elbow – I'll hate it, but I'll understand.' He just prayed with all his heart that she would not.

''Tis a bit late for that,' came her mild scolding. 'I'm as much smitten as you are.'

His face came up again, flushed by a look of reprieve as he saw that her expression belied the stern tone. And their eyes remained locked for a moment, conveying how deeply each felt.

'But your wife's family can't be pleased about ye

234

courting me.' Seeing his relief fade, she immediately guessed. 'Ah, they don't know.'

'It's not out of cowardice.' Niall pre-empted any hostile verdict, as, mindful of bumping into folk, both fixed their gazes on the way ahead. 'Even though they would probably judge it as heresy – me making a choice of my own. It's just that I can't bring meself to hurt them. Ellen's the third one Nora's lost.' He glanced at Boadicea to see her expression change first to shock, then to deep pity and understanding. 'Anyway,' he added, 'there's nothing to tell yet, is there?'

Boadicea remained thoughtful. 'So, all this time you've been making excuses to them about your whereabouts?'

'Not really. I told them I was off to the pictures, or the pub, and that was the truth.'

'And where is it that you're meant to be this afternoon?'

'Painting with a friend.' A sheepish grin seeped through his guilty expression. 'Well, it's only half a lie. I am with a friend, and we have been looking at paintings.'

She clicked her tongue at his impudence. 'Did you give this friend's name? What if they bump into him? I hope he's been primed with the same story.'

'Oh, I just made him up,' confessed Niall, then joked, 'I have to rely on these imaginary friends. Nobody else'll talk to me.'

'Eejit! Seriously, do you have many friends?' She

was always so busy talking about herself, that she had omitted to ask this before.

'Just the one.' He caught her look of amazement. 'You don't need more than one – as long as he's a good un.'

Boadicea maintained her fond smile. 'And how often do you see him?'

Niall mused. 'Oh, 'bout once a year.'

'He lives far away then?'

Niall frowned. 'No, Navigation Road – t'other end from The Angel.'

Boadicea thought this hilarious, her hearty laughter drawing curious looks from passers-by. 'Oh, Niall, you're a treasure!'

He showed no offence. 'I've got folk I see every day, but that doesn't mean they'd give me the shirt off their back like Reilly would. If I didn't see him for ten years he'd still be my friend.'

'And when was the last time you saw him?' smiled Boadicea.

'Ellen's funeral.'

She looked guilty. 'Oh . . . sorry.'

'That's all right.' His tone was warmly forgiving. 'Didn't get much of a chance to have a laugh with him, as you might imagine . . .'

This brought Boadicea back to the subject of his dead wife's family. 'How long can you keep this secret from them, Niall? Better you tell them, than somebody else. I mean, I'm hardly going to be popular if they do find out that way.'

He hadn't the heart to tell Boadicea that she

would be hated whichever way they found out about her. Even so, she should be warned. 'All right, I'll tell them. But you'd better get ready for a rough ride.'

'Just what I need.' She shook her head, and gave a little growl as they continued across King's Square, as much exasperated by the people and pigeons who got in her way as by his last statement. Then, she stopped again. 'Damn! Now you've gone and made me forget – I was supposed to get some stockings for Ma from Browns. She'll only have them from there . . .' Looking up at him, she tendered hopefully, 'Would ye mind if we go back?'

Niall did not mind at all, and took a detour along Church Street, telling her that he would wait outside the department store. 'It'll give me chance to have a fag. I'm gasping.'

Once arrived at their destination, Boadicea hurried inside, saying she would try not to be long. 'Here, take my brolly. Sure, you're half-drenched!'

'I'm not having that!' Laughing it aside, he watched her go into the store, then pressed his back to the plate-glass window, trying to gain some shelter from the ineffective overhang, and lit his cigarette. After a long, hearty drag, he exhaled in ecstasy, much relieved to have made a clean breast of things, and to have been absolved. Then he stood back to gaze with uninterested eyes at the crowd of passers-by.

That initial haze of smoke had barely dispersed when he saw through it a familiar figure coming towards him along Davygate – Gloria. There was no doubt that she had seen him, for beneath the umbrella her face underwent a sudden glow, as if bedecked with fairy lights. Niall panicked and fled into the store. Once inside, he looked round swiftly, taking in every counter and hoping to alert Boadicea, but she must be on an upper floor. Should he go up there? What if Gloria saw them together? Taking a drag of his cigarette, he wheeled to snatch a look through the window, trying to spot his admirer. Oh my God, there she was, dismantling her umbrella and making her way to the entrance! Looking about him for a sign of the men's department, he made a dash for it. At least he would have a legitimate reason for being there if she managed to collar him. However, on his way through the maze of fixtures containing female paraphernalia, he happened to spot another doorway and, making a swift decision, he rushed through this exit into a different street.

This might have confused Gloria, though it certainly did not deter her, for she simply took the identical exit, waving to him as she came. Cursing her, Niall had no option but to wait and share a few words, greeting her casually as he held open the door for her.

'Now then, Gloria, I didn't see you there!' He pulled on his cigarette and threw a quick sideways glance at the far end of the building, to check whether Boadicea had emerged, and was thankful not to see her yet. 'Not with your mam today?'

Gloria bared her false teeth, which had been brought out for the occasion. 'No, she doesn't like this wet weather! She's sent me out to get meself a pair of shoes.' And she opened a paper bag to show him.

'By, they're grand!' Trying to remain casual, he threw another furtive look towards the far door.

'Ooh, ta!' The besotted Gloria looked as if she might swoon with pleasure, then crumpled her bag shut, and cocked a hopeful eye at him. 'Are you off home? I'll walk with you!'

Niall balked. He had just caught sight of Boadicea emerging from the other door, and she was searching for him. 'Er, sorry, Gloria, I'll have to rush!' In a final act of desperation he pointed across the square to a public convenience. 'Ta-ra now!' And he galloped for the lavatory, hurrying down the steps to the very bottom, to be greeted by a smell combined of urine and disinfectant. He lingered in the lavatory's echoing tiled interior, finishing his cigarette and also relieving himself, whilst awaiting Gloria's departure.

After a few minutes had passed, he trod cautiously up the steps, allowing only his head to emerge above ground level, where it swivelled for a sighting of his wretched pursuer through the cast-iron railing. To his relief, Gloria was no longer evident amongst the crowd. But upon continuing to the top of the staircase, he saw to his horror that Boadicea had gone too.

Looking about him in a desperate search for her,

he finally saw her at the far end of Church Street, heading back for their original route home, and he hared after her, dodging in and out of the traffic, on and off the pavement.

'Where did you get to?' her face accused from beneath the umbrella, as he finally caught her up by the medieval Christ Church in King's Square. 'I waited ages – thought I'd been abandoned.'

'I was only in the lav.' Any mention of Gloria might complicate things. 'It was you who abandoned me!'

Looking happier again, she apologised for her rash departure and linked his arm, drawing him under her umbrella to walk in this fashion across the square. But once the pavement narrowed again, she was forced to lift her umbrella above the head of passers-by. Hence, with too many shoppers in their way, Niall fell back to walk in single file along the greasy wet flags behind her, returning to her side whenever that was possible. But all the while he kept his eyes alert for Gloria, for it had not failed to register that she would probably mention to Nora that she had seen him. At least he had not been with Boadicea at the time, but he would certainly have to come up with a good explanation as to why he was in town, when he should have been painting. Perhaps it was time to come clean.

They reached the shortest street in York, Whip-Ma-Whop-Ma-Gate, where a medley of horns from car and bus signalled a jam. Squeezing a passage between the duelling vehicles, Niall led his companion across the awkward, narrow junction, and on past the Old George Hotel that preceded Fossgate. Here, thankfully, they were to leave much of the traffic noise behind them, apart from a cart that came past laden with vegetables, the resounding clip-clop of the horse's hoofs accompanying them all the way past the bridge.

Before they knew it, to Niall's disappointment they had reached the archway leading to her home. Retreating beneath it, Boadicea dismantled her umbrella and gave it a shake. 'Will ye come in for a cup of tea? I can't promise I'll be able to sit with ye for long; I've to get ready for work.'

'Ooh, I'm glad you reminded me!' Niall suddenly recalled that he had left his work clothes here. 'I'd have nowt to wear on Monday. Er, you haven't got a bit of paint I could splash on 'em, have you, to make it look authentic?' And chuckling, they went into the house together.

But he did not stay long after collecting his bundle, saying warmly, 'I don't want to hinder you, so I'd better get off home, much as I don't want to leave.'

Seemingly as reluctant to let him go, Boadicea returned with him to the Walmgate end of the alleyway, where she sheltered under the arch, and he stood in the rain, not appearing to mind that his coat was by now quite damp, wanting to savour this last moment.

'If I don't see you before, shall I come same time next week?' He stood smiling, to await her answer.

Boadicea smiled back at him. She had been right about her fine hair, for it had undergone a drastic reaction to the weather, but Niall thought she looked as sweet as an angel, her twinkling blue eyes and pink cheeks framed by a curly halo of gold. 'I'll look forward to it,' she told him. 'Now I must go, or I'll be rushing round like the proverbial.'

He leaned towards her expectantly. 'Can I give you a little kiss?'

Her cheek presented, he allowed his lips to settle there, imbibing the scent of violets, and feeling his insides quiver. Then she turned tail and hurried back to the mansion.

Smiling to himself, Niall was about to proceed along Walmgate when, from the corner of his eye, he glimpsed a figure crossing the road towards him. Turning his head, he had no time to avoid the blow – in fact he only succeeded in providing a better target for the stinging slap that was dealt to his cheek, so fiercely delivered that it made him cry out.

Objecting loudly, his hand automatically raised to attend his throbbing flesh, he took a moment to right himself, then stared at the woman who had dispensed the injury, and his spirits fell. It was Harriet.

9

'Just you wait till I get home!' Harriet had warned him, as a parent might say to a naughty child. 'Me mother'll hear about this!' And leaving him in purgatory, she had minced away in the opposite direction, to resume the errand that had been so rudely interrupted by his treachery.

Thinking to cushion the impact, Niall hurried home and, after ascertaining that the children were out at play in the puddles, he stood before his mother-in-law, damp cap in hand, and blurted an awkward confession: 'Nora, I've been meaning to tell you . . . I've met somebody I want to marry.'

The unexpectedness of this had interrupted her sewing, and had forced her to give him her full attention, but after recovering from her initial shock Nora was merely shirty. 'I don't see why you couldn't trust me to find you somebody suitable,' she complained.

'It's not that I don't trust you, Nora.' Still on his feet, he had begun to explain in measured tones about how he valued her opinion, and would of course introduce her to his lady friend at the first opportunity – and at that point Harriet returned.

'He's told you then!' Eyes like marbles, she remained in the passage for a moment, shrugging off her wet coat and giving it an angry shake before hooking it over a peg.

'If you mean about the woman he's met, yes.' Nora did not sound too pleased. Then she frowned in puzzlement, as Harriet came charging into the living room and threw a brown paper parcel on the table. 'How did you—'

'Cause I've just seen him kissing her, that's how!'

'*What?*' Able only to splutter that one word, Nora turned swiftly back to Niall, who inwardly cringed in guilt.

'Where do you think he got that red mark on his face?' thundered Harriet. 'I wasn't going to stand there and let that happen!'

Seeing his mother-in-law's eyes well with anger, and hoping to fend off another physical attack from Harriet, Niall sought to explain. 'You're talking as if I've been caught in some passionate embrace – it was only a kiss on the cheek! No more than I'd grant either of you.'

Harriet made a loud scoffing noise, then bellowed disgustedly to her mother, 'Good job we ran out of material!' That which seemed a nuisance only half an hour ago, had now turned provident. 'I'd never have caught him otherwise – painting, my foot! How long's this been going on? How many more lies have you told us?'

'Harriet!' barked her mother with an authoritative glare, and immediately the tirade was stemmed.

Her order obeyed, Nora turned back to Niall, stuck her chin out, and directed a jaundiced eye at him. 'Right then, you were eager enough to tell me before we found out your true colours – who is this woman?'

Besieged by those three fierce presences, Harriet, her mother, and that oppressive black sideboard, and annoyed to hear his sweetheart referred to as 'this woman', Niall was less than co-operative.

'Her name is Miss Merrifield.' He employed a formal air, not only in an attempt to calm things, but also from an unwillingness to include Nora in his intimate knowledge of Boadicea.

But being Nora, she demanded to know anyway. 'And does she have a first name? She must have if you're on marrying terms.'

'*Marry?*' Harriet bawled at her mother, who held up a hand. Silenced again, and frustrated, the daughter folded her arms tightly under her breast, and began to prowl up and down.

'Name!' repeated Nora to her son-in-law.

He sighed and offered it reluctantly, as he bent to lay his damp cap on the hearth. 'It's Boadicea.'

'My God!' A nasty laugh from both mother and daughter. 'Were her parents comedians?'

Niall pressed his lips together, his nostrils flared. You can talk with a name like Beasty, he wanted to retort, but that would hardly encourage them to share his point of view.

'Well, she can't live round here,' frowned Nora, 'or I'd have heard of her. So where does she live?'

Harriet jumped in again. 'I can tell you that, Mam! Well, I saw which alley she went into after kissing him, so we'd only have to knock on a few doors!'

Fearing they would invade the Preciouses' home, Niall held up his callused palms. 'Now let's not get silly—'

'Silly?' Nora's repetition was laced with opprobrium. 'We won't have to get *silly* if you come clean about her.' And she cocked her head expectantly.

Ashamed and unwilling to reveal that the love of his life was already married, he granted his interrogators only those details that were innocuous. 'She's from the same county in Ireland as we are—'

'With a heathen name like that?' exclaimed Nora. 'I don't believe it!'

'Well, she had to call herself Mary over there,' muttered Niall.

'I know what I'd like to call her!' spat Harriet.

Annoyed by their sneering condemnation of the woman he loved, Niall clammed up then.

But his mother-in-law remained dogged. 'It seems a funny going-on to me. Why, you can't have known her five minutes!' Her eyes narrowed. 'Or have you? How long has it been going on?'

'Not long.'

'Where did you meet her?'

He hesitated before admitting, 'She works at The Angel.'

The room erupted, the women's shrill exclamations pinging the crystal vase on the sideboard. 'A *barmaid*? So that's what he was up to behind our backs, letting us think he was drowning his sorrows, when all the time it was to see her!'

Niall tried to beseech them. 'You're making it sound dirty, it—'

'That's *exactly* what it is!' Nora's eyes bulged.

'No!' he cried. 'There's been nothing like that between us. We just have some good conversation, and go to the pictures together . . .'

'Oh! Now it's all coming out,' crowed Harriet, nodding sagely to her mother. 'Hanky-panky in the dark!'

Niall turned on her. 'Don't be tarring me with the same brush as yourself! She's a respectable woman – she goes to Mass on Sundays.'

But Nora was not to be duped, stating grimly, 'Bernie McEvoy goes to Mass, and we all know what she is!'

Niall set his mouth in defiance. 'Do you think so little of me that I'd pick a woman of the streets to look after my children?'

'She works in a pub; it's almost as bad!' Against the pale grey of her dress, Nora's face had turned puce. 'And I'm not having my grandchildren raised by a barmaid, so you can get that out of your head straight away!'

Losing control, Harriet launched herself at the exit. 'I've never been in a pub in my life, but I'm off round to tell her employer what she's up to!'

'No you bloody won't!' Niall grabbed her arm.

Though it was not he who successfully delayed her, but her mother's command. 'No you won't, Harriet! I'm not having you making matters worse. He knows he's in the wrong, don't you?'

'*Do* I?' Niall maintained a rebellious air, though the general tone of the argument seemed suddenly to have been given a change of direction by his mother-in-law.

'Oh, yes.' Her voice might have adopted a more reasonable tone, was almost a purr, but the steely glint of her eye showed that the battle was about to begin in earnest. 'So get yourself sat down, and let's pay this matter a great deal more thought – and I don't want you butting in, Harriet.'

'It's had all the thought it requires,' Niall answered firmly. 'I know how I feel about her.' Resisting her order to sit down, he glanced at the clock. 'Anyway, the kids'll be coming in for their tea in a while. I don't want them hearing all this.'

'I'll bet you don't! And seeing as we're mentioning the children, how d'you think they'll feel?' enquired Nora, a truculent Harriet sitting in one of the heavy Edwardian chairs nearby to contribute a nod of agreement.

'They'll like her as much as I do.' Niall finally sat down in his armchair, though his attitude remained stiff.

'How do you know?' grilled Nora. 'You haven't consulted them. You haven't paid them one minute's regard.' She saw him about to object. 'Oh aye! You'll have a game of football when it suits you, and read them the odd fairytale, but young as they are, they can tell your mind's somewhere else – and now we know where! It's not even a year since they lost their mother and—'

'It was all right when you wanted me to wed Dolly, though!' flared Niall at the accusation that he was a bad father.

'Dolly's their aunt – she loves them!' Nora shouted above him. 'You don't know anything about this woman, other than your own selfish lust. Yes, that's what it is! Lust! You haven't given a thought to anybody else in this house. You say you care about your children, but you haven't given them the time of day whilst all this has been going on!'

'That's rubbish!' Niall jumped to his feet as if to leave.

'It's all very well racing through a few pages of *Mowgli*, but what they really need is somebody they can rely on.'

'They can rely on me!'

'Go on then,' needled his mother-in-law, still in her seat, looking up at him, 'tell me what Dominic's been doing with himself these last ten months.' Pleased to see him falter, she pressed forth her attack. 'No, you can't, can you? So *I'll* tell you – he's been smoking!'

Niall's jaw dropped.

'Aye, I thought that'd surprise you,' nodded his mother-in-law. 'He probably puffs off more a week than you do!'

Niall spluttered, his first instinct being to count the cigarettes in his own packet.

'Oh, he hasn't been pinching yours, if that's all you're bothered about! He buys his own.'

'Where does he get the money?' frowned Niall.

'It's what he earned from all those Requiem Masses he's been doing – made rather a pastime of it.'

'He's meant to hand any money to you!'

'And so he did,' said the boy's grandmother calmly. 'But I let him keep a copper or two for himself.'

'If you knew what he was spending it on, why didn't you stop him?' demanded an angry Niall.

'Why didn't *you* stop him? You're his father.' Nora tapped her chest vigorously. '*I* haven't stopped him because I know how the lad's feeling at losing his mother, and having a father who's too busy sniffing round barmaids to show any interest in him! And what about Brian, the poor bairn who still doesn't understand why his mother isn't coming back – how do you think he feels when his father's off gallivanting every night?'

'It's not every night!' repudiated Niall, as if to a fool, though his defiant stance was fast beginning to crumble. 'I knocked that on the head a long time ago. I only go out once a week – surely I deserve that after working so hard to provide for you lot?'

'Eh, I provide for meself, thank you very much!' objected Harriet, but was overshouted by her mother.

'It might not be every night, but I'll tell you what is!' riposted Nora. 'Wet sheets and blankets from our Judith, that's what! Stuff that I have to wash and dry every morning – or near as dammit – not you, *me*. Me, who should be enjoying a bit of rest in my old age!'

It was a gross exaggeration, but it did the trick. Completely quashed now, Niall murmured guiltily, 'I'm sorry, Nora, I had no idea . . .'

'No, because I didn't tell you! I just got on with it. Because that's what a grandmother does for those she loves. And all these months you've taken us for mugs!' She shared a look of disgust with Harriet, both sets of eyes brimming malice.

'I haven't honestly!' Niall was effusively penitent. 'I'm truly grateful for all you've done. I'm really sorry, I never thought—'

'No, you didn't!' Nora gave a curt nod. 'And believe me, I haven't told you the half of it. The number of hidings I've had to give Batty for taking stuff that doesn't belong to him . . .'

Niall groaned, and flopped back down onto the chair, leaning forward, head in hands.

But there was even more to come. 'I've had neighbours at our door complaining that Juggy's clouted their bairns—'

His face shot up, objecting, 'Juggy? I won't believe that!'

Nora craned forth to lay emphasis on her declaration. 'She's even been hitting her friends, slapping them across the face!'

'But why?'

'Don't ask me! Ask her! But she's taking her anger out on those who don't deserve it. There's only Honor that's doing any good at school, and no thanks to you. It's me who has to drag her out of bed every morning. Do you think your barmaid's going to put up with all that – or will you even bother to inform her, or is she just there to meet your requirements, like the rest of us seem to be?'

Having said her piece, the tartar sat back and fidgeted with the gold watch-band on her thick wrist, awaiting him to consider her revelations.

Consumed by guilt, during the wordless interval that followed Niall was deeply pensive, staring at his mother-in-law's masculine fingers upon that delicate bracelet, whilst mulling over the accusations of its owner. It wasn't simply that he had been taking advantage of Nora's generosity that caused him to review his situation. No, it was what she had made him see about his own behaviour towards his children. He *had* been selfish. Utterly selfish. He could dress it up all he liked, and protest that his aim was to give them a mother, but in truth, the only needs he had been concerned about were his own. For once his eyes were truly open, and he saw that the love affair had been conducted all on his part. He professed to love Boadicea, but how could he expect her to take on such awesome responsibility? There she was, a lass who had been so hurt in the past that she wanted nothing more to do with marriage, wanted to remain carefree and single, had warned him at the outset not to expect anything more than friendship – how could he have sought to cajole her into changing her mind? What had he to offer? Five troubled children was hardly an incentive to marry him, was it? No. It broke his heart to say it, but not only was this unfair, it was totally pointless. Even if Boadicea had been free to wed, he would never be able to bring her into his home without looking like a traitor to his dead wife's family.

Oh, but I want her, I need her, his heart argued.

And your children need you, came the accusing riposte.

Oh dear God, what was he to do? What *should* he do?

Watching him intently, ready to pounce again at the first sign of resistance, Nora and Harriet were finally triumphant to witness the look of surrender that moved like a shadow across Niall's face.

'You're right,' he murmured decisively, sounding calm, though his soul was overwhelmed by such a tidal wave of loss that he could never hope to describe. 'I have been thinking only of myself . . .'

Nora stopped playing with her watch and leaned forward with gimlet eyes to encourage him. 'So you'll finish it?'

Eventually, Niall moved his head in agreement, unable to utter even a yes, for his pain was so bad that it felt like his heart had been ripped from his body.

His mother-in-law's expression mellowed, and she reached out to clasp his wrist in a hand that was almost as large as his own. 'I knew you wouldn't let us down. In spite of everything I've said, you're a good lad.' She dealt him a last pat, and gestured to her daughter. 'Put the kettle on, Hat. I think we need a cup of tea before the bairns come in.'

Whilst Harriet silently complied, Nora herself deigned to offer Niall a word of encouragement to atone for all the harsh ones. 'This doesn't have to mean you'll always be on your own, you know. We weren't meaning to run your life for you, were we, Harriet? Just that we think you deserve a lot better, and so do those children.'

Niall rubbed his hands over his stricken face, immersed in regret, still unable to fathom how he could have been so neglectful of them. 'I'm sorry for taking you for granted, Nora. I promise I'll buck my ideas up from now on.'

'I don't really mind looking after them, you know.' The tyrant's voice was lighter, now that matters were once again under her control. 'I'd be lost if I didn't have any of you to look after. That's why I was so concerned. I look upon you as my own son.'

Feeling even more wretched, Niall dealt her a grateful nod of recognition.

'What you need is some time away from all your troubles,' Nora told him brightly. 'The schools break up next Friday, I'm going to write to our Beesy and tell her we're coming to stay for a week. You, me and the children.'

'Er, what about getting these bridesmaids' dresses finished?' Harriet spun round, a brown glazed teapot in her hand. 'Or had you forgotten it's only four weeks till I get married?'

'How could we forget? You never shut up about it,' said her mother, with a cryptic smile at Niall, who was to voice a different concern.

'Next Saturday?' He shook his head. 'It's short notice. I might not be able to get my docket signed in time.'

'They'll grant it.' Nora sounded confident. 'If you have any bother, refer your boss to me. I'll tell him we've got family trouble.'

I'll bet you would, thought Niall bitterly, and for a moment longer he resisted his mother-in-law's bullying plans. 'It'll cost a fair old whack.' Even as a railway employee, receiving several free passes and a heavy discount on the remainder of the tickets, he pointed out that there was still the ferry to Ireland and the train from Dublin. 'And we can't expect Beesy to keep us for nowt.'

But Nora remained unfazed. 'I've still got all that cash from when I sold the furniture.'

Sean's furniture. Remembering his own part in the looting, Niall experienced a fresh surge of shame. Thus, he was compelled to cave in. 'All right, then . . . I suppose I could do with getting away.'

'Good.' Nora looked immensely satisfied, and felt able to relax with the cup of tea that Harriet now handed to her. 'Oh, take that look off your face, Hat! Your blasted dresses'll get finished, even if I have to sew till midnight when I get back.' With her daughter pacified, she turned back to Niall. 'Right, it's settled then. You give your word you won't see this woman any more?'

'Yes . . .' There was slight hesitation, as he lifted his devastated eyes from the carpet to spill an awkward admittance. 'Only, I've arranged to meet her next week. It wouldn't be right to leave her hanging on, so I'll have to see her to let her know.' His expression brooked no argument over this.

Nora gave a haughty sniff, and raised her cup to her lips. 'If you must.'

But with her son-in-law determined upon the decent way out of this, she had to be content.

The error of his ways so graphically pointed out to him, Niall decided thereupon he must not prolong the agony for an entire week before imparting the bad news to Boadicea. He would go to the pub that same night. This intention was relayed discreetly to Nora, as his children piled in for their tea.

'But I'm only going to put an end to things,' he swore to her. 'Then it's definitely over.'

Immediately sceptical, Nora decided to take out

insurance, and eyed him shrewdly as she revealed to her grandchildren that their father would be treating them to a holiday in Ireland. Witnessing such excitement that followed this announcement, he could hardly renege now, could he?

Niall remained determined to go out. However, before doing so he was to pay much more consideration to his children than of late, and ensured that each was given his wholehearted attention before they finally went off to bed.

Only then did Niall permit himself to think of Boadicea, and to set off and see her, in parting telling his mother-in-law not to worry, for, 'It's definitely over.'

At the time of saying, he fully meant it, for Boadicea's sake as well as his children's. But when he entered The Angel, and saw her face light up at his impromptu arrival, he was so deeply affected by that smile that he could not bring himself to inflict such finality. How could he claim to love her, yet give her up so easily? Yet, he must, for his children were suffering . . .

Tongs of guilt wrenched at his gut, twisting it this way and that, as he made his approach through the crowd of drinkers.

'Can't stay away?' Her breezy greeting pierced the hubbub, now that he had managed to carve a path to the bar. 'This is a pleasant surprise – what can I get ye, me dear?' She seized a glass.

'No, I'm not stopping,' he smiled apologetically, gazing upon her as if this might be his last sighting,

and his soul wept. 'I just came to let you know . . .
I'm ever so sorry, but I've just found out Nora's
organised a family holiday to Ireland, and I won't
be able to see you next week. In fact, not for a few
weeks.'

'Ah well . . .' Boadicea's smile faded, and she
examined his eyes for a moment, her own misting
with disappointment. But this soon reverted to her
usual verve. 'Ireland, eh? Sure, aren't you the lucky
one. I wish I was going with ye.'

Oh, so do I, agonised Niall, his heart keening
its distress as he was jostled by others who were
trying to buy a drink.

It was obvious she was too busy to linger. 'Well,
have a nice time, darlin'. I'll miss ye. Come and
see me the minute ye get back!' Issuing a last
affectionate apology with her eyes, Boadicea was
forced to tear herself away then to serve somebody else.

Elbowed from all sides, tormented to his core,
Niall remained suspended for a moment, unwilling
to depart. Whilst others supped of their ale, he
drank only of her, imbibing deeply, for he might
never see her again. He should have spoken. But
he didn't. He couldn't. Instead, he tore his eyes
away, and went to confession.

His heart lamenting all that night, Niall wondered
how he would ever bear this pain; ached for any
contact with her, however chaste, could have cried
out in gladness when he did see her again the very

next day, in church. If Nora had her way, it was the only place they were ever likely to see each other from now on.

Of course, Boadicea was not to know that. Catching his eye as she emerged from her pew at the end of Mass – a pew that was almost level with the one he and his family were in – she threw a covert glance of affection across the aisle. Guilt smote him like a stab in the back. Please God, that the pain of it did not show as he returned her visual caress.

Forever watchful of her son-in-law's actions, now that his treacherous meanderings had been exposed, Nora followed his line of vision. And the moment her eyes came to engage with Boadicea's, she knew this was the one.

Her mood became dark as she finally emerged from church, linked her arm somewhat possessively through that of her son-in-law, and proceeded to follow others along the street, noting the way he cast one last look at Boadicea, who travelled in the opposite direction. And her voice had a meaningful edge to it as she declared, 'Now there's somebody with a past!'

'How the hell can you tell that?' A shocked Niall tore his eyes away to scoff at the woman gripping his arm.

'So, it *is* her,' said Nora, eyeing him shrewdly.

He didn't bother trying to argue, but simply dealt her a brusque nod.

'Just as well you're out of it then,' said his

mother-in-law as they continued arm in arm. 'I should say you've had a lucky escape.'

Niall clicked his tongue with exasperation, glad that his children could not overhear, for they were some way ahead with their Aunt Harriet, all eager for breakfast. 'She's as respectable as you or me!'

'Then why didn't she didn't go up for Holy Communion?' queried Nora.

Her demand caused him to meditate, though it was soon to be answered by Nora herself: ''Cause there's some sin that prevents it! She's got something to hide.'

'What absolute rubbish!' snapped Niall. 'I know more about her than I do about meself! I've never known anyone so open with information.'

His elder showed more perspicacity. 'She only tells you what she wants you to know. It prevents the need for awkward questions.'

Robbed of all happiness, her son-in-law was close to losing his temper. 'I'll ask for her credentials next time then, shall I?'

'Next time?' Nora's glare reminded him that this was meant to be over.

Thoroughly exasperated, both by her and his own inability to solve this awful predicament, Niall gave a dramatic sigh. 'Oh, don't worry! I've done as you ordered.'

And this served to quieten her, as they proceeded home.

But he hadn't though, had he?

10

Faced with the choice of performing their journey most of the way by land or sea, as usual Nora made the decision for everyone, opting for the shorter and less traumatic sea route from Holyhead to Dun Laoghaire. 'If I have to put up with Juggy throwing up over me like last time, I'd prefer it to be three hours rather than nine.'

But whatever the method, it turned out to be an arduous journey for the adults, encumbered as they were with food and drink and apparel for five children, and constantly having to shepherd their charges together. Preferring to take a morning ferry, they departed from York railway station as late in the day as possible, so as to travel through the night. And what a night it turned out to be, having to rouse the youngsters from their sleep in order to change trains, and procuring tearful, quarrelsome behaviour, then trying to settle them again. Able to grab only the shortest, most uncomfortable of naps after midnight, and wearing the imprint of moquette upon his cheek as he stumbled bleary-eyed from the train, Niall felt he had not slept at all, when they finally arrived in the early hours of the next morning at Holyhead.

Even before they had embarked upon the Irish Sea, he felt exhausted and irritable. Had it not been for Nora, who kept them in line during breakfast at a café, he would gladly have strangled his offspring who, having slumbered quite well, were now buoyant once more about their holiday, and pestering to know when they would get there.

At last the time came to board, and, thankfully, the mist lifted to reveal a fine warm day, projecting a relatively calm crossing. Kept pacified with barley sugar and other titbits from their grandmother, and intermittently entertained for much of the three hours by a kindly priest who asked them all about themselves and cracked ancient jokes, the children were to provide less trouble than they had on the train. Granted breathing space from having to occupy them himself, Niall was finally able to roam along the deck, for a while looking out to sea, and appreciating the feel of the salt-laden breeze against his face, then wandering below to explore. Aside from the nuns and elderly ladies who sat in serene contemplation, there was an air of excitement amongst the passengers, flocks of young Irish men and women, forced from their homeland by the need to find work in England, now shiny-eyed with happiness at their return. Some were fuelled by more than excitement, even at this early hour staggering red-faced and merry from the bar. Wandering past there, Niall was assailed by the clinking of glasses and loud bursts of laughter, bringing instant reminder of the one he was supposed to forget. Hence, when back on deck, and a cry went up to signal the row of mountains rising out of the sea, his was the only pair of eyes that failed to focus on them, turning wistfully instead to the land he had left behind.

Trying very hard to fight his personal gloom and physical weariness, Niall sought to match his children's excitement, as the boat negotiated the rocky coastline, and eventually arrived at the rather old-fashioned-looking port, to be cradled into the arms of its twin piers, where the passengers disembarked. When the customs officer asked, 'Anything to declare?' instead of replying that he was heartily sick of this already, he answered with a simple, 'No.' Then, laden with baggage, trying to keep the excited children in order, he and Nora made their way into the railway station that was similarly quaint, here catching a train to the city where they would meet the connection for the final leg of their journey.

With everyone safely on board, only then were the adults allowed brief respite, each slumping back with a grumpy sigh of relief, as the train set in motion. His head tilted wearily to one side, his dark hair plastered skewwhiff from its uncomfortable resting place of the night before, Niall stared from the window. Up ahead, he could see the engine, and hear it chug as it followed the curving track around the wide expanse of Dublin Bay, and through an open window came the acrid smell of its smoke, and flecks of soot that settled on everyone's clothing. But, feeling claustrophobic enough in his mother-in-law's domineering presence, Niall resisted the urge to close the vent, for it also admitted the evocative tang of brine. The sea felt almost close enough to touch, separated only from the railway by a low stone wall. The tide had just begun to ebb, licking at rocks garlanded with seaweed, and clumps of black mussels. With the sky a bright blue, and the sun twinkling the water, only the heaviest of hearts would not have lifted at the sight of it, and soon Niall found himself infected by his children's air of anticipation, at least until he arrived in the city.

Then, for a time, it was back to the bad-tempered scolding, as he and Nora struggled to shepherd their grubby young charges through the crowds, first to find dinner, and afterwards to the correct departure point. The children were still merry and chattering throughout, attempting to read aloud the street names that were reproduced in Gaelic, until they were bundled onto another train, bound for the West.

It was time for tea when they arrived in Ballyhaunis, though it felt like a lifetime had passed since leaving home. With no one at the tiny railway station to meet their crumpled detrainment, and too drained by this summer heat to undertake the last few miles on foot, especially as it was uphill, Niall was forced to hire a wagonette, to convey his family and their luggage to their final destination. Alas, upon those hard wooden seats, this was to prove the most uncomfortable leg of their journey, not only for their buttocks, but on their jaded senses too; the driver, taking them for tourists, was as talkative a chap as ever drew breath.

For a time, Niall remained polite enough to attend the man's loquacity. But once away from town, and grown impatient with the blarney, he folded his arms and sat back in silence, allowing others to respond if they wished. In truth, the driver seemed content with the sound of his own voice, and the other occupants of the wagonette fell mute as it turned off the road and went creaking and jingling along a narrow, unpaved lane that was hardly wide enough for one vehicle, their weary eyes familiarising themselves with the undulating countryside.

At leisurely pace, the horses' hoofs making dull thuds upon the hardened earth, their vehicle trundled between rolling green fields that were divided by grey dry-stone walls furred with moss, with brambles and blackthorn catching at the wheels. Here and there a small whitewashed cottage with a thatched roof, around the bumpety bend a little shrine of rocks and a statue of the Virgin, a bare-footed boy perched on a donkey, which was also laden with panniers of turf. Then the verdant fields gave way to wild stretches of bog and gorse and heather, the horses labouring as the road inclined. It was always the same when coming here, thought Niall, jolted back and forth by the uneven ground. There was something ancient about the place. For all the traditional songs and customs at home, for all his undiluted Irish blood, he never felt truly Irish until he returned here – and yet at the same time an impostor.

Still, whatever he was, his hosts made him feel very welcome. The cottage enjoying an elevated position, and its residents maintaining a lookout over its half-door, Beesy hurried forth the instant the wagonette appeared between the trees that shaded her front garden, her husband not far behind. He in rough homespun waistcoat and corduroy trousers, his boots muddy from the field, she with plaid shawl about her shoulders, a white apron covering her long black skirt, and her grey hair scraped into a bun; both were short of stature, and as slender as reeds, and both inflicted with arthritis, but with a lively youthfulness about them as they beamed fond greetings, and hopped from foot to foot in their eagerness to be at their visitors.

'Sure, and why didn't ye tell me you were relatives of Mrs Cronin!' complained the gabber who had conveyed them, watching kisses being planted as each one was almost dragged from his vehicle. 'I'd nivver have wasted me breath.' But he was philosophical in accepting a lower price than he would have charged had they been strangers, and helped unload their luggage, before finally driving back to town.

'Oh, God love him, look how he's growed!' Beesy reached out to cup Dominic's face in both bony misshapen hands, her eyes a vibrant blue, her sentences swift and her tone marvelling. 'Why, he's tall as a house! And barely four years gone by since last we saw yese.' Then she went along the line, making similar comment on each smiling child, making the shy and quiet Honor blush by announcing that she had grown 'into a proper little lady! Like a filum star, she is'; introducing herself to the two little boys, whom she had not previously met – 'Bartholomew and Brian, there's grand names for you!' – before bending to the last in line, squashing Juggy's cheeks between two rough palms. 'And surely this cannot be that little child who was no higher than a donkey's knee? I'd never have known ye! Do you remember your Aunt Beesy, now?'

Juggy squirmed and grinned at having such attention. She could not truthfully say she did have any recollection of the old woman, but there was one thing she did retain from her previous visit. 'You've still got your fairy tree.' A small finger pointed to the hill at the rear of the house to where a lone specimen stood, its thorny branches fashioned by time and weather into a shape not unlike Beesy herself.

'Sure, and we have!' Beesy's tone indicated a certain dread, not entirely jocular. ''Tis in fearsome trouble we'd be with the leprechauns if we chopped that down.'

Then, after all the smiling exchanges with the children, she turned back to Niall, whom she beheld with exaggerated sympathy. 'And here's your poor father looking so sad and forlorn . . . How are you bearing up to your loss, Nye?'

He had been wondering whether his mother-in-law had divulged in her letter the true reason for bringing him here; from the benign way his hosts were looking upon him, he guessed not. He was about to reply, when Nora cut in.

'Oh, he's bearing up remarkably well,' she informed Beesy.

Her sister-in-law failed to sense the irony. 'Good, good. A terrible business for all concerned.' She pressed a hand to Nora's, conveying stoicism. Then, slightly arthritic of movement, she turned back to the children, a tear in her eye as she indicated Honor. 'And here's your eldest grandchild, the very image of her mother, God be good to her. 'Tis proud poor Ellen would be of them all.'

But then her voice became cheerier. 'And our own young ones are that excited at seeing you again – 'tis here they'll be first thing tomorrow! Now, away inside with you all.'

About to turn, she stopped to cast an eye at

the grizzled figure in his homespun waistcoat and corduroy trousers, who waited patiently by for instruction. 'Austin, what're ye doing, hanging there useless as a broken tail on a hound? Get along and fetch their cases!' This stern admonishment seemed at odds with such a gentle spirit, and those who saw through it smiled.

But, surrendering to the dominant personality, her husband hurried to do as he was told, whilst the women and children moved to enter.

'Eh, don't be giving yourself a hernia,' said Niall, beating Austin to his suitcases and grabbing two of them. 'I'll carry 'em.'

'You will not,' said the elderly man, whose slenderness was offset by huge ears, and a big hawkish nose, all of which were scarred from a life out of doors. 'I'd never hear the last of it from Bridget were I to let a guest tout his own luggage.' And with hands the size of shovels, he grabbed the cases back.

'But—' Niall was stopped in mid-protest by a firm demand from his host.

'How long have you been on this earth, Nye?'

'Thirty-four years,' he replied, after a puzzled moment.

'And you haven't learned the rules yet?' quipped Austin. 'Anything for a quiet life, that's the motto! Do as you are told, and never answer back.'

'That's where I must be going wrong then,' muttered Niall, with a cryptic glance at Nora's armour-plated figure, before it disappeared into the cottage, and finally he allowed the elder man to take possession of his luggage.

Whilst everyone else filtered indoors, for a moment he himself held back to reappraise the sun-dappled setting, a dozen hens pecking and croaking and scratching around him as he stared. Nothing had changed since last he had been here, save possibly the addition of a fresh coat of white-wash to the cottage walls. The thatched roof; the tiny windows, each no bigger than a chess board; the green planking of the door, which was divided horizontally like that of a stable; the stack of peat set out to dry, its original lush blackness turning gradually to brown under the sun; the sow in her sty built of old doors and corrugated iron and bits of bedstead, with half a dozen meaty piglets running riot – all were exactly the same as they had been, probably for centuries. So was the garden, totally lent to vegetables – for who needed flowers with such picturesque natural surround-ings, thought Niall, as he lifted his abstracted gaze to the hillside beyond the fence. What a lovely peaceful place this was. In years gone by, he had thoroughly enjoyed each of his sojourns, but this time . . .

Feeling a tentative tweak of his trousers, he looked down at his small assailant. The red hen looked back at him, cocking her head and surveying him with beads of curiosity. He gave a sigh, and vowed to try his best not to spoil his children's holiday.

With everyone now entered, so too did he, booting out the chicken that would have followed him, sending her into a clucking panic, before closing the lower half of the door against her. A pleasant coolness overtook him, emanating from the stone floor, and infiltrating his sweat-drenched clothes like a welcome breeze. With only two tiny windows, even with the upper half of the door still open, the interior of the cottage was dim, and it took a moment to adjust his eyes. Then Niall saw that everything in here was as he remembered it too. There was the Sacred Heart in its little shrine set into the wall; the religious pictures on the walls; the religious relics amongst the pots on the dresser; and the four brass candlesticks that shone like beacons, even with no sun to catch them. There was the wooden bench by the hearth, and several more around the large table; suspended from a crane over the fire was the black cauldron, which was giving out the most delicious smell of Irish stew, and on the table a stack of soda bread accompanied an array of best china.

Now that Beesy's guests were arrived, the meal was quickly served. Having expended her excitement, she wrapped the plaid shawl about herself, and joined Austin and the others at the table, a quiet dignity about her as she clasped her hands to pray.

'Can I say grace, Aunty Beesy?' exclaimed Juggy.

'Why, to be sure you may,' agreed her great-aunt.

The child lowered dark lashes, and pressed her palms together. 'Jesus, Mary, Joseph, bless this lovely food we are about to receive, bless this house and all the people in it, and bless Aunty Beesy and Uncle Austin for letting us come here on our holidays.'

Beesy crossed herself, and, with a misty smile, leaned over to pat the child. 'God love her little Yorkshire voice.' Then she bade her guests tuck in, and returned to her quiet everyday mode, sitting in silence and allowing them to eat in peace.

Austin too was a man of reserve – at least until a hen fluttered up to perch in ungainly fashion on the half-door, where it flapped and muttered for a second in trying to keep its balance, before fluttering down amongst the guests. Whereupon he gave an oath, and jumped from his bench to chase it round the room, the creature squawking and scattering feathers until he managed to grab it and threw it back from whence it came.

This caused the children no end of amusement, their widowed parent heartened to hear such bubbling laughter.

'That will be your job from now on!' Austin warned those who giggled.

'I'm having t'first go!' announced Dominic, which did not go down well with his siblings who began to bicker then, earning a scolding from their father.

'Remember you're guests in this house!' Niall interrupted his meal to warn.

'And remember why you're here too,' muttered Nora, with a telling glance that brought him quickly back into line.

If Austin noted the coldness that emanated from her eye, he refrained from mentioning it, but concentrated on the children, wagging a finger, and putting an end to any bad feeling over who was to take charge of the hens. 'Sure, you will all take your turn! Those creatures could provide work for an army.'

The children were to find out this was true when later, after tea, they were allowed to run up and down the hill, and about the garden, helping their great-uncle to round up the hens for the night. After that, apart from a few words with the sow and her piglets, and a quiet stroll in the field as the sun went down, they were too exhausted to do much else, and were soon in bed.

Weary and despondent, their father was not long behind them.

Surprised to find he had slept soundly, even wedged alongside his boys in the smaller of the two bedrooms, Niall woke quite refreshed and alert the next morning. He had no idea what time it was – this room was without a window – but it was obviously very early, for no one else stirred, not even Beesy. She and Austin had given up their own bed to Nora and the girls, and had spent the night in a recess of the living room. Niall lay there for a while alongside his sons, acutely aware of their breathing, of his own wrongdoing towards them, yet tortured and brooding also over his lost love. After a while, unable to get back to sleep for thinking of her, he inched as carefully as he could from the bed, trying not to rouse the other occupants, who, thankfully, were still flat out from their journey of the day before. Tentative of movement, donning each item of clothing with infinite care, ever conscious of any change in his children's breathing, he finally sneaked away as quietly as he could.

In the rustic living room, in danger of stumbling into something in the dark, he waited for his eyes to adjust. What sky that could be seen through those tiny windows was uninviting, like a charcoal-grey blanket. Niall underwent a moment's contemplation. Should he go for a walk as intended, and perhaps in lifting the latch disturb his hosts, who slept soundly beneath their patchwork quilt in the recess? Feeling so low, he had no wish to converse with anyone. But if he did mismanage his exit, Beesy and Austin would wonder who had been so ignorant as to disturb them. The least he could do was to have the fire going in case they arose. Deciding on the latter course, he moved cautiously through the gloom to the hearth, crouched over it, and as gingerly as he could, raked aside the white ashes that had been used to damp it down the night before.

A tiny red glow appeared. Niall sat back on his heels to stare at it for a pensive moment. Then, bending his face to its warmth, he used his lungs as bellows, offering first gentle encouragement, then more passionate approach, until it radiated new life. His emotions mixed, he took a slab of turf from the basket beside the hearth, and laid it gently upon the fire. Momentarily, the glow was gone, though he knew it survived, for smoke began to creep around the edges of the dry slab, curling and drifting incense-sweet against his nostrils. Experiencing a raw moment of anguish, he tore himself away and, not caring whether he made a noise now, anxious only to escape, he lifted the latch and strode out into the morning.

It was very cold. Hunching himself into his jacket, he made his way to the lane. Not a street-lamp in view, he must be careful not to trip in the gloom. Once away from the trees, he could see there was light on the horizon now, and a bird sang. Apart from this, and the sound of his own boots prowling the stony ground, it was deathly quiet. The land still bore tendrils of mist, as did the lane ahead of him, vaporous wraiths that spiralled sluggishly upwards to meet a bleak sky. A small furry creature dashed from a crack in the dry-stone wall and ran across his path to disappear into the tangle of briars on the other side. Niall could hear it rustling as he passed, and paused to investigate briefly, before moving on.

Eventually coming across a side-track, he took it, and squelched aimlessly along, staring out across the brown peat bog in a state of melancholy, agonising over Boadicea. He tried to remember what his life had been like before she had suddenly appeared in it, but could remember only darkness of spirit. Not wanting to revisit that place, in an effort to drive the demons from his mind, he strode on, leaving the imprint of his boots in the sponge-like carpet of moss.

Somewhere, the sun had risen, the sky was lighter in shade, though in hue it remained a drab slate, and the coldness and emptiness of the land was such that it penetrated his soul. Having never really noticed before how depressing this region could be, today Niall was granted an insight into why his ancestors had left. This was what it was truly like to eke out one's daily life here.

Unaware of how far or how long he had roamed, past tremulous swathes of bog cotton, thickets of gorse and desolate spaces, he came eventually to a lake, and paused to watch a furtive figure amongst the reeds – a heron stalking its breakfast. Under his weight, the moss began to exude little puddles of brown water that formed and trickled around his boots. There was barely a sound at all now, so hushed that he could hear the lightest of breezes rippling the grass, and the sound of his own heart crying for Boadicea. He was meant to be with her. What the hell was he doing here?

A child's voice called faintly in the distance, reminding him. 'Da-ad! Daddy, where are you?'

Sighing to himself, Niall threw his eyes heavenwards, holding this position for a number of seconds, as if appealing for an unguent to his pain. Then, turning, his hunched figure slowly made its way back.

When he returned to the cottage the heavy incense of the peat fire had increased, providing a more welcoming atmosphere than the bleak outdoors. Everyone was up, and seated around the table, his children eagerly expectant of their cousins' arrival.

'Ah, here it is you are! Didn't we think the bog had swallowed you up.' The gentle Beesy bade Niall sit down with the others. Bacon was thrown into a pan, but barely had time to sizzle before it was whisked onto the plate, the fat still as white and soft as when it went in. ''Twas very early up you must have been – was your bed uncomfortable?' She looked most concerned that her hospitality might not meet the grade.

'No, no, it was grand, Beesy. I slept like a log,' Niall assured her as, rubbing his hands, he sat down to eat. 'Sorry if I disturbed anybody. I just woke really early and couldn't get back to sleep.' He felt his mother-in-law's eyes on him. Guilty conscience, she would liked to have said.

But just at that point her nieces Mary and Nancy arrived with their horde of children – Johnny and Clare, Patsy and Deirdre, Molly, Jimmy, Bridget and Peggy – prompting both he and Nora to rise and greet them, the house becoming a bustling throng of excitement.

'Ah, still as shy as ever!' With a teasing smile, and sturdier by far than her parents, having first greeted her Aunt Nora, Mary took hold of Niall's cheek between forefinger and thumb, her sister possessing an obvious fondness for him too, for both gazed long and admiringly into his face.

'Can't a man have his breakfast in peace?' complained Austin, overrun by his grandchildren, but mainly referring to his guest.

'Aye, leave the lad alone,' Beesy told her daughters. 'Sure, he's just this minute sat down.'

Niall said he didn't mind, though he blushed like a youth under the women's laughing blue eyes, and he could not help comparing them to Boadicea. A similar age, they were even less sophisticated in the dresses they wore, the shapeless low-waisted fashion of a decade earlier, the shoes with straps across the instep, the bare legs, the short brown hair all curly and untamed. Yet he knew them to be kind and pleasant girls, and he put up with their teasing for a while before reminding them they had husbands.

'And when are we going to see Fergal and Con?' he said, in the hope of diverting their attention from himself.

'Sure, haven't they work to go to!' Copying her sister, Mary bent her curly head to exchange greetings with each of Niall's children, the room resounding with kisses as Nora underwent the same with her nephews and nieces. 'You'll be seeing them tonight, I've no doubt.'

Austin groaned at the thought of being even more overrun. The greetings were still going on around him, Niall addressing the native children now, remarking on how they had grown.

The smaller members of his own offspring, to whom this was all new, had been staring with fascination at their cousins, whose ages ranged from five to twelve – the whole posse of them barefoot, their calves covered in splashes from the mud of the bog. But soon the watchers found themselves being herded towards the door, as the young mothers bade Niall and their Aunt Nora resume their breakfasts.

'Get along now, you children, out to play and get to know each other!' Nancy banished the two tribes into the garden, though they needed no encouragement.

Breakfast recommenced, Nancy and Mary partaking of a cup of tea whilst the rest ate. It had not progressed far when Juggy burst in, announcing excitedly: 'Dad, our Brian's taken his shoes off!'

'That's all right.' Niall chewed calmly. 'He just wants to be like his cousins.'

'But you said only gypos ran about wi' no shoes on!'

Under accusing laughs of the host family, Niall looked deeply embarrassed and tried to cover his gaff, quickly explaining to Juggy, 'Things are different when you're in the country. Go on, out now!'

'Can I take me own off then?'

'Yes! Now go on, before I take your blasted head off!' Hardly able to look at his hosts, he gave a self-conscious laugh and muttered, 'Kids, eh?'

Things were to get little better from here. After breakfast, when Austin went off to work, Niall remained to chat for a while with Nancy and Mary, but, with the conversation turning to feminine subjects, he was soon to fall back into his normal quietness. Envious of their musical Irish accents, he began to feel even more of an interloper, and loath to interject his unattractive Yorkshire vowels. This threatening to plunge him back into despondence, he rose from his chair as unobtrusively as he could, and wandered over to the door to look out over it.

But Nora was keeping an eye on him, interrupting the conversation to ask, 'And what will you be doing with yourself this morning, Niall?'

He started at her voice, then went back to watching his children playing with their cousins, all of them barefoot now, as they swung on a rope that dangled from one of the larger trees. 'I was going to take the kids for a walk . . . but I think I'll let them play whilst they're happy.'

'Well, don't think you have to hang about here,' said Nora. 'I'm sure Beesy will understand if you feel a bit outnumbered among all us women.'

'Aye, specially as we're gypos,' teased Mary, to

an embarrassed laugh from the one who had made such a gaff.

Wondering whether Nora wanted him out of the way so she could spread her nasty gossip, Niall glanced around the room as if seeking some outlet. His hosts could barely read, so there was no book about the place to occupy his mind. 'I might as well make use of meself and give Austin a hand,' he elected.

And so, for the rest of that day, whilst his children had a great old time playing with their cousins, and the women constantly fed each other on bits of family news, Niall helped Austin tend the fields. It might not be much of a holiday, but the physical labour did serve to divert his mind from Boadicea, and tired him out so that he could at least sleep at night.

But in the early hours of the morning, there she was again, the first thing on his mind.

Whether or not his mother-in-law had broadcast his treacherous behaviour, Niall could not say, for the family's generosity towards him was to continue unabridged. But then, Beesy was hospitable to everyone, however irksome, he noted when, three days into his supposed holiday, another branch of the clan arrived unannounced from Ballina, and these too had to be put up. This involved some ingenious rearrangement of beds. The woman and her daughter being allocated the one in the living-room recess, Beesy and Austin were now relegated to the roof space over the pigsty, poor Austin having no say in the matter at all.

'Well, they are city people like yourselves,' explained Beesy in a whisper, when Nora commended this self-sacrifice after breakfast, the latest guests enjoying a garden stroll in the morning sunshine. 'They expect the best. 'Twill do us no harm for a couple of nights.'

'No harm, says she,' muttered Austin to Niall, scratching the mat of grey hair that protruded from his open-necked shirt, as they prepared to set out to work after an uncomfortable night. 'Then there's no harm in we men taking ourselves to market for a spot of drinking the day.'

But when he made his voice audible, it was for Beesy's benefit. 'If 'tis helping me you'd be again this morning,' he said cheerfully to Niall, 'you can help load the pigeens into the cart for market.'

Seated at the table with her brothers and sister, still eating their porridge, Juggy overheard. 'Aw, you're not selling 'em?' came her lament.

'Sure, and how do you think we'd make our living if we didn't?' her great-uncle called to her, whilst lacing his boots. 'They're big enough now to leave their mother.'

'Can't we keep just one?' wheedled the child, fixing him with disappointed eyes and inclining her head beseechingly, a ploy that usually worked with her father.

'We can not,' Austin apologised, then rose and

went to a tin on the mantelpiece and fished out a halfpenny. 'But here's a picture of some wee pigs for ye.'

Accepting the coin with polite thanks, Juggy turned it over, grinning at the sow and her piglets on its reverse, whilst similar denominations were handed out to her brothers and sister.

Batty had turned his attention to his father, asking eagerly, 'Can we come with you to town, Dad, so we can spend 'em?'

'Would you rather not play with your cousins?' Aunt Beesy intervened. 'Sure, their mothers will be bringing them over any time now.'

'Well, I don't mind—' Niall began to say that he would not mind taking them all, but Austin grabbed his arm to still him.

'Take thirteen children to town?' he growled from the side of his mouth. 'Is it mad you are?' Then he raised his voice to instruct the others, 'They'll be safer here. Sure the market's a dangerous place, what with all them creatures leppin about.'

Beesy saw through him. 'Don't be thinking 'tis stout you'll be tipping down your neck all day long,' she said firmly. 'There'll be drinking enough at the shindy.' A party in honour of the guests had been arranged for the end of the week.

Her husband might take umbrage, but Niall smiled and asked his children which they would prefer. 'If you want to stay and lark with your cousins, I'll take you to town later in the week.'

When they opted for this, he turned to his mother-in-law. 'What about you, Nora, do you want to come?' He hoped she would refuse.

And so she did, though her reply was to spark mixed feelings. 'No, it'd be rude to go just as Beesy's relatives have nicely arrived.'

Turning glum, Niall offered to stay too, but Nora was keen to explain that her words had not been meant as a rebuke. 'It's going to be all women again here,' she told him. 'It'd not be much fun for you. You might as well make the most of your freedom whilst you can.'

Seeking a double edge to this pronouncement, Niall locked eyes with her, but only for a second. Then he was away with Austin, glad to be out of her company.

Unlike some who lived far away and had been up before sunrise in order to travel to market, the occupants of this house had only a few miles down the road to go. With a good breakfast inside them, and a great stack of bread wrapped in a cloth to take for lunch, Austin and Niall, with some help and hindrance from his children, loaded the litter of pigs into the donkey cart. Then, with each man alongside it, they set off for town on foot.

It was a day for selling livestock, but the market was very different from that of York, for few of the animals were penned, save for those trussed up in donkey carts. The square was lined with such brightly coloured little vehicles, some containing a single pig, others an entire litter; lowing herds of cattle that blundered on and off the pavement, herded by drovers with pipes in their mouths and blackthorn sticks in their hands. But except for the panting dogs with fanatical eyes, no one seemed unduly hurried, drifting along as if they had all the time in the world, giving an occasional idle poke of a red-speckled hide, or a white one, or a brown. There were donkeys everywhere, some with panniers, some hauling carts laden with turf, or vegetables, or pigs. The crowd was composed mainly of men, though there were one or two old women with shawls over their heads, travelling sedately along the street, as deals went on all around them amid a great deal of spitting and slapping of palms.

His piglets sold by mid-morning, Austin made a beeline for a pub. Niall's protestations that it was much too early for alcohol were ignored, and he was dragged off the street into a tobacco-stained room that was hardly bigger than his own front parlour. With two small tables and eight flimsy chairs, and a wooden counter loaded with trays of sweets and all manner of unrelated objects, the place itself did not seem to know whether it was a pub or a shop. And there Niall and Austin were to sit for the rest of the morning, sinking pint after pint of Guinness, whilst others came and went in their dung-stinking boots and their trail of pipe smoke, until Niall began to feel light-headed and refused to touch another drop before some of it had been soaked up with the wedges of homemade bread.

'I think I'll just go for a wander round town while I can still stand,' he eventually told Austin, who was remarkably unaffected. 'You stay here as long as you like.'

'I intend to.' Ruddy-faced and cheerful, Austin took another greedy gulp of his stout. Shaking his head in wonder at the slender man's capacity, Niall re-emerged into the sunshine, and proceeded to go about the town, pausing occasionally to look into a shop window, or to buy some sweets and comics for his children, and a book for himself, but mainly to wander aimlessly, and to wonder what was being said about him in his absence.

Back at the cottage, five other women seated around the table with half-prepared vegetables and scandalised expressions, Nora had finally divulged her true reason for being here.

'An *affair*!' Beesy stopped grating the potato to gape in disbelief, then turned to examine the others, who were similarly shocked, her daughters hardly able to utter a word from excitement. 'No, it cannot be, not Niall – why, he's quiet as a mouse!'

'Huh! And you know what they say about the quiet ones being the worst,' retorted Nora, slicing her way through a pile of scallions, the smell of them taking over the room. 'So . . . much as I love coming to see you, Beesy, we're not just here for a holiday – it's to get him out of the clutches of that one!'

After a further series of indignant gasps, the culprit's name was raised and ridiculed.

'Boadicea Merrifield?' repeated Beesy's latest visitor, also called Mary, a prim-and-proper kind with a superior air. 'What kind of a stupid name is that? Did she concoct it herself?'

Nora shrugged, and continued slicing the onions.

'I'll never understand the English.' Old Beesy shook her head, her vivid blue eyes momentarily clouded by these troubling thoughts, as she went back to using her grater, slivers of potato dropping into her bowl. 'Cursing a child with a heathen name like that.'

'Oh, she's not English,' informed Nora, reaching for another onion.

'Then where is she from, Aunt Nora?' enquired Nancy, her own knife fallen idle.

'That I can't tell you, except that it's this county—'

'Ye mean, she be Irish?' shrieked her niece Mary, almost slicing through her finger along with the cabbage. 'With a name like that?'

'Well, as I heard it from Niall,' proceeded Nora in confidential manner, 'she's known as Mary by some—'

'Sure, aren't most of us?' The woman from Ballina interrupted with a little laugh at her own daughter, who shared her name, and also at Beesy's daughter.

'—but she prefers the fancier title,' continued Nora. 'Her father must have been English, with that surname, but she was definitely born here because she's got the accent.'

'And ye've no idea what parts she'd be coming from?' asked Beesy.

'No, only that it's County Mayo – but I'd dearly love to, so's I could find something out about her.' Nora's attitude grew darker by the minute, her knife slicing briskly through one onion after another. 'Niall cracks on that she's told him all about herself, but there's something shifty about her—'

'You've seen her for yourself then?' put in Beesy.

'Yes! She goes to our church. Bold as brass and brassy-looking with it. Got the nerve to stand making cow's eyes at him whilst Father Finnegan's taking Mass!'

'Shame on her!' breathed the listeners.

'Well, that's what you get from the kind of woman who pounces on a man the minute his wife dies.' It was not just the onions' astringency now that brought tears to Nora's eyes.

'And sure, there's no accounting for what a man will stoop to.' Beesy extended a hand across the table to comfort her. 'We'll pray for him, darlin'.'

There were pious murmurs of accord from those others round the table.

Sufficient potato in her bowl now, Beesy's gnarled, arthritic hands set out a linen cloth, then tipped the gratings into it, wrapping them into a bundle and squeezing this over the bowl. Watching those deformed fingers having trouble in milking out the moisture, Nora offered to take over. Her own large fists pressed to the task, and the bundle so malevolently set upon, it was not hard for others to visualise this as her son-in-law's neck.

'Aw, those poor wee children o' his!' Beesy clutched her pendulous breast. 'The more I think about them, the nearer I'm to weep. Just lost their mother and now another trial. Do they know about their father's wickedness?'

Nora shook her head. Her mouth was set in an unforgiving line as she tipped the contents of the cloth into another bowl, and handed this to Beesy, who waited with the flour. 'And if it's up to me, they never will.' Her eyes held a plea. 'That's why I need all the help I can get.'

'You shall have our prayers,' promised Beesy, mixing in the flour and salt, these words supported by all who were round the table.

'Thank you, Beesy, but I meant more tangible help. I think I've managed to make Niall see the error of his ways, but that one might still want to get her claws into him, and if she does then I need to have the ammunition to stop her.'

'With such a name, there's someone sure to have heard of her,' announced Mary from Ballina. 'I'll be after having a word with Father Kelly when I get back. Maybe he'll be enlightening us over your mystery woman, if it is true she comes from this area.'

Nora thanked her, but, 'I don't hold out much hope. Our own priest couldn't tell me any more than I already knew.'

'Ah, but Father Kelly is very well-appointed with the bishop,' declared the woman, the glint of surety in her eyes as she levelled them at Nora. 'If he cannot find out, no one can.'

Then her look of self-importance was deflated by the intervention of a church bell, and everyone fell silent; she composed herself for prayer.

With the sun directly over the bustling market town came the tolling of the Angelus. As one, the crowd paused in their dealing and bargaining and shopping, each woman religiously crossing herself, each man removing his hat and bowing his head, all devoting their attention to God. Standing at the top of Main Street now, Niall removed his own cap, bent his head and crossed himself, and waited in reverential silence whilst the bell continued to toll, only the lowing and snorting of beasts intruding upon the sacred moment.

The clanging finally stopped, and in a trice, or so it seemed to Niall, everyone returned to what they had been doing, whether gossiping, or cheating . . . or thinking of some forbidden love. Lifting his head, he replaced his cap, but instead of moving on, he stood to watch them for a while, pondering the vagaries of humankind. How could they carry on so unaffected whilst for him the Angelus had driven home the message of his sinfulness as effectively as a nail through his heart? His anguished eyes fell upon a green post-box set into a wall, causing him to wonder if he should write to Boadicea. It might be easier to inform her of the situation by letter . . .

With an inward sigh, he began to move back down Main Street, his gaze straight ahead now. But suddenly he was to undergo an eerie flash of recognition, and everyone around him was to vanish. The trip to town had been intended to lift his spirits, but for Niall, this parade of shops was so like Micklegate, the cobbled road having a gentle curve to its descent, and the buildings on either side possessing a similar feel of antiquity – even if not so tall and grand – that for a moment he was magically transported there, and hurrying home from work in anticipation of an evening with Boadicea. They could drag him a thousand miles, they could drag him ten thousand, but his mind would remain in York.

This preoccupation had not gone unnoticed by his host. Working alongside Niall in the fields the next morning, the constant click of their hoes the only sound shared between them, Austin said nothing for a long time. His frame, like his wife's, was arthritic. Such outdoor work must have induced considerable pain, though he did not show it; and neither did his failing eyesight prevent him from seeing another's.

Only after they had toiled many lengths of the

field, however, did he make a rare pronouncement. 'I'm thinking we must have you to the matchmaker while you're here, Nye.' His tanned wiry arms wielded the hoe along the rows of healthy seedlings, carefully turning and sifting the soil until, halted by Niall's glare, he added in guilty afterthought, 'Aye, well, maybe it is too soon after poor Ellen . . .'

Niall came upright. 'She's put you up to this, hasn't she?'

The old man looked up under the peak of his cap, his face bemused. 'Who is that?' he asked.

'My bloody mother-in-law!' snapped his accuser. Then he gasped his frustration to the sky, where great banks of cloud sailed gently past. 'I knew there was summat going on when we got back from town yesterday; they were all looking at me in a funny way. I guessed Nora'd been up to skulduggery!'

'Why not at all . . .' Austin's weather-beaten face, with its big nose and ears, continued to look thrown. ''Twas just myself thinking to ease your misery, son.'

Niall threw down his hoe. 'I wish every bugger would stop interfering!'

'I'm not, truly I'm not!' protested Austin.

And, upon studying the old man's baffled expression, Niall's glower began to fade, and he bent to pick up his hoe, mumbling, 'Sorry, Austin, I just thought . . . well, Nora's tried to fix me up with a couple of women, and we've fallen out over it.'

'I swear I never heard a breath of it,' vouched Austin. 'The matchmaker was my own idea.' Then he eyed his companion with sympathy. 'But, from the cut of your face 'tis obviously too soon to engage his skills.'

'Well, Nora reckons it is.' Niall remained pessimistic.

'That would be understandable, Ellen being her daughter.' The old man took off his cap and scratched his scalp through the curly grey hair, pondering on his own words, before going back to work, his hoe once again striking stone. 'But now ye have me totally confused again. Ye say 'tis her who thinks 'tis too soon, yet she's the one who's been coming up with marriage candidates.' He adopted a reasoning tone. 'Did ye not think to accept one of them? I know what a loss it must have been, but a man needs a wife to look after him, Nye, and the children a mother.'

'It depends what sort of wife.' Niall lifted his eyes to follow a hooded crow that balanced on a thermal overhead, its gliding form etched against the cloud as it watched them from above. Then he drove his implement at the earth again. 'Nora's choice doesn't coincide with mine.'

'Well, like I said,' panted Austin, 'we've a fine matchmaker down the road.'

Niall cast his mind back to his first time in the motherland, when he had thought it odd not to see any courting couple as in York, nor any Monkey Run in the town for a chance to pick a mate. Nowadays, he understood how things were done in Ireland, that such important matters were left to wiser beings. But as he told Austin, 'It'll be a waste of time. Anyhow,' he dashed a hand at his sweating brow, 'Nora reckons we've got her to look after us; we don't need anybody else.'

'We've heard a lot of what Nora reckons.' Still perplexed by these contrary declarations, Austin continued working along the row. 'But what do you feel yourself?'

Had it been any other male, Niall would have welcomed this opportunity to get things off his chest. But Austin was his wife's uncle, if only by marriage. Thus, not wanting to insult Ellen's memory, he responded with a non-committal shrug. Still toiling, he lifted his eyes and looked away across the field to where his children were once again in the company of their cousins, and taking it in turns to lead the donkey up and down, one of them on its back. He could not, though, prevent his thoughts from straying to Boadicea.

Involved though he was in his work, the old man must have interpreted that secret smile. 'Could it be,' he said, 'that you've already found a match?'

Niall stopped hoeing and looked back at him quickly, his expression turning apologetic.

'You've no call to pay penance to me,' Austin reassured him.

'Sorry for being so cagey, Aust. I'm surprised you didn't know already.' Returning to his labours,

Niall gave a mirthless laugh. 'That's her whole reason for bringing me here, to get me away from a scarlet woman.'

The old man sucked in his breath, finding this a good enough reason to stop work. 'Scarlet woman, begor?'

'In my mother-in-law's opinion.' Niall stopped hoeing too, smiling wistfully as he informed his companion, 'Ah, she's not really. She's a lovely lass. Everything I want. It's just that everyone thinks it's too soon, and maybe it is . . .' Turning sombre, he leaned on his hoe, resting his chin on his hands.

Austin was firm, pointing a thick horny finger as he declared, 'If your mind is set on it, then 'tis not too soon! Don't let yourself be bossed about like I am – why look at me, driven out of my own house to make room for people I've never even met. Not yourselves! I mean those two biddies from Ballina. Having to move because her ladyship objects to sleeping on the other side of the wall to the pig! Who the blazes is she anyhow?'

'Nora told me it's Beesy's cousin twice removed,' explained Niall.

'Well, I wish some bugger would be so kind as to remove her a bit further!'

Chuckling genuinely now, Niall told him, 'You'll be glad to hear we'll be out of your hair in a few days.'

'Aw, my brother-in-law's family can stay as long as they want to! Dominic was a good man, God rest him.' Talk of relations led Austin to another question. 'Tell me, and how is your own brother these days?'

'Your guess is as good as mine,' tendered Niall. Then at Austin's bewildered frown added, 'Surely you heard?'

'About the unpleasantness?' Austin nodded. 'Aye, we did. But sure, that was over a year ago, was it not?'

Niall looked rather sheepish. 'I haven't spoken to him since he left. I don't even know where he is . . .'

The hooded crow had come to land and now strutted in a nearby furrow, swaggeringly confident that the two men were too involved in their conversation to notice him.

'You have lived amongst the English for too long,' censured Austin. 'A man should let nothing come between he and his brother – especially if he has only the one.'

Niall accepted the criticism. 'I feel guilty the way I treated him, particularly since I now stand accused of the same crime.'

'To be sure, you two will make it up. Come on then!' cried Austin excitedly, as he launched back into his work, arms flashing like whipcord for a few seconds before slowing to a more manageable tempo. 'Do tell us all about this secret lady friend of yours – how much land would she be having?'

'None, as far as I know.' Niall jabbed and sifted with his hoe.

Again Austin stopped, his exclamation almost a shriek. 'No land – sure what use is she to a man?'

'She pulls a good pint,' joked Niall, pausing with him.

'Ah well, I suppose that's to her favour,' acknowledged the old man thoughtfully. 'But tell me, how does a fellow manage in York with no land to his name?'

Niall gave a careless shrug. 'We have to rely on the shops.'

'Aw, 'twouldn't do for me!' Austin dashed the back of his calloused hand under his nose to remove a dewdrop. 'A man should grow his own food if'n he's able. Ye've not even enough to run a few fowl, ye say? The divil!' He shook his head, dumbfounded. 'Sure, I'm grateful to know where my eggs be coming from.'

'Same place as the ones we buy – up a hen's arse,' teased Niall, his mood much improved at being able to discuss this with someone who did not condemn him as evil simply for wanting to remarry.

'There's nothing much wrong with you now, cracking jokes!' The old man wagged a dirt-stained finger.

'I can tell you, Aust, I feel a hell of a lot better for talking to you,' confirmed Niall.

'Well, I'm glad I'm useful for something,' declared Austin.

'I didn't know what to do with meself when I came here.'

'And now ye do?' quizzed the weather-beaten old face.

Niall looked away again to where his offspring frolicked, a sight that inspired his decision. It was all so simple. All these months he had been considering the wrong people, worrying about what Nora would think of Boadicea, when all the time he should have been asking his children. How could they form an opinion unless they met her? He was not to reply for the moment, for at this point the Angelus tolled, both he and Austin removing their caps, and standing with bowed heads to pray, as did the children, the only creature moving being the crow.

But this time, as the bell resounded it did not condemn, and the moment it fell silent, Niall gave his reply. 'Aye,' he told the other, his voice quiet, but its tone resolute, 'I know exactly what I'm going to do.'

'The scarlet woman, is it?' Austin gave a whoop of glee, that sent the hooded crow cawing and flapping into the air. 'Begod, I wouldn't like to be in your shoes when Nora do be finding out!'

11

Determined that Nora would not have the chance to interfere again, at least not until he'd had time to consult those more important to his plan, Niall kept his change of heart under wraps. Proceeding as the day before, he drifted quietly and unobtrusively through the rest of his holiday, only allowing his lighter mood to permeate the solemn façade when playing with his children, and at the ceilidh that was thrown to mark his family's departure. It was obvious by now that everyone had been informed of his affair, for whilst they behaved exactly the same towards him as before, he was viewed with very different eyes, some deeply suspicious and protective of their wives, others holding a quiet admiration, as though they had not known he had such devilment in him.

Encouraged by his participation in the rousing get-together, watching him sing and clap and dance to the fiddle-playing with her kin, Nora congratulated herself on a job well done. She had steered

Niall through his trial and safely out the other side; he had finally come to accept where his loyalties lay. Little did she guess that such happiness as he portrayed was not for reason of anyone here, but because he was going home to Boadicea.

Came Saturday, and he was there at last, back in the land of promiscuous bill-stickers and noisy pubs; the squelching acres of bog and green undulations replaced by serried ranks of grimy terraces that served to trap the August heatwave, adding to the claustrophobia; the gentle glow of the peat fire, the fresh air and idle pace, a distant memory. As on their outward journey, they had undergone a gruelling return, having to travel through the night from Ballyhaunis in order to connect at Dublin for the morning ferry. Which was why Nora was most put out that there was no meal waiting when she and Niall finally entered a somewhat dingier-looking living room that evening, their clothes sticking to them, covered in soot and exhausted, with five ravenous and irritable children to placate.

'Well, I didn't know what time to do it for!' Harriet defended her own laziness. 'I'd offer to cook you something now –' the fact that she had on her gloves, and was slinging a handbag over her arm, belied this – 'only Pete's expecting me.'

'I suppose I'll have to do it meself as usual then,' snapped Nora, ignoring her daughter's apology, trying also to deafen herself to the pestering whines of her grandchildren. Throwing open a cupboard, and finding little more than the tin of peaches which Mrs Hutchinson had brought months ago – the ones she had sworn never to eat again – she made a sound of disgust.

After a quick glance at the clock, Niall clapped his hands together and gave them a hearty rub, as he cut in, 'Who fancies fish and chips, to save your granny cooking?'

There were cries from the children of 'Me! Me!', Juggy and Brian jumping up and down.

'Right, wash your hands and set the table, and I'll be back in a flash!' And he beat Harriet to the door, and sped off to Walmgate.

Almost ready to go herself, Harriet moved closer to her mother so that the children could not over-hear, and spoke from the corner of her mouth. 'How's he been behaving himself? Do you want me to follow him?'

Gathering a fistful of cutlery, Nora was aloof as she marched on the table. 'I thought you were in a hurry to see your fancy man?'

'Fiancé!' corrected Harriet, her angular jaw turning sulky. 'I hope you're not going to refer to him as that when he comes to meet you tomorrow afternoon.'

'Oh, we're finally to be honoured, are we?' Nora remained sour. 'Anyway, get yourself gone. The other fella doesn't need shadowing. He's learned which side his bread's buttered – which is more than I can say for some. God help this chap you're marrying if you can't even find the ruddy bread bin.'

Harriet gave a click of her tongue. 'You won't let me forget it, will you!' And she flounced out, calling a cheery goodbye to the children as she went.

Luckily for Niall, his sister-in-law was too intent on making her appointment to waste time investigating the fish and chip shop as she hurried along Walmgate, for she would not have seen him there.

Instead, he had cantered straight past, and across the road, for to his delight he had spotted his favourite barmaid making her way to work.

'Bo!'

She wheeled at the sound of his voice, her face breaking into one huge grin of delight, and her arms opening to envelop him as he arrived, as naturally as if they were wed. Not caring that anyone might see them, Niall swept her up and buried his face in her neck, lifting it only to plaster her cheek with kisses, then swinging her off her feet, such was his ecstasy at seeing her.

She laughed, almost tearfully, her eyes reflecting his happiness. 'Oh, Niall, I had an awful feeling I'd never see you again!'

'Well, you have, and you will! I'm never going to be parted from you again.' Unwilling to release her, he dealt her one last hearty kiss and a final squeeze, then drew her away from the curious stares of passers-by into the darkness of a covered alleyway, here to kiss and embrace more intimately. 'We've just this minute got back, but I had to come.' His breath was hot in her ear. 'It's been murder . . .'

'Ye didn't care for the old country then?' Her muffled jest emerged from his neck, to which her mouth was pressed.

'I've never looked forward so much to leaving it.' His voice was low and gentle as he dabbed her head with kisses.

'If I didn't know already, I could tell you'd been to Ireland,' murmured Boadicea, her cheek still pressed to the crook of his shoulder.

'How?' asked Niall, with a tender kiss, though was more concerned with the feel of her.

'The scent of the peat is woven into your clothes.' She lifted her face and smiled.

Feeling himself become too aroused, he unlocked one of his arms from around her, and took a sniff of his cuff, inhaling the lingering scent of Beesy's cottage, before nodding in recognition. Then, he took hold of her hand as a prelude to his explanation.

Gripping her fingers, and speaking with his face close to hers, briefly he gave account of the situation that had sent him to Ireland, about Harriet seeing them together a fortnight ago, and Nora's emotional blackmail.

'Sure I knew something was up,' she murmured thoughtfully, 'from the look on your face the last time I saw ye. It nearly was the last time, wasn't it?'

He displayed anguish. 'Only because I was worried about what I was doing to the kids. That's the only reason I let myself be persuaded to go.' He continued to grip her hand, and shook it to inject her with belief. 'But the moment I was there, I knew I'd made a big mistake, that I couldn't live without you, that I'd do anything to have you back, even if it meant upsetting my kids – but then, how *could* they be upset if they've never even met you? So, I've decided,' he dealt her hand a pat, 'they *are* going to meet you, and I know they're going to love you just as much as I do.'

'Ye can't be certain of that, Niall.' After the prior look of shock at the thought of being presented to his children, a film of worry had drawn across her eyes.

Again he patted her hand. 'Well, it doesn't really matter if they do or not, because I love you, so they'll just have to put up with that. I've got to live my own life, Bo. I'm sick of creeping around for fear of upsetting folk. That's why I'm going to put everything on a firm footing, fetch them to meet their new mother—'

Still worried, she bit her lip and shook her head. 'Begod, you're like a whirlwind.'

He denied her implication that he was moving too quickly. 'It's not going to happen for a fort-night – that's when Harriet's wedding is, and I want to get that out of the way first. For one thing, I don't want to spoil her day – that'd be a rotten trick – and for another, the lasses are that looking forward to wearing their bridesmaids' dresses. I daren't do anything that's going to upset the apple cart – I can't even promise to call in on my way home from work, not now they know where you live. They wouldn't think twice about upsetting the Preciouses. So . . .' he beheld her with earnest expression, his eyes full of love as he gripped her hand, 'if you can wait a little bit longer before seeing me again, it'll all be worth it in the end.'

Boadicea nodded.

'You can?' He pretended hurt. 'I'm not sure I can. It feels I've already spent a year away from you, not just a week.' And he let go of her hand, to embrace her long and tightly, as if to boost himself for the sacrifice ahead.

Almost at once, though, he was forced to tell her, 'I'll have to dash in case the Vir—' he broke off, and began to shake with laughter. 'I meant to say "in case the Merchant of Venice sees us and demands her pound of flesh", meaning Harriet, and it nearly came out the Virgin of Menace – but that fits her to a T!' His laughter infecting his companion, they shook for mirthful seconds, tears coming to their eyes. 'It was only a slap she gave me last time, but she's sure to extract the full pound if she catches us again. I dread to think where she'd take it from.' Still grinning, he wiped his eyes. 'And I'm only supposed to be out for fish and chips.'

Boadicea drew away with loud grievance. 'Sure,

is that all I'm up against, feeding your belly? Get along out o' here!'

But he knew her well enough now not to take offence, and, with eyes that twinkled like her own, he gave her a last passionate kiss before both finally tore themselves away.

'Is it back at work on Monday?' asked Boadicea, receiving a nod. 'Oh, I almost forgot!' She put out a hand to stop him going. 'Did ye see in the paper, they managed to shoot that wolf o' yours?'

For a second his smile waned and he gave a little sound of disappointment. But then he was philosophical. 'Oh well, I suppose it had to cop it some time. Right, I'd better get off before I get meself shot. Don't sit anywhere near me at Mass tomorrow!' He threw a warning grin as he made across the road. 'Nora'll have her eyes peeled for any false move, so you'll have to forgive me if I ignore you. We don't want to make trouble for ourselves before we have to. I'll be seeing you, soon as I can!' And blowing her a kiss, his face wreathed in delight from this brief reunion, he departed.

Back at work on Monday, his disappointment over the slaying of the wolf in his absence was quickly to be assuaged. It was true, his mates informed him, the creature had been shot, for a trail of its blood had been found in its wake. But no one had found a body. And as livestock was still being terrorised, they must assume that the hunter's gun

306

had not inflicted a mortal wound and the wolf was still at large. Back to its old tricks maybe, but wise to all its pursuers' techniques, never again did Niall see the wolf in daylight.

But then he was hardly to miss it, with such momentous issues on his mind. Less than forty-eight hours had gone by since he'd lain eyes on his loved one – for, aware of Nora's observation, he had not even been able to look at Boadicea in church – but no one could stop him thinking of her. He couldn't have stopped thinking of her if he'd tried. Being stuck in the house yesterday had felt like prison, although in the afternoon there had been an amusing diversion when Harriet brought her fiancé, Pete, to be introduced to his prospective mother-in-law. Presented with a spivvy-looking, bumptious type, whom one might have expected as Harriet's choice of partner, Niall had wasted no sympathy on him but took great pleasure in watching the fellow's confidence shrivel under Nora's eagle eye, and the expression on his face as he wondered what he had got himself into. Was the groom still looking forward quite so much to his wedding? Niall himself was looking forward to it immensely, for it would mark a new beginning for him too. But until then, the days were simply crawling by.

Finally, though, the big event did arrive, and with it, Dolly – which was a somewhat embarrassing encounter for both her and Niall. Luckily, they did not have to be together long, for he was ordered to visit the barber, thenceforth to stay out of the women's way whilst the bride and her maids of honour got themselves ready.

Apart from Harriet's friends and workmates, her other sisters and their husbands, another forty of the Beasty clan turned up, though none from Ireland, the latter being unable to make the journey. However, Beesy and Austin's sons, who lived in Leeds, came with their families to represent their parents, and Beesy did send generous gifts in their stead.

'I wonder how much she paid for it?' Bedecked in white gown, the others gone ahead to church and only she and Niall left in the house, Harriet inspected Beesy's linen, comparing it favourably to some of the other gifts that had been laid out for display. 'A lot more than Mrs Lavelle, that's for sure. Those tea towels couldn't have cost more than a tanner each. They'll be threadbare before I've been wed a month.' Tutting, she turned back to Niall. 'Come here, then, let's have a look at you before we set off, check you're up to standard.'

With no father or brother to give her away, she had bestowed this honour on Niall, who now stood under inspection.

'One and six,' he told her with straight face as she cast her critical eye over him.

'What?' she frowned.

'You were looking at me new tie. That's what I paid for it – just in case you were going to ask.'

Seeing he had a twinkle in his eye, she smacked him playfully. 'Well, I'm glad you paid a lot more than that for my present!' She indicated the carving knife and fork with antler handles. 'No, they're smashing, those; they'll last for years.'

Niall had the decency to blush, and felt a twinge of guilt over what was to happen once Harriet was safely away on honeymoon. That was the only reason he had bought her such a decent gift.

His sister-in-law's flippancy belied her wedding-day nerves. After a last critical inspection of her floral headdress and veil in the mirror, Harriet turned back to him, asking anxiously, 'Do I look all right?'

'You look smashing,' came his gallant assurance.

For once, Harriet bestowed a genuine smile, and her eyes misted over. 'Thanks, Nye, and thanks for the present, and for giving me away . . .'

His blush deepened.

'I wish me dad could have been here, but I know he's looking down on me and saying he couldn't have picked a better stand-in . . .'

'Steady on, Hat, you'll have me roaring.'

'Aye, me and all.' Harriet straightened her shoulders, and with a deep breath to steady her nerves, she grabbed her bouquet with her usual no-nonsense approach. 'Come on then, let's get this done.'

And walking as if she meant business, she preceded him from the house.

Thereafter, he was to take her arm, and escort her past an audience of well-wishing neighbours, through the network of terraced streets, and onwards to the church. It had seemed silly to hire a vehicle to carry them only a hundred yards or so, and Harriet was not averse to having as many folk as possible admire her on the way.

It was a very fine day, with not a cloud in the sky – though perhaps too hot, thought Niall in his starched collar and dark suit, and he was glad they were almost to the church. Its stone walls presented a brighter patchwork in this afternoon sun, the smoother of the blocks still buttery as new, providing great contrast to those rougher ones that were engrained with almost a century of soot. Finally he and Harriet reached its entrance, to excited exclamations from those who clustered within its low outer walls, awaiting the bride. Niall offered a few words of calm to the smaller bridesmaid, Juggy, who was jumping and twirling in her pale blue gown, which threatened to dislodge the flowers in her hair. She was not the youngest bridesmaid, for another niece, aged five, was there to balance the wedding photographs. But she was certainly the most giddy, and at Niall's directive, the sensible Honor and her Aunt Dolly – also in pale blue – took the seven-year-old in hand, and steered her into position behind the bride, and in front of the other maid of honour, a friend of Harriet's, at the same time showing her how to hold her posy.

Standing prepared now in the cool stone entry, Niall and Harriet took simultaneous deep breaths, and shared nervous smiles. Then, as the organ struck up, they became serious again, and embarked towards the large stained-glass window over the altar. Moving slowly to the accompaniment of the music, Niall felt a thrill as he imagined another, dearer, arm in his, but this was only to last a few moments, for at the end of the aisle his role was over as he handed his sister-in-law over to her groom. From then on, he took a step back, and paid solemn heed to the Nuptial Mass.

Following what seemed like hours of serious matters, he and the rest of the congregation finally moved on to a reception at a Co-operative hall above a parade of shops. As weddings go, thought Niall, it was a very nice do, though much of his own enjoyment was coloured by the thought of what the morrow would bring. Which was why, at the end of the sherry-soaked reception, when he and others went to the station to wave the happy couple off on the train to Scarborough, the smile on his face was as wide as if he himself had been wed.

Up until half-past one in the afternoon, that Sunday was the same as any other: Nora first up to light the fire and to make sure Dominic arrived on time for his duties as altar boy, to help the little ones dress for church, to cook the dinner, which was eaten at the same hour. The only thing different was that Harriet was not there to wash up afterwards. Still, there was a capable thirteen-year-old, Honor, to help her grandmother, and Niall made sure he did his part by helping to stack the pots and carry them to the scullery. After everything was done, he sat down to read his paper, and to let the meal digest, Nora eventually doing likewise, the children settling down to read until it was time for Sunday school.

But today, when Niall found himself succumbing to the afternoon heat and his head began to loll – at which point he would normally have drifted off to sleep – he chose not to allow his eyes to close; instead, from the corner of them, he watched Nora's grey head nodding this way and that, as she drifted towards slumber. Two flies zizzed lazily around the light fitting, occasionally colliding, and the sound of this brought her suddenly back to consciousness. Eventually, though, her head came to rest.

Carefully folding his paper, Niall murmured to the children, 'I think we'll give Sunday school a miss, and have a walk to Rowntree Park instead, what do you kids reckon?'

Roused from her encroaching slumber by the eager yells of acceptance, Nora pressed her hands to the wooden arms of her chair as if to rise, though her eyes were dazed. 'I'll just have to splash some water on my face . . .'

'Oh, you don't have to bother yourself, Nora.' Niall gently pressed the elderly woman back into her chair. 'Stay here and put your feet up. I'll see to them.' The children's hair and dress was still neat from their morning trip to Mass.

She looked grateful, but was concerned enough to ask, 'Can you manage them all on your own?'

'Aye, you stay and have a nap. Honestly, we'll be all right. I've got Honor to keep the little uns in line.' Satisfied to have pacified their grandmother, he turned to the children. 'Now then, you can all get yourselves to the lav before we go.'

There was an immediate dash, though Honor dallied to ask: 'Can we take our swimming cossies, Dad?'

'Not today, darlin'.' He hated to see her disappointed face. 'But I promise we'll go again soon, and you can take your cossie then. Now, go and hurry that lot up, will you?' There had come the sound of arguing over the use of the lavatory.

Appeased, she straightened her white broderie anglaise dress, then tripped into the yard.

'Tell you what I will take, though,' muttered Niall, and grabbed his Kodak from the sideboard to examine the film counter. 'We'll use the last of this film up, so's I can get it developed and we can see our holiday snaps.' He slung the camera around his neck, looking forward to having a photograph of Boadicea that he could treasure in her absence.

'Can we take some bread for t'ducks, Gran?' Waiting her turn for the lavatory, Juggy ran in to ask.

Nora had settled back again, her eyelids heavy and her voice weary. 'Well, there's some stale stuff I've put aside, but you'll have to do without your bread and butter pudding.'

That was good enough excuse for Juggy, who hated the dish. She ran off to get the bread. Then, after what seemed like an eternity to Niall, his children were ready to go.

'Come on now.' He herded Batty, Brian and Juggy to the door. 'Let your gran rest in peace.'

'You make it sound as if I'm dead,' chuckled Nora, her eyes closed now.

It would be a lot easier if you were, thought Niall, smiling as he left.

With Dominic striding ahead, the sensible Honor in charge of Batty, and Brian riding on his father's shoulders, Niall used his right hand to hold the youngest steady, whilst his left was grasped by Juggy. Thus he escorted his brood towards Walmgate.

'This isn't the way to Rowntree Park,' pointed out Honor when, at the end of the street, her father whistled to alert Dominic, and redirected him across the main road and towards town. 'We normally go down past church and over Castle Mill's Bridge.'

'I know, but there's somebody else coming with us, and she lives at t'other end of Walmgate.' Niall braced himself for the explanation to come.

'Who is it, Dad?' Juggy squinted up at him through the sunshine as she swung along on his hand, hopping and skipping.

He had wanted to be further from home before he told them. Upon learning it was a woman they might take fright and run to Nora. Still, he'd never find out their opinion by pussy-footing around. 'It's somebody I want you to meet,' he began, as they passed the King William, the smell of ale gusting from its open door. 'A lady. She's really nice . . .'

Dominic's bold stride faltered. He turned and paused to examine his father. 'Are you gonna marry her?'

'No!' Niall laughed away the boy's suspicion, and, unable to deliver a touch of reassurance, for both hands were occupied, he tried to convey it in his expression. But then he sought to be more truthful. 'Well, not today . . . I might do in the future.' He snatched an examining glance at each of the other children, apart from the one travelling on his shoulders, whom he could not see. All appeared similarly confounded, and had fallen quiet. He decided to add a few words of explanation. 'It's a long time since your mam died – I'm not seeking to replace her, I could never do that – it's just that I've met this lady, and I like her very much, so I want you to meet her and tell me what you think, that's all. Don't worry, I won't be getting married tomorrow.'

Noting Dominic's sullen expression, he became slightly uneasy. Having not figured largely in his plans before, his children's behaviour had greater bearing now. What would happen if Boadicea didn't like them? But of course she would. Anxious to dispel his own fears as much as theirs, he offered words of encouragement, and hurried the youngsters to the other end of Walmgate, then through the alleyway to Boadicea's lodgings.

Here there was to be a comical moment, when he knocked at the door and Ma Precious answered, in her usual sergeant-major style. His children's faces fell, thinking that this was the woman he wanted them to vet.

'Now then!' boomed Ma, above the yapping of her ginger Pomeranian. 'Brought your tribe with you, I see. Herd 'em in, then!'

'No, we don't want to bother you,' began Niall.

'Good, 'cause I won't let you!' came her cheerful holler.

Used to her by now, Niall laughed, and lifted Brian down from his shoulders, reassuring him that the dog, which sniffed around his ankles, would not bite, before speaking again to its owner, 'No, I just meant we're off to Rowntree Park, and we've come to ask Boadicea along.'

'Can I come for a ride on the swings?' Ma suddenly bent towards the children, bringing her face down to theirs and unsettling the smaller ones, though Juggy made laughing retort.

'You'd break 'em!'

Ma came upright in mock offence. 'Are you saying I've got a big bum?'

Then even the more timid children laughed, causing the dog to emit its high-pitched yap until

Mrs Precious stuck her slippered foot under its rear. 'Shut up, you noisy beggar!'

'What's going on here?' By now Boadicea had appeared in the background, having somehow heard Niall's voice amid the ruckus.

'They've come to take you to Rowntree Park!' Ma told her.

'That's very kind!' After slight hesitation – her eyes flitting over the neatly clad brood, the girls in white dresses, the boys with shirts and ties – Boadicea came forth, beaming.

'Kind?' scoffed Ma. 'No fat bottoms allowed, apparently!' But the children could tell from the way their father laughed that this was not someone to be afraid of, even though he had not introduced her.

He seemed eager to introduce the other woman, though. 'This is Miss Merrifield, who I was telling you about—'

'Boadicea – but you can call me Bo!' Smiling, she leaned forward to shake the eldest child's hand. ''Tis such a mouthful otherwise,' she said to Honor, engaging with the others too, before turning her beam on Niall. 'Thanks for the warning – just as well I had on my best clothes!' She tweaked the puffed sleeves of her dress, which was basically pale turquoise, but with a rich network of navy and green upon it, so that it looked as if she were wearing a section of butterfly wing. 'And I see you have yours on. Just hang on, I'll only be a few minutes!' Her toes peeping through white sandals, she tip-tapped up the stairs to her room.

Niall eyed her fondly as she fled, knowing her well enough now to guess that her flamboyant performance hid a bundle of nerves, and admiring her for overcoming them. Had he been the one under scrutiny and the children been hers, he would never have been able to appear so natural.

'And you can come in while you're waiting!' ordered Mrs Precious. 'Georgie'll want to meet this lot.'

Niall steered his children ahead of him, issuing a greeting to the occupants, first Mr Precious and then the others. 'We're not here to spoil your peace,' he was quick to tell Mr Yarker, whose face had turned even sourer than usual upon being interrupted from his after dinner nap. 'We're off as soon as Boadicea comes.'

'Pity, I was hoping for a game of skittles,' murmured Yarker, eyeing the band of children uncharitably, though Mr Allardyce offered a less facetious smile.

The children were looking nervous again as they came further into the room to be surrounded by all its bizarre objects, staring round-eyed at the stuffed animals under glass, Brian tripping over the dog-skin rug, and having to be picked up and set on his feet again. But all were soon put at ease by old Georgie, who obviously loved children, for he came grinning forth with a large jar of sweets in his gnarled, stained hands.

Not all the children had pockets, so Mrs Precious instructed her husband, 'Go find some bags and share 'em out – but none for brass-face here; she says I've got a fat bottom!'

Juggy giggled nervously, hoping this was only a joke, though she was none too sure, until the kind old man summoned her along with the others to help share out the sweets.

Brian seemed entranced by all the stuffed creatures in the room, and by the Pomeranian, who was now attempting to mount the head of the dog-skin rug, as it lay unresisting with glazed eyes.

'Is this a zoo?' he asked his father.

'What an astute boy,' commended Mr Yarker, whilst the adults sniggered. 'I sometimes wonder myself.' And he distracted the dog from its crude attentions, by a swift jab of his foot.

'What's funny?' Boadicea came back into the room, carrying her handbag.

Red with mirth, Niall shook his head and changed the subject, instead offering her an apology. 'Sorry for not giving you prior notice, but I just had to grab my chance.'

'That's all right! I'm pleased to meet your children any time.' The brave performance might be a little contrived – it was easy to see how Boadicea coped so well as a barmaid – but the smile she gave was genuine. 'They're very well behaved, like their father.' Then she spoke to them directly, 'I believe it was your aunt's wedding recently – did you girls enjoy being bridesmaids?'

Honor and Juggy merely nodded, too busy eyeing the fair-haired woman up and down to concentrate on what she said.

'Ooh, I made a lovely bridesmaid,' Mrs Precious told Juggy, quite seriously, 'not that *you*'d believe it.' Then she gave a sly wink at Niall.

'Right, we'd best be off, then,' he said brightly, seeing Boadicea was poised with her handbag on her arm.

Unnoticed before, Batty had threaded a length of cord through the dog's collar, and now began leading it towards the door.

'Oy, where do you think you're going with that?' demanded his father, Boadicea most amused. 'It's not yours!'

'Can't we just take it for a walk?' tendered Batty, stroking the animal protectively.

But his father was adamant. 'I can't handle you lot and that as well.'

'Besides, he's my baby, aren't you?' sang Ma, and, scooping the little ginger dog to her proud bosom, she snuggled her face into its fur.

Eyelids heavy, Mr Yarker threw a look of disgust at the scene.

Niall responded with an apology. 'Sorry to disturb your nap, Mr Yarker! Batty, put that cord back where you found it. See you later, Ma. Thank Mr and Mrs Precious for the goodies,' he added final instruction to the children.

Then, all niceties conveyed, he and Boadicea made for the outside world.

'And where is it you're taking me, did Ma say?'

'Rowntree Park. Just t'other side of the river,' he explained to her. 'It's a memorial for all Rowntree's blokes who were killed in the war. There's a lake and lovely gardens, fountains—'

'Sounds grand,' interjected Boadicea, with an enthusiastic glance at the children.

'—tea room, stuff for the kids to play on,' continued Niall, 'Bowling greens – ooh, all sorts.'

'Swimming baths,' put in Honor, who had not spoken until now.

Niall glanced down at his eldest child, seeking chastisement in her tone. 'Aye, well . . . we couldn't really go in there today.'

Boadicea seemed to sense his unease, saying cheerfully, 'Because of me? Why, ye should've said – sure, I love swimming!' And addressing herself mainly to Honor, she added, woman to woman, 'We must definitely take our costumes next time.'

Then, taking the younger children's hands between them, the elder ones remaining aloof, Niall and Boadicea shepherded them from the alleyway, to be rendered half-blind as they came into brilliant sunshine, then across the road, and following the tramlines into the short stretch of Merchantgate. Thenceforth they made their way up its gentle incline, skirting the black and white timbers of the Red Lion, and turning left to head in the direction in which Niall had just come – though by route of Piccadilly rather than Walmgate, the two roads running parallel for fifty yards or so, until Piccadilly veered away and curved around a grubby row of warehouses, finally to merge with Fishergate. Then came two bridges to cross, first over the Foss, with its industrial barges, then the wider Ouse, which had pleasure craft and rowing boats too, followed by a stroll along the bank amongst dozens of others in their Sunday best, beneath the dappled shade of an avenue of trees.

Whilst Boadicea expressed vast relief at escaping the fierce sun for a while, smiling and chatting with Niall, Honor took command of the smaller ones and walked slightly ahead, occasionally snatching a glance over her shoulder at the woman who walked alongside her father, as if trying to gauge the depth of their relationship. Cheeks bulging with sweets, the boys seemed to have lost interest in Boadicea now. Dominic swooped on a stick, and, pretending it was a sword, served his smaller brother a series of thrusts in the chest, which sent Batty complaining to his father that he wanted a stick too, forcing Niall to search. Then, of course, Brian had to have one, which all added time to the journey.

'What is it with boys and sticks?' demanded Boadicea, laughing at Niall's sons up ahead as they crossed swords, thrust and parried. 'They're never happy unless they've a weapon in their hand.'

'Don't get in people's way!' ordered the boys' father, then shook his head with a weary smile at Boadicea. 'Well, I'm glad you're amused. I thought you might never speak to me again after meeting that lot – oh Christ, he's nearly caught that old chap round the whatsit. Right, put them sticks down now, or I'll take them to thrash you with!'

This appeared to make his partner even more amused, for she broke into chuckles. 'Oh, Niall, ye make yourself sound like the biggest thug, when those children have you eating out of their hands!'

'What?' Niall gasped, but played along. 'I'll have you know it's a good job you were here, or they'd be flayed alive!'

They eventually reached the iron gates of the park, some twenty minutes after leaving the Preciouses. Behind the avenue of large trees that juxtaposed the river lay over forty acres of ornamental gardens, set out in a maze of pathways that meandered through separate areas of recreation. Each section was enclosed by a neatly clipped hedge, one housing an ornamental pond, another a fragrant mosaic of flowers and benches from which to admire them, another just a statue or a sundial, but all of these leading to a lake.

Released from their father's control, the children thundered down the path bordered by shrubs, racing, their laughing efforts drowning out the sedate tap of wood on wood from the bowling greens. Keeping an eye on the youngsters careering ahead, Niall and Boadicea proceeded in leisurely fashion towards the half-timbered dovecote at the far side of the park.

'Don't go too fas— oh too late!' Niall groaned,

as Brian tipped headlong and a wail pierced the air. He went hurrying up to set the little boy on his feet, saying briskly, 'You're all right, no need to cry, it's nobbut a scratch.' But Brian thought there was reason to cry, and let go at full pitch.

Boadicea hung back at first, agitated by the piercing screams, yet reluctant to interfere between father and child. Then, moved by the little one's distress, she took a quick step forward. 'Here, let me.' And with a lick of her handkerchief and a series of gentle dabs at the scuffed knee to remove the beads of blood, Brian was soon up and running full tilt through the dovecote and towards the small bridge that crossed the lake.

Niall alerted Honor, who, fortunately caught the lad in time to prevent an accident, and held his hand at the water's edge to watch the swans until her father caught up, thenceforth to give them some of the bread Juggy had brought. The moment a crumb had hit the brown water, squadrons of ducks appeared from all sides of the lake, surging forth and leaving wide ripples as they converged on the bread-throwers. And for a while, the man and the woman were to stand there, inhaling the earthy, slightly fishy aroma of the lake, each providing a safe pair of arms to some of the smaller figures, who might have thrown themselves in along with the bread.

Soon, though, the boys began to clamour for the playground, but were overruled by their father who warned, 'I don't want you scrowin' round in t'muck or your gran'll kill me.'

'Scrowin' round in t'muck?' mimicked Boadicea, hoping the children would be amused, which they were. 'Sure what sort of talk is that?'

'It's York talk!' Niall pretended to cuff her, which also brought laughter to his children's faces – even Dominic's – this in turn sending a flood of happiness through their father's veins. It was going to be all right. They liked her.

Despite her elder brother's entreaties to hurry up, Juggy was still carefully dividing her bread into tiny, equal portions. 'We've got to keep some for the bunnies!'

Niall informed Boadicea that across the other side of the park were large cages, in which was a varied collection of rabbits and whatsits.

'Whatsits?' Boadicea cocked her head at the children. 'Sure, that's a funny kind o' name for a creature.'

Niall recalled the name he had been seeking. 'Golden pheasants, I meant.' He dealt her a scolding grin – then suddenly remembered he was carrying his camera. 'Tell you what, though! Before we go there or anywhere else, let's take some photos while this lot still look half decent.'

Arranging them all in a group, with the dove-cote in the background, and a cluster of its cooing residents atop its tiled roof as a bonus, he took a couple of snaps. Yet there was still available film on the camera, so, to his two elder sons' disgruntlement, Niall led the search for another suitable background, Dominic and Batty dragging their feet behind.

'This would be good!' Finding a hedged enclosure free of others, at least for the moment, Boadicea pointed to its ornamental pond, and gathered the children to her. 'Should we stand in front or behind?'

'If you all sit on the edge,' instructed Niall, 'I can get the fountain in behind you.'

And so they did, lining up to perch on the low wall containing the pond, on which also sat a collection of stone fish, each of the latter aiming a spout of water at the bronze statue of Mercury in the centre.

'Aw, can't we go to t'swings now, Dad?' demanded a bored Dominic, when his father had taken two photos, and seemed intent on dallying over another.

'Go on then!' permitted Niall, lowering the camera with a sigh of submission.

'We've got to feed the rabbits yet,' put in Juggy, but two of the boys had already run ahead.

'Don't worry!' sighed Niall, at her crestfallen expression. 'We'll get to see t'rabbits before we leave. Honey, you go with them to the playground. I've just got a couple of snaps left to take; we'll catch you up later.' And as Honor and the rest of his children galloped off, he murmured to Boadicea, 'I want to get one of you on your own, so I can keep it in me pocket.'

'Then I'll take one of you,' she said eagerly.

'Nay, you don't want one of my ugly mug!'

'I won't argue that you're ugly,' her expression was prim, 'but if you can have one of me, I can have one of you!' Eyes flickering, she returned to the pond and took up a pose on its wall, gathering her dress in case it trailed in the water, and arranging it so as to display her knees in their suntan stockings. Then deciding this made them look too fat, she quickly changed her position, legs stretched out and ankles crossed.

Grasping his camera at waist level, Niall squinted down into its viewfinder, using a hand to shield it from the sun, shuffling back and forth so many times that his model was forced to complain.

'Did ye know these fish were once real?' she asked brightly, patting the stone scales of the ornament on the wall beside her. 'They were just made to wait so long for somebody to take their photograph that they got bored stiff.'

'Don't make me laugh!' he shushed her, still trying to get a decent snap. 'It'll be all blurred . . .'

'There'll be people coming by in a minute! Sure, I'm not sitting here like a drip all day!'

Nipping his tongue between his teeth, Niall finally gave the order for her to keep still, and – 'Got it!'

Hearing the shutter click, Boadicea leaped up laughing, 'Thank God!' And she grabbed the camera off him, determined to do a better job.

Finally the roll of film was used, which was just as well, for some people did come by, inducing Niall and Boadicea to move on. Smiling and contented, Niall hooked the camera strap back over his neck, and, saying the children would be all right for a while with Honor, he took hold of Boadicea's hand. Tucking it under his arm, he proceeded to lead her on a gentle saunter around the gardens, through rose pergolas, around the lake, and towards the bandstand.

The discordant tones of brass instruments told that the afternoon concert was due to begin, and quite soon it did, a lively march causing Niall to act against his normal reserved nature and bob up and down alongside his companion.

'It must be a law of nature,' he told her, both of them smiling broadly. 'The minute you hear an oompah you have to walk in time to it.'

They paused for only a while at the bandstand, though, for Niall said they had better check that the children were where they were supposed to be. 'Ellen'll never forgive me if—' he broke off, with an embarrassed look at Boadicea. 'Sorry . . .'

'You are allowed to mention your wife, Niall,' she told him kindly, patting his arm and speaking over the noise of the band.

Feeling wretched, he wanted to explain, but walked on for a while, waiting until it was no longer necessary to compete with the band. 'It's just that she was always so protective of the kids,' he finally told Boadicea as they strolled amongst the perfumed rose beds.

She sighed. ''Tis a big hole she's left. You can't help missing her.'

Steeped in even more guilt now, Niall felt it was time to confess. 'Well, that's just it . . . I don't. I've never been happier in my life than I am with you.'

Boadicea did not answer, but allowed her eyes to respond for her, her fair lashes slowly descending and then opening again to convey harmony.

'But sometimes it feels like she's still there,' he murmured. 'I suppose it's all the reminders – not just the kids, but having her mother living with me . . . I'm dreading what Nora's going to do when she hears I've brought them to meet you. Probably stop my pocket money, for a start.' He managed a weak smile. 'I dare say she'll start mentioning Ellen's name in every sentence just to make me feel guilty . . .'

'Well, there's no reason for you to feel guilty at mentioning her in my presence,' vowed Boadicea.

'There is, though.' Niall hung his head, and primed himself for an adverse response. 'I wished it upon her, that accident – well, not wished,' he said quickly, at Boadicea's horrified frown, 'but imagined, imagined what my life'd be like if she wasn't in it. All the years of nagging – not just from her, that wouldn't have been so bad, I could've coped with that, but there were four of them constantly at me – her mother and sisters – you've no idea what it's like to be a man in a houseful of women – not to mention when they had a get-together with the rest of her sisters, all treating me like I was some sort of pathetic . . .' Inferring from her knitted brow that his explanation was less than coherent, his voice trailed away.

But after deep cogitation, it returned. 'I suppose I *am* bloody pathetic. What bloke would stand by – no, not stand by, *join in*, while his brother gets robbed of all his furniture and virtually evicted from his home?' He looked sick with self-reproach, all this whilst others went about their recreation all around them, the thwack of tennis rackets from the courts, the happy squeals of children . . .

'This is the brother ye don't see any more?' Since last mentioning the subject, Boadicea had not questioned Niall again, the very mention of his sibling having obviously struck a nerve. Now she understood why.

He dealt her a glum nod as they stepped around a half-eaten ice-cream cornet, dropped by some unfortunate child, and now melting on the path. 'I've no idea where he went. I feel awful . . . all the things I said to him about him not waiting till his wife was cold before finding somebody else . . . and she looked a really nice lass, the one he took up with, but I were that rotten to them both.' He glanced at his companion, his words heartfelt. 'He asked me to put meself in his shoes. I couldn't associate with such behaviour then, thought I was above it. I know how he feels now. By God I do.'

She interjected with a loving pat, but allowed him to continue, strolling quietly by his side.

'Me poor mam'd be that ashamed of me . . .'

'We all do things we're ashamed of, Nye.'

'Aye, but to wish your wife dead!' His face crumpled in self-disgust, and he took a few more thoughtful paces before speaking again. 'I hadn't intended to tell you any of this when I came out. I were just looking forward to a nice time with you and my kids – I *was* having a lovely time, watching how well you got on with them, and them with you. But I think that's what set me off. I thought, how can I keep this to meself, when you've been so open with me? I had to let you know what I'm really like . . .'

'I already know what you're *really* like, Nye,' she reassured him softly. 'I won't think any the worse of you, and I take it as a compliment that you feel able to trust me with your secrets. You think you're the only one who has such awful thoughts? Well, I can tell ye, you're not. When I was first with Eddie—'

He flinched at the first use of her husband's name, but she didn't seem to notice.

'—I used to be that anxious whenever he was out later than usual, wondering if he'd had an accident, imagining him lying in the hospital . . . everybody does that, I should think. But when things started to go wrong between us, I took to using that same thought in a different way, employing it as a yardstick, as it were, to measure my feelings for him, wondering, would I feel as heartbroken as in the old days if he didn't come home? Well, he eventually didn't come home, not because of any accident, but presumably because he didn't want to. I guess he'd had the same kind of thoughts about me.' A corner of her lips turned up in self-disparagement. 'So don't go tearing yourself apart that it's only you who thinks that way.'

Niall gave a respectful murmur on her honesty, and took another few unhurried paces, before admitting, 'I did feel sad when she went. I didn't think I would, but I did.'

'So did I, when he left,' murmured Boadicea. Then, finding that with this dispiriting conversation her shoulders had begun to sag in the butterfly-coloured dress, she brought herself suddenly erect and enlivened her pace. 'But I'm not any more so come on now, cheer up and let's go see what the kids're doing!'

Finding his offspring still enjoying the swings and seesaws, and reluctant to leave, Niall and Boadicea looked around for a bench on which they might sit and wait, but all were taken. So he led her to a large expanse of grass nearby, there to spread the jacket of his suit for her to sit upon.

'Can we just put it under there?' Boadicea re-directed him into the shade of some trees. 'Else my face will look like a Swan Vesta by the time I go home.'

Across the park, the band struck up another number, though it interfered little in their conversation now, as they sat beneath the green canopy watching Honor trying to keep the others in order whilst they awaited their turn on the slide, the boys play-fighting and tumbling about on the grass, barging into others in the queue.

Niall took a deep breath, inhaling the scent of crushed grass. 'What do you think of them then? Do they come up to scratch?'

'They're horrible little divils.' Then she laughed, and added warmly, 'Ah sure, they're a grand bunch – as they would be with you for a dad.'

He was gratified that she liked them, but, 'Apparently, I'm no such great shakes as a father.' And he related what Nora had told him before the trip to Ireland, about each child's problem, whilst Boadicea listened in sympathy. 'I gave Dominic a stern talking-to about smoking, and he's managed to cut it down to sixty a day.' He threw her a smile. 'No, I think I managed to put the fear of God into him. Batty'll never alter. He's always been a light-fingered little devil; it's nowt to do with losing his mother. As for Juggy and Brian, poor little buggers . . .' he shook his head, 'the only thing wrong with them is that they're missing their mam.' Thankfully, the bed wetting seemed to be over with, he added. Then he became cheerful again. 'Anyhow, I'm glad they behaved

themselves for you, and they seem to like you –
not that it would matter.'

'Of course it matters,' she corrected him.

'No, I meant it wouldn't change the way I feel
about you. It just makes it a lot easier if they like
the woman I'm going to marry.'

Boadicea made a sound of impatience. 'Niall,
you know the situation . . .' Her spirits slightly
flagging again, she slid her fingers across the grassy
space between them, gripped his hand and shook
it, as if to dissuade any talk of matrimony. 'Don't
go getting them all fired up about something that
might not happen for ages – might never happen.
Let's all enjoy the afternoon.'

'How can I enjoy it when you've just throttled
another of my proposals?' he demanded quietly.
'It might suit you to carry on like we are, going
home to our separate houses after every meeting,
but I can tell, you, it's doing me no good at all.'

Understanding his frustration, she gave his hand
a squeeze, though failed to come up with a solution.

However, after a lengthy period of thought,
Niall offered one of his own. 'You could at least
make enquiries about getting a divorce.'

She showed weariness at his audacity. 'You
make it sound so easy, when ye don't even know
the first thing about it.'

That was true. Divorce was a term one only
ever read about in the newspapers, when some
society figure had been caught out, a term for rich

people and totally unheard of amongst his own class and religion. No one of his acquaintance had ever even uttered the word, except in the context of denouncing some libertine or harlot. He felt a pang of conscience then, for his own narrow view. This was no loose woman who held his hand. He stroked her fingers, his eyes still on the children, who were now on the 'witch's hat', clinging on for grim death as it hurtled round and round. 'I know enough to realise it'll cause a bit of a scandal, not least from the Church—'

She interrupted with a bitter laugh. 'That's an understatement! We're for the flames, more like.'

He conceded that this was a very serious situation for two Catholics. But despite all that had been drummed into him since childhood, he told her, 'I can't believe a merciful God would punish me for loving a woman so much that I can't see any point in life without her.'

Boadicea was softly condemning. 'Ye shouldn't say that, blessed with five beautiful children.'

'Aye, and I'd give my life for them too,' swore Niall. 'But they'll grow up and I'll grow old. I couldn't bear the thought of old age without you. That's why I can put up with anything the Church or anyone else throws at me. I'm prepared to risk anything, because of the way I feel about you. Question is, do you feel strongly enough about me to put up with it?' He turned to examine her again.

'I surely do.' It was obvious, both from her

tone and the depth of longing in her blue eyes, that she spoke the truth.

'Then we have to find this bloke and set you free.' Niall refused to use the deserter's name. 'I don't know the first place to look, but I'll help you if—'

'No, that's all right,' she hastened to say, bracing her shoulders as if to get ready for action. 'It's my job to do this. I'll consult a solicitor first, find out how to go about it. Better for you to stay in the background for now. It wouldn't look too good, would it?'

Pleased that she was at least making a move towards the enablement of their marriage, at least a civil ceremony, he gave a smiling nod, his eyes gleaming with love for her, and Boadicea's shining back. There was nothing more to be said then, for Juggy came tumbling across the grass to ask if she could feed the rabbits as soon as her siblings joined them.

At Niall's consent, and the others' arrival, Boadicea leaped up to brush the bits of twig from her dress, saying to the children, 'Right, it's off to the rabbits – and on the way, we'll have an ice cream!'

'Oh, I'm not sure we can afford—'

'Please, Niall,' Boadicea gripped his arm, delivered a firm look, then took out her purse. 'Let me pay – not that I'm trying to bribe them or anything,' she muttered, with a sly grin.

So with his agreement, they were to move *en*

masse towards the elevated building that was the tea room, the purchase of their ice creams leaving just enough time to visit the shady corner of the park with its large cages of rabbits, and exotic-looking golden pheasants, so that Juggy could finally dispose of the bread she had clutched in her hot little hand. Then they made their way back to Walmgate.

The table had been set for tea by the time Niall and his children got home. 'Oh, here you are!' said Nora, 'I thought you'd got lost!' At their entry, she had risen immediately to uncover the plates of sandwiches and cake on the table. 'I hope they haven't turned dry. I thought you'd be home ages ago. I bet you're all starving.'

'We've had an ice cream,' boasted Juggy with a grin.

The hawkish face groaned, but Nora directed her mild rebuke at Niall. 'I've told you about spoiling their tea, you monkey—'

'It's half an hour since they had it,' he had begun to explain, when Batty piped up: 'A lady bought 'em!'

'What lady?' To Nora's consternation, her eldest grandson was quick to inform her.

'The one me dad's courtin'.'

Nora flushed an angry red and all jocularity ceased. 'You swore to me!' she levelled an accusing finger at her son-in-law. 'You said you'd put your children first!'

'And I have.' Niall ordered himself to remain calm, and rolled up his sleeves, intending to wash his hands. 'I decided to ask their opinion. And they've no problem with my seeing Boadicea. So neither should anyone else.'

With her puzzled grandchildren hanging on her every word, Nora was forced to contain behind gritted teeth all the things she would like to have said. But as she barged off to the cupboard, swiftly to return, there was message enough for Niall in the brightly labelled tin that was slammed down on the table.

'Maybe your father'd like some of these!' she announced to the children.

Whilst his children remained bemused and uncomfortable, Niall stared long and hard at the tin of peaches, fully aware what this represented. His mother-in-law had sworn never again to touch the fruit that Ellen had been on her way to buy on the afternoon of her death. This was her way of reminding him.

12

He had expected a full-blown row with Nora once the children had gone to bed. Or at least, to experience another serving of her own inimical brand of persuasion. But his mother-in-law seemed finally to have grasped, from the determined front he presented, that there was little point. Not that she had given up. This he knew all too well from the way she flexed her jaw as she sat opposite him, ostensibly darning a sock, but underneath concocting some plan of action.

He was to find out on Monday night what course that plan would take.

With no need to be secretive now about his romantic meetings, and no call to ration them, he had decided to take full advantage of Harriet's absence, and visit Boadicea, for he was anxious to know if she had consulted a solicitor about the divorce. Not long after the children had gone to bed, he made his move.

Her disapproving eyes watching him as he put

on his jacket and combed his hair, Nora had no need to ask, though she did anyway. 'Where do you think you're off?'

'I think we both know,' he answered quietly.

She got to her feet, a challenge in her tone. 'And who'll be looking after your children? I can't do it; I'm going to visit our Peggy.' And stabbing a silver pin through her old-fashioned hat with its artificial roses, she began to tug on summer gloves. 'Sorry if that ruins your little designs!'

'It won't,' he answered blithely. 'I've just looked in on them – the little uns are flat out. I've told Honor to fettle them if they cause any bother. I'll only be half an hour or so.'

'Long enough for the house to burn down!' Without further ado, Nora grabbed her purse and departed, with the epithet, 'And we'll all know who to blame!'

Simultaneous to the slamming of the door, Niall closed his eyes in exasperation. 'Enjoy yourself, you old sod,' he muttered.

She was right, of course. However, there was an easy solution. Tucking his comb into his pocket, he went next door to enlist a custodian.

Even before he had posed the question, Gloria's limpid eyes enlivened at the mere sight of him framed in her open doorway, and she hurried to invite the adored one in.

Niall knew well enough to address himself to the mother first. 'Hello, Mrs Lavelle, sorry to disturb you. I just wondered if you'll be going anywhere this evening?'

'The only place I'll ever be going is me grave, lad.' From an armchair came the martyr's sigh.

'Not for a long time yet,' Niall assured her. 'Er, I've just come to ask if Gloria can do me a big favour. Me mother-in-law's gone out and I need to nip out as well, but there's nobody to sit with the kids—'

'I'll do it!' Gloria almost swooned at being presented with this chance to help the man she so admired, and turned to her mother, lisping beseechingly, 'If you'll be all right on your own, Mam?'

Niall reinforced the daughter's plea 'I'll only be taking her away for half an hour or so, Mrs Lavelle.'

'Take her for as long as you like, love,' said Mrs Lavelle, with a telling look at Gloria, which he chose to ignore.

'Thanks – right then, Glo,' he backed out, 'I'll get off . . .'

'I've made some scones.' Seizing a tin, Gloria pursued him, keen for any association. 'I'll have one waiting with a cup of tea for when you come in!'

Thanking her, and opening his own front door for her to enter, he hurried away with a smile of anticipation at seeing Boadicea, which was also mingled with satisfaction. Let Nora do her worst. So long as it did not upset the children, he could cope with all her silly goings-on.

Nora did not regard them as silly. There was a determined strategy to her behaviour, as she hovered inside the confectioner's on the corner of the street, bemusing the shopkeeper by her inability to choose between the jars of aniseed balls, sherbet lemons or toffees, whilst darting looks out of the window; finally having to confess to the woman that she was only waiting for Niall to pass. 'The minute he comes by, I'll be out of your hair, Mrs Dalton! I just want to see how long the beggar stops out for.'

Barely had the words left her lips than Niall appeared, causing her to duck her head until he had loped past. Then, muttering thanks to the shopkeeper, she emerged and scuttled back down the street towards her home.

'What the hell are you doing here?' She stopped dead on seeing Gloria seated in Niall's chair – as if wrapped in his arms – her demand wiping the beatific expression off the poor woman's face. 'Don't tell me, I already know!' she added, as the baby-sitter rose to offer an explanation.

Gloria's toothless face had begun to sag with disappointment over the shattering of her dream of spending time alone with the object of her desire when he returned. 'Niall said you were going out, Mrs Beasty.'

'I only said that to test him! I wanted to see how low he'd stoop!' Nora seemed furious as she ripped off her gloves, then her flowered hat. 'And you're not to do this again, do you hear?' she told

Gloria. 'He's taking advantage of your good nature!'

'I don't mind,' protested the gummy mouth.

Setting her hat firmly on the sideboard, Nora wheeled. 'Oh, so you don't care that he's using your services as a baby-sitter, whilst he goes out canoodling with his trollop?'

Gloria was too shocked and hurt to answer.

'Well, I *do* care!' raged Nora. 'And I'm telling you, you're not to do his bidding any more. Have you got that? Anything he asks you to do, you tell him no!'

Gloria nodded and picked up her cake tin, her eyes focused upon it, so that Mrs Beasty would not see that they welled tears.

'You're a good lass, you deserve better,' stated Nora, cooling down somewhat, as she propelled Gloria firmly towards the door. 'But don't you say anything to him, just leave him to me.' Yet at least, she recognised, Niall had had the decency not to leave his children on their own, as he was intending to do before she had pricked his conscience; she could put that to her advantage.

Once Gloria had been ejected, Nora snatched an angry glance at the clock, wanting to check the duration of his tryst.

In the meantime, she made herself a cup of tea, then sat down and penned an urgent letter to Beesy, asking if she had heard anything from her cousin in Ballina, and pressing her to hurry with this vital

343

information. By the time she had finished the letter, and tucked it into her pocket for tomorrow's post, she had reached another decision. It was futile to waste her breath on more argument tonight. Until she received a reply from Ireland, she would allow her son-in-law the rope that would, with luck, hang him.

Niall had shown no surprise, when he got home later that evening, to find Nora sitting there and not Gloria, for he simply assumed that his mother-in-law had sent her home. What had slightly unnerved him was that there was no tongue-lashing as he might have expected. Although the silence was almost as bad.

'I won't be going out again till Saturday,' he had told her, in somewhat duller mood than when he had gone out. Boadicea had failed to visit a solicitor, seemingly in not as great a rush as he to obtain her divorce. It had rather flattened him.

'Suit yourself,' Nora had sniffed, as she finished plaiting her hair and retired to bed. 'You always do.'

But apart from this, and a refusal to converse with him on an evening, he had noticed little difference in her behaviour towards him throughout the rest of that week, a meal being on the table every night as usual.

On Saturday morning, though, there was the hint of something else in the air, as Nora looked keen to pounce on the letter that Niall had just picked up from the doormat, on his way to the breakfast table.

'Oh, it's from Beesy,' he said, seeing its Irish postmark.

Still bleary-eyed, for it was very early, she had nevertheless become instantly alert, and snatched the letter. 'Get your porridge, or you'll miss your bus.'

'Aren't you having any?' Seating himself, Niall sprinkled sugar over the contents of his bowl.

'I'll have it after you've gone.' Pouring them both a cup of tea, she sat away from the table in the old Edwardian chair with its barley-twist legs, and opened the letter.

'Are they both all right?' Niall sought to enquire over his shoulder, between mouthfuls.

'Yes,' said Nora, reading on.

'What does she have to say?' he asked, when she did not volunteer any information.

'If she wanted you to know she'd have addressed the letter to you,' mumbled his mother-in-law.

Niall gave a laugh. 'I was only asking.' Nevertheless, he got on with his porridge.

Nora allowed no expression to cross her face that might give the game away, but her heart was filled with cheer, as she raced through Beesy's news. The latter had just received word from her cousin Mary in Ballina about 'that woman', the information provided by Mary's 'very good friend' Father Kelly, who had seen it as his duty to act upon this immoral relationship, and whose correspondence with the bishop had revealed that the one under investigation had gone to live in a small town in Lancashire when she had left Ireland. So, armed with the damning information provided by Nora, which had been embellished by her allies, Father Kelly had written to that diocese to see what he could unearth. That was all Beesy could tell her for now, though she would post the results as soon as they were known.

Disallowing this note of anticlimax to upset her, and inscrutable of feature, Nora folded the letter away and slipped it into her pocket. Until the receipt of concrete evidence that would unveil the true character of this Boadicea woman, she must suffice to destroy this corrupt relationship by increments.

Little did Niall suspect this, as he took his empty breakfast bowl to the sink and got ready for work, though before too long he would interpret what was afoot.

Almost ready to go, he pointed out what he thought to be a discrepancy. 'I was just going through my drawer, Nora, and I didn't notice a clean shirt. I thought maybe you'd put it somewhere else . . .'

Setting out bowls ready for when the children came down, she paused to stare him in the eye. 'Is it for church you'd be wanting it?'

He met the gaze that so frightened others. 'That as well.'

'As well as tonight, you mean, when you go to

see your friend – aye, I thought that's what you really meant!' His mother-in-law added a curt nod. 'Why don't you give them to *her* for washing then? Seeing as she's the one getting the benefit!'

Niall remained perverse, and calm. 'But I don't hand my wage packet to Boadicea, do I?' he said, slinging on his haversack.

The name was a red rag to a bull. 'I don't mind washing the clothes of a man who does an honest day's toil! But if you think I'm slaving away to whiten your collars just so's you can go visit your Jezebel, you've got another think coming!'

Concerned that his children might now be awake and overhear, Niall drew the argument to a halt. 'I'd better pay somebody to do it then.' And he went away to bundle up a dirty shirt and two collars, telling Nora as he left, 'I'll drop them off somewhere on my way to work.'

'Be my guest!' invited Nora. But he did not see her triumphant smirk as he marched next door.

Gloria seemed different today when she answered his knock, and not just because it was early morning. Her apology was not so cringing as usual, at being unable to fulfil his request. 'Sorry, Niall, me mother says I can't do it for you.'

Momentarily stunned, Niall held those placid blue eyes, which today almost had a hint of rebellion in them. 'But how did she know I'd ask?'

'Mrs Beasty told us all about your—'

'Gloria!' came a sudden interruption from the

other end of the passage. 'You're not talking to *him*, are you?'

'Yes, Mam!' Gloria lisped back, without pause.

'Well, shut the door!'

And muttering a final, insincere apology, Gloria did just that.

Gritting his teeth, Niall underwent a few seconds' thought over how many others Nora might have told about his affair. Then, not to be beaten, he went along the street and knocked upon another door.

'Sorry to bother you, Mrs Whelan!' He directed an engaging smile at the one who answered. 'But I wondered if you could do me a favour and wash and iron a few things for me – just a shirt and couple of collars? I'll pay you anything you ask.'

A beneficiary of his kindness for many years, the drab-looking housewife was all too ready to help him, especially if it would bring in an extra shilling to a tight budget. 'Of course, love, when do you want them doing?'

'Today. I know it's Saturday, but well, there was a bit of a mistake at home, and my mother-in-law forgot to wash my decent shirt and I need it for church.'

'Yes, I heard about your bit of bother, love.' The expression on the woman's face showed that Mrs Whelan was not to be hoodwinked.

'Oh . . .' Niall looked slightly shamed. 'Well, if you'd rather not—'

'What business is it of mine who you want to

take up with?' came her light reply. 'I've said I'll do them and I will. On a regular basis if you like.'

'You're a treasure!' Niall handed over the bundle.

Mrs Whelan accepted it with a smile. 'With grand weather like this we'll have them dry by noon, and ironed by tonight.'

Reiterating his thankfulness, Niall went off to work, imagining Nora's face at having the wind knocked out of her sails, when he announced that he had found someone to help with his washing.

After spending the morning at work, and not arriving home until two, he knocked at Mrs Whelan's door on his way past, in the hope that his small bundle of washing would be ironed. Some of his children were playing further along the street with the Whelan children, the boys with a cricket bat, Juggy and her friend with skipping ropes. The instant he caught his daughter's eye with a wave, she broke off her game and pelted towards him. Awaiting her, he grinned, and was still wearing this expression when his knock was answered.

'Ah, hello, Mr Doran . . .' Mrs Whelan did not seem too happy at having to convey her information. 'No, I'm afraid I wasn't able to do your washing after all.'

Niall grunted as Juggy's small body slammed into his thigh, and he bent to pet her. But his words were still for Mrs Whelan. 'Don't tell me – you've had a visit from my mother-in-law.'

She confirmed this with a shameful nod.

'Oh, well,' he sighed and nodded, stroking the child's warm head thoughtfully. 'That's all right, love. I can understand you might not want to get involved in our row.'

'Oh, it's not that, pet,' she hurried to assure him, handing over his unwashed bundle of clothes. 'I've told you, it's none of my business who you take up with. It's just that Mrs Beasty has made it very clear that if I do help you, she'll let the Assistance Board know, and Norman'll get his benefits stopped, you see. We can't afford to get into trouble. Eh, I feel awful after all the rabbits and coal you've brought me over the years . . .'

'Don't you worry yourself about it, love!' With this assurance, Niall hoped to disguise his fury, for Juggy had been listening intently. Telling Mrs Whelan that it was quite all right, he would find someone else to do his washing, he waited for her to go inside, before turning his attention to his child.

'Right, you go back'n play with Kathleen now,' he instructed, trying to sound cheerful, for she seemed to know there was something amiss. 'I've just got summat to do before I have me dinner. I'll fetch you some goodies when I come back!'

Then, with no other recourse, he hurried back up the street, and directly to the Chinese laundry – though it was to cost him dear if the proprietors were to rush his shirt through their process, so that he could wear it that night.

* * *

As ever, Niall was forced to wait until his children were in bed before confronting Nora. Pre-empting her cry of reproach at the sight of him wearing a clean shirt, he warned his mother-in-law, 'It wasn't Mrs Whelan who did it, so you needn't think she's gone against you! Bringing that poor soul into it – as if she hasn't enough on her plate with half a dozen kids and an unemployed husband!' He made a sound of disgust. 'You've frightened her half to death with your threats.'

'I wouldn't have to threaten her if you had any sense of decency!' expostulated Nora. 'Do you think I enjoy broadcasting my business to all and sundry?'

'Well, before you start going round putting the fear of God into any more of our neighbours, I'll save you the bother!' retorted Niall. 'I'll be taking my washing to the Chinese laundry in future – see how *they* deal with your threats!'

'Oh, *well*!' Nora ejected her corseted rear from the chair, and charged to where she kept the dirty linen, coming back to hurl a large bundle at him. 'If they're happy to do your shirts, you can take your sheets and towels as well!'

'I will!' Niall shot back, but he left the dirty articles scattered on the floor, and stormed off to see Boadicea at the pub.

'You should have brought them to me,' the latter told him sympathetically, after he had related all that had gone on that day, whilst she pulled him a pint.

'Nay!' Looking weary, he waved this offer aside. 'There's sheets and all sorts. She's been doing them up to now, I suppose, because the boys sleep in my bed, and by depriving me she'd be depriving them. But I've gone and shot meself in the foot by saying I'll take them to the Chinks. Anyway, I can't expect you to do them.' Exchanging the money in his hand for the glass of beer, he took a sip.

Boadicea clinked the coins thoughtfully. 'You'd expect it if we were married.'

'Yes, but we're not, are we?' Niall's voice had turned dull, partly because she had made no headway in finding her errant husband. 'And if Nora has her way we never will be.'

Immediately he found his hand pressed by a gesture of affectionate encouragement. Then, having conveyed this, Boadicea began to dry the selection of glasses she had just washed, keeping her eye out for anyone who required serving, for the bar was quickly filling up. 'When I said you should have given them to me, I meant I'll shove them in with mine – Ma sends all ours to the laundry.'

'I can't have her paying!' he objected.

Boadicea bent forward to murmur. 'Niall, don't ye know she's filthy rich?'

'Is she?' He looked astounded.

'Yes!' Ensuring there was no one to overhear, and also alert for the landlord, who would maybe give her a ticking off for slacking, Boadicea continued the pretence of drying the glass in her hands, as she went on, 'How do you think she affords to give us such good quality meals on the board we pay her? Her parents left her a fortune. You might not know it from the state of the house – it's an untidy wreck of a tip, I know – but that's just the way Ma is. She's got money stuffed all over the place. I argued with her about it when I first came to live here and found a wad of fivers tucked under the carpet in my room. I thought she was testing my honesty, d'ye see. But no, that's just the way she is – hates visiting the bank. I'm telling ye, she's rolling in it.'

'You never said owt before—'

'And when would I tell ye?' she asked him. 'In here, or in the pictures, and be overheard by some villain who'd rob her? I didn't see as it was any of our business.'

'No, you're right it isn't,' he nodded, and took a drink.

'So just give your washing to me. I can ask her permission if it makes you feel better.'

Niall said it would. 'And I'll make what contribution I can. Nora's not going to beat me.'

This might hold true, but he knew that his adversary would have a damn good try before giving up. Moreover, she was to possess the ammunition, for, added to her current embargo over his laundry – which caused Niall difficulty enough – some outrageous news was to arrive in Tuesday's afternoon post.

Cock-a-hoop at its receipt, Nora could barely wait to inform Niall of the letter's contents, although somehow she managed to hold her tongue long enough to make an all-out display of it.

To Niall's dismay, Harriet was there when he arrived home that evening, here on her first visit as a married woman. Obviously informed that Niall had taken up with Boadicea again, she was on her feet and yelling at him the minute he came in. Thank God the children were out playing.

'I bet you couldn't wait to get rid of me!' she railed, before he'd hardly had time to hang up his rucksack.

'Had a nice honeymoon, Hat?' Sweating and weary though he was, Niall tried to sound bright as he interrupted her flow with a sardonic smile. 'Where's Pete? Got sick of you already, did he?'

'Thinking I wouldn't say owt if you bought me off with a fancy carving knife!' continued Harriet. 'Well, you can have it back! I want nowt of yours, you two-timing sod!'

'I take it your mother's told you then that the kids have approved Boadicea.' His tone still even, he went to wash his hands.

'There's summat I haven't told her, though.' Nora beheld him strangely as she placed his meal on the table. 'And something your fancy piece hasn't told you either.' There was the gleam of victory in her eye. She pulled a letter from her pocket and wagged it at him as he came out of the scullery. 'She's *married*!'

Harriet sucked in her breath at her mother's coup, and listened as Nora read out extracts from the letter, both women eventually turning to look at Niall with expressions that said, how do you like that?

Inwardly it felled him that she had gone to such lengths to employ spies. Outwardly he remained undisturbed, as he told them, 'There's nowt in there I don't already know.' And he sat down, and began to cut up his potatoes, releasing small puffs of steam.

At first astounded, then infuriated, Nora lost her air of triumph and went for him. 'You mean to tell me, you were aware you're consorting with an adulterer—'

'Eh, now, I won't have you talk about her like that!' Niall used his knife to point. 'The man she was married to deserted her, so it's none of her fault. Anyway, I've told you there's no how's-your-father going on between us.'

'Well, I'm glad to hear it! But that doesn't change the fact that she's a married woman – and how do you know there hasn't been any *hows-your-father* with other men before you met her?'

'I know.' Niall growled with certainty, and carried on slicing.

'I mean, she swans in here from nowhere,' Nora proceeded, 'hasn't been here five minutes before she's picking up fellas – who is she anyway? We know absolutely nothing about her except her name—'

'You don't need to know anything.' Niall maintained his level argument. 'I'm the one who wants to marry her.'

'How can you marry her, you fool?' yelled Nora. 'She's already wed! Good grief, what have you got yourself into? Men, you're all the same, brains in your pants!'

Niall felt his temper beginning to rise, but said evenly, 'I can marry her when she gets a divorce.'

For a moment his mother-in-law could only gasp in outrage. '*Well!* Well, I've never heard . . .' And she looked at Harriet, who was equally dumbfounded. But their shocked trance did not last for long. 'Now I know you've gone completely barmy!' proclaimed Nora. 'The Church doesn't recognise divorce, you fool. You'd both be adulterers. What the hell were you thinking, getting involved with her?'

'I was thinking it's none of your business!'

'Of course it's my business!' Nora was echoed by her daughter. 'It's my son-in-law she's trying to get her hooks into, going against his family, against his religion. You'll be barred from the Church, you know!'

'Well, if that's the case, so be it,' declared Niall, finally managing to eat a portion of his meal.

After another series of exhalations, Nora could only stare at him in anger and pity. 'Well,' she said finally, 'Beesy said she'd pray for you, and my God, I'll pray for you as well, because you'll need all the prayers you can get.'

And then Harriet started on him. 'Prayers? I'll give him prayers, the lying, cheating sod, him and that bitch of his!'

'I'm not listening to this!' Abandoning his meal, Niall knocked back his chair and strode from the house, slamming the door on his way out.

'Well, he's going to have to listen,' stated Nora to Harriet, the strength of her intentions writ large upon her face. 'Because I'm off to inform Father Finnegan about this, right now.'

After swift consultation of a clock in Walmgate, Niall went straight to The Angel to inform Boadicea that her marriage was no longer a secret. Fortunately, she was the only one in the bar when he entered, the normal clientele probably still eating their evening meal. Even so, he kept his voice low to convey the bad news.

'I'm really sorry,' he said, having forestalled her delighted exclamation with the announcement that someone had betrayed her. 'It's Nora what's sprung all this on me! The interfering old . . . she got a letter from Ireland this afternoon; must have been wittering on about it to Beesy while we were over there. I'm really sorry.' His eyes confirmed this.

'And what did this letter say exactly?' Boadicea's tone and demeanour had become wary.

'I haven't read it,' said Niall. 'I didn't have a chance. Her and Harriet set on me the minute I was through the door – didn't even give me time to have me tea!'

357

'I'll make you a sandwich,' she said at once, and disappeared into the kitchen, leaving Niall to fume.

When she returned with a ham sandwich, he bit into it gratefully and asked for a pint to go with it. 'I'll have to pay you later.'

'Don't worry about it.' Boadicea obviously had more on her mind as she held a glass under the pump. 'So, you were saying about the letter . . .'

'Aye, as I said, I didn't have chance to read it. She just picked out what she saw as the juicy bits.' He curled his labourer's fingers around the pint glass she handed him, and took a gulp from it. 'Apparently, this relative of Beesy's had been talking to her own priest, and he to the bishop—'

'Oh, great!' She pushed herself away from the bar and turned her back on him for a couple of seconds, clasping her hands to her face. They were still pressed there, when she turned back. 'And I suppose he'll now be writing to Father Finnegan to stop me going to Mass, not to mention anything else . . .' Allowing her hands to fall to her sides, she concluded in dull voice, 'Oh well, I suppose I should be thankful I got away with it for so long.' The marks of her fingers still on each cheek, her eyes studied him hopelessly. 'I'm not sure about you, though, Niall. Have you thought what it would mean, consorting with the likes of me? Ye might find yourself barred from Church.'

'Well, what do I care about that?' His disdainful tone rejected this as a silly argument.

'It's not just you, Nye, it's your children – your

whole life! People would snub you in the stree—'
She broke off as the landlord poked his head into
the bar.

'Oh, it's me laddo, is it?' A dour-faced Mr
Langan nodded at Niall, then spoke to his barmaid.
'I thought I heard sounds of trouble.'

'No, it's just us having a chat!' Boadicea
smiled reassuringly, and the landlord retreated.
The moment he had gone, she returned to her
topic, hissing, 'I'm telling ye, Niall, they'll snub
ye!'

He swallowed his mouthful of sandwich, then
washed it down with another couple of gulps of
beer. 'They're not like that round here.'

'And what about the people your mother-in-law
managed to browbeat?' Her question was punctuated
with a cynical nod. 'They're like it anywhere, Niall,
and they'll need no encouragement, believe me.'

She said it with such conviction that he had to
ask: 'Why, what did they do to you?'

But she picked up a cloth and started polishing
the bar. 'I'd rather not go into it.'

''Course . . .' he shrugged, and took another
drink, but he wished she would tell him about it.

'It was too horrible,' was all she would say. 'I
just want to put it out of my mind.'

'As you'd managed to do before Nora stuck her
oar in.' Niall sounded regretful. 'I'm really sorry
about all this, Bo.'

'So am I. I like York. I wouldn't want to move
away. And now it's started again.'

He tried to cheer her up, 'Nay! We can put up with the gossips—'

'It's not just tittle-tattle, it's everything! You don't know how powerful the Church can be . . .'

'Oh, I do.' Niall had turned thoughtful, imagining himself being caned so hard he could not sit down for hours, just for not attending Mass, even though that had been no fault of his own. Faithful to his religion, that did not mean he was blind to the streak of vindictiveness that ran through some of its purveyors. Much as he loved her, he did not want his children to suffer because of this. 'But maybe it won't come to anything,' he said comfortingly, before taking another bite of his sandwich.

'I wish I had your faith.'

Niall watched her, saying not much else until he finished his sandwich. 'Thanks for that. I was starving.' Then another thought occurred to him. 'Are you going to have to tell your employer?'

She shook her head. 'Not unless I'm forced – though I'll certainly have to warn Ma and Georgie that they might be looking at trouble.'

'At least that's one set of folk you can depend on,' he opined.

'I'd like to think so.' Though Boadicea's expression showed one could never quite be sure.

Niall sighed, and took a long pull at his pint, emptying his glass. 'Chalk me up for another one, love. I'm damned if I'm going home yet.'

* * *

Unfortunately, he had to go home some time, though his pace was retarded by a series of angry thoughts. He had put up with Nora for almost eleven months, out of respect for her dead daughter, his wife. But, understandable though her behaviour towards him might be, and beholden as he was for past kindnesses, he could not put up with this indefinitely. At some point, he must ask her to leave – after all, the mortgage was in his name, though he was the one made to feel like a lodger! Well, for a start, thought Niall, as he ambled down a terraced street that led to his own, he could refuse to be handed out pocket money from his own wage packet. Maybe that would convey to his mother-in-law that he was about to take a stand.

The week going by as usual – Nora speaking little to him, he having to collect his laundry from the Preciouses on his way home – Friday was to mark a difference. Like every other man in the neighbourhood, he had always surrendered his unopened wage packet to the female of the house. Not tonight. Tearing it open in front of her, he began to sort the notes, silver and copper coins into piles, finally handing an amount to Nora. 'There you are, that should do for your house-keeping,' he told her firmly, putting the rest into his pocket.

She flexed her masculine jaw, and glared at him. 'And what about the mortgage, and the bills?'

'I reckon I should be attending to all that.' Niall was calmly defiant.

Nora snorted. 'So you'll trust a woman you hardly know, but you won't trust me.'

'Now, be fair,' said Niall. 'I've been trusting you for years. I just think it's time I had a say in my own matters – I mean, this is my house after all.'

'Oh, *your* house, is it?' Nora scoured him with eyes of steel. 'You didn't seem to mind when me and the girls spent years cleaning it, did you? On my blasted hands and knees, and this is the thanks I get!'

'Don't bloody clean it then!' he retaliated.

'And does that extend to the children as well?' demanded Nora. 'Or the cooking? Or everything else I do for nowt?'

'I'm not having that – you've lived here rent free for years!'

'Rent free? What about the contributions our Harriet and Dolly made to the budget when they were working?'

'I'd say it was only right they paid their share – and we're not talking about them, we're talking about you!'

'Well, I'm sorry!' She was not sorry at all. 'I might not have brought any shekels in, but without me to juggle the wage packets you'd have been in a sad mess after Ellen went – as we *all* will be if you start thinking you can take over the running of the house!'

'Well, it's my house and I'll do as I like!' She was always mentioning Ellen's name, trying to make him feel guilty, and succeeding. Even so, that would not stop him. In danger of losing his temper, Niall fought to inject a note of reason. 'Look, Nora, I'm very grateful for all you've ever done, but all this hostility . . . wouldn't you be happier living with one of your lasses?'

'Huh! I know what you're after!' threw Nora. 'You want to get rid of me so's you can move your bit of skirt in.'

'Don't be so disgusting!' But she was right in a way, for with his mother-in-law here he could not even invite Boadicea to tea.

'Who'd look after Ellen's children?' Again, Nora used his dead wife to batter him. 'You needn't think I'm deserting my grandbairns!'

'You could see them whenever you like.'

'I know I can!' volleyed Nora. ''Cause I'm staying put!'

Unable to eject her bodily, Niall did not know what to do, matters growing steadily worse over the weekend. In times gone by, a trip to confession would make him feel cleansed, but not this Saturday, not for many Saturdays, for there could be no absolution for one who was intent on condemning himself to hellfire. And one look at Nora's face was to be instantly reminded of his sins. The children could not help but be aware of the atmosphere now, and obviously talked about it between themselves, though they clammed up whenever interrupted by an adult. Having decided it was best not to involve them until the argument with their grandmother could be resolved, Niall had gone alone to his meetings with Boadicea. However, even this was to require an explanation.

On Sunday morning on their way to Mass, whilst her elders were still lethargic from lack of breakfast, Juggy was her usual talkative self. 'Can we go see Bo this aft, Dad?'

There was a horrified silence, everyone glancing round at Nora, who marched behind with a determined glower. Then the little girl received a sharp dig from her thirteen-year-old sister and was told to 'Shush!'

Hanging on her father's left hand, rosary beads clutched in her right, Juggy looked up at him, her blue eyes quizzical. 'Haven't we got to talk about her?' she asked rather sadly.

'Best not,' muttered her father, but he was to pacify Juggy with a wink, as they came to the church gates.

Thenceforth, there was no chance for such discussion. The two girls went in ahead, to sit with others from their school, the younger boys remaining in their father's charge. As much as he detested his mother-in-law, Niall retained enough manners to stand aside and wait for her to catch up.

But instead of polite thanks, Nora made an irritable gesture for him to proceed. 'Don't be expecting me to rush!' And so he went in, escorting Batty and Brian ahead of him.

September warmth gave way to the chill of stone,

the smell of fried bacon from neighbouring homes to the scent of polish and candle wax, though sunshine did manage to penetrate this otherwise dim interior via a stained-glass window, a ray of it catching the gleam of polished brass and the fine carving of the rood screen. Both boys having to be lifted up by their father, Niall's sons dipped their fingers into the holy water and crossed themselves, then were handed over to their grandmother, whilst their father did the same. Then Niall led the way up the aisle, his eyes flicking to right and left, investigating each stone vestibule, Nora taking up the rear with the two boys. Dominic was already in the sacristy in his duty as altar boy.

There was only a short way to travel, for the church was not large, which was how it was quite easy for him to spot Boadicea. Positioned at the far end of a row, she was on her knees at the moment, head bent. With a generous expanse of pew directly behind her, it seemed only natural for Niall to insert himself into it. Genuflecting before the altar, he moved in behind her. His mother-in-law lipped a protest at this diversion from her usual place. Nevertheless, after bobbing in respect, Nora ushered the two boys into place, and moved along the pew herself. But when the woman in front lifted her head from prayer, and turned her face slightly, so that Nora caught her profile and saw who it was, there was even more intake of breath. You've engineered this, her eyes said to Niall.

Hearing this chuntering, Boadicea shot a furtive glance around, and immediately smiled at the sight of Niall and his children moving into position behind her. Batty grinned back, though was soon looking guilty, as his grandmother dealt him a prod with her knuckle, and directed them all to their knees. Whereupon, Boadicea turned her eyes straight ahead, allowing Niall the privacy to pray, though she was to remain acutely aware of the mother-in-law's presence, even as Mass began.

The congregation rose as the priest entered attended by the altar boys. Catching sight of his family behind Boadicea, and his grandmother's grim expression, Dominic was so busy reviewing the situation that he trod on the back of Father Finnegan's heel, causing the priest to stumble and to turn around and deliver a ferocious glare. Not until his heel had been slipped back into its shoe, could the procession continue.

Solemnity restored, there came a rustle of clothing, as the worshippers knelt *en masse*.

'*In Nomine Patris, et Filii, et Spiritus Sancti. Amen!*' chanted Father Finnegan, his singsong echoing from the stone walls. '*Introibo ad altare Dei . . .*'

Head bent, Niall crossed himself and, for the next hour or so, was to lend himself totally to prayer, occasionally shifting on his knees, or easing his buttocks on the hard pew, but dutifully uttering each response without a thought for the woman in front, confessing to Almighty God, and to the

Blessed Mary ever Virgin, and to Blessed Michael the Archangel, and to Blessed John the Baptist, and to the holy Apostles, Peter and Paul, and to all the angels and the saints, that he had sinned exceedingly in thought, word, deed, and struck his breast three times – *'mea culpa, mea culpa, mea maxima culpa!'* – and beseeching the holy ones to pray for him, and crossing himself once more, as the walls resounded again to Father Finnegan's Gregorian incantations, that they might all be granted pardon, absolution, and remission of their sins. 'Amen!'

The congregation fell silent, as the priest moved to the altar and kissed it. Then came more chanting, and responding, mainly from the altar boys, and from a few like Niall who had been an altar boy himself and knew the Latin Mass off by heart, the rest of the congregation praying in silence, and then it was time to stand for the Gospel, and then to sit for the sermon . . .

Four-year-old Brian had begun to fidget, and scrambled to kneel on the pew, staring over its wooden back at the person behind and causing them much annoyance before his grandmother deftly reached across and dragged him off. And for an age he was forced to listen to Father Finnegan ranting on, trying to whip up the congregation into contributing as much as they could, for, 'The stone work has fallen into terrible disrepair, and I know you'll want to put this right . . .'

Through all this talking, and the reciting of the creed, the congregation alternately sitting and standing, Brian continued to wriggle in boredom, at one point slipping off the pew and moving to stand behind Boadicea, tapping her on the shoulder with a grin, until yet again he was forcibly hauled back by his grandmother – much more roughly this time – as a bell sounded.

'Behave, Jesus is coming!' hissed Nora into the child's ear, at the same time nipping him to order.

'*Suscipe, sancte Pater, omnipotens aeterne Deus*,' chanted Father Finnegan, presenting the host to the altar . . .

Standing by with his little jug of wine, intrigued by what was going on behind him rather than the boring Mass, Dominic found his eyes straying once again to the pew where Boadicea sat directly in front of his grandmother. So busy was he, concentrating on this, that he almost jumped out of his skin when a chalice was thrust under his nose and shaken furiously. With a swift, repentant glance up at Father Finnegan, whose face rebuked him a second time for this dereliction of duty, he was quick to tip wine into the chalice, and after that, to keep his head down.

It was time for the offertory. Niall arched his aching back, then sat patiently to wait as the collection plate chinked its way towards him, passing from pew to pew. A faint smile played about his mouth for Boadicea, though she did not turn to see it, but sat quietly waiting as others in front dropped silver and copper onto the plate, then passed it along the row. Finally it came to her.

Being at the end of the pew, it was incumbent upon her to offer the plate – now heavy with donations – to the person behind, and for them to hand it back along their row. But as it reached her, and she was about to make her own offering, an arm shot out from behind as if to grab the plate in her stead. Guessing who it was, she reacted swiftly and held onto it, determined that the Beasty one should not win. There was a challenge in Nora's eye as she used two hands to snatch possession, her thumbs and fingers clamped firmly on the rim of the plate, but Boadicea was equally firm in her grip – hence a tug of war began, both women pulling it this way and that, each unwilling to let go – until one of them suddenly did.

Boadicea could not help a covert grin at Niall as his mother-in-law staggered backwards, the plate still in her hand but its contents hurled high above the pews, coins flying through the air, to come clattering and clinking onto the tiles and to roll beneath the pews. All heads turned – including Father Finnegan's. Amongst a great deal of hissing and clandestine tittering, Niall's children joined others who began to scramble on their hands and knees for pennies, but were soon hauled and nipped into line by their humiliated and furious grandmother.

Sharing the quiet but firm discipline of his children, Niall then pursed his lips at Boadicea to throw her a twinkling look of reproof. The money being eventually collected from the floor and returned to the plate, the service could be resumed, and to the smaller ones' discomfort there was yet to follow another episode of incomprehensible chanting, and more bells ...

'*Sanctus, Sanctus, Sanctus* ...' chanted Father Finnegan, which begat more kneeling and praying, and beseeching, and praising and crossing of breasts ... and eventually Communion of the faithful.

Niall's mother-in-law had not yet recovered from her humiliating ordeal, and kept her head down as she moved to the altar rail, to receive the body and blood of Lord Jesus Christ, with others – though not Niall, nor Boadicea neither, Nora was very quick to note. After many more words of prayer, ablutions, pleas for mercy and Hail Marys, Mass was finally over. Niall rose to join the slow exodus from church. Still angry at being made the centre of attention by his fancy woman's stupid antics, Nora was first out of her pew. She shoved the boys ahead of her, but was only able to go so far, for those nearest the door were causing an obstruction, as they lined up to share pleasantries with Father Finnegan. Allowing his irate mother-in-law to barge to the fore, Niall waited for Boadicea to reach the end of her pew, and when she did, he took her arm, unashamed of being seen with her. Honor and Juggy shared a half-worried, half-pleased smile. Then the elder girl laced her fingers through those of her sister, and, with Niall cupping a gentle hand to Honor's skull, all four of them moved slowly to the exit.

Over the tops of shorter folks' heads, Niall could see his mother-in-law's twitching impatience to be out and away, though she was to remain trapped, for Father Finnegan was spending rather longer talking to Mr Langan than most. Finally though, the priest grasped the landlord's hand, shook it, then released him, allowing the flow to resume.

By the time Niall and Boadicea got to the door, Father Finnegan's patience appeared to have worn thin, for he spared them barely a smile, though he did hold Niall's gaze as he said, 'I'll be wanting to talk to you later, Mr Doran – maybe tomorrow night, if that suits?'

'I'll be in, Father,' murmured Niall, with some misgiving, and with that he and his small party were out of the church.

'Juggy was asking whether we could see you this afternoon,' he paused in the morning sun to ask Boadicea, Nora having shot off home to prepare breakfast, dragging the boys with her. 'Maybe go to the park again?'

'That'll be grand!' She smiled down at the little girl, who grinned back, and at Honor, who gave only a tight little smile, then looked away to follow her grandmother's robust departure.

'Right, well, we'd best be off!' beamed Niall. 'The smell of that bacon's making me famished – see you later!' And to his daughters' astonishment he dealt Boadicea's cheek a kiss, before accompanying them home.

13

On Monday, when Niall arrived home for his evening meal, who should be seated at the table but his parish priest. Having hoped to enjoy his tea before the expected arrival, he was therefore peeved, not least because alongside Father Finnegan was Harriet and her husband, plus of all people, Dolly. All raised a cheery exclamation at his entry, but, knowing them to be reinforcements, Niall saw it for the ploy it was, and was not overly warm in returning their greeting as he went straight through to wash his hands.

'This is just like the old days!' claimed his mother-in-law, using an oven-cloth to place an earthenware pot of stew at the centre of the table. 'Me and my lasses back together. I've invited Father Finnegan to stop for tea with us, Niall,' she threw this casual addition, 'seeing he was good enough to come round.'

Good enough to come round, retorted Niall to himself – come early on purpose so he could get fed into the bargain.

'I fed the children earlier,' continued Nora. 'They're all out playing, so we won't be disturbed. Now, come and sit yourself here, and get that down you . . ,'

'This is nectar indeed, Mrs Beasty!' Father Finnegan gave an appreciative sniff as a plate of the Irish stew was doled out to him. A pleasant-looking man, he appeared five years younger than Niall, the hands upon the cutlery unused to manual labour, his cheeks round and smooth and retaining a boy's innocence, though the exceedingly sparse brown hair that failed to hide his scalp told that he was over forty. He was also possessed of a smile that warned any observer it would be difficult to pull the wool over this one's blue eyes; eyes that were shrewd and candid, as they levelled themselves at the man who had just sat down beside him. And there were faint traces of County Cork as he said: 'You don't know you're born, Niall! A grand cook like this at your disposal.'

'I must say, I've missed your cooking, Mam,' admitted Dolly, in agreement with the priest. 'And she does a lovely cottage pie, Father!'

'Harriet must've inherited your knack, Mrs Beasty,' contributed Peter, bumping an affectionate shoulder with his spouse.

'Well, it's nice to know you appreciate my daughter, Pete,' returned Nora.

It was all very amiable – for the duration of the meal at least – but only an idiot would not guess that all the compliments were for Niall's benefit, to make him see the error of his ways.

After the plates were cleared away, though, there was a very different tack. Instead of washing up, Nora made them each a cup of tea, then sat down again alongside her daughters and sons-in-law and the priest, and gave Father Finnegan a nod to show he had the floor.

'Care for a cigarette, Niall?' The cleric took a packet of Woodbines from the pocket of his soutane, and stuck one between his lips.

Niall shook his head. 'No, thanks, Father.'

'Anyone else?' The packet was whizzed around and shoved away so quickly that, even if they had wanted a cigarette, no one would have had a chance.

Dolly jumped to her feet and struck a match for him.

'Thank you, my dear.' Inhaling deeply, the priest narrowed his eyes against the smell of sulphur, then, through a cloud of tobacco smoke, said, 'You know this can't go on, Niall, consorting with a married wom—'

'Sorry, Father,' his victim forestalled him, 'I'm pleased enough to see you, but if you're here to give me a lecture, you'd be wasting your breath.' Niall sank half the contents of his cup in one go, not caring that the tea was too hot, just wanting to get out of here.

'I don't see it as a waste at all, Niall.' Father Finnegan spread his legs beneath the cassock, and leaned on his knees, the cigarette untouched and its smoke curling lazily to the ceiling. 'I'm here to stop you committing yourself to the fires of eternal damnation – because that's where you'll be going if you continue to dally with the likes of Mrs Dunne. Nora was concerned enough to tell me all about it.'

The surprise of hearing Boadicea's married name for the first time prevented Niall from responding for a moment.

'He says he's going to marry her when she gets divorced, Father,' Harriet butted in, yet her face was respectful.

'How can you marry her, Niall?' The priest looked dismayed. 'You know the union would be adulterous. The Church doesn't recog—'

'Recognise divorce – yes, I'm fully aware of that, Father.' Niall's mood was growing darker by the minute. 'But don't ask me to choose between Boadicea and the Church, because I don't think you'd like the answer.'

'May God forgive you,' came the reply, the priest's blue eyes, and everyone else's, condemning him.

'I love that woman!' protested Niall, glaring back at him, then looking round at all his accusers.

'You may think you do, Niall,' a grave Father Finnegan shook his balding head, 'but it's not pure love you feel, the kind a man feels for God, the kind he feels for his children. Would you truly violate the teachings of Christ, those things you've held dear since you were a little child like Brian, for the sake of carnal desire?'

Niall shot to his feet. 'I've told them and I'll tell you, there's nothing like that going on!'

'Is this why you haven't been to confession in many a week?' remarked Father Finnegan. 'Because you were fully aware that an imperfect confession would make it impossible for you to take Communion, that I would never permit you to accept the body of Christ if for one second I thought you were violating that holy Body with adulterous association?'

'There is no adultery!' maintained Niall.

'But don't you see,' Father Finnegan tried to impress upon him, 'it's what's in your heart that's just as bad, encouraging the woman to get a divorce—'

'I just want to be with her. Why is that so terrible?' pleaded Niall, his face tormented.

'You don't really need to ask, Niall.' Father Finnegan shook his head. 'Marriage is out of the question – and if you're contemplating taking this relationship further, then—'

'I'll find myself excommunicated,' snapped Niall.

'No, no!' Father Finnegan held up his hands in denial, knocking the ash from his cigarette to the rug. 'The door of the Church is always open to those who desire reconciliation, and so long as you avoid adultery then you'll be open to receive the sacraments – so will she. But you don't appear to have considered there's the woman's spiritual welfare at stake here as well. It's hardly the mark of true love to condemn her to the flames because of your selfish goings-on – though I'm minded to say she's not entirely blameless, and I shall be having a chat with her too, if ever I can catch her for five minutes.' The priest looked long and hard at Niall, satisfied that he had done his best. Noticing that the cigarette was almost burned to his fingers, he took a last drag and threw the butt into the fireplace. 'Now, I've said what I came to say.' He looked at Nora, and around at the others, then back at the subject of his lecture. 'There's all these good people here to save you from straying off the righteous path, I hope you'll not let them down. For the good of all, you'd be advised to stop your gallivanting, Niall.'

Niall adopted a deliberate air of calm then, looked the priest in the eye and included the others in his defiant response. 'Well, thank you all for your concern, but I'll gallivant where I want – and if you don't mind, Father,' he snatched his jacket from the back of a chair and shrugged it on, 'I'm about to gallivant there right now!'

He tried to walk out his anger on the way to the pub, having no wish to take it out on poor Boadicea, who seemed in for a religious lecture too. He had marched all the way there and right up to the bar before remembering what night it was.

Hovering uncertainly at the bar, still jittery with indignation, he was reluctant to make a purchase if she was not here to keep him company. Instead he apologised to Mr Langan, as the latter came to serve him. 'I feel that daft! I forgot it was Bo's night off.'

The landlord nodded, appearing subdued and slightly edgy today. 'Can I get you something?'

Immediately, Niall backed away from the bar. 'Maybe later – I've just summat to do first.'

And he went straight to the Preciouses' boarding house.

Several minutes later, he was standing in its shabby hallway, Boadicea having answered his knock, for she had been expecting him. The dog came with her to the door, but upon sniffing Niall, it ceased its yapping. However, Boadicea was to receive an even louder assault on her ears when she revealed to her visitor, before he was only halfway to the sitting room, 'I've got the sack.'

Already seething from his encounter with the priest, Niall stopped in his tracks, then exploded. '*What*?'

She gave a helpless nod. 'Father Finnegan had a word with him –'

'Oh, he's good at having words! I've just had some dished out to me!'

'Calm down, Niall. You'll get the dog barking again!'

'So what was said?' demanded Niall.

She took a breath. ''Twas when I went in for

my lunchtime shift. Apparently, pressure was brought to bear on Mr Langan, the gist of it being that if he didn't get rid of his barmaid, it *might* be taken to mean that he was condoning this immoral relationship, and the rest of Father Finnegan's congregation *might* have to be instructed not to frequent that particular hostelry.'

'The blackmailing sod!'

'You've heard what that lily-livered wretch has done then?' Ma had come into the hall to join them. 'Sacked the lass just for following her heart!' Informed all about Boadicea's shady past now, she saw no wrong in this liaison, only deep romance.

Boadicea had a more philosophical slant. 'Ah well, no one could blame the man for wanting to protect his livelihood,' she sighed.

'*I* bloody can!' A furious Niall was immediately turning tail and making for the alley.

'Give him a thick ear for me!' bawled Mrs Precious.

'Ma, don't encourage him. Niall, it'll do no good losing your rag!'

The dog yapping behind her, its claws scrambling for a hold on the lino, Boadicea tried to prevent the hothead from storming off, but his only response was: 'I'll be back!' And his stride was so urgent as it carried him towards Walmgate Bar that it was almost a run.

The saloon bar was still as quiet as when he had left it. That was a shame. Niall would have preferred there to have been witnesses to the shamefaced expression he was about to extract from the agent of Boadicea's distress.

He banged his fist down on the counter, rattling a collection of ashtrays and causing Mr Langan to take immediate notice. 'You didn't tell me you'd bloody sacked her, did you? What sort of treatment is that to show a loyal worker?'

Whilst the landlord did have the grace to look shamed, he remained firm in his decision, as he told Niall, 'I didn't want to do it, but I had no choice. Father Finnegan warned me he'd announce it at Mass that all his—'

'I *know*!' incised Niall. 'He'd tell all his parishioners to stay away from here unless you got rid of her – you bloody coward!'

'It wasn't just that!' The dour face provided solid argument. 'He said he'd sprag me to the police for staying open after hours – I'd've lost my licence! I know she's a lovely lass, but I've a business to run, I can't let sentiment ruin it . . .'

'So you threw her to the wolves! Who do you think's going to employ her now?'

'Oh, don't talk daft!' scoffed Langan. 'She's a good worker, she'll get bar work anywhere – and she doesn't have to stay round here.'

Niall's mood blackened further. 'Let herself be driven out by bigots? She might – I won't!' And with that, he picked up the nearest thing to hand, a glass ashtray, and aimed it at the mirror behind the row of optics.

'Don't you bloody d—' But the landlord's

warning fell on deaf ears, and he was forced to duck as the missile flew past him, smashing into bottles of gin, whisky and rum, glass and liquor exploding everywhere, before the perpetrator turned on his heel and stormed out.

'You bloody hooligan! I'll have the coppers on you – get back here!'

But Niall ignored the command, and, almost swinging the door off its hinges, its handle gouging a chunk of plaster from the wall as he threw it aside, he strode back to Boadicea's.

'Aw, you're a good man for trying anyhow!' On his breathless return with the news that he had failed to get her job back, Boadicea tried to soothe with the aid of grateful caresses.

'Aye, well, don't heap too much praise on me, I've probably spoiled any chance you might have had of talking him round.' Niall confessed to having broken a mirror.

'He's lucky that's all you broke!' bawled Ma, who had been hovering to hear the outcome. 'I'd have put him on crutches.'

Bo seemed more concerned about the broken mirror. 'I should hate to think you'll be getting a visit from the police.'

Niall heaved a sigh. 'Well, I suppose I'll have to pay the fine and lump it.'

'Aw!' Between them, Bo and Ma drew him into the living room, where, after relating the incident for the benefit of Georgie, and Messrs Allardyce and Yarker, Niall settled down to a more agreeable evening.

Plied with chips, bread and butter and tea by Ma, fond words and the occasional petting from Bo, by the time an hour had gone by his anger had abated. Still, fearing that he would kill Nora if he said one word to her that night, he stayed a good while longer, relaxing amongst friends, and being further salved by Georgie's love songs.

Upon going home he did not enter the living room but crept straight up to bed, not because of Nora but mindful of disturbing his boys. But the moment he laid his head alongside Brian's, the earlier events were to return with a vengeance. It was hard enough to get to sleep at the best of times, what with little boys' legs twitching and occasionally lashing out over some dream. That night was worse than ever, his mind regurgitating both upsetting episodes with the priest and the landlord over and over again until it was almost dawn.

When he rose the next day his eyes felt as if they contained a ton of grit. His mind, however, was crystal clear.

'Right, that's it, Nora.' He was casually ominous as he finished his breakfast and began to get ready for work. 'Thank you very much for the porridge, and for all you've done in the past, but when I come home tonight, I don't want to find you here.'

'You've tried that before,' she smirked.

'Well, I'm trying it again, and this time I'm

deadly serious.' His dangerous look confirmed this.

'There'll be no one in when the children come home from school!'

He buttoned his jacket, seemingly unaffected. 'Honor's old enough to manage them while I get in.'

'She doesn't get home till after four! What about Brian?'

It had slipped his mind that his eldest was at grammar school. But fortunately Brian had been going to Baby Class since the beginning of autumn term. 'Dom can see to him. They'll only be on their own for half an hour till Honor gets in.'

'And will she feed them and all – and put them to bed if you're late?' Nora stood firm. 'I warned you before, I'm not abandoning our Ellen's children!'

'You can still see them,' he told her, darkly cheerful as he stuffed the sandwiches she had made him into his haversack, and slung it on his shoulder. 'They can come to visit you every weekend.'

'And where am I supposed to go?' she demanded.

'There's half a dozen places you can live – your Harriet's, for one. She's got that big new house standing half empty at Tang Hall. You can go live with her – after all, you're *her* mother. Tell you what – I'll let her know you're coming!'

And with this he went off to do just that, no

matter that he would be late for work in taking a detour of over a mile, so as to bang on Harriet's door and warn her in rude terms. 'Your mother's coming to live with you – she'll need a hand to shift her stuff!' And, as an afterthought he cast an addition at the speechless, bleary-eyed Harriet over his shoulder, before slamming the garden gate. 'And if it's not done today, you'll find her on your doorstep tomorrow morning!'

Fully anticipating that Nora would do the same to him as she had to his brother, Sean, expecting also that when he opened the door that night it would be to a room denuded of furniture, Niall was taken aback to find everything in its place – including Nora.

'Some of us are as good as our word.' She issued this edict from her Edwardian throne. 'I told you I'll go when I'm good and ready, and not before.'

Niall's heart sank. Short of man-handling her from the building, what was he to do? As long as her grandchildren were there, so would she be. In that moment of despair, he saw that there was only one solution. He himself must move out. But, damn it, why should he? He had been born in this house, his father had struggled to buy it. All right, Harriet and Dolly's wages had gone a long way to helping him keep up with the mortgage, and Ellen had maintained – but that was no reason for him to abandon it to their old tyrant of a mother.

But devious as she was, his mother-in-law did not have a monopoly on wily behaviour, and in that second of inspiration, Niall's despair turned to glee. What he was about to do might seem a lot of upheaval, but not half as much trouble as the real thing, and it would certainly be worth it. He would make out that he was leaving, pack as many things as he could, and take the children to stay with Reilly for a day or two – there would be no need to ask; his friend would gladly put them up. Once Nora had got the message, and had seen that there was no point to her being there if her grandchildren were gone, then she would leave, and he could move back in!

'What's so funny?' Watching his expression turn from annoyance into something akin to amusement, Nora eyed him curiously.

Niall forced himself to appear sombre. 'You should be pleased,' he told her. 'You've won – if you won't move out then we'll have to.'

She looked startled. 'What? When?'

'No time like the present,' snapped Niall, and he went to drag two suitcases from the understairs cupboard, and took one of these up to his room.

Unnerved at having her bluff called, Nora went to the foot of the stairs and cocked her ear, trying to gauge what he was up to. Then, upon hearing him coming down, she scuttled back to her chair.

But Niall simply deposited the heavy suitcase in the passage, then proceeded to fill the other one with bric-a-brac – photographs of his children and parents, mementoes of Ireland, all the personal things that Nora would know meant so much more than furniture.

'You can't take them!' she objected.

'Stop me,' he challenged, still collecting things. Finally, he packed his camera into the case, then snapped it shut and upended it to stand alongside the other. 'Right! I'll just get the kids in to say good night – and you'd better not say anything destructive to them . . .' He levelled a last warning glare at her, before going to summon his children from the street.

'Where's Dom?' he asked Honor, when all but one came running.

'He's on the allotments . . .' She knew from his face that something was badly amiss.

'Well, go fetch him,' commanded her father. 'Oh, here he is!' And he called to the boy at the end of the street, 'Dom, get yourself here!'

His face apprehensive, socks round ankles, and knees scrubbed by dirt, Dominic pelted to join the others.

Niall took a deep breath. 'We're off to live with Uncle Reilly,' he told them, before they came over the threshold. 'Your granny's staying here, so run and give her a kiss before we go.'

Knowing from his tone not to ask questions, they went indoors, and, under their father's stern supervision, dutifully lined up to exchange kisses with Nora.

As stunned as she was at being outwitted, the despot's jaw was unyielding as ever, as she grasped each child by the shoulders and pressed her lips to his or her cheek in so vigorous a manner that it was more like an assault than a kiss. 'Look after yourselves,' she told them, with a grim look over Brian's shoulder at Niall. 'And don't let anybody stop you coming to see your granny.'

'That won't happen.' Niall was quick to reassure them. 'You can see each other whenever you like. Right, come on, we've got to go!' And, with a suit-case in each hand, he steered them from the house.

'Aren't we never coming back?' Batty posed a worried question to his father, once they were in the street. 'What about all me cigarette cards?'

Having previously witnessed his mother-in-law's scorched earth approach, Niall could not promise that the little boy's collection would still be there when the family was able to move back in, and so hedged around his question. 'We'll only be away for a few days.' His brow became furrowed as he tried to think of a way to tell them. 'It's hard to explain . . . your granny's going to live with Aunty Harriet . . . she just needs time to pack her things.'

Only Dominic was brave enough to broach the true reason for this exodus. 'It's because of her, isn't it? Boadicea.'

His father simply nodded. 'Sometimes, you have to choose between people, Dom . . .'

'I've got a funeral to do on Friday,' the altar boy reminded his father.

'Don't worry,' sighed an irritated Niall. 'I'll make sure you're not out of pocket.'

'I just don't want to let Father Finnegan down,' lied Dom.

His father gave him a look that said, *I know you better,* but, 'You won't have to,' he told the boy.

Nothing much else was said for a while, as the family made its way through the network of terraced streets towards Reilly's, the children become very quiet and worried.

But as they reached Walmgate, Juggy could contain herself no longer, and burst into tears.

'Eh, eh!' Niall dropped the suitcases and squatted to comfort her. 'I promise, you'll be going home again in a few days – and I'm not taking you away from your gran. You'll still see lots of her and your aunties, if that's what's worrying you!' He pulled out a grubby handkerchief, the others waiting solemnly as he dabbed at her eyes. But Juggy shook her head, to indicate it was neither of these things that concerned her.

'Then what? Aw!' He pulled the little girl into his chest and cuddled her. 'Tell your dad. You know he can fix it.'

'You can't fix this!' sobbed Juggy, her skinny body heaving.

Only after much more coaxing did she finally blurt out her awful dilemma. 'I don't want you to burn in the fires of hell, Dad!'

Niall could have sobbed himself then – but he tried to brush it off with a quip, for his other children were on the brink of tears too. 'Neither do I particularly,' he chuckled, as he held her close, 'And I don't intend to. You're worrying your head about nothing, darlin' – all of you.' He glanced up to embrace them in a reassuring smile. 'Our Lord knows what's in a man's heart. He wouldn't let a thing like that happen. Who's been filling your head with such rubbish?'

'Sister Mary Magdalene!' Juggy's face was mottled and anxious, her voice still juddering with emotion. 'She said, she always thought you were a very nice man, but you could be as nice as you like but it wouldn't save you from eternal torment for being naughty with that woman.' She gave a huge sniff, and shuddered. 'Did she mean Bo?'

Niall gritted his teeth at the thought of his little girl being so manipulated by the one who was meant to educate her. And, though years of Catholic indoctrination caused him to dread the flames of hell for such trespass as he proposed, he refused to inflict this on ones who were innocent. 'Bo's done nothing wrong,' he told Juggy and the rest of his children firmly. 'And neither have I.' This was not the time or place to explain about a man's love for a woman – they were in the middle of the street, for pity's sake – but he did go as far as to say, 'I'll be straight with you. You were right about me wanting to marry her, Dom, and that's what all this is about—'

'Doesn't Granny want you to marry her?' asked an anxious Brian.

He looked at the wide-eyed four-year-old. 'No, son, she doesn't. She's very angry with me.' Having managed to dry Juggy's tears, Niall set her on her feet and rose to flex his aching legs. 'But that doesn't mean I've done anything bad enough to go to . . . that awful place, so stop all your worrying.'

'So you haven't had your wicked way with her?' tendered the eldest boy suspiciously.

I should be so lucky, thought Niall, wanting to laugh, but to Dominic he replied with amazement. 'I certainly have not!' Then he frowned slightly. 'You know about such things, do you?'

Dominic turned red and hung his head. 'Me mate says it's what happens in adultery.'

Niall did not know whether to explode with anger or laughter. 'Look here! I don't know what people have been saying, but I promise you all that your father's not wicked in any way. You know me better than that, don't you? Now, come on, let's get to Uncle Reilly's.' He picked up the suitcases and moved his children onwards, trying to cheer their spirits as they went. 'Eh, Aunty Eileen'll be that glad to see us! She's been on at me to fetch you round for ages. I wonder where she'll put us all, though? Mebbe one of us'll have to sleep in the rabbit hutch – hope it isn't me!' And with the little ones giggling over the vision of their father crammed into a hutch, they proceeded on their way.

* * *

In another five minutes or so, they were standing outside Reilly's dank and grimy little house. Whilst their father knocked and waited, a serious-looking Dom leaned like a street loafer against the century-old bricks, brushing his palm over the coating of salt that defaced them. Immediately, Brian copied this, though went too far and used his tongue, and had to be attended by Honor's handkerchief, the rest standing obediently to wait with their father.

Eileen was indeed delighted to see them, and opened wide her door, beckoning to them all, 'Come in, come in, my little chickens! About time your dad brought you to see me!' And in they streamed, the girls presenting their cheeks for a kiss, the boys trying to dodge this, and the lot of them moving into her living room, where they quietly jostled for chairs.

'You might not be so glad when I tell you we'd like to stay for a few days,' murmured Niall, leaving his children for a second and following her to the kitchen, where she had hastened to grab a cake tin.

Momentarily startled, she soon recovered. ''Course you can! But for heaven's sake, what's driven you from your own home?'

He spent a few moments telling her the essential points of his dilemma.

'By, you dark horse!' Eileen tapped him with a grin, upon hearing about Boadicea. 'What a fancy name – is she posh? She can't be if she's dallying with you! You'll have to tell me all about her.'

'Not till the kids are in bed,' he murmured with a smile. 'Oh, they know I'm going to marry her, yes, and they've met her – but they've had enough upset for tonight.' Quickly he inserted the bit about their father burning in hell. 'So, we'll just keep the conversation light, if you don't mind?'

'You know me, love! Shallow is my middle name.' Eileen set two cups plus a row of glasses on a tray, then carried it into the sitting room where the children were making themselves at home, as they had been invited to do. 'One of you, get that florin off the mantel and nip and get two bottles of pop!' She set the tray down.

There was a brief kerfuffle amongst the children over what flavours would be bought.

'Well, you lot seem to be settling in all right!' observed Eileen, pretending to scold. 'Get one of orange and t'other of dandelion and burdock – that's your Uncle Reilly's favourite.'

'Where is himself?' enquired Niall.

'He'll be in any min— oh, speak of the devil!'

With the opening of the door came a robust figure, a large cheerful face and a look of surprise. 'My God, we've been invaded – they're moving in for the kill!' As the children converged upon him the large, unshaven man fell to his knees with a castrato yell, surrendering to their rough and tumble with great exaggeration, rolling about on the floor with the little ones climbing all over him. The antithesis of Niall, Reilly was a loud, rumbustious fellow, the sort who would show one up in public, and the type from whom Niall would normally run. But having past experienced his immense kindness, and knowing him to have his quieter moments, he was more than willing to overlook this fault.

For a time he continued to smile upon the scene, but eventually, exasperated by the din, he called a halt. 'All right, that's enough, let poor Uncle Reilly free.'

The last child to obey, Brian delivered a final harmless punch, then allowed the heavy figure to stagger to his feet.

'That's what I like about your children, Mr Doran, they're so shy.' Panting, Reilly pushed back his dark tousled hair, his face the colour of beetroot as he came to deliver a light punch of his own. 'Nah then, you old bugger!' The name was Irish, but the accent was Yorkshire. 'What're you after? Well, it must be summat – you only come when you want owt'.'

'You'll never guess,' smirked his wife, then said to the children, 'Go on, you bairns, get your pop, then you can have some cake when you get back!'

They tore off to the shop, lending the adults sufficient time for Niall to outline his tale of woe.

'Married, eh?' breathed his friend thoughtfully, at Niall's conclusion.

'Aye, but he turned out to be a bad un,' explained Niall, 'and she's going to get a divorce as soon as she traces him.' He took a deep breath, his thoughtful eyes fixed on the stain that ran around the lower half of the living room, a water-mark of previous flooding. 'Trouble is, we don't know how long that'll be . . .'

'Well, we don't mind putting you all up till then—' began Reilly.

But Niall cut him off with a laugh. 'Oh no, I didn't mean that! It should only take a couple of days for Nora to take the hint and clear out. Soon as she does, we'll be out of your way. I can't tell you how good this is of you both.'

'You stay as long as you want, son!' said the other firmly. 'Your house is my house – no sorry, I meant my house is your house. Nora's got your house, hasn't she?'

'All right, don't rub it in, you old sod,' laughed Niall.

'No, I mean it,' said his friend more sincerely, echoed by Eileen. 'Stay as long as you like. I ask but one thing.'

'What's that?' Niall knew it could not involve finance, Reilly being the most generous man he knew.

'That you fetch this lass to meet us this very night,' said Reilly. ''Cause I won't believe it till I hear it with me own lugs that somebody could really be called Boadicea!'

But Reilly was to find out later on that there truly was a woman named Boadicea, and she was every bit as lovely as his old friend Niall had described. Whilst Aunt Eileen put the children to bed – a squeeze for sure, but nothing worse than they had experienced at home – Niall went to the Preciouses' to collect his lady love, and fetch her back to his new lodgings, using the money Reilly had given him to buy some bottles of beer on the way.

Naturally, within minutes, they were getting on famously, Reilly having a similar sense of humour to Boadicea. Even so, the latter initially showed reluctance to use just his surname, saying the least she could do was append a Mister. 'I can't just call you Reilly! 'Twouldn't be right after all this hospitality you've shown Niall and myself.'

'Why not?' enquired Reilly. 'Me wife does. No respect at all. You call me what you like, blossom.'

'He's trying to avoid telling you his Christian name, love,' Eileen informed her. 'He won't let anybody use it, not even me.'

'Sure, it can't be worse than mine,' laughed Boadicea.

'Well, no, that's true,' Reilly accepted this, then kept his face straight to joke, 'But I'm obviously not as amenable to ridicule as you are.'

'Oh, that's a good one!' she parried. 'With an accent like that!'

Eileen shared her amusement. 'Aye, it is funny when you think of it: all these Irish names round here – and every accent a Yorkshire one.' Then she looked sympathetic and shook her head, 'Eh, it was a dirty trick of Father Finnegan's, making you lose your job . . .'

'Isn't it just,' agreed Niall. 'Still, I suppose I

should be grateful Mr Langan isn't the vindictive sort. If he'd been going to involve the police I would have had a visit by now. And being objective, I can see there was nowt he could do really against Father Finnegan's blackmail. Well, he needn't think I'm off to Mass on Sunday. If that's how he's going to treat a faithful Catholic . . .'

Boadicea passed him a cynical smile. 'I think you might be missing the point here, Niall – it's because I'm not a good Catholic, and neither are you.'

'Aye, well . . .' Niall gave a snort. 'I'm not off to his bloody Mass anyroad.'

'What about the kids?' Eileen asked him.

'They can still go. I don't want them getting a clattering on Monday at school because of me.'

'They can come with us,' she offered.

Niall was quick to accept this. 'Aye, thanks. If there's nobody with them Nora might kidnap them – well, why not? She's taken everything else.'

Everyone moved their heads in agreement, then fell silent for a moment.

Then Boadicea drained the last drop of stout from her glass. 'Well, I shall have to pay a visit. Is it in the yard?'

Reilly jumped up to point the way to the lavatory. 'Shall I put the outside light on?'

'No, I can see, thanks!' She disappeared.

'Stick it on anyway,' Eileen advised her husband. 'She'll be tripping over summat. Eh, the nights are drawing in now, aren't they, Nye? There's a right autumn feel to the air – soon be Christmas.'

'It's nearly four months off yet, you daft bugger!' complained Reilly, sitting down again.

'Eh, the way he talks to me!' But Eileen was used to it.

Reilly returned to the topic of Boadicea's unemployment. 'Is it bar work your lass'd be wanting again? I might be able to help.'

'Seeing as he's always in one bar or another,' vilified Eileen.

Niall laughed. 'I suppose so – but, truth be known, I think she could get any job she went for. She's that bright – not just to talk to, but on paper as well. I know because she got all these qualifications at school. She wasn't boasting, she just let it slip when we were talking about our education, as you do. So I don't know why she'd prefer being a barmaid, but if that's the sort of work she likes . . .' He shrugged, then spoke of something else that puzzled him even more. 'How anyone could leave such a lovely intelligent woman—' he broke off and smiled as the back door opened, and Boadicea returned to sit by him.

'People clam up at your entry?' Boadicea posed the question to herself. 'They must have been talking about you!' But she smiled at her audience.

'Don't worry, love,' said Reilly. 'It was all good – and I have to agree with every word he said! Actually, we were just on about finding you a job. Niall tells us you prefer bar work.'

'Ah, well, I do,' replied Boadicea, 'though it's

more a case of expediency. It lends you the opportunity to move at short notice if trouble arises. Landlords tend not to ask for references, being cute enough judges of character in their own right.'

'The last one wasn't a very good judge of character,' Niall reminded her.

She turned to him. 'He was saving his own skin, Nye. That's understandable.'

Reilly finished his piece, 'Well, any way that me and Eileen can help you, we will.'

Glad that there was someone of his close acquaintance who got on with Boadicea, later that night Niall took her home, and shared a lingering kiss before returning to partake in a cup of bedtime cocoa with his friends.

'Well, what do you think to her?' he saw no harm in asking.

'As honest as the day is long,' announced Reilly with great certainly. 'You can tell by her eyes. We were just saying, weren't we, Eileen? The pair of you are made for each other. Aye, you've found yourself a good un, Nye.' His voice was laden with approval. 'Not just a nice lass, but quite a beauty an' all – and she's fair smitten with you.'

Having been unsure, so many others against this relationship, Niall was glad of confirmation that he had not been imagining it, that Bo really did possess the same noble feelings that he had for her. His chest swelled with relief and happiness – though there was still one important hurdle to clear.

And as he dragged his weary body off to bed, he hoped that it would not be too long before Nora saw sense, so that he might repossess his home.

Alas, three nights later, Niall and his family were still living with the Reillys. Passing close to their old house every day on their way to school, the children would have liked to call in on their grandmother, but their father had forbidden it, at least for the time being.

'As soon as she's living with your Aunt Harriet, you'll be free to visit her,' he told them. For, if Nora was given the idea that she could have her cake and eat it, she would stay exactly where she was.

However, this was not to say he was unconcerned over what might be taking place in his property, and therefore he was to keep his eyes and ears open for any signal that Nora had vacated it. But even this did not prepare him for the sight of his own wardrobe on display in Walmgate, as he went home from work that Saturday afternoon. A distinctive piece, its ornamental pediment being very familiar after twenty-five years staring at it from his bed every day, he recognised it at once, and stood there gawping at it for a moment in the dealer's window, before going inside – only to spot many more items of his furniture within, including his personal armchair. He tried to tell the new owner that they had not been Mrs Beasty's to sell, but this was to hold no sway, and he was forced to leave.

'That's why she's taken so long to shift!' he damned Nora to his hosts, upon his indignant arrival home. 'She's been biding her time, getting rid of all my stuff!'

Reilly sympathised; his wife too. 'But look on the bright side,' soothed Eileen, 'if most of your furniture was there, it must be a sign that she's finally gone.'

'That's true. Right, I'm off to have a look.' But it was not an encouraging task, and Niall betrayed nerves as he steeled himself to go.

'Do you want me to come with you?' Reilly offered.

'No, it's all right,' murmured Niall. 'Just keep the kids from following me.' They were playing out in the street with some new friends. 'I don't know what I'm going to find.'

It was worse than he could have imagined. Everything of value had gone, but so too had the faded curtains, which could be of no use to anyone. Even the lino had been removed. That which Nora had been unable to sell, and which she did not require herself, lay smashed upon the floor – old crockery and pictures, not one item undamaged. Apart from the rubbish littering its floor, the place was entirely empty. She had even taken the children's beds and their few toys. How could the spiteful old witch deprive her own grandchildren?

Left with not even a sweeping brush, and knowing that any request to Mrs Lavelle would receive short shrift, Niall used his boot to scrape the shards of pottery and glass into as tidy a pile as he could. His friends would help him do it properly later on.

Then, with a sigh, he stood to think. How could he bring his children back here when there was not a stick to sit upon? And yet, and yet . . . even in her evil deed, his mother-in-law might just have done him a favour, thought Niall. For, standing in that living room, its awful monstrosity removed – not just Nora, but her colossal sideboard – he felt it could have been a brand-new house, the light flooding in and reaching all corners of the room, making it look much larger, more welcoming than it had ever felt in Nora's presence. Moreover, he had got his front parlour back. All right, it would take a lot of money to replace the furniture, and yes it had been an awful assault, but it was not the end of the world. Now he could begin his new life.

Going to collect Boadicea, Niall took her first to see his empty house, and then to have a cup of tea and a very late lunch with the Reillys. Over sandwiches, there was to be much discussion about what might be done. Naturally, he and his family would have to stay here a while longer, but Reilly and Eileen refused to be fazed by this.

'We've told you, stay as long as you want,' said Eileen. 'You can't go back till you've got some furniture.'

It would be impossible to buy back his own from the dealer, for that would require a large outlay of cash, which Niall did not have. The only way forward seemed to be hire purchase. 'I wish I hadn't ripped out that old Yorkshire range now,' he sighed. 'At least we'd have something to cook on.' Nora had even removed the gas oven.

'You can get a gorgeous seven-piece suite at Jay's for a few bob a week.' Eileen turned dreamy, having coveted the items on display.

Reilly issued a confidence to his friend. 'She's not very good at cookery,' he said in a loud whisper, before turning to his wife and mouthing cheerfully as if to an imbecile, 'This might come as a surprise, but you can't fry an egg on a seven-piece suite, love.' He procured the laugh he desired, though suffered a slap from his wife.

'It'll still be a tight old squeeze on top of the mortgage,' worried Niall. 'It's the bed situation mainly – for the kids, I mean.'

'You can have our spare bed,' offered Reilly immediately. 'Till you can afford some of your own, anyroad.'

Niall looked grateful. 'Nay, we'll manage somehow.' Then he smiled at Boadicea, who was sitting next to him on the sofa, and took hold of her hand. 'The main thing is, I've got my house back. Now we can get other things cracking.' He squeezed her fingers. 'Have you had any luck with a solicitor, by the way?' He was not speaking out of line, for she had been open in discussing this with Reilly and Eileen.

She brightened. 'Oh yes! Today, as it happens, I've found a good chap. Well, he seemed nice enough, but then we'll only find out if he's competent when he gets the results. Anyway, he's begun a search.'

Niall's face broke into a wide grin. 'Ooh, that's got me all enthusiastic. Tell you what, shall we go into town and have a look at that furniture Eileen was on about? I'm not promising to buy it, mind, only to look!'

Boadicea jumped up in readiness. 'Why not? I've enough time on my hands.'

'Don't worry, love,' he comforted. 'You'll soon get another job.'

She did not seem too concerned. 'Maybe sooner than we both thought. Mr Yarker says they were run off their feet in the Five Lions last night, so he's going to put in a word for me. Right, then, let's be off. Shall we take the kids?'

'You are joking! You thought it was bad enough keeping them in line at the park – oh, that reminds me, I'll have to pick up my photos from the chemist.'

Boadicea was only half listening to him, her interest lured by Reilly and Eileen, between whom there had been a whole lot of whispering. 'What are you two plotting?'

Breaking away from his wife, Reilly stood and hoisted the leather belt of his trousers, as if about to make an important announcement. His voice was rather grave. 'Now I'm gonna say summat, I'll only make the offer once, so be careful how you reply. Me and the missus, we've got a bit of money put by, about five pounds or so, and we want you to use it to get yourselves back on your feet – don't interrupt! I said I was only going to say this once,' he rebuked Niall. Then he went to fetch a tin, one that seemed heavy and which rattled as he took it from its hiding place, indicating that it held the cash to which he was referring. 'Now then, take heed. You can pay me back when you can – I don't care when that is,' he cut short another protest, 'I'm only putting it by for my funeral.' He cocked his head as if thinking about this, then added drily, 'Mindst, if I die tomorrow and you've got the cash for this grand coffin I'm planning, I'll be spitting mad.'

Everyone laughed loudly, including Niall, who, knowing better than to offend, accepted the heavy tin, offering in return his deepest thanks. Turning to Boadicea he said, 'See, that's what I mean about a friend.'

'Has he been cracking on we're friends?' Reilly projected false astonishment. 'Nay, I hardly know him. I'll be expecting interest on that! Don't be laughing, I'm serious,' he warned them, whilst they continued to chuckle. 'Let's see, there's five pounds in there,' he pretended to tot up the figures in his head, 'at fifteen per cent that's—'

'Behave!' Eileen punched him, saying to the beneficiaries, 'Eh, he doesn't half go on.'

Transferring some of the money to his pocket, Niall handed the tin back for safekeeping, then tried to reiterate his deep gratitude. 'I've got an insurance policy that'll mature soon; I can pay you back then . . .' but this was again brushed aside by Reilly.

'Whenever you can . . . Now, I thought you two were off to town?' A large hand upon each back, he pushed them towards the door, Eileen opening it for them.

Even as he made his exit, Niall was still trying to thank his benefactors. 'We'll pay you back as soon as we ca—'

Reilly held up his palm. 'We trust you!'

Niall turned to Boadicea with a wink. 'Now about that Caribbean cruise . . .'

It was unfortunate that they were still laughing as they emerged into the street, for just at that moment, who should come towards them but Harriet.

Niall could tell from her face that this was no accidental passing, for she left the animated group of nephews and nieces to whom she had been talking, and now headed straight for him.

Swiftly, he put himself in front of Boadicea, to prevent an assault on her.

'Oh, don't worry!' The boxlike face was mocking. 'I just came to give you this!' And she thrust a key into his hand. 'Me poor mother won't need it, now she's living with people who care about her. I could've thrown it in the river, but I suppose your fancy woman might as well have it.'

'You didn't just come out of your way to give me this.' Niall fingered the key, wary of any quick movement, wishing his children were not there, and signalling for them to come in.

'No, you're right I didn't!' Harriet seemed to have no care for his offspring's sensitivities, as they filed past their father and into the house. 'I came to tell you what a pig you are!'

'I'm not the one who deprives children of their toys and beds,' shot Niall.

'We haven't deprived them!' retorted Harriet. 'Everything's been stored at my house, ready for when they come. I've just been telling them—'

'Well, thank you very much, and now you can go,' said Niall.

'Not before I let this one know her days at that house are numbered!' Harriet jabbed a finger at Boadicea. ''Cause nobody round there'll talk to you after what you did to me mam; they won't even give you the time of day!'

'We'll take our chances,' Niall finished quietly.

'Well, don't think this is over,' yelled Harriet, retreating. 'We're not going to forget what you've done to our family.'

14

Harriet might as well have thrown the key in the river, for Niall was falling for none of her pretence. 'The minute we move back in,' he told Boadicea, 'they'll be round and chopping up all my new furniture. No, I'm having the locks changed!' And he had, before installing so much as a stick.

'She's right about you having a key, though,' he added, five days later, when the house had been put to order – which had taken a great deal of work between the pair of them, and Eileen and Reilly – and all the furniture had arrived, some new, some second-hand, along with a gas oven, allowing him finally to move in. Boadicea had kindly supervised this whilst he was at work. 'Yes, I know you're not living here,' he pre-empted her objection, 'but you're going to be giving me a hand with the kids, aren't you?' Whilst still unemployed, she had promised to be there every day to provide a meal when his children came home from school. 'So you'll need one to let yourself in.'

'Your neighbours'll think I've moved in!' she offered slight objection.

He laughed. 'Bo, how can it get any worse? They're already not talking to us – *about* us, maybe.' The only ones who still gave him the time of day were old Mrs Powers and Mrs Whelan, most of the others in the street being Nora's cronies. He studied her. 'You're not really that bothered about what they think, are you – 'cause I can move?'

'No, I couldn't care less.' She shook her head, trying to display nonchalance, but felt less than enthusiastic about the hostile neighbours.

'Good, so you can have a key. I'm never leaving this door open again.'

This in mind, he gave the children a serious talking-to. 'And you're not to let anyone in here, not even your granny – yes, you *can* go and see her!' He forestalled the question they were obviously bursting to ask.

'When?' asked Honor. They had not even seen their grandmother at church, for she attended a different one now.

'Just let's get sorted out, and get the weekend out of the way and you can go any time you like, as long as you let me know first. But we have to stick to some sort of routine, 'cause I can't be worrying about what you're up to when I'm at work. Now then, this is what'll happen.' He had already outlined the rota, but did so again just to reassure them. 'I'm going to get your breakfasts, then Aunty Eileen'll be coming round to see you off to school, and she'll be here to give you your dinner, and to see if you need owt. Then Bo is going to make our tea.'

'What's your favourite meal?' Boadicea asked instantly, speaking to Niall mainly.

'Roast beef and Yorkshire pud,' he declared.

'Ye would say that!' she remonstrated with a tap. 'Why couldn't it have been Irish stew? I can cook that. And here's me taking you for a man that loves all things Irish.'

'Well, some of them I do.' His eyes twinkled with affection for her. 'But if you can't do roast beef . . .' he sucked in his breath and shook his head, teasing her, to the fascination of his children, 'I think we'll have to have a change of chef.'

'Sure, the beef's no problem! 'Tis those blessed Yorkshire puddings I've no idea about. Does this mean you'll not be taking up my kind offer of assistance?'

He pretended to think deeply about this. 'Well, maybe through the week – but not on Sundays.' Then he chuckled. 'No, I'm only having you on. Whatever you do will be great.'

The children seemed not to share his sentiment. For Boadicea's first attempt at providing for them was to cause much suspicion.

'Eugh,' frowned Batty, home from school and going straight to the table to peer under the muslin cloth that was covering a bowl.

In the middle of doing something else, she rounded on him, though her scolding was mild. 'Don't say it like that – as if you've found snot on your sleeve!'

Most of the children fell about laughing; even Honor dropped her air of reserve.

'Don't ye like boxty?' they were asked, to which came murmurs of affirmation.

'Well, that's what it looks like raw,' Boadicea told them. 'But you're going to have to wait till your father comes in to eat it.'

'Aw, do we have to?' moaned Dominic, leaning heavily on the table, and propping up his chin with a filthy hand. 'I'm ravished.'

'I think you mean famished,' corrected Boadicea, catching a handful of Brian's jumper as he clambered onto a chair. She turned to the eldest, who had reverted to her quiet state, not wanting her to feel excluded. 'Will your father mind if we don't wait for him, do you think?'

Honor shook her head. 'Me gran usually feeds us beforehand, so me dad can eat in peace.'

Boadicea gave a decisive nod. 'Then, I'd better make them now, hadn't I?'

Whilst the elder children refused to allow their pleasure free rein, still not wholly comfortable with this situation between their father and this woman, the younger ones displayed an eagerness to sample her cooking.

Juggy formed a look of eager anticipation at her siblings, rubbing her hands to emphasise her delight, and grinning at the cook. 'Me Aunty Beesy makes boxty!'

Boadicea dealt her a smile. 'Well, I'm not promising to do as good a job as herself, but I'll give it a try.' Under the critical eyes of onlookers, she placed a recently purchased frying pan on one of the rings of the gas stove, then melted some butter in it, and let in sizzle for a while, before ladling in dollops of the mixture, a wonderful smell of fried onion and potato soon beginning to tweak their nostrils.

By the time the pancakes were cooked, and sprinkled with sugar and more melted butter, their mouths were watering, and they could hardly contain themselves, digging in with their forks and puffing and blowing to avoid burning their mouths.

'Mm, not bad,' Batty permitted grudgingly, once he had taken his fill.

'Oh well, I'm glad you like it!' the cook thanked him sourly, but smiled to herself at having cleared another hurdle.

And when Niall came home, he was pleased to find such a happy household. 'Well, I'm thrilled to see the house hasn't burned down,' he announced.

'You cheeky article! Are you commenting on my cooking again?'

'No!' He laughed. 'But it's Friday the thirteenth, I felt summat must go wrong.'

'No, something's gone right for a change,' she

contradicted. 'Mind you, I can't vouch that it'll be the same on Sunday.'

She was to be right, for her Yorkshire puddings turned out like biscuits. With Eileen and Reilly invited to lunch after taking the children to church, Boadicea gave a groan of frustration. 'Sure, I followed Ma Precious's recipe to the letter!'

'Is this the same Ma Precious as cracks on she does all the cooking, when actually it's Georgie?' Fork in hand, Niall was trying his best to help by mashing the potatoes, his sinewy wrists working the mash manfully round the saucepan.

'But there's hardly any ingredients!' railed Boadicea. 'How can it be so difficult? What's the blessed secret?'

'Hang on.' He stopped mashing and beheld her with a mocking eye. 'I'll just go to Tang Hall and ask Nora – how the hell would I know?' He laughed. 'The only thing I can cook is a cup of tea. Well, maybe a bit of toast. Don't worry about it, Reilly won't mind.'

Reilly did not mind, upon hearing from his hostess the very moment he entered that the meal was hardly fit to eat; nor did his wife, the latter seeking to offer kind instruction.

'I bet you used self-raising flour, didn't you?' she asked Boadicea.

'Sure, how else would I make them rise?'

'Half the knack is to let the mixture stand for half an hour,' revealed Eileen.

'And what's the other half?'

'You have to hold your gob like that when you're mixing it.' Reilly's big friendly face contorted its mouth to one side. 'But never mind!' He sat down with the others to consume the flat Yorkshire puddings along with the rest. 'You won't have to cook for us next Sunday. LNER are doing a Sunday excursion to Scarborough. We thought we might take the kids for a tri—' He affected to be knocked sideways by the cries that greeted this announcement. 'Steady on! You nearly blew me out of me chair!'

'Well, we thought it'd give you two a bit of peace,' Eileen explained to Niall. 'God knows you deserve it after all you've been through.' Her eyes moved to the frameless photograph of Boadicea on the mantelpiece, which Niall had leaned there. 'You're beginning to curl up, Bo.'

All heads turned automatically to look at it. 'Better curled up than ripped up,' murmured Niall, between mouthfuls. 'Lucky it was in my pocket when the vandals did their dirty work. I shall have to get a frame for it.'

Eileen's fork paused mid-air, dripping gravy. 'Maybe we've got one . . .' she began.

'Why don't you just back the furniture van up to our house?' joked her husband vigorously. 'Aren't we doing enough for them in taking this blasted lot to Scarborough?'

Knowing him for a jester, the children merely grinned.

'Don't you listen to him, love,' Eileen instructed Niall and Boadicea, as she resumed her meal. 'Get your feet up, the pair of you, and enjoy your bit of peace while you can.'

By the following Sunday, though, Boadicea had found herself more bar work, so disappointingly, Niall was left on his own for much of the day. However, he arranged to have his dinner at the Preciouses; Ma would be saving a plateful for Boadicea after her stint ended at half-past two, so Niall had said he would keep her company. But, for this morning, after Reilly and Eileen had taken the children, straight from early Mass to Scarborough, he preferred to go back to bed with the papers and a bacon sandwich, and be thoroughly idle for once. Oh, but it was bliss!

Inopportunely, this peace was to be interrupted towards midday by a sharp rap at the door. Though Niall was up and about by then, he was loath to answer the knock, interpreting its delivery as another hostile intrusion – for no friend would knock like that. Going to the window, he peered out, then groaned. There, outside his door, were Nora and Harriet in their Sunday best. He ducked back out of sight, but too late.

Catching the movement, Harriet said to her mother, 'He's in – knock again, Mam!'

Is there no escape from that bloody family? thought Niall, going reluctantly to the door, and beholding the pair with weary disdain. 'Forgot to take the whitewash off the walls, did you?'

'I've come to see my grandchildren!' Nora set a confident foot over the threshold, but Niall barred her way.

'They're not here!' Without use of arms, he eased her corseted body out.

'I don't believe you! You're trying to keep them from seeing me!' Nora tried to get in again, but to similar effect.

'I'm stopping nobody from seeing anybody!' said Niall, his palm still aloft. 'They've gone to the seaside with Reilly. The only reason they haven't been to visit you yet is because it's taken us a while to get settled in, and they've got their grandma to blame for that.'

Having heard the altercation, Gloria's face appeared round her own door.

Nora immediately enlisted her help. 'He says the children aren't here! Have you seen them go out?'

As usual Gloria did not have time to answer, Mrs Lavelle bustling importantly to say, 'Hello, Mrs Beasty! Yes, it's right what he says, they went out early this morning with that friend of his.'

Nora and Harriet were momentarily thwarted. Then the senior demanded, 'And has he got that other one in there?'

Niall had barely time to voice his indignation when Mrs Lavelle replied, 'No, the last time we saw her was at five o'clock yesterday afternoon – would that be right, Gloria?'

To Niall's growing outrage, the middle-aged daughter scuttled off briefly, and returned with a crumpled piece of paper, which was consulted. 'Yes, that's right, Mam. She was here a couple of hours.'

'And have you written in your dossier how many time she visited the lav? You bloody cheeky – I can't believe this!' Niall was still stuttering his resentment, when another figure joined the gathering, the appearance of Father Finnegan causing him even further dismay. 'Oh, for pity's sake . . .'

'Good day to you, Mrs Beasty, Harriet, Mrs Lavelle, Gloria . . .' The priest nodded his balding head along the row, finally reaching the occupier. 'It's yourself I've come to see, Niall, but I'm glad I found you all together.' For the moment he digressed: 'And how are you going on at St Aelred's, Nora? It's been strange not seeing you at Mass.' But at this point he turned back to an angry Niall. 'I was hoping to see you there, Niall. It's been a week or two . . .'

'Well, we all know why that is, Father.' Niall remained dark.

'And that's what I've come to see you about,' announced Father Finnegan. 'Can we go indoors?' He made as if to enter, Nora and Harriet to follow.

But their way was barred by a stiff-sounding occupant. 'No disrespect, Father, but I don't want any of you in here.'

Father Finnegan's expression turned impatient. 'As you will, Niall, but if only you'd told me at the beginning we could have avoided all this unpleasantness! I must say, I'm very surprised neither of you said a word, and I'll be taking this further with Miss Merrifield—'

Sensing danger, Niall held up a hand to prevent any indiscretion, for his mother-in-law and Harriet were hovering like vultures, their eyes sparkling with greed, ready to pounce on any rancid bit of gossip. Mrs Lavelle and Gloria were still present too, and to them he announced in brittle manner, 'Thank you, you've made your report. You can go in now!'

But his admonition had little effect, and he was forced to tell Father Finnegan, 'Whatever it is, I've no wish to hear it!'

The priest was terse. 'I'd have thought you'd be glad of any opportunity to put the record straight. It must be devilish hard to be shunned by your neighbours and family, and to no good purpose—'

Nora could not help an indignant exclamation here. 'I beg your pardon, Father! But we've every right to shun him!' The three other women reinforced this with nods.

'Well, I'll grant you, Nora,' Father Finnegan pressed her arm, 'you've every right to be upset that he's wanting to marry another woman so soon after poor Ellen. But the situation is altogether different when that woman is not as she was painted. It's rather ironic that it was at your insistence I made further investigation—'

'Are you *still* trying to dig up dirt?' Niall's face was etched in a deep scowl now, as he turned on his mother-in-law.

'I wouldn't have to dig if it was on the surface, would I? And there wouldn't be any to dig if she was all you say she is!'

'Please, Mrs Beasty,' said the priest, with faint disgust, 'a person is entitled to their privacy. However, as you were the one to instigate matters, it's only right that you should be made aware that, through my various contacts, I made a significant discovery. It appears,' he told the astonished listeners, 'that she isn't married after all.'

Niall's mother-in-law begged to differ. 'I'm sure she is, Father. My relative was quite—'

The priest stopped her by the mere use of his eyebrows. 'What I mean to say is, there was never any marriage – it was annulled.'

In all her machinations, Nora could never have hoped for this! For it was obvious from Niall's face that it was just as much a revelation to him.

'Didn't I tell you there was more to that one than met the eye?' Sharing this news with an astonished Mrs Lavelle and daughter, Nora and Harriet were jubilant.

Presented with Niall's shock, and others who seemed to delight in it, Father Finnegan became stern. 'Yes, well, I don't think you've anything to be proud of, Mrs Beasty. It was because of you I was grossly misled into chastising Niall when he spoke the truth. There is nothing at all wrong about his friendship with Miss Merrifield.'

'There is if they're living over the brush!' persisted Nora.

'You'll try anything, won't you?' The rate of Niall's pulse was fit to deliver a stroke; he could almost hear the blood gushing round and round his brain. Why had Boadicea not revealed the news that would allow them to wed – for surely one person in a marriage could not have it annulled without the other being aware of it? But he trained his frustration on Nora in lieu. 'You can ask your spies here. They'll tell you that Boadicea has never slept under this roof!'

Under the strict eye of their priest, Mrs Lavelle and Gloria were reluctantly forced to concede, 'Well, that's true, Father.'

But Nora hadn't finished. 'Slept, no – but there's a lot of other things she could've done, the mucky trollop!'

'That's enough, Mrs Beasty!' Pre-empting a furious response from Niall who looked dangerously close to losing his temper, Father Finnegan took the sturdy shoulders and firmly turned her around. 'Harriet, I think you'd better take your mother home before she says anything she might regret! Mrs Lavelle, Gloria, inside with you all now.'

The latter two complied, but, bitterly complaining, Nora refused to leave the scene. 'Look at him, Hat! That's taken him down a peg or two, hasn't it? It's obvious he knew nowt about this neither!'

Too stunned to deny his ignorance, Niall defended the woman he loved. 'It can't be the same person.' But his explanation sounded foolish.

'Not the same person – with a name like that?' the iron jaw scoffed. 'There's no mistake. I told you she was taking you for a mug!'

Father Finnegan's youthful face projected sympathy at Niall. 'Is it true? That this is as much of a shock to you as it was to them?'

Niall blustered. 'It wasn't up to me to tell anybody Boadicea's business! Even you, Father. I'm sorry if you were misinformed.'

'Well, I'm sorry too, Niall, that you and Miss Merrifield had to put up with all that unnecessary mess – but it was of her own making. It's a great shame that she had to lose her job—'

'She didn't lose it, she had it taken away!' an angry Niall reminded him.

'Well, that's as maybe, but sure, it'll give her the chance to find work more befitting her sex.' Father Finnegan projected slight remorse. 'If only she'd told me before—'

'Yes!' Another broadside of spite came from Nora. 'And what was her reason for having him believe she's still married?'

To Niall it could mean only one thing: Boadicea had said it because she did not really want to marry him. But devastating and perplexing though this might be, he continued to uphold his defiant façade in Nora's presence. 'I think the shame of having her marriage annulled might be a good enough reason.'

'But *why* was it annulled?' volleyed his mother-in-law.

'I told you before, he deserted her. Now will you please *leave* me alone!'

Hearing the desperation in Niall's voice, the priest used his body to steer Nora and Harriet away. 'A decree of nullity is a highly unusual situation,' he told them. 'I've never had one granted to a parishioner in all my years in the cloth. But if this has been sanctioned by Rome, then who are we to argue? Come away now, ladies, we'll let the poor man be – but I just want you to know, Niall,' he turned to deliver a comforting tap on his arm, 'that I'm here should you need to discuss things, as you probably will after you've spoken to the young woman herself. And there's an end to it!' he warned Nora and Harriet sternly, as he managed to remove them and himself from Niall's presence.

Nevertheless, this was not an end to it for Niall. Totally confounded, his heart racing, he shut the door, then leaned against it for a good many minutes, wondering why on earth Boadicea had not told him. And the more he thought about this, the more he saw that she could not allege ignorance. For if the Church had granted an annulment, that must surely mean she had also obtained a divorce in the civil courts! So, her claim of still been married was a downright lie.

Desperate to hear the truth, yet afraid of what it might be, he launched himself from the door to wash and to shave, which would lend him more time to ponder on this.

But still, after he had scraped off his whiskers and had wiped away the remaining lather, and the beads of blood that trickled throughout, he could not tear his stricken eyes from that equally stricken reflection. Nor had he been able to think of what to say when he was face to face with the one responsible.

It turned out that he could not bring himself to say anything, at least not while they were having dinner – of which he ate hardly a morsel – he and Boadicea sitting in silence in the dining room, the rest of the boarders having eaten earlier.

'Was it too dried up for you?' boomed Mrs Precious, upon witnessing his unfinished meal scraped onto the dog's plate.

'No, it were lovely, thanks.' Niall sounded subdued. 'I just don't seem to have an appetite . . .'

Mrs Precious immediately slapped a hand to his forehead, almost knocking him backwards as she tested his temperature. 'Well, that's as cool as our Rusty's nose, so you're not sickening for anything! Better sit down, though. You're a bit pale.'

'It's too nice to sit inside.' Boadicea sounded cheerful. 'We're off to enjoy the last of the good weather; the fresh air will do him good. Is it the park, Nye?'

'I thought we'd just have a stroll on Low Moor,' he put forward. In such wide open space there would be few to interrupt them.

'Good, somewhere new – the moor it is!' Happy with his decision, Boadicea went to change her shoes.

Then off they went, sauntering along Walmgate in the direction of the limestone barbican. Long before reaching it, though, they cut down a side street and passed beneath Fishergate Bar instead, then through the deserted cattle market. At the crossroads, they were forced to wait for a regiment of soldiers marching from their barracks at Fulford to another at Strensall. Then they continued straight across, finally to embark on a road lined on one side with bay-windowed Victorian villas and neat front gardens, and smaller versions on the other, with shops at regular intervals. With a hundred yards still to go before they reached their destination, Boadicea chattered away about her shift in the Five Lions, its landlord, and the people who frequented it, Niall simply nodding and donating the odd question. But there was little unusual in this, and she was not to guess for a while that something dreadful had occurred.

The road was very quiet, only one car driving past, followed by a hay cart. The pavement gradually rose beneath their strolling feet. Finally reaching some allotments, Niall led her across the road towards a five-barred gate. It was impossible to see the full expanse of Low Moor from here, its entrance situated between the grounds of a private asylum and a cottage, and more like a farm track at present. Steering his companion through the gate, he shut it again with a clatter.

'Not much of a moor,' laughed Boadicea, taking his arm and pressing herself close, so that they might continue to walk side by side along this narrow stretch of hardened earth bordered by nettles and docken and the scent of forest greenery. Even beyond the gate, the true size of the moor remained hidden, at this point no more than fifty feet of grass to their right and only six to their left.

Flanked by a hedge on one side, and a high wall on the other, Niall undertook the slight gradient, pointing to a crest that was some yards ahead, and murmuring an explanation to her. 'It'll widen out when we get to there.'

And so it did, the breeze hitting their faces as they came over the hill, and seventy-seven acres of moorland sloping downwards into the distance, though for now, with the wall continuing alongside, and a small forest of mature trees growing from the other side of it, the way ahead was to retain its oblong shape, a natural corridor. There were trees on this side too, a dense collection of ancient oak, ash, elm, beech and horse chestnut that marked the path all the way into the distance, some with trunks as thick as dinosaur limbs, the sound of the wind rustling their leaves invading Niall's already confused mind with a noise like rushing water. He had chosen the moor so there would be little danger of interruption, but it was hard to know how to begin, when about to call someone a liar.

The shape of the moor altered course slightly as they came upon a series of allotment gardens, marked by rickety fencing. For now, the herd of cows that grazed upon the common land were right across the far side out of view, and would pose no problem, other than leaving behind a series of crusty, fly-laden pancakes.

Releasing her tight hold on his arm for a second, Boadicea tiptoed daintily around yet another mound in her path, stumbling through a patch of rough tussocks, before eventually linking up with him again to laugh. 'Ye should've warned me – I'd have brought my galoshes!'

Then on they strolled down the damp grassland path, squadrons of crane flies rising before them, the whirr of their wings audible in the quiet of the afternoon, rising and settling time after time, long legs a-dangle. One chose to hang from Boadicea's fringe, the rest of its ungainly limbs suspended over her nose and obscuring her vision. With a shriek she brushed it away, shivered in disgust, then laughed at herself and at her escort. But he barely cracked a smile.

'Is that the cemetery behind those gardens?' She gestured at the allotments, beyond which the tip of a large monument could be seen.

He nodded.

'You're very quiet today,' she eventually said.

'I'm always quiet.' He cursed himself for not seizing this chance. But he was to be granted another.

'Aye, but not usually as quiet as those fellas in there!' Again Boadicea gestured at the cemetery. Then, when he failed to laugh, she examined his face with a look of slight concern.

This was his opening. He wasted no further time in asking, 'Is it true your marriage was annulled?'

Though his attitude was in no way accusing, she looked as if he had hit her, and stopped dead, not responding for a few moments; when she did, her eyes held the look of defeat, and her tone was dull. 'So, your spies finally caught me, did they?'

'They're not my spies!' Niall came to a dead halt too. 'I'd never stoop—' Remembering his part in Sean's downfall, he reddened and shook his head vigorously as if to clear his thoughts. 'They're Nora's spies – and it wasn't her, but Father Finnegan who told me. But never mind all that! What I'd like to know is *why*?' His face and voice were anguished. 'Why did you lie to me, Bo?'

'Would you want to admit it?' At the change in his expression, she gave a terse knowing movement of her head. 'No, you wouldn't. You'd want to keep it damn quiet. You've no idea what I suffered, Nye.' She began to walk on down the slope.

He strode after her, and caught at her arm. 'But

you've let me go through all this – not to mention putting yourself through it. You said he'd left you—'

'He did!' Boadicea stopped again and spread her hands beseechingly.

'—that you didn't know where he is!'

'I don't! I haven't seen him for years.'

Niall frowned. 'Years . . . so how long ago did all this happen? You've never really told me and I've never asked but, well, I wouldn't mind knowing what's bloody going on!'

'I'm sorry, I'm sorry you had to find out like this. I should've told you – I wanted to . . .' Her repentance seemed genuine, for she stroked his arm pleadingly. 'But I was scared that telling you would ruin our lovely friendship.'

'*Friendship?*' Niall sounded amazed, and insulted. 'I think it's a bit more than that! At least it was to me.'

'And me too!' she cried with conviction. 'This is the first time I've got close to a man in years . . .' Her voice trailed away, but seeing that he was waiting for an answer, she gave an exaggerated sigh. 'All right, ye want hard details: it was over here that I met and married Eddie—'

'Well, obviously! They're not going to grant you a divorce in Ireland, are they?'

She closed her eyes against the hurt, before continuing. 'I was eighteen, he was twelve years older. Eighteen months later, he left me. After that I never saw him again. So I was telling the truth, Niall, when I said I've no idea where he is now.'

'Well, you might have been!' He did not sound convinced. 'But when we first met I asked you a straight—'

'You asked me if I'd ever marry again and I answered truthfully – I won't! No matter that I might desperately want to!' Her eyes tried to convey the battle that was going on inside, feelings that she could not possibly explain. But her attempt was not good enough for Niall.

His face had suddenly turned cold, his attitude slightly contemptuous. 'So, it was just to keep me from pestering you that you said you weren't free, that you made up all this cock-and-bull about a solicitor?'

'It was easier than turning you down!' she objected. 'You just kept pushing and pushing – I never meant to hurt ye, Nye.'

'Well, you *have*!' His enraged shout pierced the quietude, startling a blackbird, which flew with a *dic-dic-dickery-ickery-ickery-ickery* cry of alarm to a far-off tree.

'Oh, don't! Don't be angry with me.' Tears welling, Boadicea grasped both his arms, dragging on them and looking pleadingly into his face, trying to make him embrace her.

And eventually, after glaring at her for what seemed like hours, he did pull her to him, but there was a residue of anger in the bear hug, and accusation in his voice. 'All right, I did keep pushing – but you knew how I felt about you!'

'And you knew how I felt about marriage!' She lifted her face to protest. 'But you wouldn't let it go. Would you have preferred it if I'd kept turning down your proposals?'

He shoved her from him again, holding her at arm's length, his voice angry and confused. 'See, *that*'s what I can't understand! Why you'd even want to turn me down, knowing how much I want you. I'd never desert you like he did . . . I love you.' This was the first time he had declared it, and it had taken anger to draw it forth.

Far from being encouraged, Boadicea seemed to be in turmoil. 'I know . . .'

'Is that all you can say?'

She was crying silently now, the tears trickling down her cheeks. But it appeared that the words had to be dragged out of her, her face contorted with anguish. 'I think the world of you too. I'd like nothing better than to be able to marry you –' at the brief spark of optimism on his face, she rushed to moderate it – 'but this changes everything, doesn't it?'

When he failed to answer, she withdrew her gaze, allowing it to drift beyond his shoulder. The wall was lower here and topped by iron rails through which could be seen the tranquil, manicured gardens of The Retreat. But there was no tranquility for her. She sniffed and used a hand to dash away the tears. 'Come on, let's walk,' she said quietly, pulling out a handkerchief as they set off.

Niall allowed her to link arms and, totally despondent and disturbed, he covered her hand with one of his. 'I can only think it must've been really horrendous to make you not want to marry again.' At her miserable nod, he asked gently, 'What happened?'

She unlinked her arm for a moment in order to blow her nose, this and her eyes being red with emotion. 'I'd rather not go into it.'

'No, I'm not having that,' he said firmly. 'You fobbed me off with that before, but if I'm to understand I have to know the truth.'

Boadicea shook her head, more tears welling.

They walked in silence for a while, the extensive wall of The Retreat finally ending and the green corridor opening into a truer stretch of moor. Their way intermittently hampered by tussocks of rough grass and clumps of thistle, a flock of goldfinches swooping and veering in front of them occasionally to land upon the prickly plants, they continued across the marshy centre of the moor, not a care for their shoes, both deep in thought, yet with an eye for the herd that had begun to wend its way towards them as it grazed. There was still no one about, though male voices carried from the playing fields of the army barracks, and from overhead, the faint screeching of martins and swallows. Only a hundred yards or so now from a gate that marked the exit of the stray, and the road that ran between Heslington and Fulford, Niall decided to ask whilst there was no human to eavesdrop.

'I'm still in the dark as to why you refused to marry me, when you're obviously free to do so, if you really love me as you say you do.'

'It's because I love you so much, Niall,' came her simple reply. 'Love you more than myself. It wouldn't be fair, because I've no desire for children.'

His immediate response was to snort offence. 'And that rules me out as a candidate, me having five of my own!'

'Oh, I didn't mean that I don't like yours!' She clasped his arm. 'They're lovely – I've told ye, how could they not be with a father like theirs?'

This only slightly appeased him, for he had heard it before, and it had begun to sound very much like flattery.

'I'm not sure I could measure up to the responsibility of looking after them permanently, though . . . but that's only half the reason.' Boadicea could not meet his eye, as she continued, 'My point is, that I don't want any of my own, and I can't see as how it could be avoided – if it were to be a proper marriage, I mean.' She did chance a look at him then, darting a quick examination through her lashes, but it was enough to see she had shaken him.

For the moment, Niall was robbed of words.

He had always thought her the motherly type. Then a look of recognition came over him. Things suddenly began to fall into place. He had assumed that she had been the one to initiate the annulment, but could it have been the other way around? He put this to her, his voice laden with discovery. 'It was Eddie who was the one to apply for divorce, wasn't it?' he breathed. 'That was the reason he left you!'

Her face showed that this was the point Boadicea had been dreading. She gave a shamefaced nod, hung her head, and sighed. 'He couldn't cope with the fact that I was denying him certain things . . . things that a married man has a right to.'

Shy as he was, Niall wanted this clarified. 'You mean you wouldn't sleep with him?'

Already mottled from tears, her face turned a deeper pink, as she nodded again.

'What, never?' Niall found it hard to equate such frigid behaviour with the woman who kissed him so spontaneously in the rare moments of privacy they had shared.

She hesitated, becoming slightly flustered. 'Well, yes, we did, a few times . . . what I mean to say is, 'twas all right when we first got together, but then . . . things went wrong, and he left. He just gave up on me, I suppose.'

'Aye . . .' Niall's sighed comment trailed away, disappearing into a mist of self-examination. How would he himself measure up to the demands of celibacy? He found himself feeling sorry for the man.

She went on quickly, 'As if the divorce itself wasn't bad enough – and God knows, it was the most awful, *terrible* thing, having your intimate affairs go before the court, interrogated by strangers, told how cruel you are – if that wasn't enough, the whole lot had to be dragged up again.'

'For the annulment?' said Niall.

She gave a tearful nod. 'He found somebody he wanted to marry, and even though we were divorced, as you know, in the eyes of the Church we were still man and wife, so he took his case to his parish priest, and raked it all up again.'

'I'm not very conversant with Canon Law,' muttered Niall. 'How—'

'The gist of it was that I was deemed too young to have made an informed consent to marry – well, it was true he talked me into it, he was very good at that, was Eddie, pestered and pestered . . .' She chanced a look at Niall, trying to let him see that this was another reason she had resisted his own proposals so many times, much as she wanted him. 'I should never have married him in the first place. He was much more experienced than me. Anyway, on it went, going before tribunal after tribunal, then to the bishop, then to Westminster, then Rome, poked and picked over . . .'

'Aye, well, I've no wish to dredge all that up for you.' Niall sounded grim. 'That part of it's nowt to do with me.'

Boadicea tried to explain, twisting her hand-kerchief as she spoke. 'I've been in such a quandary, ever since we met. I love being with you, Nye. Every minute in your company is a joy. I know I should have come clean but I couldn't bear to lose that . . .'

'But see, that's another thing!' he exclaimed, his face a network of lines as he tried to fathom this mystery. 'The way you held me and kissed me, you seemed so genuine—'

'I am!' she interjected.

'—seemed to want me the way I want you!'

'I do! I adore kissing you and holding you, but I daren't take it any further, because I really, *really* don't want children!' She ended on a bitter laugh. 'So what do I do? I torture the pair of us.' She shook her head vigorously at her own inept handling of this.

'Well, I don't particularly want them either,' agreed Niall, rubbing his chin in thoughtful manner. It was embarrassing for him to say it, but, 'There's things we can do, things that don't go against the Church—'

'None of them foolproof,' countered Boadicea with an adamant shake of head. 'I couldn't afford to risk it.'

It came to Niall then, and he extended a wave of pity. 'Is it because you're frightened of child-birth?'

'Niall!' Out of sheer frustration, of pent-up longing and self-denial, she lost her temper with him. 'For Christ's sake, why can't ye just take my word for it, I *don't want* any!'

Reclaiming any sympathy he might have shown, Niall too lost control. 'I can't take your bloody word for it because you've lied to me! Not just a little fib, but a blatant, outrageous *cruel* lie!'

'I might as well go now then!' In a tearful fury, Boadicea spun round and began to march off the way they had come.

'Stop bloody running away!' He made a lunge for her, stumbled on a tussock, then managed to capture her.

'What's the point in us going round in circles?' she yelled at him, her voice carrying across the moor. 'Me standing here trying to put my case when it's obvious that, whatever I say, it's over between us!'

'I didn't say that!' Niall refused to let her go.

She stopped trying to struggle away, demanding of him hotly, 'So what *are* you saying – that you still want to marry me despite not being able to trust me? Despite me being so bloody cruel?'

'Yes!' Then just as quickly he sought to temper his impulsive response. 'At least, I want to be able to make my decision with a clean path ahead of us – so if you've anything else you're keeping from me, now's the time to spit it out!'

'I lost a baby!' She was bright red and still angry, yet a terrible sadness had come to her eyes. And to Niall's further astonishment, she revealed, 'It was conceived before we were married – *had* to get married – and after I lost it I couldn't bring myself even to look at Eddie, let alone have him touch me.'

Niall, struck dumb, only managed to open his mouth.

'Don't!' She looked on the verge of fresh tears as she held up her palms. 'Don't, I beg you, say another word, 'cause if I dwell on it I'll break down completely—'

'Oh, you poor—'

'Stop!' Wild of eye, her hand now pressed to her racing heart, Boadicea spoke hurriedly, 'I'm only telling you so's you'll know never to ask me to repeat this and I meant what I said; I could never go through all that again!'

Niall beheld with pity the face that had adopted a different emotion altogether, one that was almost frightening in its intensity. He wanted to ask all kinds of things – things that a husband should be able to ask his wife – but her attitude forbade this. She looked almost deranged by grief.

Instead, he behaved gently both in deed and word, touching her arm as he promised, 'I won't ask you anything else.'

Unable to meet his pitying observation, she kept her eyes averted. 'So,' her bosom rose as she took a deep breath, and braced herself for rejection, 'I'll understand if you want to change your mind, because no man could put up with that.'

He looked pained. 'I can't just turn off all these feelings that you've started in me!'

'And that's *exactly* the way I feel, Niall!' she implored him, beseeched with every muscle of her face. 'That was the only reason for any lies I told ye – you'd started all those same deep emotions in me and I couldn't turn them off! But at the same time I couldn't marry you knowing what I did!' She was clearly in turmoil. 'I love you, I want you – probably as much as you want me – but I just can't bring myself to – I can't!' She watched and waited for him to emerge from his inner struggle, the conflict of emotions upon his face.

Niall felt battered from all sides, asking himself, how could one stop at kisses? During the celibacy of the last eleven months, including the six since meeting Bo, having to exist on the fantasy of her naked body against his, only the thought that it would eventually lead to consummation had kept him sane – and now she was telling him that would never be! Did he love her enough to accept that awful frustration? Could he, *should* he, bear it? Seeing him ponder so deeply, she rubbed his arm and said shakily, 'Let's not talk about it any more for now. Ye've had an awful shock, ye need time to think.'

That he accepted this invitation rather said it all, and it was a subdued Boadicea who accompanied him whence they had come, retracing their stumbling path across the moor. For several minutes they travelled in silence, the only sounds that of their own tread, the screech of martins, and an occasional twittering of finches. But so numerous were his thoughts that they clattered in and out of his mind, back and forth, like shuttles in a loom. He was still a young man, how on earth could he swear to remain chaste for thirty or forty years, when the past eleven months had been hell enough? What if he did marry her, only to find that he just could not cope with the status quo, and they had to part? Would it be fair to put her through that again? And what would that do to the children? It would be difficult enough for them accepting her as a stepmother, but once they had, it would be even harder for them if Boadicea had suddenly to leave. Even if he chose to do the noble thing and keep her there, how would he himself feel? Trapped, that's how.

Yet he purported to love her. He *did* love her, not just her body, but the very essence of her. What sort of mature response would it be if he were to cast aside everything else they shared – the laughing and joking, the companionship – for the sake of that one thing? Oh, but such a vital thing . . .

Amidst this mêlée of thoughts, he even thought of asking her to move in with him – he, Mr Respectable! For, what other way to test his endurance? Then, swiftly putting this impulse to rout, he asked himself how he could assert to love her, yet seek to put her through that. And what would such an immoral situation exemplify to his children? It would tell them that he did not consider Boadicea good enough to marry – not to mention that they would suffer no end of abuse from their peers were their father to live in sin. In theory, this was not a choice between her and his children, but that was what it amounted to.

They had reached the asylum wall before Niall was to speak again. 'I swore to Father Finnegan that my feelings towards you were pure . . .' It came on a shaky laugh, a sound that was totally lacking in mirth. 'I never dreamed they'd be *that* pure.'

Precariously balanced twixt salvation and defeat, Boadicea hung on his words, desperately wanting to colour his decision, but afraid to say anything that might tip the balance against her.

'How come he never knew about all this previously?'

'I've never been to confession in years,' whispered Boadicea. 'Rarely spoken to the man. I just go to church to pray.'

He nodded thoughtfully. There were great gaps between their exchanges, each immersed in his or her own purgatory as they climbed the gentle slope.

'I love you.' His voice was thick with emotion.

'And I love you,' she confirmed, still anxious for a verdict, her heart thudding within her breast.

'I understand why you lied . . . I wish you'd felt able to tell me, but I do understand. I mean, I wasn't entirely honest with you in the beginning, was I? So I can't claim superior morals. I don't know if I can do this,' his voice was hollow, his eyes awash with woe, 'but, what I do know is, I don't want to live my life without you. The week I spent in Ireland confirmed that. Jesus, I felt like I'd suffered an amputation . . .'

''Twas the same for me.' They had reached the crest now. From one of the highest points of the city, on this fine day they had a splendid view of it spreading into the distance, on its far side the distinct outline of Rowntrees' factory, and beyond it a range of hills; but the look in Boadicea's eyes showed that her mind was even further away than this. The gate almost within reach, she stopped, as if fearing that once back on the road, her chance of redemption would be lost.

Niall paused with her, his troubled eyes on the vista before him, but like her, not really seeing it. Always quietly spoken, his pensive murmur was now barely audible above the rushing of the September breeze through the trees. 'I just keep asking meself, what if we did get married, and it didn't work out?'

'I can't advise you what to do, Niall.' She dared not even touch him. 'I've told you the way it is. Only you can decide what's best to do.' Please, please don't let me down, her heart yearned.

'I'm sure you've no wish to go through another broken marriage,' he opined.

'I have not,' she agreed. 'The Church might like to pretend that it never existed, but believe me, the pain was real enough . . .'

He searched her eyes, his own deeply troubled,

trying to divine some glimmer of hope. Maybe once they were married, and on a firmer footing, she might change her mind. But what if she didn't? Niall was not a brute to force the issue. Could he be content with companionship? Could any man? He did not know. 'I just don't know what is best,' he sighed. Then he studied his palm, using the thumb of his other hand to trace the lines and calluses thereon. 'Accepting that you don't want kids, and anything that might lead to it . . . would it still have to mean we slept in separate beds?'

She looked first startled, then wary.

'Don't worry, there's no ulterior motive,' he allayed her suspicion. 'But surely we could still be close, hold each other, fall asleep together and that . . .'

'Oh, but that'd be tempting things, Niall.' Boadicea shook her head to suggest caution.

'If I were twenty and headstrong, maybe,' he said unconvincingly.

'You're still a young man, Niall.' It was painful for her to say it, but only fair that she did. For she had felt the way his body reacted when they kissed, knew what difficulty she herself had in preventing things going further. 'Could you really make do with kisses – could I, come to that? Wouldn't you rather have a wife who could provide everything you need, not just part of it?'

'Of course I would,' he said honestly, 'but it depends what you consider to be the most important part of marriage. I'm not saying *that* isn't important, because it is – by God it is – and I still don't know if it would work between us. But what sort of bloke would I be if I gave you the elbow, just so's I could find a wife that would give me plenty of the other?'

Then, yet again, he was pulled the opposite way. 'By the same token, it's all very well being noble, but as you said, I'm still a bloke . . .'

She held her breath, dreading his farewell.

'I even considered asking you to move in with me,' he admitted. 'It would give us both a better idea of whether we could cope or not.'

Boadicea was shocked, and took a few moments to recover.

In the meantime, Niall was to fill the hiatus. 'I know,' he told her with a self-deprecating chuckle. 'I surprised meself. The things I've said about the type of person who acts like that . . .' He shook his head. 'But it's all very well to condemn others when you haven't been in their position.' He rubbed his hands briskly over his face. 'Oh, I don't know! What do you think?' He handed the problem back to her.

'About moving in?' she tendered.

'Oh no, I wasn't really serious about that! No, I mean about getting married – do you think we could make it work?'

She was truly stunned now.

'I could have a chat to Father Finnegan.' Niall grasped at straws. 'Then again, I don't really care what the Church or anyone has to say. It's something I've got to handle by myself – *we*'ve got to handle.' He saw that she was in danger of weeping again. 'Oh, look, I know it's a risk,' he said tiredly, 'but so is everything. You don't have to give me an answer yet . . .' The click of the gate alerted him to an intruder, and he took her arm and set into motion again. 'Just have a think about it.'

She allowed herself to be led, giving him a murmur of appreciation. 'If you're willing to take me on, then I don't have to think about it.'

He had been distracted by the man with whom he shared a nod in passing, but now he looked back with interest at his companion. 'You'll marry me?'

'Yes,' she smiled sincerely, as they reached the gate.

15

The shock of the weekend's revelation was to linger well into the next day. For the moment, Niall said nothing to anyone about the handicapped marriage he was to undergo with Boadicea. He was not even to discuss it with her, except to say they must postpone the ceremony until a more suitable time, for next month would mark the anniversary of Ellen's death.

However, the cermony itself required some clarification, so, on Tuesday morning before work, he called in at the presbytery that was attached to the church, to seek information from Father Finnegan. As angry as he was with the man, his respect for the cloth demanded that he go to him for guidance. Niall's religion was carved into his very fibre, and as much as he might bluff, he could not ditch it as easily as other things.

At first denied entry by a disgruntled housekeeper, after much insistence he was let in, but made to wait cap in hand in a hallway that smelled of toast, whilst the grumbling woman went to gain him access to the priest. 'Don't keep the man waiting,' he heard Father Finnegan say. 'He'll be keen to get to work.' And within seconds he was being shown into an austere dining room and invited to sit at the table.

'Good morning to you, Niall – cup of tea?' Father Finnegan was unfolding a starched linen napkin that seemed at odds with the shabby surroundings.

'No, thanks, Father.' He used two hands to drag one of the heavy dining chairs away from the table, then perched on its edge, as his host proceeded to breakfast. 'You said I should come if I wanted to talk . . .'

'Of course, of course!' The priest tapped a spoon at the boiled egg before him.

'I just need a few questions answered then I'll be off.'

'Fire away!' said Father Finnegan, delving his spoon into the runny yolk, then taking a bite of toast.

'I won't beat about the bush,' continued Niall, 'you obviously know all about the situation . . .'

'I haven't had full access to the case,' admitted the priest, crunching his toast, 'just the gist of it. I'd like to have a long chat about it, when you've more time.'

Niall gave a quick nod, his eyes on a crumb that had lodged at the corner of Father Finnegan's mouth. 'Me and Boadicea still want to get married – will that be possible?'

'In church? Yes, indeed! So long as the condition that led to the invalidity of Miss Merrifield's first union is no longer present.' Under Niall's close observation, Father Finnegan stopped eating, and mopped at his mouth with a napkin, his eyes relaying his meaning. 'You've spoken to her now, so you'll know what I'm talking about?'

'That she doesn't want children?' Niall looked uncomfortable. 'Yes.'

'You say "doesn't"?' The priest's cheery mood altered somewhat. 'That would suggest to me that her allergy towards procreation still exists.'

Niall gave a nod to show he had accepted this.

'In that case, I'd warn you not to be rash in your decision.' Father Finnegan had become concerned. 'There's a whole lot to consider; it should take more than a day.'

Niall bent his head, sounding helpless. 'I gave it a great deal of thought. I can't give her up.'

Father Finnegan gave an impatient little wave, and laid his napkin down. 'You should know the full extent of your sacrifice before finalising your decision. If Miss Merrifield has told you she doesn't want children, then I'm afraid you'll be unable to marry in church.' He saw the upset that this had created on the listener's face, and responded, 'How can the pair of you make your vows before God, knowing they're lies? I'm deeply sorry for the pair of you, Niall, but there it is.'

Bitterly disappointed, Niall seemed not to know what to say.

'Don't mind if I get on with this, do you?' Father Finnegan pointed at his egg, and when the other shook his head he took another bite of toast. As he ate he studied the one who was deeply ruminative. 'So I suppose you'll go ahead regardless and tie the knot in a register office?'

At this tone of resignation, Niall looked up, his blue eyes portraying despondence. 'I don't seem to have any choice. I'd have loved the Church to recognise our marriage, but, anyway . . .' He shrugged, and tapped his cap thoughtfully against his hand. 'If we do use a register office would that affect my children? I don't want them to suffer because of something I've had to do.'

'I can't see how it would,' said Father Finnegan. 'So long as they continue to be raised in the faith.'

Niall covered every angle. 'They might be looked down on at school.'

'I'm sure not,' the priest's voice was kind, 'but I shall pass on your misgivings to Sister Mary Magdalene.'

Niall thanked him, then slowly began to rise. 'Right, well, I won't keep you, Father.'

Father Finnegan chewed hurriedly, then rose to follow him. 'Just a minute, Niall. No, no, I'm not going to try and persuade you against your wishes! I just wanted to add . . . should you go ahead with the register office, speaking personally, I'd be pleased still to see you both at Mass with your children.'

Niall's mood lightened to a small degree. 'Well,

that's something – thank you, Father.' And, in receipt of an avuncular pat on his shoulder, he bade Father Finnegan good day, and went off to work.

Despite not having worked the lunchtime shift, with several hours of shoving an iron instead, Boadicea was running late that Tuesday afternoon. It had not seemed right to continue including Niall's laundry with Mrs Precious's, so yesterday she had decided to undertake the chore – she would after all soon be his wife. But the pile of ironing this had produced for today meant that other things must suffer. The stew had only just been put on the stove and would not be ready for ages, certainly not in time for when the children came home from school.

So, when they did arrive, famished as usual, she offered to make amends for this.

'Not bothered,' sniffed Batty. 'I don't like stew.'

Boadicea ignored the six-year-old, and continued what she had been about to say. 'You can have some bread and jam to keep you going till your father gets in.'

A collection of dirty faces, tousled hair and socks round ankles, they gathered round to wait, whilst she removed several slices from a loaf and began to daub them first with margarine, then with jam.

'We'll put one aside for your big sister for when she comes home,' said Boadicea, then, noticing that a wasp had drifted in, she added a warning comment. 'Oh, look who's smelled the jam pot!' As the striped invader hovered closer, she kept her eye on it, and began to recite a rhyme from one of Juggy's books, 'One day we had a picnic with bread and jam for tea! We thought that there were two of us, but found that there were three . . .' Still reciting, she balanced on one foot and slipped off her shoe. 'For Mr Wasp had joined us, he said oh what a treat, if there's one thing I do enjoy it's bread and jam to eat – splat! No, you don't, Mr Wasp.' The little ones burst out laughing as the insect was dealt an accurate blow with her shoe, and now lay squashed on the table.

'By, you're a good shot!' came an involuntary shout.

'What's that, a compliment from Batty?' She cupped her ear, looking pleased, then admitted with a smile, 'Not really. He was drunk on apples, and easy to hit.'

'I didn't know apples made you drunk,' Batty's laughter gave way to a frown.

Boadicea took time to explain that it was only the windfalls that lay fermenting on the ground which were potent to smaller beings. 'Don't go giving yourself ideas. All ye'll get is bellyache.'

'So what?' muttered Batty, and took his jam sandwich into the yard.

Still wanting to be popular, Boadicea chose to overlook his rudeness, though could not help her nostrils flaring slightly as she put away the bread, margarine and jam. 'Could someone pick up that dead wasp for me?'

Juggy excused herself. 'I'm not doing it. Gloria says, they can still sting when they're dead.'

'Maybe Dom can do it, then,' said Boadicea, and was glad when this suggestion was taken up without too many grumbles, though only because Dom wanted to chase his sister with it.

Boadicea heaved a sigh as they charged from the house, leaving her to potter about until four twenty – at which juncture she turned on her smile again as Honor came through the front door. 'Hello, love! I'm sorry, tea won't be ready for a while, there's some bread and jam to keep you going.'

'That's all right,' said Honor quietly. 'I'm off in the front to do my homework.'

Boadicea's smile faded as the girl disappeared with her satchel and the jam sandwich. It might take a while to get to know this reserved child, but at least this was one who never gave any trouble.

However, someone else was about to give it. Boadicea had just turned her attention to another task, when a loud knock came at the front door. Upon answering it, she was faced with an immediate declaration.

'I've come to take my grandchildren for their tea!'

Taken aback, she stared for a moment at Nora's sturdy figure in its black, ankle-length coat and old-fashioned shoes and flowered hat, the determined thrust of that jaw, and the cold glint of her eye, before stating, 'You can't take them, it hasn't been arran—'

'Don't you tell me what I can and can't do!' Nora cut her off, thumping her own chest, then jabbing her finger at Boadicea. 'I'm kin, you're not!' Unwilling to negotiate, she merely summoned the children in loud voice. 'It's your gran – come on, I want to see you!'

Honor being the first to hear this altercation, and already watching from the window, she abandoned her homework and went to the yard to call the others. Then out they all filed, squeezing past Boadicea and onto the pavement.

'Your Aunty Harriet's going to make us tea,' announced their grandmother, and, grabbing Brian's hand, she began to lead them away.

An alarmed Boadicea made one last attempt as she watched Juggy go skipping down the street along with the rest of the tribe. 'Your father won't like it,' she warned, deeply concerned at having no authority to stop this.

'He knows what he can do!' A triumphant Nora waddled off with her five grandchildren, saying to them cheerfully, 'Away, let's go and catch the bus!'

Niall would normally have appreciated a quiet house when he came home, but this evening it was far too quiet, and within seconds of his entry it was to explode with noise.

'Who the *hell* does she think she is?' he fumed, hurling his haversack at the floor, and discharging his ire at Boadicea.

The latter held his dirt-streaked face, pleading, 'What could I do, Niall? I'm not their mother. I've no legal claim on them.'

'No, and didn't the old bag take advantage of that!' His greasy cap was to go the way of the haversack. But after this short outburst, he picked up the items he had thrown and hung them up, assuring Boadicea it was not she who incurred blame. 'There was nothing you could have done. For God's sake, I'm their father and she rides roughshod over me!' For a few seconds it seemed to Boadicea as if he might head out for confrontation. But after second thoughts, and a deep calming breath, Niall plumped for inaction. 'She's expecting me to go charging up there like a bull at a gate, but I'm not going to give her the satisfaction. I'll have my tea first, enjoy this bit of peace with me darlin' before I go and fetch them.' And he gave her a rough kiss and a wink as he passed her, on the way to wash his hands.

Reassured that he did not blame her, it was a happier Boadicea who served their meal, she too enjoying the fact that they could eat with just each other for company. There was a little less pleasure to be had from what Father Finnegan had relayed to him that morning. Even so, they were able to overcome their disappointment with humour, in the relaxing half-hour that followed tea, without a pile of washing-up and children to interrupt them. However, thinking she might appear selfish in mentioning how nice it was that there were only the two of them, her only reference to this was, 'At least we've still enough stew left for tomorrow's tea, and I won't have to cook.'

Seated in a battered old armchair that was not nearly so comfortable as his own had been, Niall smiled sympathetically over his cup of tea. 'Sorry, love, you must find it a bit of a push having to do for us between your shifts.'

From the table, she smiled back at him, her eyes roaming affectionately over his tanned face. 'No, 'twas just today, I had something else to do.' She did not complain that this had been his stack of ironing. 'That's why I was late in getting the meat on, and it takes so long to cook.'

'Are you having to rush off after this?' He had noticed that she was emptying her cup in erratic little sips. When she nodded, he sought to assure her, 'Well, at least you won't have to be in two places at once when we're married.'

Boadicea was quiet for a few seconds, then leaned her elbows on the table, and watched for his reaction. 'Don't bite my head off . . . but I thought I might carry on working for a while. No, hear me out, Niall.' She had seen his lips about to offer negation. 'We've got cash flowing out the door like flood water, we've still to pay Reilly what we owe him – wouldn't it be an idea for me to keep on working? It doesn't have to be the pub,' she forestalled any objection that they would never see each other. 'I could get a few hours cleaning whilst the kids are at school.'

Male pride urged Niall to make a stand, but having relied on Harriet and Dolly's wages in the past he could not honestly claim to have been the sole provider for his family. Common sense prevailing, it did not take him long to agree that it was a good idea. 'It's your life – you work anywhere you want, love,' he permitted in warm voice, 'but you'll only have to do it while we whittle these debts. I couldn't have you slaving yourself to death for us and grafting for somebody else as well. We'll soon be on top of things, if I can manage to keep on grabbing any overtime I can.'

She gave a pleased nod, which was soon to change as she became alert to the time. 'Right, I'll have to love you and leave you, my dear.' Still at the table, she picked up her bag, took out a compact mirror to check her appearance, and spent a moment smudging the merest amount of rouge upon her cheeks and lips and patting her hair, before rising with the intent of leaning over his armchair to plant a kiss on his brow.

But he rose to meet her. 'Hang on, I'll walk with you.'

And, leaving the house, they went together through the dark as far as Walmgate, whereupon Boadicea tilted her face for a parting kiss. 'I hope you don't have too much bother with Mrs Beasty.'

At this Niall's mood altered, and his face was overtaken with that wolfish menace she had come to know well. 'Don't go getting all het up, now,' she warned, as they went their separate ways. ''Tis only the kids will suffer.'

'Oh, he's finally remembered he's got children!' sneered Harriet, her square head outlined against a yellow glow of electricity, as she answered Niall's moderate tap at the door of her council house some twenty minutes later.

Under Boadicea's advice, he managed to hold on to his temper for now. 'Well, seeing as Nora said they were being fed here,' he responded tartly, 'I didn't think there was any harm in feeding meself neither – no point us all having our tea ruined.'

'They've had better than they'd have enjoyed from your barmaid!' she retaliated.

'I doubt that,' Niall remained stiff, 'but anyway, I'd appreciate it if you could send them out now.'

Nora had come to insert her rhinoceros hips next to those of her daughter, Harriet's husband standing just behind, and the glow of electricity almost blocked out by the three of them in the doorway. 'I'm not sure they'll want to leave, they've had such a good time!' she taunted.

'Who's going to fight me for them – me laddo there?' Niall indicated Peter, who appeared not to relish this thought. 'No, I thought not. Away, kids!' Unable to see them, he projected a calm and cheerful instruction over the obstacle. 'Let's be having you home.' And just as they had dutifully answered their grandmother earlier, the five responded to his call.

'Can I take this with me, Gran?' asked Juggy, clutching the toy farm her father had made for her, a plea in her blue eyes as she hovered on the threshold.

'No,' forbade Nora, 'you'll have nothing to play with when you come again.'

But, 'Yes,' corrected the child's father, averting disappointment as he pulled her firmly onto the path, the toy still in her arms. 'Because we don't know when you might be coming again, do we?' He fixed his mother-in-law with one last ominous glare, before turning towards the gate. 'I might let you come again on Saturday, if everyone behaves themselves.' And with his parting shot meant for Nora more than his children, he took them home.

Niall might have felt a sense of accomplishment at having laid down the rules, but Boadicea could not help noticing that the children he had brought home were very different from the ones that had been taken from her on Tuesday – not in their father's presence of course; they were too sharp for that, and knew that any disrespect would earn a good hiding. But, evidently under the tuition of their grandmother and aunt, they were unusually aloof with her when she came round to feed them on Wednesday – as aloof as little ones could be without forgetting to be so – and it was plain as day they had been instructed to shun the one who was responsible for their father's fall from grace.

Watching them pick at her reheated stew, Boadicea felt a twinge of annoyance, though nothing too severe, and not towards the children, for she knew who was responsible.

'It's not as good as me gran cooks.' Batty screwed his face up in the apparent torment at having to eat it.

'I'm mortally wounded,' replied Boadicea, uncaring of his attempt to insult her as she swept up some ashes from the hearth and generally tidied the place for Niall's homecoming. 'I thought ye said ye didn't like stew anyway?'

'I only like me gran's.'

Adopting a more adult approach, Honor instructed her brother, 'You should eat something, or you'll starve.'

Boadicea appreciated this help. 'Yes, there'll be nothing else,' she warned.

Juggy too chipped in with sage advice to her brother: 'Me gran says, you should be polite and eat stuff even if you think it's horrible.'

Pursing her lips, Boadicea continued to tidy, and the meal was eventually consumed, though with no end of sighing and face-pulling.

'You can go out to play now,' she told them dispassionately, after Honor had helped her clear away the plates. But left alone, she could not avoid a feeling of dejection, at having spent much time in trying to create a rapport with them, only for their grandmother to demolish it in hours.

After the washing-up was done, there was another hour or so before Niall would get home. Desiring to make the most of the last bit of summer, Boadicea wandered to the open front door, and leaned there watching the street scene for a while, enjoying the gentle rays upon her face. In the middle of the road, Honor was winding her skipping rope, the neighbour, Gloria, holding the other end, and both of them lashing it as fast as they could, whilst Honor's friend jumped up and down doing 'bumps'. Gloria had been having fun until now, but, catching Boadicea's observation, she delivered a dirty look that compelled the watcher to turn away.

This provided no escape, for others were intent on registering their combined disapproval of her too. A monkey-like woman, Mrs Hutchinson, and another Mrs Dunphy, both of whom Boadicea knew to be Nora's cronies – though only after Niall had spoken to them in her presence and both had cut him dead – had broken off their gossip to look down their noses at her, both with pursed lips. And again, Boadicea tore her eyes away.

This time, she was met by a smile and a wave from old Mrs Powers, who had dragged a chair onto the pavement to enjoy the sunshine and to watch the children.

Grateful for this show of support in the staunch

Beasty stronghold, Boadicea waved back, then watched the children too. Along the street, the boys were taking turns on a friend's trolley, careering up and down on it, socks round ankles, a madcap gleam in their eyes, whilst little Brian hopped about on the periphery, dying for a go. 'Will ye not let your brother have a turn?' she called to Dominic eventually, when the four-year-old ran to her whining.

'Go get football press,' muttered Dominic, with a sly grin at his pals.

'What was that?' Unable to decipher the vulgarity, but guessing that the laughter was at her expense, Boadicea clicked her tongue and went to fetch a halfpenny from her purse. 'Here you are, Bri, run and get yourself some sweeties.'

Easily bought, the little one forgot all his grandmother had told him, and for one second his face lit up for Boadicea, then he grabbed the coin and ran.

Keeping her eye on the little figure, whilst he scampered up the street and through the open door of the shop, Boadicea then turned her attention to Juggy, the child for whom she felt most affection, who was seated on the kerb with an old knife, meticulously carving moss-laden chunks of soil from between each flagstone. These narrow strips of green were then transferred to what looked like a shallow tray.

'Tidying up the pavement, Jug? That's a good lass.'

There came a heavy sigh. 'No, it's for my farm! And my name is Judith.'

'Sorry, my mistake. Is that the one ye brought back from your aunt's?' Boadicea had briefly wondered what was in the case, of which Juggy was so protective.

'Yes.' The small hand continued to slice along the flags with her blade. 'I'm making a field.'

Boadicea came to squat nearby, her fond blue eyes examining the 'farm'. An ingenious contraption made by Niall, when closed it looked like a wooden suitcase that could be toted around with the animals inside; but when the catches were flicked, its two halves opened to reveal a walled farmyard, with little pens for the animals. Not that there was much stock at the moment. Boadicea smiled to herself as she watched Juggy's small hands press the strips of moss firmly into position; then, satisfied with her field, the owner began to place lead animals on it: one cow, one sheep, and a camel.

'That's a rare breed ye have there. I should think that's the only camel in Yorkshire.'

Feeling herself the object of Boadicea's amusement, Juggy pushed the dark brown hair away from her cheek, streaking it with dirt as she looked up, her expression daring the woman to laugh. 'Me teacher says a camel can survive anywhere.'

'Sure, what would I know?' Boadicea pleaded ignorance. 'If they can have a wolf in Yorkshire, they can have a camel too. Hey, you'd better take care of that sheep in case the wolf should come and eat him! Maybe I should buy you a few more when I go to town, just in case?'

Knowing her grandmother wouldn't like it, Juggy tried hard not to smile, and concentrated on her farm, as she murmured, 'Me gran says, I shouldn't ask people to buy me things . . .' There was a long pause. 'But I wouldn't mind a pig, if you're off.'

'A pig it is!' Boadicea rose to stretch her legs, happy to have found some leverage against Nora. Then, receiving another dirty look from Gloria, she sighed to herself, checked that Brian was safely home from the shop, then went indoors to reheat the stew for Niall's tea.

With Juggy in receipt of the little toy pig, the rest bribed with sweets, by Friday Niall's children were once again becoming acclimatised to Boadicea's presence. Alas, Saturday brought another visit to Tang Hall. And, with the latter becoming a regular event, it appeared that this was to be the way of things for some time to come: Boadicea using the week to try to rebuild some empathy with those who were eventually to be her stepchildren, Nora destroying it in one fell swoop, and generating a lot of hard work and not a little bribery for the week ahead.

Try as she might not to let the childish comments affect her – in the knowledge that they were being used by one who should know better – as the insults began to pile up like threatening letters from the bailiffs, Boadicea could not help feeling a little aggrieved towards Niall's brood. Consequently, it became a pleasure to have them out of the way on a Saturday afternoon, and to have Niall to herself. With all parties warned that Honor must bring them home at a prescribed time – and so far this being adhered to – Niall had no need to trail the mile to Tang Hall. Hence, he too seemed happy enough with the arrangement, though ever since Boadicea's revelation on Low Moor, he had been slightly different towards her, becoming fidgety when they were alone, and more prone to drifting into bouts of abstraction, as if he might be reconsidering his plans to marry her.

Had she dared to ask, she would have found that this was not the case at all. Though Niall was certainly in a state of limbo, it was merely the time of year that was responsible for his introspection. September was drawing to a close, the screech of martins beginning to fade, only a stalwart few remaining to scythe the clouds, and finally these too dispersing for warmer climes. In the ancient graveyard opposite the church, leaves began to tumble from the overhanging sycamores, filling the air with their pungent perfume, and the gutters knee-deep for the sport of children. The skies became leaden, tipping their contents o'er distant hills, and sending a rush of water into the Vale of York, to threaten the banks of Ouse and Foss. However unwelcome all these signs, to most, they constituted naught more than a typical autumn, but for Niall they marked the anniversary of his wife's death.

Thus, he was particularly glum as he travelled home that Friday, knowing what heartache Monday would bring for his much-loved children, and his mood exacerbated by the weather. Night was coming in as he and a mass of others – on bicycle, bus, by car and on foot – splashed their way home through the city. Even through the smoke of countless chimneys, which mingled with falling darkness to create a denser pall, the Minster still dominated the backdrop, a monument to a faith that was not his. His own little church was tucked out of sight, behind that city wall towards which Niall was quickly making his way. And, as he went, oppressed by the rain and the noise of traffic, he could not prevent his mind's descent to all things funereal, reliving that fateful afternoon that had ended in tragedy, but had started out with laughter over his wolf. Nothing had been seen of the predator for months now, nor word either, both hunters and journalists grown bored with its fate. Perhaps it had died from its wounds in the summer after all, thought Niall. If not, it would be awfully bedraggled living under such conditions – or even washed away.

Beneath Skeldergate Bridge over which he strode, the ever-rising river glistened like a black swollen snake, ready to burst free of its skin. Before him, the limestone keep atop its grassy mound had already gained liberation: the grim outer wall of the castle that had once obscured it now virtually demolished by the tide of progress that was sweeping the city. Progress, sighed Niall to himself – would that a little of it might affect his own situation. Hurrying from the bridge, he twisted his mouth in discomfort as the rain suddenly intensified, and prayed that there would be drier weather on Sunday. Needing no persuasion, he was allowing Nora and Harriet to take his children to lay flowers at the cemetery. It would have been hypocritical to go himself, but he could not help feeling a certain sadness over Ellen, the mother of his children. Pray God the poor little buggers would have some sunshine to lighten such an awful occasion. His prayers included Boadicea too, for it was she who had to suffer each time the youngsters returned from their grandmother's influence. Bo thought he did not see, but he had noticed how subdued they were in her presence, and how hard she tried to forge a bond. But so long as they were under Nora's sway, their loyalties would remain divided.

Striding on through the dark over another bridge, his head down against the rain, he had almost reached the lock gates at Castle Mills – at which point it was his habit to cross the road – when a quick glance to right and left brought a familiar figure into range, and he started in recognition.

'Sean!' Experiencing a burst of hope, he

accosted his brother, who had been heading straight past towards Fishergate, and waited for him to look back.

Sean did cast an involuntary response over his shoulder, but held this only briefly; upon seeing who it was, he maintained his pace.

But Niall persisted, 'Hang on!' And he stretched out his arm as if to detain the other. 'I've been wanting to bump into you for ages. I didn't know where you live or I would've been to see you!'

With a large gap between them, Sean did deign to pause then, but his attitude was not one of welcome, his eyes narrowed and his cap tilted against the driving rain, as he waited only to see what else would be said.

'Where did you move to?' Niall approached, to portray the anxiety of an older brother.

'Alma Terrace,' came the grudging information.

'Where's that – oh, up near Fulford barracks, isn't it?' Niall's nod mirrored Sean's. 'I think I've seen it when I've got the ferry across to South Bank. Nice street.' He conveyed admiration. 'So . . . how are you then? You're looking well.'

'We're all right, thank you.' The reply was coolly formal. 'Both of us, in case you're interested.'

Niall looked suitably repentant, tapping his rain-soaked boot and staring down at it, as he murmured, 'That's why I've been keen to see you, to say how sorry I am for what I said, and for letting Nora ruin your wedding day. It was unforgivable.'

'Yes, it was.' Having uttered this Sean turned to go.

'Aw, hang on!' His whole attitude begging forgiveness, Niall caught hold of the other's wet sleeve, but lightly, so as not to provoke annoyance. 'Just let me tell you – you'll get a good laugh out of it, if nowt else.'

'I doubt it,' said his brother, poker-faced.

'I mean you'll be pleased to hear I got my comeuppance! She did the exact same thing to my house.' Having succeeded in regaining Sean's attention, even if this was resentful, Niall carried on in stilted fashion. 'Robbed me of all my furniture, dragged my name through the dirt – everything she did to you she did to me . . .'

'So now you know what it feels like,' responded Sean, his hands thrust deep into the pockets of his mackintosh, his shoulders hunched and his face puckered against the cold rain. 'And I suppose I'm meant to be all understanding and say, "Oh, it's all right, let's be pals again"?' He curled his lip. 'You've got a bloody nerve!'

Mirroring the other, Niall shoved his own hands into his pockets, and hung his dripping head, submitting totally, whilst his brother berated him.

'You let me down!' accused Sean, as cars, buses and lorries splashed through the puddles, competing to drown out his voice. 'You're my brother, you were supposed to be on my side, but, no! You preferred to side with that vicious lot! All I wanted to do was to marry the lass I'd chosen. You didn't have to like it, but you could have trusted me – *should* have trusted me – to make my own choice, even if you disagreed with it.'

Niall made a complete surrender, not responding at all, his downcast eyes remaining fixed upon the black pavement that was sluiced with rain, whilst his brother harangued him. And eventually Sean's temper was to be dampened too.

The lips might have stopped ranting, but the resentment was still evident; lifting tentative eyes now, Niall was to see it simmering upon his brother's face, which was highlighted by one pair of headlamps after another, as the traffic continued to drone past. 'I read about Ellen in the paper,' muttered Sean. 'Must be almost a year now?'

Niall gave a solemn nod.

'I suppose you've found somebody else, have you? That's what all this is about?' Sean received another sign of affirmation. 'Aye, well . . .' His jaw twitched, and he looked away. 'I'm sorry for your loss, but it obviously didn't hurt for too long then, did it?'

Even accepting that he deserved every ounce of this, Niall wanted to pre-empt any hostile word against Boadicea that might be thrown in revenge. 'I was bloody stupid, I said some rotten things, and I want you to believe how sorry I am, Sean, I really am. You were right, it's only now I'm in your shoes that I can see how terrible it was for you both . . . she looked a nice woman, your wife.'

'She is,' snapped Sean, irritated as much by the noise of the traffic as by his brother.

'So is mine,' said Niall. 'At least, she's not my wife yet, but we'll be getting wed in a month or so – not that I've given the kids a definite date. You're the first person I've told, so if you should happen to see them—'

'Where the hell would I see them?' Sean's anger erupted again, and at once Niall was contrite, for there was pain in his brother's voice. 'That's what hurt so much when you cut me off! You knew how I loved them kids of yours!'

'I know, I know.' Niall closed his eyes to show exasperation with himself. 'I can't tell you how sorry I am. I was wrong to keep them from their uncle, and you can see them again any time you like. They'd love to see you – you're welcome any time.'

'Aye, well, mebbe . . .' Sean was not wholly responsive, his tone sullen as he looked away again, to scan the darkness of the swollen river and its imperilled barges.

'I know Boadicea'd like to meet you – that's her name.' Niall gave an clumsy grin. 'Bit of a mouthful, isn't it? But she's a lovely lass. The kids like her, so there shouldn't be too much of a problem with us getting married, if Nora leaves us alone.' His brother's reaction was simply to harrumph. But noting that Sean had stopped hopping from foot to foot as if to escape, Niall sought to enquire about his sister-in-law. 'Emma, yours is called, isn't she? Did you have any family with her?'

There came a shake of head, Sean's response made doubly sombre in the knowledge that he himself was to blame for the lack of fertility. He did not say this to Niall, for was it not obvious?

However, there was to be no commiseration from his brother, not even the batting of an eyelid, for his pity would not be welcomed. 'There's heaps more I want to tell you,' tendered Niall, the rain dripping off him. 'Will you come for a drink with me, for old times' sake?'

'What, now?' Sean swiftly negated this with a look of disdain. 'No, I've got to be home. Emma'll wonder where I am – besides, I'm pissing wet through.'

Thoroughly dispirited by the rejection, Niall gave a forlorn nod, and made as if to let his brother go. 'Aye, well, it was good to see you, kid . . .'

But his unusual meekness in accepting the chastisement, had obviously had an effect. 'You can come round next Sunday for a cup of tea, if you like,' came Sean's gruff invitation, along with an address. 'That'll give me enough time to talk the wife round.'

Niall flashed a relieved smile of gratitude. 'Shall I bring the kids?'

'Well, seeing as they're the only reason I'm even bothering to talk to you, yes,' grunted Sean, as he moved to be on his way. 'Whether Emma will is another matter. Better bring your lady friend, an' all. I'll need to give her the once-over to make sure she's the right sort.' And with this sarcasm, he splashed away.

By the time Niall arrived home that night, he had chosen to delay the announcement of Sean's invitation to his children. Knowing they would relay this to their grandmother during Sunday's visit to the cemetery, he preferred that Nora did not hear of it just yet, at least not until he had been able to cement the reunion with a visit to his brother's house, for Nora would do all she could to spoil it if forewarned.

But it wasn't only Nora who would be unhappy about the reconciliation. As Niall arrived with Boadicea and his offspring at Sean's door the following Sabbath, he saw that the chestnut-haired Emma was far from pleased about it either. He supposed that was to be expected, after what he had put her husband through. Her smile for him was manufactured, as he was shown into the living room of a house similar in size to his own, yet much more desirable, and both these facts caused to make him feel awkward.

'You've got a front garden,' he pointed out unnecessarily, kneading his hands, after first shaking hers. 'Bo'd love a house like this, wouldn't you?' He turned to the one with whom he felt most comfortable, his eyes remaining on her, as if for reassurance.

Emma was smiling much more kindly on his fair-headed companion. 'I'll show you round later if you like – not that it's anything posh.' She gave a self-effacing shrug, to which Boadicea responded with a compliment. But when Emma's eyes returned to Niall they lost their sparkle, and threatened a very uncomfortable afternoon.

Even the children did not know how to behave after fifteen months of being incommunicado with their uncle. Invited to sit down, they left the chairs for the adults and settled in a well-behaved circle on the carpet, from where they offered the occasional shy smile at Uncle Sean, and the aunt they had not previously met.

'Well, shall we have a cup of tea?' Emma addressed this, as all her comments, at Boadicea, hardly looking at Niall, and she appeared glad for this opportunity to escape.

'Shall I help?' came Boadicea's offer.

'Yes, go on then.' Emma smiled at her, then cast a glance at the children. 'Is pop all right for you kids?' With their bright nods, she and Boadicea went to the kitchen.

'Good to see the blessed rain's stopped,' commented Sean, looking out of the front window. Having had a week to think about the situation, he was to be politely amicable towards his brother. 'I might manage to get into the garden tomorrow, tidy all them leaves up. Everything's so soggy, isn't it?'

'Aye, it's all dying back . . .' Niall continued to rub his hands, and followed his brother's gaze. Both were conscious of the gulf that remained between them, and it was difficult to know what to say, their faltering exchange further inhibited by the youngsters' presence. Though in the respect of breaking this uncomfortable silence, Sean was to find his nephews and nieces useful. 'So, what have you kids been up to?' Receiving only a collection of shy, smiling shrugs, he added, 'I suppose you'll be at grammar school now, Honor?'

The thirteen-year-old offered her uncle a nod, then lowered her eyes and went back to her thoughtful tracing of the pattern on the carpet with her finger.

'Aye, I knew you'd pass your scholarship.' He gave soft praise and threw a look of approval at Niall, who displayed his pride in usual reserved fashion.

'I'm at school as well,' piped up Brian, a wide beam on his rosy cheeks.

'He's only in Baby Class,' provided Batty.

'It's still school,' reproved his Uncle Sean, before returning an agreeable gaze to the youngest. Then, 'What about you, Dom – are you still an altar boy?'

'Yes, I've got to be back for Benediction,' answered Dominic, then saw his father's look of admonition, and added quickly with his sunny grin, 'but that's hours yet.'

'Good!' exclaimed his uncle. 'I thought for a minute you were going to run off before we've had a chance to hear all your news.' But even now, there was not much information to follow, the elder children remembering all the nastiness of last year, and being rendered inarticulate by it.

Juggy was finding it hard to sit still, and shuffled nearer to her uncle to fiddle with his shoelace, poking its tip into the tiny holes that patterned his brogues. 'We didn't know we were coming here till we set off.'

Sean threw a shrewd glance at his elder brother, guessing the reason why. But he made no comment on it, for at this juncture a tray of teacups was rattled in by Boadicea, followed by Emma with a plate of biscuits and buns. 'Oh, here's your Aunty Emma – you jump up and help yourself,' he told Juggy, extending this invitation to the rest. 'All of you, that's it, tuck in . . .'

Seated on the carpet again, and biting into her iced bun, Juggy made a sound of approval at their lightness. 'These are nicer than me gran's.'

This invoked a warning glare from Dominic, but soft laughter from the adults. 'I don't think she was supposed to say that,' Boadicea leaned over to murmur with a smile of fellow feeling at Emma, and at least here there was the sense that these two were capable of firm friendship.

This being so, it seemed incumbent upon them to do all in their power to repair the situation between their men. And from then on, the ice being broken and such nuggets from Juggy helping to smooth the path towards reconciliation, the rest of the visit was to pass quite harmoniously. The attempts at humour might still be a little tense between Niall and his brother, but by the time they parted, they were on good enough terms for Sean and Emma to extend today's invitation to something much less formal, and for Niall and Boadicea to reciprocate.

'Drop in any time!' they were told, upon parting.

'But I don't think he will,' murmured Niall, as he gave a final wave before he and his family turned out of Sean's street. 'By, that was bloody hard, wasn't it?'

Boadicea nodded. 'But it's a start,' she injected with quiet confidence. 'It's a start.'

16

Not until late October, though, did Sean and Emma feel able to make the visit to Walmgate. Even then, it was only performed out of courtesy – for how could Sean say outright that he had no wish to see the place ever again, and thereby insult his elder brother? In effect, this visit was only a gesture, born of the belief that continued alienation would have upset the one who had borne them. Unable to bear the thought of meeting their mother after he died, to face her disappointment in him, that was why he had forgiven Niall. Forgiveness maybe, but things could never be the same again. Yet it must be obvious to his host that his wounds were not as healed as he pretended. This might well be the house where he and Niall were born, but for Sean, any nostalgia was quashed by unhappier memories; and although it was much changed, Nora's sideboard being replaced by a lot of unfamiliar furniture, throughout the time he and Emma were there, Sean could never quite relax.

His visit was made all the more unpleasant by the knowledge that his ex-mother-in-law was in the house next door. Informed of the brothers' reunion, and alerted by one of the children to this Sunday rendezvous, Nora had chosen this afternoon to call upon Mrs Lavelle, her voice raised to full pitch so that the neighbours might hear her spleen vented through the walls.

'Tarred with the same brush, the pair of 'em! No sense of decency, running after tarts . . .' The insults were clearly audible, and were to go on intermittently for hours, and no matter how the adults tried to joke about this, the children were naturally ill at ease. It was just as well Uncle Sean had something up his sleeve to remedy this: four complimentary tickets to Bertram Mills' circus, which had taken up temporary residence on St George's Field.

'I thought me and Emma might take you and Bo on Saturday,' he mused tongue in cheek to his brother, before his face cracked with amusement at the looks of dismay that this had provoked amongst Niall's younger children. 'I'm only kidding, you daft devils!' he chuckled, as their disappointment turned to pleasure, and was unable to resist a final tease. 'But if we're taking all you kids, you'll have to save up for three extra tickets; me and Auntie Emma can't afford to buy them.'

'Dom'll pay,' said Niall with a wry grin at his

son, as he lifted his teacup. 'He's loaded from all these funerals he's been doing.' And there followed a minute or two of jocular chat between nephew and uncle, the latter having also been an altar boy and knowing every wheeze there was to make money from it, or to get off lessons.

'Before any of you go to the circus, there's a slight problem to be solved,' murmured Boadicea. Reminded by the sound of Nora's voice through the walls, she spoke mainly for the adults. 'The kids'll be at Mrs Beasty's on Saturday; we'd better instruct her to make sure she sends them home on time.' Looking around at her silent audience, she laughed. 'Well, don't all volunteer at once.'

'She won't like that,' posed Niall, uncaring that small ears were listening. "Specially if she knows it's our Sean getting the pleasure of their company. She might be bloody-minded enough to keep 'em late on purpose.' His children smirked at the swear word.

'Best you don't tell her at all then,' suggested his brother.

And this was to be the general consensus, Niall somewhat needlessly instructing his offspring that they would not be able to visit their Aunt Harriet and grandmother next Saturday. However, this was to provoke little disappointment in them, with a circus to attend.

Sean and Emma were to stay until after dark, partly because the smaller children had pestered their uncle to read a bedtime story, but also because Sean was waiting for Nora to leave first, having no desire to bump into her, her voice through the walls having been threat enough. With Boadicea being granted an evening off from the pub, the two couples were able to enjoy a more adult conversation, and naturally, talk came around to Niall's wedding.

'Have you set a date yet?' asked Sean, playing with his tie, still not fully at ease with the one who had let him down.

Niall's face consulted Boadicea, who gave him a nod of permission. 'We're thinking around Christmas, or December at least,' he told his brother, his face bearing a look of self-consciousness as he added, 'Thought we'd better leave it a while till after . . . well, you know.'

Sean gave a pensive nod, inferring the tacit cause. 'I'll pray Nora doesn't ruin it like she did ours. By God, once you upset her . . .' He shook his head, begetting a lengthy denunciation of his ex-mother-in-law. 'And the laugh is, she never really made me feel like part of her family. I was always on the outside—'

Niall responded with a fraternal nod. 'You and me both.'

'—yet when I want to make meself a permanent outsider, she takes umbrage!'

Again, his elder brother moved his head.

'Anyway,' concluded Sean, 'good luck with your wedding. Make sure you send us an invite.'

Boadicea replied for Niall that of course they would.

'Right . . .' With the conversation petering out, Sean consulted his watch, saying lightly to Emma, 'We'd better get going, missus. We don't want to outstay our welcome.' And he eased himself from his chair.

'No danger of that,' Niall growled soft reassurance, and rose with him, Emma and Boadicea rising too, the latter to fetch their coats.

The brothers shook hands at the door, with the parting arrangement that Sean and Emma would be here to pick up the children on Saturday at a quarter past four, the first performance beginning half an hour after that. 'And thanks for tea!'

Niall and Boadicea stood close together on the doorstep to wave them off, the latter asking quietly as she fluttered her hand, 'Do ye think he was fishing?'

'For what?' Niall gave one last salute as Sean and Emma vanished into the darkness.

'To be your best man.'

'Do you have a best man at a register office do?' enquired Niall. 'I wouldn't have the foggiest – but if he was, he'll be disappointed.' He turned indoors, indicating for her to go first. 'I'll be having Reilly.'

'I know your friend's lovely.' Boadicea lingered in the doorway. 'But Sean's your brother. Might he not be upset at being shut out again?'

Niall looked pain-faced, and shrugged. 'Can't help that. I know some folk'd frown on me, but

I'd be a hypocrite if I were to ask him just for the reason he's my brother.'

'Would it be so bad to be a hypocrite for once?' Her voice was soft, but meaningful.

Niall thought this over. 'Aye, well, I suppose it's not as if I haven't been one before. Maybe I do owe him . . .' He puffed out his lips, and stood to brood for a moment, mulling over the afternoon: Sean's words had been more significant than perhaps his brother realised. Or had there, indeed, been a deeper message in them? Having both felt like outsiders under Nora's rule, should they not have stuck together; should Niall have not defended his younger brother? Feeling wretched for his own disloyalty, he changed the subject. 'Speaking of brothers, hadn't I better meet yours – and your dad? I've still to ask him for his daughter's hand.'

Knowing the last bit to be frivolous, she graced him with her twinkly smile, and linked his arm as they went back to the living room and their still-warm chairs. 'Right, I'd better take you to get the once-over, then. Will we all of us be going over to Manchester? Sure, it'll cost an arm and a leg.'

Niall informed her that he could get reduced travel, but joked that, 'It'll also put your dad off before he's had a chance to get to know me if we land him with them five arabs. No, I think we'll go on our own one Sunday, leave them with one of their uncles.'

She gave a smiling nod, adding softly, 'I think you'll like my dad, and Arthur. They're good men.'

'They must be to have you.' His warm eyes held her face.

She studied him for a while, her face correspondingly loving, yet there was something behind her smile, as if she ached to pose some question. Eventually, it came. 'There's still time for you to change your mind . . .'

'About marrying you?' Niall was quick to shake his head. 'No, once I make my mind up, I stick to it.'

Boadicea shook her head, with a pained little laugh. 'Ye have such a knack of making a woman feel special.'

'What have I said?' He looked genuinely confused.

She shook her head despairingly, but her smile was tender. Still looking baffled, and fearing that he might have upset her, Niall suggested they move to the sofa, and here they were to sit for a while, his arm around her, drawing her close to him, her head on his shoulder, to chat about the day, occasionally to kiss, until it was time for her to go.

The following Saturday afternoon, with four hours before the circus was due to perform and five excited children to manage until then, whilst Niall took his boys to visit the barber's and to buy the eldest one new shoes, Boadicea invited the girls to come with her into town.

'I'd like your opinion on some fabric I have to buy for a winter outfit,' she explained, as they went, not revealing that this was to make each of them a dress for the wedding. Having found a seamstress, she intended to keep this a secret – though she would have to think of some way of obtaining their measurements without giving the game away.

Both Honor and her younger sister agreed that the deep blue velvet was an excellent choice.

'I wish it were for me,' said Juggy, to the conspirator's greater glee.

Glad to have so quickly found something that matched the light blue tailored costume she intended to buy for herself, and to have such easy co-operation from the girls, Boadicea was full of beans as she took them off to a café for a cream cake treat, which was more than enough to enamour her to Juggy, and even the more serious Honor dropped her guard.

Afterwards, as they strolled home, wanting to maintain this feeling of camaraderie as long as possible, Boadicea was to whisper with a grin, 'It's good not to have the chaps with us sometimes, isn't it? Shall we stay out a bit longer, pop in and show Mrs Precious what I've bought?' An idea had occurred as to how she could get their measurements – she would ask Ma to pretend that she was knitting cardigans for her nieces the same size.

Unwitting to her reason, but knowing there

would be more treats at this address, the girls were more than amenable, and, whilst Honor upheld a more dignified deportment, Juggy went tearing gaily ahead, momentarily disappearing as she reached the other side of the little humpbacked bridge over the Foss. 'Probably going to jump out at us from a doorway,' winked Boadicea to Honor, who smilingly agreed.

But no, Juggy was not hiding in some doorway. Upon mounting the bridge they saw that she was standing on the pavement, being accosted by her grandmother and Aunt Harriet. Immediately alert, Boadicea dashed forth, but was not quick enough in the opinion of some.

'This is how you look after my grandchildren, is it?' Both angry women turned on her as she thudded down the slope, Nora being the spokesperson. 'Letting a little lass go by herself!'

'She wasn't by herself!' objected a breathless Boadicea, coming to a halt, Honor arriving simultaneously.

'*Anyway!*' snapped the one in the old-fashioned coat and hat. 'We're not standing here arguing with the likes of you. What we want to know is why we had to come trailing down here at all. They were supposed to be coming to us this afternoon! We've had to come looking for them. Where are the lads?'

'They're at the barber's,' Boadicea rushed her explanation to Nora, for it seemed that Harriet was intent on leading Juggy away. 'I'm sorry, they can't come today! We didn't think it would cause such a problem.' She reached for Juggy's hand.

But Harriet jerked the child out of range. 'You can't—'

'Yes, I can!' Boadicea was firm as she tried to take charge. 'They've a circus to go to this evening. We thought they might not be home in time from your hou—'

'I don't care about that!' Nora remained bullish, competing for Juggy's hand, and eventually grasping it, Harriet still holding the other one. 'Saturday's our day to have them, and they're coming with me – and if me laddo thinks he's cheating me out of seeing my grandsons, he can think again! You can send them down when they've been to the barber's. Come on, Honor!' And she made to lead the girls away.

Boadicea saw the look of desperation on Juggy's face at the thought of missing the circus. 'Mrs Beasty, you can't be so mean as to—'

'Mean? I'll give you mean!' Harriet let go of Juggy and advanced on Boadicea, her bunched fist in contrast to the rather elegant swagger coat she wore.

'Go on then!' Boadicea braced herself with a meaningful look on her face, which caused Harriet to think again – though she did not back off, but glared at her opponent as if ready to fly at her any minute.

Juggy had started to weep, Honor putting an arm round her, and both anxiously awaiting the outcome. Passers-by had stopped to goggle too, passengers craning for a last look as their bus drove past. Boadicea was deeply embarrassed – but more than that, she was furious.

'Look at the poor child – can't you see what you're doing to her?' she berated the women.

'She'll live!' came an acid retort from Nora.

'I shall tell the police!' bluffed Boadicea, stumbling off the kerb as she tried to get around Harriet to rescue the crying victim. 'Their father's entrusted them to me!'

But this only drew more sounds of contempt from Harriet and Nora.

Persistently, she ran around them and tried to bar their way, but they just barged straight through her, taking the girls with them.

'One moment, madam!' A stentorian voice was to hinder the attempted abduction, Nora and Harriet both halting as the imposing figure stalked up to them, his arrogant bearing and perfect elocution commanding respect. 'I have reason to believe you are attempting to remove these children from their guardian, and I must ask you to accompany me to the police station!'

'I'm their grandmother!' objected Nora, though under the authority of the plainclothes officer, her confidence was fading to bravado, 'and this is their aunt.'

'And as I understand it,' snapped the man with the sour, cadaverous face, indicating Boadicea as he laid down the law, 'this is the individual who has been appointed by their father to look after them, therefore you would be committing an offence in taking them away. Now, kindly hand them over!'

Nora and Harriet were no shrinking violets if their opponent was an equal, but presented with such officialdom, their stand was to be exposed as bluster and, with grim faces, mother and daughter abandoned the girls and marched away – though not without a series of muttered threats over their shoulders.

'No wonder we won the war with men like you!' Boadicea heaved a sigh of relief, as her fellow boarder escorted her and the distressed girls through the alleyway and into the mansion. 'Thank you, Mr Yarker. I don't know what I'd have done without ye.'

'What an objectionable pair of hoydens,' opined Yarker, his mouth contorted with its usual look of distaste. 'Don't mention it, my dear – but do please attend to that snivelling.'

Boadicea quickly stooped to mop Juggy's eyes with a handkerchief, finally to receive the shuddering question, 'Why did me granny not want us to go to the circus?'

'Aw! It wasn't that she didn't want ye to go,' her guardian told her gently, as she dabbed the mottled cheeks and patted them.

'Are we still off then?' Juggy still vibrated with emotion, yet there was a glimmer of hope through her tears.

'Of course you are!' Though the incident had thoroughly disconcerted her too, Boadicea tried to sound bright as she steered the two girls to where an impatient-looking Yarker held open the door for them. 'But there's ages yet, so come on, let's go have a cup of tea and a bun with Ma. She'll make ye feel better – and best not mention this to your daddy when we get home. He'll only be upset.'

Nevertheless, she herself would be obliged to tell Niall some time, for this situation was intolerable. It was fortunate that Sean and Emma came to collect the children at a quarter past four, thereby lending Boadicea time to enjoy a peaceful tea with Niall, before having to reveal what had happened, prior to her leaving for work.

As expected, he flew into an immediate rage.

'That's it!' He shot from his chair. 'I've bloody had it up to here with that lot. Right, I'm off up to Harriet's now and tell 'em they're not seeing my kids again!'

'Oh, Niall, could ye just hang on till tomorrow?' Looking worn down, Boadicea jumped up too and held on to his arm.

But he fought her. 'No, don't try to stop me!'

'I'm not bloody going to!' Still annoyed and shaken by this afternoon's episode, she had no wish to urge caution this time, for it was obvious that the Beastys understood only one language. 'But I was hoping you'd come with me to the pub and have a few drinks before the kids get back. If you leave Nora till tomorrow night, then I'll be here to look after them . . .'

And so, under her pleading gaze, Niall accompanied her to the Five Lions to douse his anger with a few pints, and to spend an hour chatting to her, until compelled to go home in time for the children's return.

The next evening, however, was to be less recreational.

Knowing Niall to be more than a match for the Beastys, and having heard what he proposed to say, Boadicea could not help a smile of satisfaction at the thought that this nastiness would soon be dealt with, as she saw him off on his crusade that Sunday night.

Her mind's eye picturing each stage of his progress, as she went back and forth, helping the little ones to get undressed for bed, she was to become so abstracted that she forgot to undo the buttons on Brian's jumper, and in trying to tug it over his head she lifted him clean off his feet.

'Sorry, Bri! Did I nearly strangle ye?' At his muffled squawk, she pulled the jumper hastily back into place, and unfastened it properly before taking it off, but even as she helped him into his pyjamas, she was thinking of Niall – now he was through Walmgate Bar, now along Lawrence Street, march, march, marching with deep intent, now surely at Tang Hall, and finally at the Beasty one's door – she could almost hear his words . . .

'Bring your mother out, Harriet!' commanded Niall, facing his sister-in-law across her doorstep. 'I'm not repeating meself!'

And when a tight-lipped Nora barged forth to demand, 'What do *you* want?' he was to tell her, in no uncertain terms.

'You know why I'm here! You've been warned about taking the kids without permission, but you obviously can't be trusted! So until you can keep to the rules, you're not going to see them any more. When I entrust them to Boadicea, I don't expect somebody else to come along and drag them away, upsetting them – not to mention her – and if you try it again there'll be trouble!'

'You might trust a barmaid to look after them, but I don't!' bellowed a furious Nora. 'For a start, she's not their mother—'

'But she soon will be!' shot Niall, pushing his wolfish features towards his mother-in-law and enjoying the look on her face as he informed her, 'We're getting married in December.' He did not give precise detail, for she would be sure to ruin his day. 'And then she'll be their legal guardian, so if you try to take them without her permission I've told her to report you to the police!' And after waiting a second for his warning to sink in, he spun on his heel and made for the gate.

'It'll be us who's sending for the police!' bawled Harriet, stalking after him to clatter the gate into place, and to lean over it and hurl insults as Niall strode away. 'That filthy trollop couldn't manage dishwater, let alone children!'

But Niall knew that these were words of desperation, for when he had left Boadicea half an hour ago she had been managing very well indeed. Thus he threw Harriet and her mother a last caution. 'Well, she seems to be doing a better job of it than you – so stay away, 'cause I won't tell you again!'

'Batty, I won't tell you again! Put that book down and get up at the table like I told ye ten minutes ago!' A slightly irritated Boadicea finished plaiting Juggy's hair, then dealt her a gentle shove towards the table where the others sat drinking their hot beverage. Finding herself ignored, she added, 'I'm going to tip your cocoa down the sink if you don't come and drink it!'

'See if I care,' mouthed Batty from behind his tome.

'What was that?' Boadicea put her hands on her hips and directed herself at the one in the armchair. 'I think ye might care when your father comes home and finds out how rude you've been.'

But the six-year-old was obviously wise to her, knowing from the lack of a good hiding from his father that she had not informed on him before. One might have hoped that last night's trip to the circus would have induced good behaviour, but the boys had been giddy as clowns since Niall had gone out. Boadicea suspected this obstructive behaviour was due to the girls giving their brothers an account of yesterday's commotion between herself and their grandmother. Even in her absence, Nora made herself felt.

With a hiss of impatience, she made for the stairs. 'One last time! If you're not up at the table by the time I've sorted out your dirty clothes for tomorrow's wash, you're for the chop!'

Overhearing yet another impudent comment as she left the room, and sniggers from the others, Boadicea stomped upstairs and began to go about the bedrooms, collecting things to wash and muttering to herself, 'What sort of idiot am I? Here am I cooking for the little swine, doing his washing – and him treating me like dirt!' Still, as she went through Batty's trouser pocket to check for unwanted articles in her washtub, she could not help but laugh to herself as she read his childish scrawl upon the bit of paper that fell to the floor, along with a few pebbles and matches.

Her amusement was curtailed by a knock at the front door. With a sigh, she made towards the staircase. However, Honor was to beat her to it. 'I'll go!'

'Thanks, Honey,' Boadicea called back, smiling again as she tucked Batty's list into her own skirt pocket, and continued to gather the clothes – that was, until Honor hissed up the stairs: 'It's a policeman!'

Boadicea's heart skipped a beat – she was almost sick – and for a second she could not move.

There came a pounding up the staircase, then

Honor poked her pretty freckled nose round the door. 'Did you hear me?' And she stared at Boadicea, who seemed frozen to the spot. Her mind a cauldron bubbling with thoughts, Boadicea tried to fight her way to the surface, turning vacantly to the speaker and attempting to sound calm, though her heart was beating so quickly that it brought her dangerously close to fainting. 'Yes . . . yes, I'm coming . . . I just wanted to finish off up here.' Struggling to compose herself as she went, she followed Honor downstairs and, whilst Niall's elder daughter went into the living room, she moved like an automaton to the door. By the time she reached it, she had managed to fight off the tide of panic, though her face remained pale and her legs weak.

'Is this the home of Bartholomew Doran?' enquired the policeman.

Warily, Boadicea gave affirmation.

'Then I'd like to speak to your son, please, Mrs Doran.'

Too concerned to know why the officer was here, she did not correct his misassumption that she was Batty's mother, but said, 'I'll fetch him.'

But as she turned and went to the kitchen, without invitation the policeman followed her. 'Come in, why don't ye?' She was now sufficiently recovered to offer sarcasm, her eyes fixing him as he stood in the middle of the living room as if he owned the place, but he ignored her and continued to examine each of the other occupants.

Prepared by their sister for the policeman's entrance, most of the children returned his mistrustful scrutiny with awe, all except Batty in his armchair, who continued to read, his face hidden behind the large book.

Boadicea gave swift instruction. 'Would you take your books upstairs, please – not you, Batty! The policeman wants to speak to ye.'

Dragging their heels, the children made their exit, Boadicea giving the last one a helpful shove then closing the door on them, before standing with arms folded to hear the accusation.

'This afternoon,' began the officer, his worldly eyes impaling the small brown-haired boy, 'we received a report that a collection of garden tools had been stolen from a shed at the rear of Margaret Street. A number of boys were seen loitering in the vicinity on Saturday morning and were chased away by the owner, who only discovered the theft around two p.m. today. A witness gave your name as one of those seen running away yesterday. So, Master Doran,' he concluded sternly, 'what have you to say to this?'

'Weren't me.' The six-year-old's blue eyes beheld him ingenuously.

A period of interrogation was to ensue, an anxious Boadicea standing by to hug herself and to listen as Niall's son insisted, 'I've been at church today.'

'And what about yesterday?'

'I went to get me hair cut with me dad.'

'That would take all of ten minutes – where were you the rest of the day?'

Batty appeared thoughtful. 'Me uncle took us to the circus.'

'And what about the morning?'

Batty shrugged. 'I was just here, with her.'

'You can vouch for your son's whereabouts, I suppose, Mrs Doran?'

Only now did Batty betray a hint of anxiety. Studying Niall's son for that fleeting moment, Boadicea read what was there and responded unequivocally to the policeman, 'Yes, it's true what the lad says. He was here with me the entire morning.'

'What, every second of it?' The constable looked disbelieving.

It was obvious that Boadicea had little respect for the police, but until now fear had caused her to remain civil. She narrowed her eyes, and her chin came up. 'Would you be calling me a liar?'

'Certainly not.' He shook his head, though his own blue eyes remained shrewd as they adhered to hers, exacerbating her discomfort as he plainly saw through her. 'I just find it strange for a lad his age to be stuck in the house on a Saturday.'

'There's nothing strange about it.' Boadicea kept up her resistance. 'He was ill in bed.'

'Not ill enough to keep him from the circus.'

'That was five hours later! I didn't want to keep him from his treat. He was all right after he vomited. I had to clear up after him, that's why

I can vouch so surely – so the one that says they saw him is the liar.'

'Well . . .' the man in blue continued to eye her, clearly disbelieving a word she said, 'the witness couldn't be entirely certain it was him.'

'So we've been put through all this by some eejit who needs his eyes testing?' scoffed Boadicea. 'It's funny how my lad was the only one named. Sounds like somebody has it in for him, if you ask me.'

'All right . . .' he procrastinated, his eyes still not leaving her, 'but I'll just have a quick look in your coalhouse to satisfy myself.'

'To see there are no stolen goods, ye mean? Be my guest.' Stalking ahead on her green suede high heels, Boadicea escorted him into the yard, then gave a theatrical presentation of the coal bunker, and hovered, hugging her body against the cold whilst the policeman shone his torch into it, then moved to a shed to flash it over the array of tools therein.

'Every one of those belongs to the boy's father.'

The officer withdrew, his tone and attitude lacking any form of apology. 'Right, I can see there are no gardening implements.'

'That's it then, is it?' she enquired tersely, as he switched off his torch.

'Yes, I'm obliged for your co-operation.' He eyed her with slight contempt.

'You can leave this way if ye like.' An angry Boadicea hurried to open the rear gate. It was bad enough a uniformed figure coming to the front door in the first place; she did not want him leaving that way too. The instant he was through, she slammed the gate and rammed the bolt home.

When she returned to the kitchen, Batty was still seated there, head in his book, the epitome of virtue. 'Right,' she said to him, quietly menacing, 'let's be having it.'

He looked up to perform a theatrical frown. 'What?'

'Don't come the injured party with me, Stainless Stephen – it won't wash! Where have ye stashed the goods?'

The boy turned fierce. 'I never stole owt! I knew you wouldn't believe me!'

Arms folded under her breast, she said with weary patience, 'Batty, if you're ever to become a master criminal it's not a good idea to keep a list in your pocket with the heading "BURGLAR GANG" – and your name in top position.' She saw his look of shock, and drove her accusation home by brandishing the slip of paper. 'Yes, I just found it minutes before the policeman came when I was sorting your clothes out to wash! I thought it was just some game – little did I know. Now come on, let's have this out before your father gets in. I don't want him worrying about it!'

'You won't tell him then?' Batty's expression changed from defeat to optimism.

'Do you really think that good man wants to hear that his son is a thief?' Boadicea flung at him.

The boy hung his head.

'Haven't you anything to say?'

'Sorry,' he mumbled.

'A thank you might be in order too!' Her voice and eyes were scathing. 'I've made myself a liar sticking up for you.'

At last he looked suitably grateful, his remorse genuine. 'I won't do it again, I promise.'

'Damn right you won't! I'm hanging on to this list, and if I ever get to hear you've been in any kind of trouble again it'll be shown to that policeman.' With great deliberation she folded it back into her pocket. 'What the devil do you want with garden tools anyway?'

Shame upon his pixie face, the little boy shrugged. 'We just wanted some weapons of war.'

'War, is it? Sure, your father will give you war if he ever finds out!' She caught a look of fresh alarm. 'Ach, don't fret, he won't find out from me. But tell me, then, where did ye stash them? They'll have to be returned somehow.'

'We shoved 'em under a boat in Danny Wrigglesworth's yard,' he confessed.

'He's your fence, is he?' Boadicea clapped a hand to her brow. 'God help us!' Then she heard the front door open. 'Ssh, your father's here!'

Both turned to present a smile to Niall as he entered, but his face did not reciprocate.

'How did you get on with Nora?' she asked immediately.

'She's been put in her place – but never mind her,' he said. 'What's been going on here?'

'Why, nothing at all!' Boadicea issued lightly.

Detecting subterfuge from both the woman and the boy, Niall looked grim as he took off his jacket. 'I've just been informed by Gloria Lavelle that we've had a copper here – couldn't wait to tell me.'

Boadicea sagged, then overcame her reluctance, and blurted, 'It was all a mistake! Someone claimed they saw Batty and his friends stealing some garden tools. I said it couldn't have been him because he was with me all morning yesterday.'

'But we both know that isn't true, don't we?' Niall accused the conspirators. Still wound up from his encounter with Nora and Harriet, he expressed his rage to the ceiling, then shouted at her, 'For Christ's sake, can't I leave this house for one minute?'

'So what did you expect me to do?' Boadicea protested. 'Hand your son over to the cops?'

'I don't expect you to lie for him!' Niall's glare was filled with revulsion. 'You should have waited till I got in. If my son is a thief then I expect him to be pun—'

'Don't say another word!' She flushed with anger, her eyes holding a threat. 'Before you start clambering into your pulpit, throwing recriminations, think very carefully about this: it isn't just Batty that'd be punished, it's the entire family who'd have to live with the shame, his father

498

dragged through the courts, your name in the newspapers, made to look like an unfit parent – *that*'s what I was trying to spare ye, Niall. And small thanks I get!'

His glare no less corrosive, Niall wheeled on his son. 'See what trouble you've caused? Well, mister, you can thank Bo for saving your neck—'

'He did thank me,' she intervened swiftly.

'—but you needn't think it's saved your backside!' continued Niall, and, seizing the child by one arm he hauled him from the chair and delivered three hefty slaps to his pyjama-striped buttocks and almost threw him at the stairs. 'Now, get to bloody bed!'

Following Batty's tearful exit, the father rocked his head in his hands. 'Christ, what else could go wrong?'

'Don't say that,' murmured Boadicea, still annoyed with him. 'In my experience, something always does.' She was now by the fire, prodding it with a poker, though it was merely for something to do rather than necessity.

'I'm sorry I shouted at you,' he sighed as he watched her.

'That's all right.' Still levering the coals with the poker, she shrugged forgiveness, though the fact that it was not really all right was evident in that she remained aloof.

'Come and sit down and give me the full story,' he suggested gently, and when she had related it, said, 'You shouldn't have to put up with this.'

'You're right there!' came the pithy rejoinder. Niall's mother-in-law might have been thwarted in her attempts to ruin Boadicea's chances with him, but his children were doing a pretty good job of it themselves. 'Anyhow,' she added, as if hoping to bring the matter to a close, for the episode had upset her greatly, 'I don't think Batty'll do it again. He had such a fright.'

'I'll bet you did too,' observed Niall.

She nodded, though did not tell him how much of a fright, and from then on an uneasy truce came into force, with Niall eventually coming to understand why she had covered up for his son.

'But I'll still have to go round to the Wrigglesworths and get these tools back, and try to return them to the owner,' he said at the end of it all, and, weary of face, he slapped his knees and rose.

'Niall,' Boadicea projected weariness too, 'can't ye forget about being Mr Honest for one blasted day? Leave matters be, I'm begging ye. Sure, ye might get caught with the tools and ye don't want the police involved again, do ye?'

Barely faltering, he shook his dark head.

'Let the cops find the wretched things themselves.' She came to stroke his arm. 'Batty's had his clattering, let that be an end to it. He's not a bad lad. And now you've warned his granny off, and she can't exert her influence, things can only improve.'

17

Whilst Boadicea's relationship with the six-year-old was certainly to improve, and Brian and Juggy were not too difficult to handle either, there were still two others with whom she had yet to break down the barriers. Even without their grandmother's manipulation, Dominic and Honor continued to be somewhat reserved in their attitudes, neither willing to approach Boadicea for anything they might need, no matter how friendly she tried to be. Dominic was often so bad that she wondered if he were visiting his grandmother in secret, though she chose not to divulge her suspicions to Niall. In a way, though, he was still easier to deal with than his elder sister, for at least Boadicea could chastise him for his cheek. A much quieter individual, Honor's only form of rebellion, if she did not concur with something that Boadicea had said, would simply be to remove herself from the room. How could one deal with that?

In comparison, decided Boadicea, the neighbours

were merely tiresome, and, unless Mrs Beasty decided to pay a visit to the street and stir things up again, their nastiness was restricted to cool looks. So long as this was the depth of their toxicity, she would find them no more discomforting than the weather. Besides, with Reilly and his wife, Sean and his, the Preciouses and her fellow boarders, she had many more friends than enemies. Moreover, she had found a soul mate in Emma, who herself had been an object of Nora's venom, and, still now getting to know Niall's children, could sympathise with all that Boadicea had to tolerate from them.

'But for all that, it's Honor my heart goes out to,' lamented Boadicea, as she stood on the table and gazed from Emma's window at the gloomy scene beyond, the pink and bronze chrysanthemums, bedraggled in the November fog. 'As much as she tries to play the little woman, 'tis obvious she's in desperate need of a mother's affection, the age she's at, somebody who can give her advice on female things. I mean, I fully agree with Niall not letting Mrs Beasty and her daughters see them until they can keep their poisonous thoughts to themselves, but Honor's been left with no one to answer her questions – she's not going to come to me, is she?'

Agreeing it was an awfully confusing time, being half-child, half-woman, Emma took pin after pin from a small cushion and inserted them through the hem of the silky jade-green dress, whilst Boadicea performed a slow rotation. 'I don't think you have to worry too much yet about her going with lads, though. She tells me she's off mischiefing with her pal tonight.'

Her Irish friend responded with a groan. Having not previously heard of this local custom, it befell Emma to explain that November the fourth was designated Mischief Night, when the native children would get up to all sorts of impishness. 'Just harmless stuff,' she told Boadicea, 'pinching rubbish from people's bonfires, or tying a few front doorknobs together, so the occupants won't be able to get out tomorrow morning . . .'

Boadicea gave a circumspect laugh. 'Well, if it gets no worse than that, I'll be happy – do you want me to turn again?'

'No, all done.' Positioning the last pin, Emma stood back to check that the hem was level, and lauded the overall result. 'Oh yes, very à la mode – Niall's not going to be able to keep his hands off you in that!' She saw the other blush in getting down from the table, and was swift to apologise, biting her lip. 'Sorry, that was a bit cheeky. I just feel I've known you ages.'

Boadicea waved aside her own embarrassment, and used both hands to smooth the material that clung to her hips, studying the reflection of her ankles in the mirror that Emma had propped against the wall. 'I wish I had known you for ages, or I'd have commissioned your services before.' It was only by accident that she had discovered Emma's talents – not that it would have been right to ask her to sew the girls' dresses. 'That's perfect, thanks. Not like Mrs Precious would do it. I've trusted her before and it's turned out all wonky – mind you, that could be my needlework.'

Emma smiled. 'Well, you don't have to worry about sewing it.' This matter had already been co-ordinated. 'I'll do it for you this afternoon.'

'Aw, no rush.' Boadicea would not need the dress for a couple of weeks. Both she and Niall having managed to arrange a day off, she was finally taking him to meet her father and brother a week on Saturday. Having written to warn them of this, she had just received a warm response. But she mentioned none of this to Emma, for Niall was undecided yet who should look after his children. She referred to the dress again. 'I know it's only an inch too long, but it makes all the difference between looking like a woman of style or an old granny, with it flapping round my ankles like it did. I should have had it altered when I bought it. I knew it was too long but loved the colour. I was after buying a new one when I remembered this had been hanging in the wardrobe for months and I came over all wasteful.' Careful to avoid the pins, she slipped the clinging garment over her head, and handed it to Emma before pulling on a tie-necked jumper and pleated skirt.

'So will you be wearing it anywhere special?' Emma gave the silken article a shake.

Boadicea replied with a white lie and a grin. 'Not that I know of – not a secret wedding, if that's what you're thinking.'

'Drat!' Emma looked beaten. 'And here's me thinking I'm being all subtle'

'Don't worry, as soon as we make up our minds on a date, you shall be informed.' Boadicea made a move for her coat and gloves. 'Right, I'd better be away to my shift. Is there anything else I should do in preparation of this Mischief Night, apart from pray for rain?'

'That won't keep 'em indoors.' Emma wrinkled her nose. 'No, just make 'em a bit of bonfire toffee. That should please.'

Boadicea threw her eyes to the ceiling – 'A good job it's my night off' – and she asked for the recipe.

Emma went to dig it out. 'Oh, and tell them me and Uncle Sean'll be round with a bag of fireworks tomorrow, but only if they've behaved themselves.'

'I shall cross my fingers.' Thanking Emma one last time, Boadicea left.

That same Monday evening, only the elder children being allowed out after dark, Honor's friend Vera called for her at half-past six. Having been forewarned by Emma, Boadicea welcomed Vera in to wait, offering her some treacle toffee whilst making sure that Honor had warm gloves and coat to put on, even though this seemed to be resented as fuss. The same went for Dominic, though he was to exit alone. Their father had words for them both.

'If you're off mischiefing – yes, I *do* know what date it is,' he said with a warning twinkle in his eye

– 'keep well away from this street. We've got enough enemies already without you creating any more – and don't go setting any bonfires alight, Dom.'

'No point going out then,' said his son, with a laugh as he went.

Niall shook his head in fatherly despair, then jumped along with everyone else in response to a canon-like boom, the result of someone shoving a banger down a drain.

''Tis like blasted Waterloo!' Boadicea clutched her chest, then chuckled to reassure the younger ones, and was aided by their father, who gathered them round for a bedtime story as compensation for not being allowed the same privilege as their older brother and sister.

Outside, the darkened streets were populated with furtive figures, in balaclavas, wellingtons and gabardines, some pushing wheelbarrows, old prams and trolleys, collecting rubbish for their bonfires – or stealing it from rivals – others not satisfied with bits of wood, but detaching whole gates from their hinges, and spiriting them away.

Honor and her friend were to remain in their own street for a while, huddled against the cold and giggling as they concocted the rude note that would be shoved through Gloria's door. Using the wall on which to rest her paper, licking her pencil to make the message more legible, Honor scrawled away in the darkness, 'Dear Miss Lavelle, I have heard that you do not wear knickers, if this is true, please be so kind as to stand at the window tomorrow morning when I come by, and I will show you my willie, signed, The Milkman . . .'

On his way to meet his own friends, as ever, it was to be profit that was Dominic's chief motive for mischief. Hearing the clink of coins from an alley, he pressed himself to the brick wall and sneaked a look round the corner, to see a group of men playing pitch and toss under a streetlamp. With their inefficient lookout being distracted by lighting a cigarette, an impish Dom took advantage, by suddenly shouting, 'Police!' – and the group scattered into the darkness, abandoning their coppers. Thus the cheeky perpetrator could dash in, scoop them up and flee, before anyone could notice his ploy.

Laughing to his pals some minutes later outside a corner shop, and chinking his coins as he related his audacious exploit, Dom only realised his act had been witnessed when a man came out of nowhere, grabbed him, and dragged him yelling into the darkness. His friends did the only thing they could. They ran and left him to it.

'Did you see your brother on your travels?' frowned Niall, when it was thirty-two minutes past eight and Dom was two minutes late. Honor had been in for some time and was seated in her nightdress with a mug of Ovaltine, in her usual ladylike fashion, looking as if butter wouldn't melt in her mouth, though apart from writing the letter to Gloria she had knocked on many doors and run away.

His daughter was still in the act of shaking her

head when a slight click and waft of cold air indicated that the front door had opened. Boadicea exchanged a knowing look with Niall, then, when no one came into the living room, she went ahead of him to check the passage – and found the boy trying to sneak up the stairs.

'And where d' ye think you're off?' she demanded with a grin. 'Any later and you would have been in trouble – but come on now and have some Ovaltine.'

Slightly hunched, and walking in an odd way, Dominic tried to avert his face as he demurred her offer and continued for the stairs, but at his father's summons, he was compelled to follow her into the light of the living room.

Boadicea put both hands to her mouth as Niall jumped up and accosted his son. 'Who did this to you?' he demanded of the bloody face, whilst Boadicea and Honor looked on in horror and sympathy.

Dom could hardly get the words out, so swollen was his mouth, and from the protective way he hugged his body, it was obvious he had been beaten about other parts too.

'Who, did you say?' yelled Niall, bending close to his son's face. 'That bloke who lives at thirteen? What did he hit you for?'

The father might have difficulty in making out what was being said; however, Boadicea had no trouble deciphering his motives. 'Niall, wait!' she cried as he launched himself at the door. 'It's dark, you don't know for certain who it was – you could be arrested if somebody witnesses you hitting him!'

'Then I'll make sure I'm not seen!' Niall hurled over his shoulder, before running from the house.

'Christ Almighty!' Boadicea uttered a sound of frustration, then hurried to fetch a wet cloth and made to tend Dom's wounds. But he brushed aside her attempts, and she was forced to hand over the cloth so that he could do it for himself, wincing along with Honor as both stood to watch him dab at his mouth.

'What on earth did ye do to anger the brute?' she breathed.

'Nowt,' shrugged Dom, then instantly regretted it, for his face showed that every movement hurt.

'Oh dear, ye poor thing.' Boadicea stood by, her face a picture of compassion. 'Take your shirt off and let me have a look what other damage he's done.'

She moved as if to help, but Dom lurched away, emitting yet another groan of pain.

'Well, your father will have to have a look when he comes in!' she scolded in frustration.

Dominic was not keen to wait around for his father to return, and tried to slope off, but she bade him sit by the fire and handed him a cup of Ovaltine, and was to pace anxiously until Niall returned some ten minutes later.

'Couldn't ye find him?' she asked immediately. 'You weren't long.'

'It didn't take long.' His face still dark, though

much of his fury had been worked out in giving the man what he deserved, he rubbed his grazed knuckles. 'Don't worry,' he forestalled her look of anxiety, 'he won't tell the police. They were gambling and Dom pinched their money – Norman Whelan saw it, and he confirmed who it was. Luckily I found the bugger straight away.'

'Did ye do much damage?' Noting that Dom had finished with the cloth, Boadicea took it off him and handed it to his father, in order that the latter might tend his knuckles.

'Well, I saw a couple of teeth fly out,' admitted Niall.

'Serve him right,' she nodded with satisfaction, and went to lay a tender hand on the victim's shoulder. 'A good hiding is one thing, but that's assault what he did to poor Dom.'

Niall's beneficence was not to last. 'Aye, well, poor Dom'll be getting another pasting – from me, if he pulls that one again!' He included Honor in his next instruction, 'Come on the pair of you, off to bed now.' And obediently they went.

He and Boadicea left alone now, a tired-looking Niall examined her face as she went about clearing the mugs away, and his tone was one of despair. 'I'll bet you're thinking you've made a big mistake in taking me on, aren't you?'

She looked at him sharply, for indeed, she did often feel as if she were reaching the end of her tether with these incidents. It was only because of her adoration of Niall that she put up with them.

But her face softened, 'Aw, well, he might be a little divil, but the prank didn't warrant such a thrashing.'

Niall continued to rub his knuckles as he spoke, his expression become distracted. 'I'll go up and check him in a minute, see there's nowt broken. Same can't be said about t'other fella.' For a moment he looked sinister, then this was repealed as he gazed upon her again. 'You won't give up on us, will you?'

She came to him immediately, and put her loving arms around him. 'So long as you won't give up on me.'

'A saint like you?' he said, with a heartfelt kiss. 'Never.'

This beatification that Niall had conferred was to come in most handy the next day too, for it was Honor's turn to reap the results of the previous night's mischief. The smell of bonfires and gunpowder already in the air, Boadicea had become concerned that the eldest child had not yet returned from school, and poked her head into the street to see where she might be, only to witness sparks of temper flying from next door.

'No good hiding up there!' Bereft of teeth, Gloria was inflicting her vocal impediment on someone who was apparently lurking at the top of the terrace. 'Get yourselves down here!' And as the two reluctant figures approached, Boadicea was alarmed to see that one of them was Honor.

'Thought you'd sneak out this morning before I could catch you,' lisped Gloria as the schoolgirls arrived. 'Yes, I know it was you, milady! Even though you tried to disguise your handwriting, I know it well enough.' She brandished the incriminating note at Honor, who, with her friend Vera blushed in shame. 'That's disgusting that is! Well, if you think I'm teaching you to dance now, you've got another think coming. In fact, I've a good mind to tell your father . . .'

Boadicea sought to intervene at this point, and, with the rest of her charges having followed her to investigate the noise, she stepped onto the pavement. 'Is there some kind of trouble?'

Gloria turned to flourish the note under the intruder's nose then, her gums spraying spittle over the group of listeners. 'I should say so. Just have a look at that!'

'The rest of you, go get your coats, then you can clear off to play,' Boadicea commanded the ones who had followed. Then, in calm manner, she took the note, her lips twitching as she read it, finally to look up and say, 'Well, I'm very, very sorry, Miss Lavelle, it must have been awfully upsetting for ye,' here she gave a stern look at the schoolgirls, who continued to hang their heads whilst the rest of the children gawped from afar, 'but I don't think there was any malice intended.'

'Oh, well, I might have known!' lisped Gloria, her toothless cheeks pink with outrage. 'They probably learned that sort of language off you. They were never like that before you came along!'

'Yes, well, I've said I'm very sorry.' Boadicea set

her mouth, and shoved both girls into the house before she lost her temper.

'I'll have that note back!' demanded Gloria. 'I want to show it to her father.'

'I can do that perfectly well, thank you,' came Boadicea's crisp response, before slamming the door.

In the living room, Honor and her friend were to remain shamefaced under Boadicea's mild chastisement. 'It's not the sort o' thing your parents want to hear, is it?' she asked them softly. 'I'm surprised at ye.'

'Sorry,' came the quiet joint apology.

'Ah, well, that's enough for me.' Boadicea's warm tone signified that the matter was over and done with, and she threw the note on the fire. 'So long as you've learned. I'm not condoning it, mind! It wasn't a very nice thing to do, and I can't say I liked having to deal with it. But I think you've had enough telling off now, and your father shan't know about it, Honor, nor yours, Vera – unless that soft biddy next door cares to give you away.' Amusement had begun to tweak her lips, as she told the pair with some indignation, 'Imagine her thinking I'm the one who taught ye such rude words – the cheek of it!'

Honor and Vera were still blushing, but relieved enough to display similar amusement.

'And what was all that about her teaching yese to dance?' Boadicea asked them.

'She was going to show us how to do that jazzy stuff,' Honor revealed.

There was a cynical laugh from Boadicea. 'And

where would Gloria get any dancing practice, with no teeth to her name? If it's jazz ye want ye should've come to me. They say I'm not a bad dancer. I'd be happy to teach ye.'

Sitting on the arm of a chair now, and swinging her black-stockinged leg, Honor showed appreciation for this, thinking that her grandmother must be mistaken about this woman, who was really quite kind. Then, she added rather sadly with a look at her friend, 'But Gloria's the one with the gramophone.'

'Not the only one,' announced Boadicea, with a proud air. 'Don't I have one myself back at my lodgings? I shall get your father to carry it over – that's provided he's still talking to us if he finds out about your little contretemps with Miss Lavelle – and I'll teach you all the moves. See, who needs Gloria when ye've got me!' And giving them a smile, she announced, 'Right, I'd better have a look how those baked potatoes are getting on for your Bonfire Night tea!' And she disappeared into the scullery.

'She's lovely, in't she?' Vera was overheard to say. 'I'll bet you'll be glad when she comes to live here all the time.'

Pricking up her ears for the answer, Boadicea waited in suspense.

'It's not the same as your own mam, though,' lamented Honor.

As if there had not been enough fireworks already, true to Emma's word, she and Sean were to turn up after tea with a paper bag containing the real thing. With Reilly and Eileen making a contribution too, the small back yard was to resound with colourful explosions for a good hour after tea – thankfully none of them from Gloria, who was content to have said her piece. It was a pity that Boadicea was the only one who had to go to work, and, added to Honor's declaration, this left her feeling rather out of things for a day or two.

But there were bridges to be built, and as an adult Boadicea must be the one to construct them. Thus she was to follow through on her promise to have Niall transport her gramophone here on Saturday, and spent much of that afternoon conveying dance steps to Honor. At the end of which, Niall remarked that, notwithstanding his daughter's natural reserve, he could sense a definite improvement between the pair.

Satisfied that everything was coming together, she and Niall began seriously to discuss a date for their wedding, so that they might inform her father during the coming visit – though the latter presented a slight problem in itself, for Eileen and Reilly had been put in charge of Niall's children so much lately, it seemed almost indecent to ask if they would perform this courtesy yet again, and for an entire day.

Circumstantially, they were spared having to do this, for it was they who would be performing the favour. Under onslaught from months of rain, York's rivers could finally take no more. With the Foss Basin overflowing into his home, along with much sewage, Reilly was obliged to call upon his friend to help transport as much furniture as possible to the upper floor before the deluge struck, and to seek temporary accommodation. This was to be gladly given, Niall having the greater obligation for favours past, and welcoming him and Eileen into his home, for as long as necessary.

Whilst this would likely only be for a few days, Reilly had an idea how to make things more comfortable for everyone. 'It's worked out quite well in a way,' he said, after an exhausting evening of shifting furniture, to much ironic laughter from his wife. 'No, listen, woman. Niall and Bo are off to Manchester tomorrow. It's a bloody long way to go for the day.' He addressed himself mainly to Niall now, 'why don't you stay overnight, and make a weekend of it? Then me and Eileen can have your bed,' he ended with a crafty grin at his wife.

'Eh, you're not so daft as you look.' She nodded approval.

'He is,' returned Niall, with his customary dry wit. 'My bed comes with a little lad in it.'

'Oh, he'll be locked in the shed along with the rest of 'em the minute their father's out the door,' said Eileen matter-of-factly, before responding to the genuine issue. 'No, but he's right, Nye, you'd be mad to rush there and back in a day. We don't mind taking them to Mass and everything. We love having them, don't we, Reilly, as long as we can give them back?'

Though the idea was greatly tempting to Niall,

he was unsure how to answer for Boadicea, who was presently at work, and would be working on Sunday, as far as he knew.

'Surely she can get dinner time off,' appealed Eileen. 'Even if she still has to work the night, if you set off from Manchester after Sunday dinner you could be back in time for her evening shift.'

Niall wondered whether Bo would think there was something underhand in his query over whether her father had enough room to put them up overnight.

'Well, there's one way to find out,' said Reilly, his big face showing enthusiasm as he began to rise. 'You and me'll go and ask her—'

'Oh yes!' Eileen exclaimed knowingly. 'And leave me here to mind the kids.'

'Just for a last half,' wheedled her husband. 'There's only an hour till closing.'

'Last half my foot,' said Eileen to Niall. 'I've known him get three pints down his neck in a fraction of that time.'

'Well, I'm going to need summat to send me off to sleep,' objected Reilly, 'if I'm having to kip on the floor.'

'Oh, you poor hard-done-by soul, go on then!' She gave a smirk and, with great amiability, shooed the men from the living room. 'And I'll put my time to better use, shall I, in making up a bed for us in the front room?'

Reilly clapped his hands in a rapid little gesture of success, as he and Niall headed for the pub.

'Sorry I can't give you my bed till tomorrow—' began Niall to his friend.

'Ah, doesn't matter!' Reilly nudged him and laughed. 'Eh, you'll have to get rid of Brian out of it when you get married, though.'

Niall laughed too, and said not one word to the contrary.

It did not go down too well with the landlord when Boadicea asked during that very busy Friday night, if she might skip her Sunday dinnertime shift as well as the two Saturday ones already granted.

'Tell you what,' he hinted, in less than helpful tone, 'why don't you take every night off? There's not much point me having a barmaid who's never here.'

And so, in the knowledge that she would soon be handing in her notice anyway, upon marriage, Boadicea felt it only fair to enact this suggestion, thus leaving the landlord to bemoan his loss, for her affable and garrulous nature had earned popularity amongst his customers.

It was as well that she was such a good talker, thought Niall, upon finally getting to meet her father the next day, for William Merrifield was a man of few words. Obviously this was not through any form of shyness, for he had a cheery and efficient air as he welcomed in his guests – and his marble-green eyes spoke volumes as they took the prospective son-in-law's measure. Still, the stockily built man had little to say for now, and it was clear that

Boadicea had inherited her fluency from her mother, similarly her looks – for which Niall was most grateful, for ex-Sergeant Merrifield had a head like a bullet and a face that was heavily creased from his wartime experience.

Arthur's appearance was nothing like as hard, and he shared the blue eyes, fair hair and fresh complexion of his sister, though not her loquacity, for he was as unforthcoming as his sire. With Niall himself being the shy type, it was left to Boadicea to promote conversation, and this she was to do most admirably.

But, as uncommunicative as Mr Merrifield and Arthur might be, they showed great decency towards their guests. No matter that their red-brick terraced house had only two bedrooms, upon hearing that Niall and Boadicea would now be staying the night, they refused to show inconvenience, her father saying immediately that he and his son would move in together, his daughter could have his bed, and there was a comfortable sofa in the front room for Niall.

'I'll get your Aunty Violet to cook dinner for us tomorrow, as well,' said Mr Merrifield, his accent a strange mongrel mix, due to living in various barracks amongst all different types. 'She insisted on coming to do tonight's tea for us when she heard you were coming – said me and Arthur weren't up to providing anything decent – so she can ruddy-well do us dinner as well.' He threw Niall a sardonic smile, his eyes less critical of the visitor now.

Arthur too dropped his reticence, his sentence

exposing an Irish twang. 'We'll be having a night out an' all, as you're staying.'

Boadicea took no time at all to agree. 'Oh, can we go somewhere there's dancing?' The recent practice with Honor had fired her up.

Her father did not know of such a venue, but Arthur said there was a large pub that catered for such tastes. 'There's a good band playing – do you like dancing, Niall?'

'Aye . . .' Niall was quietly keen, raising his thick eyebrows to display accord.

Arthur must have noticed the gleam in his eye. 'Sure, don't think you're dancing with my sister all night,' he berated, causing Niall to suspect he was only half-joking. 'I haven't seen her in ages, and I intend to make the most of it.'

Niall took this in good part, though when evening eventually descended, and the four went out to the pub – after they had been treated to an exceptionally nice meal from the aunty – it appeared that Arthur had been serious about wanting to partner his sister. For he was to claim the first two dances with her, and her father the next, leaving Niall to sit at the side and covet the one in the jade-green silk, which clung to every part of her body, and he with nothing more exciting than a pint of beer to curl his hand around.

Boadicea sought to apologise for this, when she was finally allowed to flop beside him to catch her breath after a lively series of footwork. 'Ye'll have to forgive them, Niall, they see so little of me –' her smiling blue eyes adhered to him, as she performed an unconscious tweak of her silken lap to smooth away the ruffles, completely unaware how alluring the swish it made as it brushed against the stockinged thigh beneath was to Niall's ears, '– but I swear, the next one's for you.' Her eyes became stern as she moved them to her father and brother, including both in her light rebuke.

'I'm not sure I'll be capable of standing up, let alone dancing, the way your dad's treating me,' laughed Niall, as Mr Merrifield placed another full glass before him, and he sipped it slowly, so as to make sure this debilitation did not come to pass.

And when the band struck up a blues number, he was quick to stake his claim, grabbing Boadicea's hand and leading her to the floor, and from then on there might have been only the pair of them in the room. The fingers that had a moment ago met only hard glass, now enjoyed warm flesh. Urged on by the soulful music, its seductive rhythm, Niall pressed his hand to the small of her back, caressed its curve through the silk, then drew her gently against him, so that he could feel her belly against his as they swayed from side to side, and cheek to cheek, warmth against warmth, every nerve aware of her, bringing such ecstasy . . .

Correspondingly entrapped by the moment, Boadicea gave way to its rapture, closed her eyes and allowed herself to savour the hardness of his jaw against her cheek, the fiery heat of his hand on the small of her back, even though it was winter outside, and the similar burning heat in her groin. Not caring who looked on, nor how unwise it was to let herself be so intoxicated by the music, she sashayed her hips in time to his, deafening herself to the warning voice in her head that demanded she hold him at arm's length, but instead giving in to a deeper need, which made it impossible to tear herself away from this man she loved and desired above all. However much it might torment each of them afterwards, knowing it could lead nowhere, they were desperate to take solace in any form of contact, both in thrall to that seductive rhythm until its very last note.

It was the only dance they were to enjoy. Upon returning to his seat, releasing her fingers that had been so lovingly entwined in his, Niall found another drink pressed into his hand, and for the rest of his time there, this was all that was on offer to him, save for the joy of sharing her gaze.

Their tongues loosened by the beer, father and son were to be quite conversational with Niall, as all returned home, where Boadicea made them a plate of sandwiches before finally deciding it was time for bed.

'Thanks for a lovely night. Shall I make the sofa up before I go?' she asked Niall, then vanished for five minutes, returning to say that the bed was made. 'Good night, all!'

'Night, Bo,' said her father and brother in unison, but made no move to retire themselves, though Mr Merrified apparently decided that he had been trussed up too long and he began to strip off, throwing both his tie and his collar aside, and rolling up his shirtsleeves to display tattooed forearms. 'Ah, that's better!'

Niall felt relaxed too, due as much to the drink inside him as the cosiness of the room, and this inducing him to lounge in his armchair as if at home. For a short while he was to recline there with the men, their sparse comments about football and horse racing interjected by the puffing of cigarettes, and the creaking of floorboards as Boadicea moved about the upstairs room.

Imagining each stage of her undress, and in danger of driving himself mad with it, Niall finally announced that he too should retire. Exchanging a civil good night with his hosts, he went first to the outside lavatory, then to the front room, leaving Mr Merrifield and Arthur enjoying their final cigarette of the night.

Only when he had been tucked up for half an hour on the sofa did Niall get what he had been expecting all day, though it came in a rougher fashion than he would have preferred. His drowsy thoughts ripe with imaginings of Boadicea, he was disturbed by a sudden shaft of light, that quickly vanished again as someone came into the room and closed the door behind them. But he did not realise that both father and son were present, until one of them grabbed his shoulders and the other pinioned his legs to the sofa. Disconcerting and uncomfortable as this might be, he chose not to struggle, as the interrogation began. It was obvious they had been waiting for Boadicea to go to sleep before making their move – or at least to see if Niall would attempt to sneak into her room.

'We don't want to disturb anybody.' This quietest of threats came from ex-Sergeant Merrifield, the one pinning his legs and whose bullet head leaned close enough for his victim to smell the beer he had been drinking. 'We just want you to answer a question for us: why do you want to marry our lass?'

Whilst Niall accepted this as a perfectly natural question for a father to ask, he found it difficult to respond on such an intimate level to someone he had just met, and under such physical handicap. 'I would've thought that was obvious . . .' he said.

The old ex-army sergeant was quietly intimidating. 'It isn't just because you want her to look after your five kids, is it? 'Cause we wouldn't want—'

'Whoa!' Unable to rise, Niall used his voice in an attempt to muzzle the other. 'I can look after me own kids, thank you very much. I'm not marrying her for that.'

'Ye do know she doesn't want any of her own?' Arthur took his turn at quizzing.

Niall glanced up at the eyes of the one who pinioned his shoulders, that glittered through the dimness. 'Yes, I am aware,' he said calmly, before having to reattend Merrifield senior.

'See, we can't work out why you'd still want to marry her, if you know you're not going to be able to touch her – and if you think that's going to change once you get a ring on her finger, then think again, mister. If I hear you've tried to force—'

'I wouldn't!' Niall sounded bruised, as he engaged the father's eye, hoping to appear as determined as Merrifield. 'I wouldn't do that to any woman, least of all one I respect as much as Bo.'

'Talk's cheap,' warned the ex-sergeant, in the quietly menacing tone that had disciplined troops. 'I saw how you looked at my lass, the way you held her while you were dancing, and I want to make sure you've fully grasped how difficult this is going to be. In fact, one bloke already found it impossible. So you'd better be sure, because she's had her heart broken enough. We're not going to let that happen again. Do you get my drift?'

Annoyed as he was at being threatened with violence, Niall gave a genuine nod. 'You've nowt to fear. I swear on my children's lives. I think the world of that lass.'

Only then did they let him loose, both men standing back and allowing him to rise if he wanted to. 'Aye, well,' came an explanatory growl from the ex-soldier, 'she's thrilled to twitters with you an' all – her letters have been full of you – but we had to make sure for ourselves.'

'Does that mean I pass muster?' chanced Niall through the dark, easing the pressured muscles of leg and shoulder.

'Not yet,' said Merrifield, stern again, as he opened the door and summoned Niall to follow. 'There's a bottle of whisky waiting to be drunk.

Let's see if you still give the same answers after you've had some of it down you.'

Niall was to have no clue whether or not he had given the same answers, for by the time he was returned to his sofa he could remember little of what had gone before, and he slept until eleven the next morning. He must have passed with flying colours, though, for there was no recrimination when he finally dragged himself to the table – except from Boadicea and her aunt for the three examples of soused manhood for whom they must cook dinner – and when he finally boarded the evening train, her father and brother were both extremely genuine in their handshake.

'See you at the wedding!' called Boadicea, waving madly as the train chugged away from those loved ones on the platform, and her next words were for Niall as she gave a last flourish. 'Didn't I say they'd like ye?'

They arrived back in York to a traffic jam, their bus from the station taking an age to reach home, due to the spectacular event of the last electric tramcar being driven before it. The tram bedecked with lights, the Lord Mayor at its controls and the tramway men in fancy dress, this procession was to travel ahead of Niall and Boadicea's bus for most of the way, along a route lined with hundreds. And as if this were not obstruction enough to those weary from travelling, as their vehicle crawled past St George's Field, they were to see that the Martinmas fair caravans were yet marooned, the illuminations from the procession glistening on the flood water and signalling to Niall that he would be spending another uncomfortable night amongst house guests.

Still, he could not object after they had done him such a favour, and, after another day or two, the flood was to recede, permitting Niall to reclaim his overcrowded home, and allowing the Reillys back into theirs – though only after a massive bout of cleaning had been performed by all.

In reward for this assistance and for giving them lodgings, towards the end of that week Niall was to be presented with a Readicut rug kit.

'I know there's no need,' said Eileen, at his objection. 'Call it an early wedding present if you like. It'll give you something to do on a night when you're married.' She cocked an eyebrow in Boadicea's direction. 'Well, she won't be letting you out, that's for sure.'

Both fully aware that her quip held more truth than Eileen could ever be told, Niall exchanged a self-conscious glance at his wife-to-be, who poked gentle fun at the gift. 'Sure, is this supposed to be a hobby? Looks like more work to me.' Having quickly replaced her bar shifts with four hours of daily cleaning at the school, to fit in with the children's attendance, after only a day Boadicea was finding it very tiring.

'Yes, but think what you'll have at the end of it! There's a hook in there for each of you, so if you go at it hard enough you might get it done for the wedding,' suggested Eileen, with a wink at Reilly. 'When did you say it was?'

Niall had been hoping to announce the news to his children separately, but as the Reillys were close friends, and the youngsters were present, it seemed a shame not to take advantage. 'Well, as you ask, and as we've got everybody together . . .'

'Uncle Sean isn't here,' pointed out Juggy.

'Never mind,' said her father, with an affectionate look at Boadicea, who drew nearer to him, 'we'll tell him soon.' And using his eyes to include the children in this joyful announcement, he revealed, 'We've set a date – seventh of December.'

'That's only two weeks on Saturday!' Whilst the dark-haired Eileen gave a childlike squeal and an excited hug of both, and Reilly pumped Niall's hand, the happy couple waited for reaction from his children. With none of them appearing to be actually displeased, Boadicea and Niall must be content with that.

It was imperative that Nora did not get to hear about the wedding before it actually occurred, otherwise she would surely spoil it. So the children were instructed not tell anyone until after the event.

'Especially not Mrs Lavelle and Gloria,' Niall impressed upon them, for the news would be quickly passed on. He himself had thankfully not bumped into Nora since their showdown, and he had no wish to hear her response to his marriage.

'You can rely on us not to say a word,' said Eileen, with a nod from Reilly, to whom she made a jocular addition. 'Well, come on, my lad, we'd better make tracks so these two can start on their rug.' And on this, they were to depart.

However, after their friends went home, instead of the rug, Niall and Boadicea thought to pay a little more heed to the children, telling them that the wedding would involve a party, with lots to eat and drink.

'And go see what's in the front room!' invited Boadicea, with a mysterious smile to the girls in particular.

There were gasps of delight, as Honor and Juggy undid the brown paper parcels that contained their blue velvet dresses. 'It's that stuff we chose!'

Their stepmother-to-be chuckled in appreciation. 'Yes! Go try them on, let's see what they look like – and there's rig-outs for the boys too!' And though these were only composed of white shirts, ties, shorts and socks, Niall's sons were pleased enough to have new clothes.

The dresses were a perfect fit, and the next ten minutes were given to disporting them, though eventually a smiling Boadicea had to apprehend Juggy, who was twirling like a dervish, and say, 'We'd better put them away for the time being, else you'll be sick of them before the wedding.' And she folded them carefully into their tissue paper.

'The house could do with sprucing up too.' She turned to Niall then, having been eager for some time to put her own stamp on what had been his first wife's domain. 'D'ye think we could have a few rolls of wallpaper for the living room? I've seen a lovely leaf design . . .'

Niall was more than happy to accommodate her. 'You get it and I'll stick it on at the weekend – no next weekend, 'cause I'll have to scrape the old stuff off first.'

'How many rolls?' she cast her eye over the drab walls.

'About five,' he calculated.

'It's sixpence ha'penny a roll, so that's . . .' totting up on her fingers, she announced with pleasure, less than three bob!'

'Two and eightpence ha'penny,' said Dom, more precise.

'Oh, we might have known me laddo would have it down to the last farthing,' laughed his father.

Boadicea looked amused. 'Right, I'll get it tomorrow – oh, and isn't that handy?' she beamed at her audience. 'I'll have five children to help me tear the edges off.'

The next afternoon being Friday, upon coming home from school, the children were presented with a roll of wallpaper each, and set to work on carefully removing the half-inch selvedge from one side. This was to be considered no chore at all, for when the strips were all removed and wound into a tight spool, they could be used as streamers. Thrown and rewound, and thrown again, there was much fun to be had with these until bedtime.

There was more on Saturday, when their father

employed them in removing the old wallpaper, so many little hands ripping and picking and tearing at the walls he had dampened, the job was done by late afternoon. Then it was bath time for the grubby crew, and the long tin receptacle was dragged before the fire, the girls bathing first whilst their father and the boys waited in the front room, then Boadicea taking them into the scullery to wash their hair, whilst Niall and his sons had theirs.

With no pub to go to, it was a mixed blessing that Boadicea could be here to participate, happy to be in Niall's company, yet finding the children an awful lot to cope with, what with all the wet towels to dry, the tangled hair to comb, the teeth to inspect. But afterwards it was rather nice to see them all seated around the table, their faces all scrubbed and shiny as pink apples, as they waited to be served with bacon sandwiches for tea.

Handing these out, Boadicea came to stand behind Niall's chair and placed a hand on his shoulder. 'Now,' she asked gaily, 'is that to everyone's satisfaction?'

'It smells lovely, thank you.' In an automatic gesture of affection, he covered her hand with one of his, startling his children, for they had never seen him do that to their mother.

Equally unthinking, Boadicea lowered her head to inhale him. 'Mm, you smell lovely too – all of yese,' she added to the children, as her face came up to beam at them. And for the first time, she experienced a wave of affection for them all, and began to feel like their mother.

Even so, it was nice when they had gone to bed and all the washing-up was done and she could sit with their father alone. Niall obviously enjoyed this cosy feeling too, but, 'I suppose we should do some of this blasted rug,' he sighed after a while. 'Seeing as how they were so kind to give it.' And so, they pulled two dining chairs before the fire, seating themselves opposite each other, and close together – for it was only a small rug – then, with the canvas spread on their laps, they began to work from either side.

It was a slow and boring process, the tufts of wool remaining one colour for several rows, though eventually it was to become more interesting when the pattern began. A picture of the finished article showed a formation of flowers, in shades of pink and green and red and lilac – far too feminine for a labourer's hands, and Boadicea could not help smiling affectionately at the contrast. To prevent the rug-making from becoming too laborious, there was discussion of their wedding.

'How many bottles of port should we get?' she enquired of her husband-to-be, the reflection of the fire flickering in her blue eyes as she patiently worked. 'And what kind? They start at three bob, though I don't really want to buy cheap stuff . . .'

'Pick a middling one, about five bob then.' Niall tweaked another tuft of pink wool through an aperture in the stiff canvas. 'I reckon three should do us.'

'Are we having a cake?' She paused to ease her fingers that were beginning to hurt from manipulating the hook, and watched as he carried on.

'Have anything you like, love.' Niall had left his first wedding arrangements to the women, and this one was to be no different – only in the way he felt. He glanced up to caress her with his smile, the fire glimmering his own eyes, before he reached for another strand of wool.

Boadicea braced herself. 'It has to be said: where will I be sleeping?' One cheek red from the fire, her other slowly coming to match it as embarrassment took over, she covered her sudden bout of shyness by continuing with the rug.

Infected by her awkwardness, Niall hesitated for a moment, before hooking through the strand. 'You could go in the front room . . . but the kids don't miss a trick; they'll surely tell somebody. I couldn't stand being the object of that kind of gossip. Besides,' he looked up at her, 'I want you beside me. I promise I'll behave meself,' he added, before lowering his eyes again.

She nodded in warm agreement, and fell silent for a long time, as both pressed on with the rug.

But it was making her fingers sore, and also her spine, and eventually she stopped to ease this, leaning back in her chair as Niall continued to work. His dark head bent over, his face concentrated on his task, he seemed to regard this as the most important thing in the world. Watching his masculine fingers working upon it, the muscles and sinews in his tanned wrists, Boadicea experienced a sudden flutter of desire in the pit of her abdomen. Involuntarily, she made a little sound, and he looked across at her with love – but then his face altered, as if he could read what was there, and as he stared into her eyes that danced with firelight, his own began to darken with sexual longing. The rug was only a small one. His lips had only a short way to travel as they reached across for hers. Capitulating totally, Boadicea felt herself lost in the taste and moist warmth of him, her eyes closed in ecstasy as her lips were possessed for long moments.

Then in an instant she had torn herself away, looking flustered and not a little angry with herself. 'Time for me to go!' Throwing the rug aside, she rushed to put on her coat, and with a last quick peck, was gone.

With no other recourse, Niall lit a cigarette, gripping it between his lips as he took out his frustration on the rug, working so strenuously upon it that his fingers looked set to bleed.

18

Niall had always been a prudent man, and this was to reap rewards at exactly the right time, for, just prior to his wedding, an endowment policy came to term, to be delivered in the form of a cheque by the insurance man. For some, it might have been tempting to be less frugal with the reception, but, never one for overt display, this recipient was determined to keep celebrations to a minimum, the money better spent in repaying his friend. Still, it was good to know that apart from the usual weekly outgoings, he and Boadicea would begin their married life free of debt.

From the bride's family, only her father and brother would be attending, Mr Merrifield and Arthur staying with Reilly for the night. Naturally, Boadicea would also have to invite Mr and Mrs Precious, who treated her as kin, and because of this she felt obliged to extend the invitation to Mr Yarker and Mr Allardyce – though not Eamonn and Johnny, who might reduce the occasion to a brawl. Thankfully, only the Preciouses accepted. Added to the four whom Niall had already invited, apart from the children, this made only eight guests to be transported to the register office.

It was therefore disconcerting to find that there was to be an uninvited one upon the scene. In an act of pure coincidence, on that crisp and bright blue Saturday afternoon, as Niall and his entourage, in all their finery, emerged to meet the taxis that had just drawn up outside, who should be coming from the house next door, but Nora.

It was difficult to say who was the most discommoded, the groom or his mother-in-law. Feeling Reilly's hand upon his shoulder, Niall thanked God that Boadicea was not here to incur that same look as he was receiving; wanting to do things properly, she would be travelling from her lodgings along with Georgie and Ma, and had deputised Eileen and Emma to help Niall with the children.

Up until this point, the antagonists had not spoken in weeks, for, although Nora did still occasionally visit her former neighbour, she had come to accept that she would not be allowed access to her grandchildren until she toed the father's line; hence, in order to let the bad blood congeal, she had gone out of her way to avoid him. But that was impossible today.

A look of shock electrified her face, due to the indisputable evidence that this was a wedding party. Her eyes flitted back and forth over the guests, over her granddaughters, in the blue velvet dresses with white sashes and hair ribbons, and her grandsons, their cheeks like cherubs, in white shirts, grey shorts and blue ties, their brown hair neatly parted and slicked with brilliantine, and her eyes brimmed with tears of outrage.

Equally dismayed, Niall held his breath, fully expecting a volatile outburst. But, for some reason, perhaps because she was outnumbered, Nora suddenly appeared to shrink in stature. Moreover, she seemed mesmerised and lost for words. Unsure what to do, Niall simply dealt her a civil nod, which seemed to break her spell – for she cried at him resentfully, 'I suppose we're not even allowed to give them Christmas presents neither!' – before wheeling away and hobbling off to catch her bus.

'Of course you are!' the groom called after her, for the benefit of his worried children, as much as her. And, 'Of course, you'll be seeing your gran at Christmas,' he reaffirmed to the youngsters, as he loaded them into one of the taxis. Then, with a look of relief at Reilly that their convergence had been no worse, he pushed Nora from his mind and climbed into the waiting cab, determined to enjoy this, his happiest day.

And upon first glimpse of his smiling bride in her pert little hat upon her golden head, and the exquisite costume that showed off her figure, he knew that all was going to be well. After that one small hitch, the wedding could not have gone better, not merely because both Boadicea and Niall were elated that this had finally come to pass after so many hurdles, but because the alcohol provided by the groom had been multiplied fourfold, Mr Merrifield and Reilly seemingly determined to out-do each other in the amount they had provided, and equally resolute that everyone should participate. Even the children were indulged, no one minding that they went around examining empty glasses, their aim to find a drop unfinished and tilting back their heads to drain this down their throats. Ergo, by only seven thirty that evening, it was a very merry household, and looked like becoming even merrier.

'Go home and fetch your squeeze-box, Georgie!' commanded Mrs Precious, her voice competing with Reilly's, who had until now been the one to entertain them with anecdotes. 'Let's have some music.'

'Aw, don't send the poor fellow all the way down Walmgate,' pleaded Boadicea, above the calls of approval. 'I'm sure with Pa's voice he doesn't need an instrument to lead us. Come on Pa, start us off!'

And at this, old Georgie jumped up in his sprightly manner, and with hands clasped to his heart launched into his favourite love song: 'Roses are shining in Picardy, In the hush of the sil-ver dew.' And soon every adult in the room was swaying from side to side and joining in, rather spoiling Pa's perfectly delivered rendition with their enthusiasm, but nevertheless creating a sentimental blurring of the eye as each remembered his or her own wedding day.

Whilst the song was going on, Juggy had been studying each contributor, particularly Mr Merrifield and Arthur, who had no wife to accompany them, and, at the end of it, she finally got to question the latter. 'When are you getting married?'

To surprised laughter, he told the little girl, 'Nobody'll have me.'

A great, 'Aw!' rippled the room.

Juggy thought about this, then announced to the gathering something she had overheard,

'Me Aunty Harriet's expecting a happy event.'

'Does that mean your granny's moving out?' asked a drunken Uncle Sean, with a crafty gleam at Niall, whose snigger merged with others.

Juggy failed to understand the adult's joke. She did not even know what a happy event was, but it had obviously amused the grown-ups so she smiled.

Then, 'Give 'em another, Georgie!' whooped Mrs Precious, smacking the old man's bottom, and with this, many more love songs were to follow, the pitch growing more and more zealous.

So much so, that an angry fist thumped on the wall from next door.

'Eh up!' said a glassy-eyed Niall, shoving his hair into place, and grinning like the Cheshire cat at his bride. 'We're annoying Mrs Lavelle. I think you kids had better simmer down and think about going to bed.'

There were moans of objection, not merely from the children.

'Let 'em stay up!' said Reilly, his big face glowing like a beet.

'All right, you two can stay up a while,' the father allowed Honor and Dom, 'but the rest are already an hour past your bedtime.'

'But aren't you on early rota at Mass, Dom?' Apart from birthdays and such like, there were so many other things for Boadicea to keep her eye on. But with Dominic not appreciating this interference, it seemed expedient to let it go for now. She turned to attend Juggy, who had just voiced a bright idea.

'We could invite Gloria in – she might like to marry Arthur.'

'There's no might about it,' giggled Honor, whose tongue had been loosened by the port and the excitement.

There came a rap at the door.

'Oh, no, she's heard you,' joked Boadicea.

'I'll get it!' yelled a pink-cheeked Batty, hoping to delay his bedtime, and he raced off to admit whoever it was.

It turned out to be Father Finnegan, and at his entry all of a sudden everyone was sober, or affecting to be, though this was not very convincing.

'My, you all look as if you're having a good time,' beamed the cleric. 'I've just popped in to extend my felicitations to the bride and groom –' here he looked hopefully at the almost depleted bottles of port, '– though it might be easier with a glass in my hand.'

With the filling of his glass, and everyone else's topped up too, the priest was to remain there for a while, laughing and joking with the wedding guests, delighting the children for his presence had delayed their bedtime even further, at least until Juggy drew attention to herself.

'You've got a button missing, Father.' And when he looked down quizzically at his soutane, she added, 'There's only thirty-two.'

'And so there are!' He frowned at the one that had been lost, then his mood was one of congratulation for the child who had noticed. 'And how come you know there should be thirty-three?'

'Boadicea says, there should be one for every year of Our Lord's life on earth.'

There came a combined, 'Ah!' from the wedding guests, and not a little pleasure from Boadicea, as Father Finnegan praised the stepmother's teachings. 'I can see the new Mrs Doran will do just fine in keeping your children's faith, Niall. Er, I wonder,' he fingered the gap on his cassock, 'is she as expert at sewing on buttons?'

And for the next five minutes the bride was to

find herself searching for a button to match the missing one, and to sew this into place, before the priest decided he had taken his fill and went on his way.

'Here endeth today's lesson!' Arthur raised his glass, looking decidedly merrier at Father Finnegan's exit.

'Fancy having to sew on buttons on your wedding day!' boomed Ma Precious with indignant laughter, then threw her arms round Georgie and hugged him fit to suffocate.

Niall shook his head at the audacity of it too, then remembered the children, who were trying to make themselves look small in order to remain. 'Eh, and now it really is bedtime,' he told them.

'They're not likely to go while we're still enjoying ourselves,' proffered Sean to the other guests, his cheeks similarly ruddy to his brother's. 'Maybe we'd better make a move.'

Whilst Niall happily accepted this, Boadicea seemed awfully keen to keep them here. 'Aw, ye don't have to!' She sprang up, wobbled on her high heels, laughed and steadied herself, before adding, 'Let me make everybody some supper at least.'

'Aren't we stuffed enough already?' laughed Reilly, patting his stomach, that was swollen from all manner of pastries and sandwiches and cakes consumed earlier.

'Sure, you can at least have a cup of tea before you go.' Boadicea went to make it, warning the children as she went, 'Better go and change into your pyjamas.' When there were more objections, she nudged Honor, and murmured a suggestion, 'Maybe if ye change out of your dress, Juggy won't mind doing the same.'

At last, after a cup of tea and a final bun, the smaller ones went off to bed. However, it was a good half-hour later before the two older ones finally joined their siblings upstairs, and a good fifteen minutes after that until Mrs Precious hollered, 'Come on, Georgie, these lovebirds want to get to bed!'

And after lining up to exchange kisses – Mr Merrifield pressing supportive hands to his daughter's shoulders, and directing an intuitive look into her eyes – the eight guests finally departed and the house fell quiet.

Sagging with fake exhaustion, but her face exhilarated, Boadicea flopped onto the chair beside Niall's. 'Peace at last! Oh, but it went well, didn't it?'

He reached over the arm of his chair for her hand and squeezed her fingers, kissing them. 'Aye, I right enjoyed meself.' His tone was deeply genuine. 'I feared I wasn't going to, what with Nora popping up like that.' He had told her all about this, once the ceremony was over. 'I've never seen her struck dumb before.' He chuckled, then fell silent, rubbing his thumb along her fingers thoughtfully, as his mind turned to bed.

But his bride had not finished with the subject.

'About what ye said about letting her give them Christmas presents . . .'

Niall's thoughts were on more important matters. 'I don't see why they should go without just 'cause their grandmother's an old so-and-so. But she isn't delivering them in person, I'll go and pick them up. She's not ruining my Christmas.'

'Maybe we should let her see them again,' came the quiet suggestion.

'After all she said about you?' Jerked from his reverie, Niall's voice held amazement.

'She sounded awfully upset. I feel really sorry for her.' Boadicea had had plenty of time to calm down in the month since the attempted abduction, and now tried to persuade her husband to show some festive spirit. 'Sure, she's a horrible piece of work, but she has a right to be aggrieved when I'm after replacing her daughter in your affections – and she's a right to see her grandchildren.'

Niall studied her determined face. 'Well, if she's still behaving herself nearer to Christmas, I might think about it,' he decreed parsimoniously. 'Now come on, don't let's spoil our happy day with that old bat – eh, I hope we manage to get a decent photo for our mantelpiece! I reckon all them our Sean took'll be blurred from the amount he drank.' As intoxicated though he himself was, he noticed then that his favourite photograph of Boadicea was not in its place on the mantel, and he pointed this out to her. But she was too happy to go looking for it. 'Ah sure, it'll turn up.' And she leaned over to kiss him, then spent a while gazing into his eyes until it was no longer safe to do so, and she tore herself away. 'Right, I suppose I'd better clear up all these glasses and plates before we go to bed. I don't want to face them in the morning.'

Niall removed his suit jacket, and rolled up his sleeves, and with him to help it took little time to make the living room and scullery shipshape. Then there was nothing further to delay them.

He paused with his hand on the light, inviting softly, 'If you go ahead, I'll turn everything off.'

And so she did, he closely following. The sleeping arrangements had been altered yesterday. There was only one bed now in the room that Niall had formerly shared with his sons. And though last night he had continued to share it with Brian, it should tonight have been empty. It wasn't.

Upon turning on the light, Boadicea suppressed laughter at the vision of the little boy asleep there. Niall gave a snort of amusement too, though it was born of exasperation, and he wasted no time in scooping Brian from the mattress.

'You don't have to move him on my account,' whispered his wife.

But Niall took this the wrong way. 'You don't need a guard; I've given my word.' And he transported the sleeping child to another's bed.

She had started to undress when he returned,

but her mood was subdued. 'If this is what it's going to be like, you misunderstanding every innocent thing I say, maybe I should sleep in the front parlour after all.'

Niall was contrite, as he too began to remove his clothes, starting with his tie. 'I'm sorry,' he told her softly, fingering the tie, unable to prevent his eyes from straying to her. 'I know I'm a touchy bugger. I promise I'll try not to be.' Then, satisfied that this had served to appease her, he turned his back to lend her some privacy, and sat on the bed to remove his shirt, and to pull on the old one he wore for bed, before removing his shoes and trousers and socks.

Then they were both in bed, and lying beside each other, trying their best not to think of what could have been.

Niall reached down for her hand, pulled it to his lips and kissed it. 'Thanks for a lovely day,' he said sincerely.

'Wasn't it wonderful?' her voice shared his joy, as she returned his kiss.

Then both rolled over, and went to sleep.

Needing no church bells to rouse him, Niall was up early on Sunday morning and lighting the fire for Boadicea, who had risen at the same time and was getting the breakfast ready on the gas stove. The sticks, paper and coal took a good while to radiate any heat. Meantime, the pair of them were to shiver in the December darkness, laughing across the table at each other as their teeth chattered between each mouthful of porridge.

Then it was time to get the children up and ready for church, Niall and Boadicea to give thanks and feel that God was smiling upon their union.

From then on the day just got busier for Niall's wife, and she had little time to check on how others were feeling, though in between dinner and tea she did seek to remove the children's impression that all she was here for was to cook for them, by suggesting that they go to watch the skaters on the frozen lake at Rowntree Park.

'Maybe we'll have a go too,' she offered enticingly.

Made to sit quietly with their books since dinnertime, Niall's offspring were by now keen to escape from the house.

'Hang on, there's one of us missing.' Counting heads, Niall saw that it was Brian. 'Does anyone know where he is?'

'He sneaked outside when you dropped off to sleep,' informed Juggy.

'I did not fall asleep!' laughed an indignant father, knowing very well that he had.

'I'll go find the little fella,' smiled Boadicea, 'you kids get yourselves ready to go.' And she bustled off to look for the youngest.

It took no skill to detect him. As soon as she opened the front door there he was, with hangdog expression, sitting on the pavement, leaning against the wall of the house and tugging a handful of seedpods from the weed that was growing out of the dust.

'Ah, there you are!' Boadicea hugged herself, for the air was fiendishly bitter. 'What on earth are ye doing out here in the cold with no coat, Bri?' When he did not answer, she squatted beside him, shivering as she watched his infant fingers that were purple with cold nip open the shepherd's purse to reveal the green 'coins' therein.

'Go away, I don't like you,' he sulked, and remained intent on his task, tearing open one tiny purse after the other, then throwing them aside to litter the pavement.

'That's a shame, 'cause I like you.' It was easy to guess the reason behind his new aversion to her. She pulled out a handkerchief and tried to wipe his running nose, but he fought her, writhing his head away.

'For heaven's sake, what you doing standing here with t'door open?' Niall had come to investigate, his face distorted at being so cold.

Immediately the four-year-old's sulk turned to uncontrollable rage. 'Why do you have to sleep with her? I want you to sleep with me!'

Too taken aback to chastise him, Niall looked at Boadicea, each of them experiencing a wave of pity for the one who missed his father's closeness.

But whilst Niall's method was to say, 'Aye,

well, you're a big lad now; big lads don't sleep with their dads,' his wife's was more compassionate.

''Tis Christmas soon, Bri,' said Boadicea gently, still squatting beside him, a coaxing hand on his shoulder as she poised with her handkerchief at the ready. 'Father Christmas only comes to visit children's beds, not grown-ups'. I mean, ye can swap places with me if ye really want to, but you'd miss out on all those parcels he's bringing ye . . .'

This caused Brian to be thoughtful, and to remain still enough for her to dive on his nose with the handkerchief. This time he let her wipe it. And by the time she had done so, his mood had metamorphosed, so that he ran into the house as good as gold to join in the expedition to the frozen lake.

'See, that's all it takes,' she murmured to the child's father. 'A little bribery.'

Hunched against the cold that pierced his shirt-sleeves, Niall shoved her into the house before him. 'Aye, but how's Father Christmas going to provide all these presents?'

'Ye'd better get your hammer and nails out, hadn't ye?' Boadicea looked smug, then murmured laughingly so that the children did not overhear, 'I can knit stuff for the girls but I can't knit a garage.'

'That's what he'd like, is it?'

She nodded, and told him quietly of the one

Brian had seen in a toy shop window. 'I'm sure with your talents you can copy it.'

So, this was what Niall found himself doing in the weeks up to Christmas, after the children had gone to bed, dragging the half-finished toys from their hiding place, to measure, to saw and to paint, Boadicea beside him knitting gifts, both of them rushing to finish the tasks in time. There was no time for the rug now, nor opportunity for any sly diversion to the pub – not that he would want to go there, for this was all he had ever dreamed of: to be in the company of the woman he loved. Had it not been for one thing, he would have been ecstatic . . .

But he must try not to think of that, must throw himself into other pursuits, and try to concentrate of the festive season, which was not hard. Walmgate was even livelier at this time of year. The gypsies had arrived in their brightly painted caravans, and were camped on some waste ground down one of the lanes, their presence being objected to by some of the locals and fights breaking out at all hours of night and the day. There were huge flocks of geese being driven for slaughter, a terrible, strangled honking filling the air as hundreds met their end and yet more awaited; cattle, pigs and chickens too passing through the butchers' yards, the fortnight before Christmas one long cacophonous disruption.

Exhausted both from lack of sleep and from

his day-time work, Niall was not relishing another evening shift of making toys as he plodded home that Friday night through the busy, illuminated streets. But, as ever, all weariness was put aside upon receiving his dear wife's greeting.

'And what has Father been doing at work today?' Having hurried to divest him of his haversack and greasy old cap, she steered him to the table where his meal awaited, the look in her eyes making him feel utterly adored.

Left with nothing to do, Niall sat down amongst his offspring, smiling at them and offering a proud boast. 'I helped break a record.'

'From the boss's gramphone?' Boadicea winked at the children and sat down to join them. 'I should have thought that would get ye the sack!'

'Eh, she's a silly billy!' Niall shook his head at his brood, and set upon his fish. 'No, I mean we worked like blazes. The thirty of us took only four hours to lay eleven hundred yards of new track – that's a record, that is.'

Picking up her own knife and fork, Boadicea looked impressed. 'How about that, boys? Your father helping to build the railways. Ye should be proud. Do any of you fancy working on the permanent way when you grow up?'

'I do,' said Juggy.

The boys all laughed, Batty scoffing. 'Girls can't work on the railway.'

Juggy looked to her father, who, to her disappointment, was to confirm this.

'I'll stay home and help Bo in the house then,' offered Juggy, which earned her stepmother's praise, and a smile from her father for such co-operation.

He himself was to be less than co-operative, though, when Dominic sought a favour on his way to bed. 'Have you got a pair of trousers I can borrow, Dad?'

Almost falling asleep over his newspaper, and in the knowledge that he faced an hour of toy-making, Niall sounded rather testy. 'Trousers – what do you want trousers for?'

'Sister Bernadette asked us to bring some on Monday afternoon. We're having a dress rehearsal for the Christmas concert.'

Rubbing his eyes to prevent himself from dropping off, Niall looked vague. 'You'd better go and ask your stepmother. She knows where everything is . . .'

The excitement of the wedding over, and the reality of having a stepmother hit home, Dominic had no intention of asking Boadicea for any favour, and continued to address his father. 'But they're your trousers.'

Frowning and puffing out his cheeks, Niall racked his brain. 'I think I might have a pair somewhere – does it matter if there's a rip in the backside?'

'Who's got a rip in the backside?' Boadicea entered in a blast of cold air from the back yard, and to Dominic's annoyance his father turned immediately to her.

'The lad's after some long trousers for his concert. I've got some torn ones somewhere . . .'

'I can mend them,' she offered brightly, knowing exactly where she could lay her hands on them. 'They're under the stairs. I'll dig them out for you right now so's I don't forget.'

Dom mumbled something inaudible on his way to bed.

'What was that?' A stern Niall cupped an ear.

But Dominic had disappeared.

'That lad's looking for a good braying,' muttered Niall to his wife, who brushed aside this decree.

'Don't blame him. 'Tis his grandmother's influence.'

'Hah! She's not even seeing them and she's still managing to cast her evil eye – and you want me to start letting them go to visit her again, Lady Bountiful.' But he was not really annoyed at his wife.

'Ah, well,' sighed Boadicea, 'in a few years they'll be grown and she'll no longer have such a hold on them.'

'That's a long way off yet,' protested Niall. 'Dom's three years away from being big enough to wear them long trousers—'

'Yes, he's still a child,' Boadicea pointed out firmly, 'so just let him be. I can handle that one.'

*   *   *

As promised, the trousers were there waiting when Dom rose on Saturday morning. There had also been a moderate snowfall overnight, and, with more fun to be had outside, the eleven-year-old paid them little notice, and left them lying over the back of a chair whilst he and his brothers and sisters went out to play. Here in the street they were to stay, scraping the snow from their windowsill and neighbouring ones, and from every available surface with which to fashion missiles, until finally the meagre supply was exhausted and they turned to other things.

Their father being at work, Boadicea spent much of her morning changing the linen in preparation for Monday's wash – though she was not looking forward to trying to get it dry in this freezing weather. There were also the bedrooms to clean, before finally coming down to attend the living area.

She could hear someone rummaging in the outside shed, and, assuming that it was Dom, left him to it, whilst she dusted and swept and tidied. But noticing that the trousers were no longer where he had left them, and that it had gone suspiciously quiet outside, she went out to investigate. And there he was with the trousers spread on the floor of the shed and a paintbrush in his hand.

'You destructive little devil, what are you up to?' The boy having almost dropped the brush in his haste, she carefully removed it before it dripped any more whitewash.

'They're only his old ones!' Dominic objected.

'I didn't ask that!' Clicking her tongue, Boadicea laid the brush atop the open tin. 'I asked what are you doing? I thought you wanted these for the concert.'

'Aye, but they really need to be striped ones, so—'

'You thought you'd paint your own stripes on.' Boadicea shook her head at such daft behaviour. 'Why didn't ye ask me before you did it?'

He turned petulant 'I thought it'd wash off.'

'And who, might I ask, is going to wash them?'

'That's what you're here for, isn't it?'

She was astounded. 'Why, you cheeky—' and involuntarily she began to raise her hand.

Dom took a step back into the shed. 'I'll tell me dad you've been flirting with the insurance man!'

Boadicea hesitated only the slightest moment, before her hand struck his cheek, causing him to yelp. 'Don't you dare threaten me!' she exploded. 'You can tell your father what you like!' And looking at his attitude, the resentful way he was beholding her, she had a sudden inkling what might have happened to her photograph. 'And whilst we're flinging accusations, I don't suppose you know anything about that photo of me that went missing a while back?'

Dom was brazen. 'It fell into the fire.'

'And you just gave it a little push – well, now we both know where we stand, don't we?'

Deeply offended, she bundled the ruined trousers up and shoved them in the dustbin.

Seeing her go indoors, Dom expediently vanished too.

Though he was to reappear and be seated at the dinner table with his brothers and sisters by the time his father arrived home just after one, it did not take a genius to gauge the subdued atmosphere at the dinner table.

'Dare I ask?' Niall sighed to Boadicea, as he warmed himself through before the fire, prior to eating. 'What's been going on here?'

'I think Dom has something to tell you,' Boadicea invited the boy, 'haven't you, Dom?'

The latter looked guilty: which was she going to mention first, the photo, the trousers or the blackmail? Whichever, he began with the lesser crime. 'Sorry, Dad, them trousers weren't quite right, so—'

'They need to be striped, apparently,' cut in his stepmother, her voice turning bright, 'so I'm going to town this afternoon to buy some stuff, and I'll ask Aunty Emma if she can run a pair up on her sewing machine!'

'You don't have to go to all that trouble,' complained Niall, as he set on his meal.

'It's no trouble, that's what I'm here for.' Boadicea looked pointedly at Dom, but there was a gleam in her eye that told him he had got away with his impudence this time, but just let him dare to do it again . . .

The final days up to Christmas were to bring no further trouble, which was a great relief to the one who had all the cooking, cleaning and shopping to do. Boadicea thanked heaven she was no longer forced to go out to work, as she struggled home through a layer of slush along Walmgate, which was seemingly miles longer under the weight of bags laden with Christmas fare, having to hurry, for the schools were breaking up early that day and she must be home in time to meet the children. The street was teeming with activity. Her head already banging with the noise of cars being driven past, and the Salvation Army band, she winced at yet another invasion, the metallic ringing of hammer upon anvil, and she glanced with annoyance into the farrier's yard, where a horse waited patiently for his new shoes. Her ears hurting as much as her arms, which felt stretched beyond repair, the arrival of her turn-off was greeted with a great sigh of relief.

Still, her own doorstep was some way to go, and staggering onwards, she decided to take the back route. Heading down a lane, trying to keep her balance on the slippery granite setts, she noted a figure ahead, a foreign-looking boy, dark-skinned, with a mop of black fuzzy hair, who was loitering at the end of the back lane. Cigarette in hand, he held her boldly with his eyes, and took a casual drag of his cigarette as she passed.

Boadicea tottered on under the weight of her bags, calling blithely afterwards, 'Don't be late for your tea, Dom.'

'No, I w—' the black-skinned youth broke off, his tone stunned as he cast aside the cigarette and followed her to demand, 'How did you know it were me?'

'Sure, didn't I spend the best part of last Saturday getting blisters on my feet looking for that material of those trousers?' laughed his step-mother. Then, gauging the reason for his worried expression, she winked. 'Aw, don't fuss! I won't tell your father you were smoking – but cut it out, it'll kill ye – much as I'd like to see ye dead.'

The boot-polished face split into a white grin as Dom kept pace with her and reached for her bags without being asked. 'Here, let me carry them.'

'My own native bearer?' She sounded impressed. 'Why, I might as well.' And she shared her load with him, enquiring how his concert had gone as the pair of them made their way to the back gate.

When they reached home the others were already in the yard, and burst out laughing at their brother in his outfit from the minstrel routine, Brian wanting to try on the black curly wig, and everyone laughing again as his little face was swamped by it. But for some there were more important matters to discuss.

'Can we go see Father Christmas tomorrow?' Juggy ran to beg her stepmother.

'God love us, can ye not wait till I get in!' Boadicea led the way into the house and dumped her bags with a grunt of relief. 'Anyway, I thought he didn't come till Christmas Day?'

'No, he visits Boyes's first,' explained Juggy. 'He has threepenny gifts and sixpenny gifts – I don't mind if we only have the threepenny ones,' she added helpfully.

'That's very amenable of ye.' Having already gone without things herself in order to fulfil the dreams of others, this would be an extra burden on Boadicea. But things had been going so well between her and Niall's children and she wanted to keep them that way. 'Who'll be coming with me to see him then?'

Three hands shot up, Honor being too old to care. A glance at Dominic told his stepmother that he would have liked to come, but did not want to be considered childish. However, not wanting to be thought ungrateful, as his step-mother took the weight off her feet, he came to lean very close by her, happy now to be in such proximity – and not simply for the fact that he had accepted her into his family. Approaching manhood, despite his still boyish antics, Dom had begun to appreciate his father's attraction for the voluptuous Bo.

'Right, if it's just the three of yese I think we can manage that,' she decided, to great applause.

Then she groaned at having forgotten an important purchase. 'Aw! Juggy, darlin', can ye save my poor feet?' Taking sixpence from her purse, she begged, 'Go get me ten Players for your dad, love.'

'I'll go,' offered Dom immediately.

'Er, thanks, all the same, Mr Helpful,' Boadicea eyed him shrewdly, 'you'll have them all smoked by the time you get home.'

At this, he gave a laugh of genuine affection, and, as his little sister ran off on her errand, and Honor unloaded Bo's shopping bag, he bounded out to skid in the slush with his brothers.

Unfortunately the weather was to get worse, Saturday opened with snow and sleet, but, having made a promise to the little ones, Boadicea felt compelled to brave this icy onslaught and take them to visit Father Christmas in his grotto at Boyes' store. Setting off as early as was humanly possible to avoid the crowds, she was on Ouse Bridge at the moment of opening, but it appeared that everyone had had the same idea, for by the time they emerged from the grotto with their threepenny gifts, the store was heaving, people shoulder to shoulder in the aisles – and she had yet to buy a present for her husband. Thankfully it did not take too long to purchase underwear and a box of cigarettes, though now that the children had had their fun they were proving a burden, and so she allowed them to open their gifts, in order to keep them quiet. Quiet was not really the word, what with Brian and Batty constantly firing their guns at shop assistants, and the same enjoyment did not hold for Juggy who, having received a jigsaw, pestered to go home so she could play with it.

'We can't go home yet!' protested a tattered Boadicea. 'I've to get something for Ma. Be good, all of you.'

'Ooh, can I play with it at Ma and Uncle Georgie's house then?' begged Juggy.

Her guardian sighed and said, 'Oh, I suppose so – sure, I'll have to unload you rascals on somebody!' And, after purchasing the items for Mrs Precious, she took them there.

Everyone else out, Ma and Georgie were both in the kitchen when the visitors descended on them, he stirring a vast saucepan, she on her hands and knees carving up some old carpet with a blunt knife and her usual ham-fistedness.

'Stop barking, Rusty, you know very well who it is – he's just excited!' she informed Boadicea and the children. 'I'm making him a new bed for Christmas.' And so saying she wrenched the circle of carpet free and tried it in the dog's basket for size. 'There – how's that, little cherub?' Seizing the yapping Pomeranian she gave him a hearty kiss and dumped him in the basket.

Obviously unimpressed, the dog jumped straight out.

'There's no pleasing some folk!' complained

Ma, gathering up the remnants of carpet in her brawny hands, then clambering to her feet. 'Anyway!' She beamed upon the gathering. 'Now you're here are you stopping for your dinner? Georgie's making some soup.'

Boadicea thanked her, but said Dom and Honor would require lunch, and, 'We've got to be back for Niall.'

'What time's he in?'

'About one.'

'We'll have ours at twelve then!' bellowed Ma. 'That gives you plenty of time – you can take him and the others some home with you an' all!' Then, seeing the pile of chopped vegetables still on the table, added, 'That's if it ever gets done! Come on, Georgie Porgie, get a move on. Shouldn't these veg be in that pan?' Using her large hands as a scoop, she began to gather the vegetables as if to assist.

'Just let me fish the carcass out, dearie!' came the old man's warning, and this he only just managed to do before she started to hurl potatoes, carrots and cabbage into his saucepan.

'There!' She brushed her palms in businesslike fashion. 'We'll let it simmer for a couple of hours while we have a cup of tea – get the kettle on, Georgie!' And leaving her poor flustered husband behind, she herded her guests into the antiquated living room, the dog trotting ahead.

'Can I open me jigsaw now?' beseeched Juggy, as she and her younger brothers found themselves places to sit amidst the aspidistras and stuffed animals.

Granted permission, she crouched excitedly on the floor and displayed it to Ma, who in turn displayed amazement.

'By, that's a grand un!'

This was overstatement, and Juggy knew it. Made of wood, and consisting of only a dozen pieces, the jigsaw was not to hold her interest for very long, though it was to prove a boon for others. Having put their sopping coats to dry by the roaring fire, Boadicea saw a way of keeping her charges occupied whilst she and Ma enjoyed a cup of tea, by organising a competition to see who could construct the jigsaw fastest – Brian being given a head start as he was only little – and she and Ma acting as umpires, counting out the seconds as each competitor took a turn: 'One! Two! Three . . .'

This was to be the source of much amusement till Mr Yarker came home, his disgruntled expression forcing the jigsaw to be packed away and the children to be quiet. Assisting with the latter, ever eager to please, Georgie then took them into his workshop, which smelled of wood and oil and varnish, and showed them the array of instruments that dangled from its roof, then entertained them with a tune on one of the fiddles. Here the children were to remain entranced, until Ma bawled for assistance.

The house was filled with an appetising aroma

of soup, and also all of its residents, when the children returned. Ravenous, they needed no encouragement to enter the dining room, where the boys underwent a bout of play-fighting with Eamonn and Johnny until told to behave. Then, as old Georgie appeared, everyone became intent on the steaming tureen, which he placed on the table, all eventually being supplied with its delicious contents.

It was left to Eamonn to sum up. His bowl almost depleted, he fished out an extra content and held it aloft and dripping between forefinger and thumb. 'Great soup, Ma – but could ye leave out the carpet next time?'

With much laughter, Boadicea was to relate this incident to Niall, Dominic and Honor when she served their own portions an hour later, these having been gingerly transported home in Kilner jars. Juggy and her younger brothers were also keen to show their father the gifts they had received from Father Christmas, although not for long, as Boadicea sent them off to wash their hands and faces. For a change, this caused little fuss, for, with their father being more kindly disposed towards their grandmother due to the festive spirit, the youngsters were to visit her again that afternoon.

There was little objection to be heard from the adults either at having the house to themselves, and later, after washing up, Niall and Boadicea took great pleasure in being side by side on the sofa, lazily discussing what they would have for Christmas dinner.

'Have ye made your mind up yet – turkey or goose? I've only three days to order one. Goose is only one and tuppence a pound – half as much as turkey. Then again, turkey's nice . . .' As she chatted away, Boadicea absent-mindedly stroked a masculine forearm, that emerged from its rolled-up sleeve, brushing the dark hairs back and forth, this way and that, and seeming to have no idea that she was making its owner shiver. His resolve to remain celibate swiftly wearing thin, Niall shifted closer, and began to nuzzle at her neck, and behind her earlobes, inhaling deeply and sending a shudder through the recipient, so that when his kisses moved to her lips, she responded willingly.

So willingly, that Niall could take no more, and he jumped up to light a cigarette, then turned to observe her, unable to say whether it made things better or worse, knowing that she wanted him as much as he wanted her. 'I think I'd better just go out and cool off for a while,' he told her on a stream of tobacco smoke. And with that he left to stride out his frustration on the pavements.

If only he knew, thought Boadicea, that this was just as frustrating for her, wanting him, yearning for it to go further, yet prevented by the knowledge of what might transpire from the ultimate embrace. Unrequited passion still inflamed her lower regions. In the hope of dampening this, and putting this free time to good use, she hurried to a cupboard, stood on a chair to reach its top shelf, and took out a bag of knitting, then set to sewing up the little woollen sections of the doll's outfit she had been making for Juggy. She seemed to have been working her fingers to the bone on such things lately. But it was well worth the effort when she thought of that little pixie face illuminating on Christmas Day.

Eventually, having stitched up the final seam, she turned the red woollen coat the right way out, then went to fetch the new doll, and tried the entire outfit on it, being very pleased with her work and thinking how delighted Juggy would be too. But the sound of feet scampering through the front door sent her into a mild panic – she had not expected them back so soon. Performing with haste, she shoved the doll behind the cushion of the chair she was on, crumpled up the bag with its remnants of wool, and sat back clutching it to her breast with a smile of anticipation as Juggy burst into the room.

'Me granny says we're not to call you Mother!'

Her eyes pinned to that excited face, Boadicea's smile remained fixed in disbelief, then slowly began to fade, like the sun behind a cloud. Of all the things the child could have thrown at her, she had not expected this. Her mind enumerating the many things she had done for Niall's children – the washing, the cooking, the tending of wounds, putting up with their cheek and covering this up from their father, hearing their prayers, going without so that they might have a treat – her heart was cut to the quick. Immediately came the unwanted vision of her own lost babe, clawing at her heart – her very soul – as she tried to fight it away. These thoughts, and the sexual frustration over Niall, all erupted into one enormous grievance to drive her to the edge of tears, and, with the others following their sister in, Boadicea was compelled to turn away so that they might not see her distress.

'Sure, I never asked ye to,' she muttered to Juggy, as she rose to leave the room. 'Call me what ye like.'

'You shouldn't have said that,' Honor scolded her sister, with an eye on their stepmother's hurried journey through the icy yard. 'Look, you've made her cry!'

'No I haven't! She's just off to the lav.' But as Boadicea remained closeted for an awful long time and the reality hit home, Juggy was to become crestfallen. 'I was only saying what me gran said,' she mumbled.

Dominic looked worried too. 'We'll have to fix it up or me dad'll go nuts.'

'About what?'

En masse, his brood reddened and shrank as their father made an unexpected return. Demanding to hear what had been going on, upon their confession Niall clutched his temple in exasperation, then caught sight of the hastily hidden gift and dragged it from behind the cushion.

'Look!' He brandished the doll in its little red outfit at a tearful Juggy. 'This is what Bo's been making you for Christmas, you evil little . . .' Frustration demanded that he throw the wretched thing, but it had taken too much hard work from the woman he loved and therefore he refrained from doing so, but his grip remained tight and his eyes extremely angry as he used it to berate them. '*Weeks* she's spent making sure you all have summat nice to open – not to mention the months she's been running about clearing up after you, and feeding you, and caring for you – and this is how you repay her! I'm bloody ashamed of you!'

Never had they witnessed such rage from him, and were so frightened that even the boys began to cry as he hammered his message home. 'And there'll be no playing games for any of you during the school holidays! If you want something to do I'll make sure you have plenty of jobs – oh, yes!' They hung their weeping heads in disgrace as he railed at them, yet Niall wondered if they had grasped the true immensity of what they had done to the woman he loved. Therefore, his voice was to crack with emotion as he hurled his last words at them: 'And you can forget about Christmas – because you'll get nowt!'

But of course they did, they being only children and he an adult who knew full well where the true blame should lie, and by the time Christmas arrived all broken hearts had been mended.

After a good cry in the lavatory, Boadicea had returned to find the children repentant and a loving husband to act as mouthpiece, who took her in his arms and told her that they had not really meant it, that they were only repeating their grandmother's poison, and tried to persuade her that everything would be all right tomorrow, which it was.

And, if Boadicea was still privately licking her wounds as she returned with the rest of the family from Mass on Christmas morning, she was nevertheless gratified to see that the gifts upon which she had laboured were truly appreciated. Envisioning the day ahead as one of hard work, and expecting no other present than the stockings and bath salts she had received from Niall, she was therefore surprised and touched to find that Honor and Dominic had organised a whip-round to buy her a set of bowls for a dressing table – made of cheap green glass, but nevertheless much appreciated by the stepmother.

'We all put in a tanner each,' explained Dom quickly, receiving a commendation from his father.

'Sure ye shouldn't've spent all that money on me.' There was a tear in Boadicea's eye, and her voice was soft.

'I can always earn some more,' Dom shrugged generously.

'Anyway, me gran gave us it,' revealed Juggy,

wondering why her father and stepmother laughed so heartily.

'Poetic justice?' murmured Boadicea to Niall, in a private aside, both of them wondering what Nora would say if she knew her money had been spent on her enemy. But much uplifted by the children's gesture, she uttered profound thanks, and did not feel so put upon as she went to launch herself into the preparation of the festive dinner.

It was a strenuous morning, but worth every ounce of hard labour, for Niall announced that the goose was the best he had ever tasted, and for once every single child was in unison, not one word of insurrection to ruin the day.

The festivities were not over by a long chalk, though, for they had received an invitation to tea at the Precious household, and so there was to be no sitting down after the washing-up, but a brisk walk through the snow.

Before they had barely set off, though, there was to be a surprise. Niall was in the process of locking the front door behind them when Gloria and her mother came out at exactly the same time. The Lavelles said hello to the children, but ignored the adults – there was no surprise in this – but as Gloria and her mother went on their way, another voice assailed Niall from across the street. 'Merry Christmas, Mr and Mrs Doran!'

As Gloria and Mrs Lavelle turned to project censure for this show of disloyalty from two of Nora's stalwarts, Boadicea looked round in smiling appreciation, and not a little surprise, as Mrs Hutchinson and Mrs Dunphy, slithered their way across the road to speak to her and Niall.

'We just want to say,' offered the monkey-like woman, grasping Bo's forearm, 'that whatever Mrs Beasty's opinion, you're legally married now, and you've proved yourself to be a good mother to these kids, and they seem to like you.' Here, she bestowed a smile upon the children, who smiled back. 'So that's good enough for us – isn't it, Gladys?'

'Aye, she can be a bit over-zealous, can your mother-in-law,' supplied Mrs Dunphy in confidential tone to Niall, her arms hugging herself against the cold. 'I mean, Nora's my friend, and I can understand her being upset, but I do think the rest of us should give you a chance.'

'That's very Christian of you, ladies,' replied Niall charitably, though only willing to forgive them because they might prove helpful to Boadicea in gaining others' acceptance. Bo donated a smile of thanks too.

'Well, it's Christmas, isn't it?' responded Mrs Dunphy. 'We won't keep you – enjoy your day out!' And with this, she and her companion gave a last smile, then hurried indoors, leaving a delighted Mr and Mrs Doran to resume their journey to the Preciouses.

The family's arrival prompted a fight, thankfully not between Johnny and Eamonn, who were charm itself as they welcomed the children in with a boxful of crackers. But a series of explosions from these ignited the dog, which started to bark and yelp, and in turn attacked one of the cats, which flew at it, and a screaming, spitting, snarling mêlée ensued, the animals whirling around in a corner, the whole room turned to bedlam . . . for twenty seconds. And then it was all over with the tossing of a bucket of cold water from old Georgie. The cat fled, the dog shook itself and sneezed, and those in the vicinity were forced to change their garments.

'I do so love the festive spirit,' announced Yarker, ridding his sleeve of the droplets, as water swilled around the carpet.

There was the hint of a smile on Niall's face as he and Boadicea inserted themselves and their family into this bedlam. 'And what contribution have you made to the season of goodwill, Mr Yarker?' He winked at his wife.

The lugubrious face mused for a second, an inch of ash dangling precariously from his damp cigarette, as Yarker raised it to his lips and announced, 'I didn't kick a pigeon.'

'Did you fetch anything with you to play with?' boomed Ma Precious at the children, who shook their heads. 'Never mind, we've plenty of games in the cupboard!'

'How wonderful,' came Yarker's unconvincing comment to Mr Allardyce.

'Right, Georgie, is that tea ready yet?' bawled Ma.

'Almost, dearie!' came the voice from the kitchen.

Still bloated from dinner, Boadicea sought to suggest a little breathing space. 'Oh, we've just nicely eaten, Ma . . .' but this was to fall on deaf ears.

'Right, everybody in here then!' As her husband began to scuttle from the kitchen bearing plates, Ma's brawny arms directed all others to the dining room, sweeping them forth as if herding sheep.

Wearing paper hats that had come with the crackers, the children were helped onto their chairs by Johnny, his brother and Mr Allardyce, Mr Yarker as usual remaining aloof, though he did deign to pass a cruet when requested.

'That's my exercise for the day,' he responded to Niall.

Faced with the magnificent spread, Niall and Boadicea wondered how they were ever going to eat it, but it seemed churlish not to try when Georgie had gone to all this trouble. Even so, only a quarter of what was laid out was actually consumed, and much of it went into feeding the dog, not just the living one, either, for Niall was later to notice a mince pie in the jaws of the dogskin rug, and wondered which of his children was responsible.

And, as Ma had promised the children, after the trifle had been digested there were to be plenty of games, these being provided by poor over-worked Mr Precious. 'Don't go doing that washing-up yet!' his wife scolded. 'Get that tiddly-winks from the cupboard!' And all evening, she had him running about with nuts and glasses of sherry and all manner of festive titbits, so that even the children were outfaced.

'No, thanks.' Juggy shook her head, when a box of dates came to her. 'They remind me of cockroaches.'

'Such charming progeny,' murmured Yarker.

'I think I'll pass too,' Boadicea gave a disgusted laugh, as she tried to deter the younger brothers from jumping up and down on Eamonn. 'Come on, now, boys, don't get too giddy. Pa, if ye've got any breath left in ye, will ye not give us a tune on your concertina? It'll give the poor fella a chance to sit down,' she murmured to her husband, who sat beside her looking bloated and happy.

'He's not going to play what I think he's going to play, is he?' Niall pretended as if ready to weep. But no, there was to be a round of carols. Not until towards the end did Georgie turn senti-mental, and begin to serenade his wife with one that made grown men cry.

'"Roses are shining in Picardeee . . ."'

Though he was never to finish the song, for Brian was violently sick, and, after Boadicea had cleaned this up, Niall deemed it, 'Time to go home!'

'And a very merry Christmas was had by all,' announced the dour Mr Yarker, reaching for a much-needed cigarette.

19

After a splendid festive season, it was back to labouring on the railway for Niall, though the next working week was to be a short one too, the very eventful year drawing to a close. Only one more day, sighed Niall with gladness, as he made his way home that evening through the snow and ice, more eager than most to see the back of 1935. He was keener still for the new one to bring good things for himself and Boadicea, which, if Christmas had been any example, it promised to do, the children growing more attached to her by the day, and she to them. Similarly, the neighbours; for, apart from those who were very close friends of Nora, most had taken up the trend set by Mrs Dunphy, showing a greater respect towards the new Mrs Doran, and so finally granting he and Bo the peace they craved.

Pondering on his success against the bigots, and all the good times ahead, his mind filled with thoughts of his lovely wife and the children who awaited him at home, Niall was therefore some-what dismayed to find himself the subject of renewed interest. Across the road, undeterred by the inclement weather, two women were indulging in gossip, and following him with their eyes as he made his way to his door. Obviously it was him they were discussing, for, as he frowned back at the speaker she concealed her mouth behind a knitted glove, as if fearing he could read her lips. But the clouds of breath continued to emerge around the woollen mitt, hanging upon the freezing air, even after Niall went in.

Annoying though this was, he chose not to mention this to Boadicea, wanting nothing to spoil the happy warmth that overwhelmed him as he came through the door. The evenings with his family were short enough, without ruining it with such needless chat.

The next morning he had completely forgotten about it, as he made his way from the house into a thick blanket of fog, aware only of the cold that pinched his ears, turning them purple and making them throb as he huddled into his old mac and slithered up the street on a sheet of frozen snow to catch his bus. Feeling eyes on him again, he glanced around, but could see only the swirling icy vapour, and, thinking himself deluded, he strode on.

'Mr Doran!'

Come to fetch her milk from the doorstep, a shawl hugged about her bent frame, old Mrs Powers caught sight of him before he disappeared into the fog, and beckoned him to return, her face suggesting urgency.

'I don't believe it for one minute, but I thought you'd better know . . .' The glaucous eyes peered up at him earnestly, as she tugged at his sleeve to delay him. 'I heard an awful rumour in the sweet shop yesterday afternoon about Mrs Doran.'

Immediately, Niall bristled. Had the gossip been directed at himself it would not bother him, but his wife was a different matter, and his answer was sour. 'I won't ask who's putting it about.' Mrs Powers looked uncomfortable, but it did not take much to guess that it was Nora behind this, and so he asked quickly, 'Come on then, love, what have you heard?'

'I'm sure none of it's true,' reaffirmed Mrs Powers, 'but you have a right to know: they're saying that Mrs Doran was up for murder.'

Niall did not know whether to laugh or cry – felt as if he had been hit in the stomach. He stared at her, unable to fathom such vile canard.

'I hate upsetting you, dear – I know what a lovely lady your wife is – I just thought you should know . . .' Afraid of the mood she had created, Mrs Powers held his darkening face for a few sympathetic moments, then shivered and backed indoors.

Niall barely noticed her go, so intent was he on Nora's malice, all thoughts of work forgotten.

His loud thumping on Harriet's door was answered by husband Peter, who was knocked sideways in the rush to find the culprit. 'Where is she?' Niall bullocked his way into the living room of the council house, glared around him, then barged into what appeared to be the kitchen. When she was not there he simply bellowed: 'Nora!'

'What did you let him in for?' Still in her dressing gown, a bad-tempered Harriet chided her husband, before urging him to remove Niall.

But the latter stood his ground. 'You do and I'll bloody flatten you!' he threatened Peter. 'I'm not going till I've seen that vicious old bugger.'

'Are you referring to my mother?' Harriet adopted an air of superiority.

'Oh, you recognise the description then – where is she?' And then Niall saw for himself, as Nora suddenly entered, and he approached her so swiftly that they all feared she was under attack and rushed to stop him.

'You vile old bitch!' Niall had rarely used such a term to her face, but his manners were overtaken by fury. 'Well, you needn't think you're seeing your grandchildren again after this!'

'For what?' Nora squared up to him, her eyes blazing. 'For telling the truth! I'll be seeing them again all right – I'll be seeing them every day when I get custody!'

Deaf to such idiotic threats, Niall was in no mood for games, his fists bunched as he gave a last retort before leaving. 'You're lucky I've got work to go to or I'd . . .'

'What?' asked his ex-mother-in-law nastily. 'Send

for the police? No you wouldn't, because then you'd hear the truth! That you've married a murderer!'

'You stupid evil old sod!' Niall came back, as if to strike her, but Peter and Harriet held him off, albeit with great difficulty as he tried to be at his tormentor.

'It's right, Niall!' gasped Harriet, struggling to restrain him, 'She was up in court for killing her baby. Our Florrie knew her from Leeds—'

'You're all as evil as each other!' Niall was thoroughly shaken – not because he believed it for a second, but because of the depths to which they had sunk. 'I didn't think even you lot could stoop that low!'

'Don't believe us then!' parried Nora. 'You'll believe it soon enough when you hear from our solicitor. We're applying to have them kids taken away from you!'

Dismissive though he was of her tale, he was forced to respond to this threat. 'Just try it!'

'I will!' Nora thrust her iron jaw at him. 'You think we're making it up, but we've got the evidence! The minute our Florrie heard that name she remembered – because it was the same year as her eldest was born and it really upset her reading about it! Our Harriet sat in the library for days going through the newspapers, and she finally found out what it was that fancy woman of yours has been hiding. I can give you the name of the paper and the date and you can look it up yourself if you don't believe us.' Her armour-plated hips waddled to a drawer, from which was taken a piece of paper bearing all the information needed, and she pushed it at him, trying to make him take it, then having to shove it into his pocket. 'But it doesn't matter if you believe me or not, I'm having our Ellen's kids off you!'

'Now, we've talked about this, Mam.' Still holding onto Niall, having a care as to the invasion of her nice new home, especially with her own child on the way, Harriet proffered a word of reprieve for the father. 'We can't fit them all in here. Now that he knows what sort of woman he's married to he can do something about her.'

'I don't need to do anything about her because it's all lies. And I'm warning you,' Niall wrenched himself free and made for the door, 'I'd better not hear any more of it because, by God, you'll regret it! 'Cause I'll be the one going to a solicitor for defamation!'

Nora ignored this, to yell, 'I hope you're going home to confront her! I'm not having my grandchildren left one more minute in the company of a murderer!'

But Niall slammed the door, having no intention of falling for her tricks, instead jumping onto a passing bus that would take him to work.

As much as he might ridicule her words, though, they had made his heart thud, and his gut churn. And as much as he might try to disregard them, they niggled at him throughout the bus ride, repeating themselves over and over again. Just when he had assumed things were looking up, that old witch had to go and spoil it. Yes, that was what she was: an evil old witch, determined to ruin his life with her lies.

But what if it were not lies? Bo *had* lost a baby, she had told him so herself. He had assumed that the child had not come to term . . . but what if it had? Every time he moved in his seat, he could sense the piece of paper crinkling in his pocket, reminding him, until finally he was compelled to take it out and look at the details there, even though the very thought sickened him.

The newspaper was one he took himself, but he could not recall reading of such an event – but of course not; it covered the whole of Yorkshire and he only took an interest in local affairs. Besides, who could remember what they had read twelve years ago, which was the date on Nora's bit of paper. Infuriating as the woman was, she was right in that it must have taken Harriet ages to find it. Didn't she have anything better to do? The piece of paper still clutched in his hand, he lifted concerned eyes to stare from the window, his mind in turmoil. The bus was rolling through town now. There would be a stop coming up soon. Should he alight whilst he had the chance, and instead of going to work visit the library and see for himself?

No – he was furious with himself for even thinking to do this! For that would give it credence, and didn't *he* have anything better to do than dance to Nora's tune? Dark of spirit, acid curdling his stomach, he shoved the scrap of paper back into his pocket, and decided to remain on the bus as it travelled slowly through the thick grey blanket of fog. Only when it arrived at his destination did he alight. The fog had in no way dispersed. And neither had that sickening thought.

Due to his lateness, the other platelayers had enjoyed their bacon sandwiches and were on the point of leaving the cabin when he got there. Promising the foreman he would be there right away, Niall brewed himself a mug of tea, tipped a quick dash of condensed milk from an opened tin, and drank it between collecting his fog signals. Then he picked up his lamp and hurried after the rest of his gang into the swirling mist. It was deathly quiet, the embankments clad in a thick fleece, this and the blanket of fog suppressing all but the noisiest of sounds.

The freezing mist refusing to lift, his hair and eyebrows gathering icy droplets as he wandered along the line with his lamp, Niall was to remain on fogging duty for most of the morning. He paced several miles without even knowing it, barely aware of the shadowy figures who worked alongside him, nor that his extremities turned blue, as he fought to remain alert to his job of railway safety, whilst his mind was constantly dragged away by other things. But Nora's horrible lie was only one of them; for some infuriating reason, the words of 'Roses of Picardy' kept going round and round his mind. Round and round and round, they went . . .

For Christ's sake! Attempting to direct himself yet again to the crucial task in hand, he took out another fog signal and bent to insert this small explosive device beneath a certain point in the rail. Then, all at once aware of being watched, he raised his eyes – and came face to face with the wolf. The hair on the back of his neck stood on end. No more than three yards away, it peered at him from between two thorny bushes, its fur and whiskers glistening with beads of icy moisture as it crouched in the realisation that it had been seen. Neither of them daring to move, the wolf seemingly as mesmerised as he, Niall stared into its hazel eyes for an age, with the fog swirling around them, and the thoughts swirling around his head. Somewhere, far away, a horn sounded. He barely heard it, his eyes unable to tear themselves away from their vulpine counterpart.

Then vaguely he became aware of pandemonium, of shrieking whistles and yells of alarm, and of something else bearing down on him, something large and deadly that forced his eyes to break away, and, as he turned his head, out of the fog loomed a train.

His heart leaped, and with seconds to act, so too did Niall, hurling himself for the embankment, feeling his face raked with gravel as the wolf made a leap in the opposite direction – and disappeared under the wheels of the locomotive.

'You mad bastard!' As the train went on its way, out of the fog a series of lamps bobbed towards him, the men who carried them yelling at his insanity. 'Didn't you hear the horn? You'll have us all flamin' killed!'

Heart still racing, almost vomiting at how close he had come to death, Niall issued abject apologies to all, grabbed his fallen cap and rose, to pant, 'The wolf – where did it go?'

A dozen angry faces condemned him, but the foreman's was angriest of all. 'Do you mean its head or its arse – 'cause they went in different directions! But I know where you're going, Dolly bloody Daydream. For Christ's sake, what's wrong with you today? You're no use to anybody – get yourself home!'

And with this and other angry denunciations ringing in his ears, Niall left them surveying the bloody remnants of the wolf, whilst he himself staggered along the track to the nearest station, and caught a train back to the city.

He fought against it. He fully intended to go straight home. But Nora had seemed so very convinced, that he just had to see for himself. So, instead of heeding his own judgement, instead of taking his wife on trust, he went to the library, and asked to be shown the incriminating newspaper. When the pertinent volume was brought out and laid before him, he went straight for the date that was written on Nora's piece of paper. And there it was, as she had said – not in a great splash, just a couple of columns, for it was no one famous that had been killed, only a baby – there was Boadicea, fighting for her life, protesting that it had been a terrible accident, that after weeks of broken nights she had collapsed with exhaustion and had dropped her baby girl onto the bed, and from there, tragically, she had bounced onto the floor . . .

His scalp crawling in horror, his pulse racing, Niall pored over every word of that murder trial, growing ever more nauseated as he saw that Nora had spoken the truth – but not the whole truth, and not the whole story, for in flicking to the following day's edition, desperate to see the outcome of the trial, his heart leaped at the verdict: not guilty.

A great wave of relief washed over him. He almost laughed out loud, almost wept, right there in the library, and clamped a hand over his mouth to prevent it. How could he ever have doubted that lovely woman, believed that vicious twisted old bitch over his wife?

Leaving the musty volume open on the table, overwhelmed at the acquittal, Niall put on his cap, left the library and rushed home.

Up to her arms in flour, her hands rolling out pastry, Boadicea's face lit up at his unexpected entry, and he was filled with shame that he had believed for one minute that she was capable of such a crime. He went immediately to hug her, then stepped back and held her at arm's length, a stupid grin upon his face.

'What?' she laughed in confusion at his odd behaviour.

'I just love you,' he breathed.

'I love you too.' She gave him a playful smack with a floury hand, then, when he released her, went back to her pastry. 'What are you doing home? Not that it isn't wonderful to see my dear husband! And look at you, you're dripping – and your poor little lugs are blue.'

She made as if to rid her hands of flour and come to help him, but Niall said: 'No, you get on with what you're doing,' and he went to hang up his haversack, and his old mac, and to lay his saturated cap on the hearth, before flopping into a fireside chair to thaw out. 'Where are the kids?' He knew they should be here, for the school was still closed.

She laughed. 'They've gone with Emma to the pictures, remember?'

Niall gave a sound of amusement too at his own lack of memory, then turned more serious as he prepared to admit the discovery that had obscured it. But how could he begin? The fire had caused his nose to stream. He trumpeted into his handkerchief, then put it away, and rubbed his hands briskly over his face, leaving them there and tapping a thoughtful finger against his nose as he stared at her.

Boadicea was quick to pick up on his mood. 'What is it? Has something happened at work?'

He nodded, looking guilty, as he removed his hands to admit, 'I nearly got meself killed—'

'Oh, Niall!' Her eyes filling with concern, she abandoned her baking, and came forward to hear the rest of his tale.

'I saw the wolf, couldn't take me eyes off it, didn't hear the hooter, but that wasn't all.' He looked up at her, shamefaced. 'I've done something awful.'

She stared at him, waiting.

'When I set off this morning,' he began, 'I bumped into Mrs Powers, and she told me that Nora had put this awful, this *foul* rumour about . . .' He shook his head, his eyes turning dark in anger at the memory. 'I didn't believe it, of course,' he went on quickly, looking at Boadicea, who had become very still and quiet, 'and I couldn't have anybody else believing it either, so I went round to Harriet's and confronted her and her mother. They gave me all this bull about a court case – I knew I shouldn't have listened to a word but Nora seemed so sure. She had the name of the paper and everything . . .' Boadicea's face had turned ghastly now. 'It troubled me all morning – I know I should have taken you on trust, I know I was weak, but I just had to go and have a look for meself, if only to prove them wrong.' His face pleaded with her to forgive him. 'I'm really sorry, darlin', sorry that I ever doubted you for one second, I know they only gave me half the story . . . but I have to admit that there was a brief moment when I thought it could be true, and for that I'll never forgive myself. I know you could never have killed anyone, let alone your own child.'

There was a strained silence. Then Boadicea said, 'I did.'

It was almost a whisper, and he saw how painful it had been for her to utter. 'Yes, I know you did, love, but I know it was an accident,' he assured her quickly. 'I read to the end, I know you were acquitted.'

She performed a slow shake of head, her eyes void of all emotion. 'But I did it,' she said, in the quietest of murmurs.

Niall stared at her intently, cocking his ear to make sure that he had not misheard, and was about to ask her to repeat this. But the look in her eyes forestalled him, and then came an intense surge of shock that went right to his bowels and told him it was true, and his lips parted in horror, then just as quickly closed again as he swallowed, unable to respond.

Her hands still caked in flour, her eyes fixed straight ahead, not seeing him but something else, something terrible, Boadicea stood there, like a child made to stand before the class to recite some awful deed. 'Moira, we called her. Came out crying, she did, and almost from that moment she never stopped. Day and night, it was all she ever did. Day, after day, after day. She was such a lovely little thing when she did go to sleep – blonde hair, blue eyes, adorable as an angel – but the moment she woke up she'd start crying again, and her face would be all twisted and demand- ing, and if I didn't get to her in time, to change her nappy, or whatever, she'd get louder and louder, and nothing would pacify her, and she wouldn't feed, and I tried to put her to my breast, and she'd just go rigid, and her face would turn crimson, and she'd scream and scream, and her little hands would bunch into fists . . .' Boadicea's own hands bunched involuntarily, a sign of panic in her eyes as her voice picked up speed. 'And the more I tried to feed her the more she screamed and writhed and fought against me, and my head was going round fit to explode, as if I was going mad. I was so tired – I hadn't slept in days – and I'd just had enough – and I threw her – anywhere, and the moment I did it I regretted it 'cause I knew what was going to happen, and it did, for she hit the floor, and when she stopped crying, I knew she wasn't going to cry ever again . . .'

Despite his revulsion, Niall's compassionate heart went out to her, and he managed to speak, to clarify this dreadful misunderstanding. 'But you didn't mean it – you fainted and she bounced from the bed to the floor!'

Boadicea shook her head, almost vomiting on the emotion that she was trying to suppress – had tried to suppress for years – her eyes and nose beginning to run. 'She never even touched the bed, Nye. She went straight to the floor, and I sent her there.'

If Niall had imagined there could be no worse horror than that he had suffered this morning, he now knew there could, for here it was, magnified tenfold, and he was unable to utter a word, unable to fathom how any mother could do this, let alone the one he had entrusted with his own children, the one he had adored. In his fevered brain, a picture arose, of Ellen with their firstborn, the look of fierce maternal love on her face, the look that had said she would die to protect her baby, and it made him want to throw up, that he had entrusted her children to one who had killed her own.

'So . . . you got away with it,' he breathed at last.

Boadicea turned her face sharply to look him in the eyes, her own brimming angry tears, and her voice trembling with bitterness. 'Yes, I got away with it. Instead of hanging me, they let me go, so that I could live happily ever after.'

He met her ferocious glare. 'But you lied to save your neck!'

'And who wouldn't?' she flung at him, bashing the air with her fist. 'How dare you sit there in judgement of me when you've no idea what I was suffering – still suffer! Twelve years, and not a day goes by when I don't think of her, think of what she'd look like, whether she'd have eyes like my mother, what she'd be doing with her life if I hadn't taken it!' Her face twisted in grief and her voice cracked with an emotional plea. 'But it wasn't really me that did it – for I was out of my mind! I was eighteen! Little more than a child myself! I had no mother, no one to turn to!'

He had risen, for her tone was becoming more

and more strident, and he feared she would become hysterical. Nevertheless, he remained angry and confused. 'But you had a husband!'

'And much good he was, out at work all day!'

'Be fair!' In defending the man, Niall defended his own position. 'The breadwinner has no choice but to go out.'

'Did he have to go out on a night too?' she yelled at him. 'And every night?'

Niall struggled to come up with a reason. 'He was probably just trying to escape the noise, if she was as bad as you say . . .'

'But *I* couldn't escape! Just try to put yourself in my shoes, try to imagine what it might be like,' she insisted, forcing the words through her teeth, her eyes almost manic. 'I know you've got an imagination, Niall; haven't I heard what it's capable of coming up with?'

These last words served to shake him as he recalled how he himself had imagined Ellen dead, and that this was what she damned him with. 'But imagining's not the same!' he flung back at her.

'You're damned right it's not the same! Because you're not the one who was pacing the floor night after night, trying to comfort that tiny little thing ye'd spent twenty hours giving birth to, and two more weeks of trying everything to find out what was wrong with her – two weeks old, that's all she was but it felt like she'd been crying a hundred years! How could you *ever* imagine how it feels, to suffer the most excruciating agony of labour, feeling as if your guts are being ripped out, to be eighteen and thrust into a motherhood you're not prepared for, to be the one responsible day and night – and I'm not talking about the responsibility of going out earning a living!' She lopped his interruption with a look of scorn. 'That's the easy part – any eejit can do that – but to be a mother, to know that you're the one that child relies on, for its food, for its every need, to be at its beck and call every second of the day, to feel it kicking for nine months inside you, to feel yourself split in two when you finally can push it out, to hold its cheek against yours, to want it, to love it, to adore the very breath of it – you think that anyone sane could rob herself of that? I was mad! Deranged from lack of sleep!' And she broke down sobbing.

With such an explanation, his horrified opposition being overwhelmed at last by pity and the love he still had for her, Niall went to her then, and held her whilst she poured out her grief, cupping her skull as she sobbed against his shoulder, shaking his head as he voiced the awful truth. 'And this is the real reason he left you, not because you wouldn't sleep with him, but because you killed his baby . . .'

'*My* baby!' She tore away and thumped at his chest in fury, spilling copious amounts of tears. 'My baby, and I killed her!' And she fell against him sobbing again, and racked with torment.

Close to tears too, his face stunned, Niall held her body that heaved and writhed out its agony against him, wondering how such massive suffering could remain pent up so long behind such a blithe and witty exterior, hugging and comforting as he waited for her sobbing to end, whilst knowing that her grief never would. And only now did he finally understand the aversion she had shown when he had wanted to involve the law in certain matters, the law that had put her on trial like a criminal, when instead she was deserving of compassion.

When she could cry no more, and leaned against him, shuddering with exhaustion, he shook his head at the fact she had felt unable to trust him, murmuring into her hair, 'If only you'd explained it all at the beginning . . .'

Her face came up sharply, mottled with tears and renewed anger. 'You'd have stood by me? The same way you stuck by your brother?' She saw his face adopt a look of guilt, and pressed her accusation home, 'Yes, you faithless bloody wretch – and Sean's only crime was to fall in love! So God help me who killed a child, with you my judge!'

And he saw then that he was equally guilty of such injustice as the law had shown, and his expression begged forgiveness. 'I'm sorry!' he embraced her. 'It's not coming out right. I'm trying to get to grips with what you told me, I believe what you say, that you weren't in your right mind – God knows how you must have felt, what you must have gone through, it breaks my heart to think of it . . .'

There came the sound of the front door being opened and a cheery voice coming along the passage. 'Here we are, Bri – safe and sound!'

Acting on an impulse of panic, with a simultaneous gasp Niall and Boadicea immediately broke apart, he to the far corner of the room, she to perform a swift wipe of her face then to sit with hands folded on her lap, as Emma entered with an apologetic smile.

'Oh, hello, Nye! I didn't realise you'd be home. He got frightened by the baddy's face leering at him!' came the explanation, as Brian went straight to Boadicea, who instinctively folded him into her arms when he scrambled onto her lap. 'Set him off bawling and wouldn't stop, disrupted the whole theatre. I had to leave Honor in charge, couldn't have her missing the . . . film.' Too late Emma noticed that she had intervened on some crucial exchange, stumbling over her last word as she saw through the artificial smiling masks worn by the occupants, and the laughter drained from her face. 'Sorry . . . maybe I should have taken him to our house.'

Eyes down so that Emma could not read the pain in them, Boadicea murmured that it was all right, and pressed a comforting kiss to Brian, whose head was now snuggled into her breast, a thumb in his mouth.

Definite now that her presence was unwelcome, Emma's eyes remained on her friend's face, obviously reading it well, for she held out her arms to the child. 'Tell you what, Bri, let's go see if Uncle Sean's home from work.'

Niall saw the look that passed between the women, and, knowing of their close attachment, he wondered with a flicker of resentment if Emma had been party to that awful revelation before he had. It had also not escaped his notice that Brian had gone straight to Boadicea for comfort. Not to him, but to her. How could he ever begin to tell his children of her crime, which might yet rob them of a second mother, of whom they had grown so fond?

'I want to stay here,' whined Brian, sinking his face deeper into Boadicea's bosom. 'I feel poorly.' Then he cocked an eye up at her. 'A little snack might help me feel better.'

'I'll get ye some bread and jam,' she said immediately. 'How's that?' And, with his miraculous recovery, Brian bouncing onto his feet, she rose to do so. Only to the adults was it obvious that her mundane task disguised a fight with inner demons. 'Sorry, you had to miss the film, Em. Can I get you a cup of tea?' she asked, with manufactured brightness.

Deeply aware of the malaise now, Emma was about to refuse. 'I'm disturbing—'

'No, you're not,' Niall jumped in quickly. 'I were just off to the lav.' With a cryptic smile he grabbed a newspaper and said as he went outside, 'No need to rush off, I'll be ages.'

And indeed he was, for the main discussion could not be resumed with others attending, and would require an enormous amount of thought on his part before it was. Oh dear God, what was he going to do?

How long he had been in the lavatory he did not know. It could have been fifteen minutes, it could have been an hour with all that was on his mind, the awful events being replayed there time and again, the accusing words respoken.

When he emerged and made a tentative return to the living room, Boadicea was alone, and once more attending to her pastry on the table, if only to tidy up the mess of flour there.

'They've gone then,' he remarked superfluously.

'She took him back to wait for the others coming out of the cinema,' Boadicea explained in a dull voice, as she gathered the bits of pastry into a ball. 'Said she'd take them all to her place for tea, so's we could talk.'

'So she *does* know!' It was an accusation.

Boadicea was still shaking her head, when he added resentfully, 'Why did you feel able to tell her and not me? I'm your husband, for Christ's sake!'

'She doesn't know anything!' came the weary reply. 'All she knows is that something is badly amiss between us – and she's right! God, you're like a little child, sulking because your best friend has another best friend! You want me to give you the reason why I didn't dare tell ye – I can give you a whole list of reasons!' She had adopted the offensive now, her eyes brimming once again with tears, but tears of anger, the bits of pastry gripped in her fist. 'What was your immediate reaction when Nora told you I'd been up in court – you assumed it was true!'

'It *was* bloody true!' he volleyed.

'But your first response at my confession wasn't to pity me – it was to condemn! As I feared it would be.' She shook her head in despair of him. 'I really wish I could have confided in you, Niall. Because the way I see it, if you truly love someone, you should feel able to reveal your darkest secrets knowing that they'll still feel the same about you—'

'Well, that's what I mean!' he gave protest. 'If you'd loved me enou—'

'Do you honestly think,' she interrupted, 'that I'd wash and cook and scrub the house for you and your children, and wipe the mess from Brian's backside, and put up with all the pranks and the backchat, and the gross insults from your in-laws – is that the mark of someone who doesn't love you?' Her angry, tear-filled eyes beseeched his. 'I agree, I *should* have felt able to tell you everything, to feel certain you'd love me no matter what I'd done, the way I love you, faults and all, but—'

'Faults?' He could not help an involuntary frown, his voice disbelieving.

She gave a bitter laugh, and dashed away her tears with a hand that left flour on both cheeks. 'Despite what ye might think, you do have them – we all do. It's called being human.' Weariness having claimed her, her voice was calmer now as she resumed the clearing of the table. 'You can condemn me all you like, but you've always had someone else to look after your children, and the fact of the matter is that you've no idea how you would have reacted in that same position.'

'No, you're absolutely right, I don't,' he made earnest agreement. 'And you're right that it shouldn't matter what somebody's done if you really love them. And I really do love you, Bo, I do. I'm sorry for the way I must have sounded. I was just so shocked. I couldn't believe . . . still can't.' But he had to accept it, for the truth was laid bare, and now that it was, other things must be answered. Watching her hands scoop the flour into a mound, he prompted her gently. 'Tell me what happened afterwards with Eddie. I suppose he blamed you . . .'

'Because that's what you'd do?' she rejoined without looking.

'No! Not now you've told me how it was.' He regretted ever defending the man. 'He can't have loved you.'

'Oh, he did . . . but not enough.'

'And that's why you were never sure of me,' said Niall. 'Never sure I wouldn't let you down like him.'

Her actions absent-minded now, pushing the floury debris back and forth rather than clearing it, Boadicea voiced sympathy. 'He tried his best, poor man. He didn't blame me, he blamed himself for letting it happen. His way of putting things right was to try and give me another baby, as if she could be replaced, as if I'd want to put myself through that again. Like I already told ye, there's only so much a man can stand of being shoved away.'

'Not this man.' His voice was firm, but noble. 'I didn't marry you for that. You know very well I didn't.'

Boadicea looked at him, her face accepting this. Then she went back to her chore. 'That was before you knew you were getting a murderer, though. Aren't you worried about your children?'

'Stop it!' he warned, and came to prevent her from paying more attention to the table than to him, taking her arms and iterating his opinion directly into her face. 'That's not what you are. I know you'd never harm them, you couldn't help what you did and, God knows, you've paid for it . . .'

'I'll bet that's not what Nora thinks.' Boadicea saw that she had hit another nerve.

Niall's expression had changed, as he remembered this morning's threat. 'Aye, well, Nora can think what she likes. You were acquitted in a court of law, and nobody can argue with that.'

'But you know the truth, Niall,' she searched his eyes. 'How would you feel if it had been your child I'd killed? Could you ever look at me in the same way again? Could you, *can* you live under constant scrutiny from your neighbours?'

He brushed a strand of hair from her damp cheek. 'Is that the reason you lived in so many places, kept moving round?'

She nodded. 'And now there's not just me and you, but your kids. Once word gets round that their stepmother is a—'

'Don't say it again.' He laid a hand over her mouth, his tone emphatic. 'You're not, and I'll make sure they know you're not. I love them kids, by God I do, but if the only thing they have to face is a few cruel words, and that we have to move house because of it, then so be it. But wherever we go, whatever happens, we'll go through it together.' Gripping her arms tighter, he held her gaze deliberately. 'I love you, and nowt that's been said today has changed that, and nothing ever will.'

'So you're not going to throw me out?' She permitted a quaver of hope to infiltrate her voice.

'Never,' he swore.

Boadicea tilted her face to meet his, the grief still stark upon it, despite a smile trying to fight its way through. 'But we can't go on like this, Niall. *I* can't go on like this. It's no sort of marriage is it?' And she turned her face away.

He was appalled. After all he had said, she was the one who wanted to end it!

Freeing her arms, he allowed his own to drop to his sides, then watched with growing dismay as, unable to meet his eye, she resumed the clearing of the table, taking the pastry cutter and rolling pin to the sink, returning with a damp cloth with which to wipe up the flour.

And all the while he watched her, he could say nothing, his overwhelming heartache forming a great lump that blocked his throat, and rendered him dumb, and in danger of weeping over impending loss.

Finally, the table was cleared, but the air of doom still hung like an oppressive curtain over his senses, as he waited for her to finish her task and go. He fought the great restriction in his throat, opened his mouth to beg her not to leave him.

But as she dusted off her hands and turned to him again, he saw that she had simply been taking time to choose her words; that, by some miracle, her grief had been leavened by a glimmer of hope; that she did not intend to end their marriage, but to let it begin, as she told him, 'Now that I'm sure you'd stand by me if anything were to happen . . . then I'm ready to take the risk. And there's no time like the present.'

He could not quite believe what he was hearing, and did not respond for some seconds. When he did, his voice was cautious. 'When you say "happen" . . . you mean, if you did fall for a baby? With me?'

Boadicea nodded, but added hurriedly as immediately he moved closer, 'I'm not saying I want one, Niall. Please God it won't happen, and we'll try our utmost to avoid it.' She stroked his arm, though it was not merely an act of affection but to hold him at bay. 'I meant it when I said I could never go through that again. Besides, don't I have five of yours already to love?' Had her actions not already proved it, her eyes showed that she did genuinely care for them. 'But as they won't be back for hours . . .'

His blood was pounding as he took hold of her. 'Is the time right?'

Bo nodded, her expression equally desirous, overwhelmed with love for him. 'As right as it'll ever be, and I can't think of a better time . . .'

He heaved a sigh of relief, gazed deep into her face projecting joy and optimism for the future – and yet as much as he pulsed for this moment he held back, as if doubting such happiness was finally come to pass, afraid to be let down. 'You're sure this is what you want?' His tone was one of barely contained passion, his breath warm on her face. 'Don't do it just because you feel sorry for me—'

'Have ye heard yourself?' Her soft rebuke was almost a laugh. 'I don't feel sorry for you, eejit, I feel sorry for *me*! I love you, and I want you – oh God, if you only knew how I've wanted you so much – and if you're willing to take the risk now that you've learned the very worst about me, then so am I, and neither the Church nor Mrs Beasty will tell us how to live our lives.' And wasting no further time, she applied firm hands to either side of his head, and grappled his face down to hers. 'No going back,' she murmured, before passion took over them both. And nor was there, all the emotion of that terrible day being put to better, more magnificent, use.